Bonu
For your enjoyment, we've added in this volume
Bachelor Unleashed, a favorite book by Brenda Jackson!

Praise for
New York Times **and** ***USA TODAY*** **bestselling author**
Brenda Jackson

"Brenda Jackson writes romance that sizzles
and characters you fall in love with."
—*New York Times* and *USA TODAY* bestselling author
Lori Foster

"Jackson's trademark ability to weave
multiple characters and side stories together
makes shocking truths all the more exciting."
—*Publishers Weekly*

"There is no getting away from the sex appeal and
charm of Jackson's Westmoreland family."
—*RT Book Reviews* on *Feeling the Heat*

"Jackson's characters are wonderful, strong,
colorful and hot enough to burn the pages."
—*RT Book Reviews* on *Westmoreland's Way*

"The kind of sizzling, heart-tugging story
Brenda Jackson is famous for."
—*RT Book Reviews* on *Spencer's Forbidden Passion*

"This is entertainment at its best."
—*RT Book Reviews* on *Star of His Heart*

BRENDA JACKSON

is a die "heart" romantic who married her childhood sweetheart and still proudly wears the "going steady" ring he gave her when she was fifteen. Because she believes in the power of love, Brenda's stories always have happy endings. In her real-life love story, Brenda and her husband of more than forty years live in Jacksonville, Florida, and have two sons.

A *New York Times* bestselling author of more than seventy-five romance titles, Brenda is a recent retiree who now divides her time between family, writing and traveling with Gerald. You may write Brenda at P.O. Box 28267, Jacksonville, Florida 32226, by email at WriterBJackson@aol.com or visit her website at www.brendajackson.net.

NEW YORK TIMES AND USA TODAY BESTSELLING AUTHOR

BRENDA JACKSON

THE REAL THING
&
BACHELOR UNLEASHED

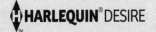

HARLEQUIN® DESIRE

ISBN-13: 978-0-373-83797-7

THE REAL THING & BACHELOR UNLEASHED

Copyright © 2014 by Harlequin Books S.A.

The publisher acknowledges the copyright holder of the individual works as follows:

THE REAL THING
Copyright © 2014 by Brenda Streater Jackson

BACHELOR UNLEASHED
Copyright © 2010 by Brenda Streater Jackson

Recycling programs for this product may not exist in your area.

Printed in U.S.A.

CONTENTS

Dear Reader,

I can't believe I'm writing about one of those notorious Westmorelands—one of the last four in the Denver Series. When I first introduced the twins—Adrian and Aidan, Bailey and Bane—I understood the pain that motivated them to create havoc in their wake. And I knew by the time I wrote their stories they would have gotten older, and improved their attitude and behavior. I also knew the person with which each chose to share their life would appreciate everything about them, and help any additional healing that was needed in their life.

I chose Trinity for Adrian Westmoreland because she was headstrong and independent. What she thought she wanted most out of life was a medical career and to live in a small town. It took Adrian Westmoreland to show her that all your wants and desires mean nothing unless you can share them with the person you truly love.

I hope you enjoy this story about Adrian and Trinity.

Happy Reading!

Brenda Jackson

THE REAL THING

* * *

To the love of my life, Gerald Jackson, Sr.

To my readers,
who continue to inspire me to reach higher heights.

To my family—the Hawks, Streaters and Randolphs—
who continue to support me in all my endeavors.
I couldn't ask to be a part of a better family.

For we cannot but speak the things
which we have seen and heard.
—*Acts* 4:20

THE DENVER WESTMORELAND FAMILY TREE

Raphel and Gemma Westmoreland

Stern Westmoreland (Paula Bailey)

Thomas (Susan)

Adam (Clarisse)

Dillon (Pamela) ①
Micah (Kalina) ⑥
Jason (Bella) ⑤
Riley (Alpha) ⑧
Canyon (Keisha) ⑩
Stern (JoJo) ⑪
Brisbane

Ramsey (Chloe) ②
Zane (Channing) ⑨
Derringer (Lucia) ④
Megan (Rico) ⑦
Gemma (Callum) ③
Adrian (Trinity) ⑫
Aidan
Bailey

① Westmoreland's Way
② Hot Westmoreland Nights
③ What a Westmoreland Wants
④ A Wife for a Westmoreland
⑤ The Proposal
⑥ Feeling the Heat
⑦ Texas Wild
⑧ One Winter's Night
⑨ Zane
⑩ Canyon
⑪ Stern
⑫ The Real Thing

Chapter 1

"I understand you're in a jam and might need my help."

In a jam was putting it mildly, Trinity Matthews thought, looking across the table at Adrian Westmoreland.

If only what he'd said wasn't true. And…if only Adrian wasn't so good-looking. Then thinking about what she needed him to do wouldn't be so hard.

When she and Adrian had first met, last year at his cousin Riley's wedding, he had been standing in a group of Westmoreland men. She had sized up his brothers and cousins, but had definitely noticed Adrian standing beside his identical twin brother, Aidan.

Trinity had found out years ago, when her sister Tara had married Thorn Westmoreland, that all Westmoreland men were eye candy of the most delectable kind. Therefore, she hadn't really been surprised to discover that Thorn's cousins from Denver had a lot of the same traits—handsome facial features, tall height, a hard-muscled body and an aura of primal masculinity.

But she'd never thought she'd be in a position to date one of those men—even if it was only a temporary ruse.

Trinity knew Tara had already given Adrian some details about the situation and now it was up to her to fill him in on the rest.

"Yes, I'm in a jam," Trinity said, releasing a frustrated breath. "I want to tell you about it, but first I want to thank you for agreeing to meet with me tonight."

He had suggested Laredo's Steak House. She had eaten here a few times, and the food was always excellent.

"No problem."

She paused, trying to ignore how the deep, husky sound of his voice stirred her already nervous stomach. "My goal," she began, "is to complete my residency at Denver Memorial and return to Bunnell, Florida, and work beside my father and brothers in their medical practice. That goal is being threatened by another physician, Dr. Casey Belvedere. He's a respected surgeon here in Denver. He—"

"Wants you."

Trinity's heart skipped a beat. Another Westmoreland trait she'd discovered: they didn't believe in mincing words.

"Yes. He wants an affair. I've done nothing to encourage his advances or to give him the impression I'm interested. I even lied and told him I was already involved with someone, but he won't let up. Now it's more than annoying. He's hinted that if I don't go along with it, he'll make my life at the hospital difficult."

She pushed her plate aside and took a sip of her wine. "I brought his unwanted advances to the attention of the top hospital administrator, and he's more or less dismissed my claim. Dr. Belvedere's family is well known in the city. Big philanthropists, I understand. Presently, the Belvederes are building a children's wing at the hospital that will bear their name. It's my guess that the hospital administrator feels that now is not the time to make waves with any of the Belvederes. He said I need to pick my battles carefully, and this is one I might not want to take on."

She paused. "So I came up with a plan." She chuckled softly. "Let me rephrase that. Tara came up with the plan after I told her what was going on. It seems that she faced a similar situation when she was doing her residency in Kentucky. The only difference was that the hospital administrator supported her and made sure the doctor was released of his duties. I don't have that kind of support here because of the Belvedere name."

Adrian didn't say anything for a few moments. He broke eye contact with her and stared down into his glass of wine. Trinity couldn't help but wonder what he was thinking.

He looked back at her. "There is another solution to your problem, you know."

She lifted a brow. "There is?"

"You did say he's a surgeon, right?"

"Yes."

"Then I could break his hands so he'll never be able to use them in an operating room again."

She stared wide-eyed at him for a couple of seconds before leaning forward. "You're joking, right?"

"No. I am not joking. I'm dead serious."

She leaned back as she studied his features. They were etched with ruthlessness and his dark eyes were filled with callousness. It was only then that Trinity remembered Tara's tales about the twins, their baby sister, Bailey, and their younger cousin Bane. According to Tara, those four were the holy terrors of Denver while growing up and got into all kinds of trouble— malicious and otherwise.

But that was years ago. Now Bane was a navy SEAL, the twins were both Harvard graduates—Adrian obtained his PhD in engineering and Aidan completed medical school—and Bailey, the youngest of the four, was presently working on her MBA. However, it was quite obvious to Trinity that behind Adrian Westmoreland's chiseled good looks, irresistible charm and PhD was a man who could return to his old ways if the need arose.

"I don't think we need to go that far," she said, swallowing. "Like Tara suggested, we can pretend to be lovers and hope that works."

"If that's how you prefer handling it."

"Yes. And you don't have a problem going along with it? Foregoing dating other women for a while?"

He pushed his plate aside and leaned back in his chair. "Nope. I don't have a problem going along with it. Putting my social life on hold until this matter is resolved will be no big deal."

Trinity released a relieved sigh. She had heard that since he'd returned to Denver to work as one of the CEOs at his family-owned business, Blue Ridge Land Management, Adrian had acquired a very active social life. There weren't many single Westmoreland men left in town. In fact, he was the only one. His cousin Stern was engaged to be married in a few months; Bane was away in the navy and Aidan was practicing medicine at a hospital in North Carolina. All the other Westmoreland men had married. Adrian would definitely be a catch for any woman. And they were coming after him from every direction, determined to hook a Westmoreland man; she'd heard he was having the time of his life letting them try.

Trinity was grateful she wasn't interested. The only reason she and Adrian were meeting was that she needed his help to pull off her plan. In fact, this was the first time they had seen each other since she'd moved to Denver eight months ago. She'd known when she accepted the internship at Denver Memorial last year that a slew of her sister's Westmoreland cousins-in-law lived here. She had met most of them at Riley's wedding. But most lived in a part of Denver referred to as Westmoreland Country and she lived in town. Though she had heard that when Adrian returned to Denver he had taken a place in town instead of moving to his family's homestead, more for privacy than anything else.

"I think we should put our plan into action now," he said, breaking into her thoughts.

He surprised her further when he took her hand in his and brought it to his lips while staring deeply into her eyes. She tried to ignore the intense fluttering in her stomach caused by his lips brushing against her skin.

"Why are you so anxious to begin?"

"It's simply a matter of timing," he said, bringing her hand to his lips yet again. "Don't look now but Dr. Casey Belvedere just walked in. He's seen us and is looking over here."

Let the show begin.

Adrian continued to stare deeply into Trinity's eyes, sensing her nervousness. Although she had gone along with Tara's suggestion, he had a feeling she wasn't 100 percent on board with the idea of pretending to be his lover.

Although Dr. Belvedere was going about his pursuit all wrong, Adrian could understand the man wanting her. Hell, what man in his right mind wouldn't? Like her sister, Tara, Trinity was an incredibly beautiful woman. Ravishing didn't even come close to describing her.

When he'd first met Tara, years ago, the first thing out of his mouth was to ask if she had any sisters. Tara had smiled and replied, yes, she had a sister who was a senior in high school with plans to go to college to become a doctor.

Jeez. Had it been that long ago? He recalled the reaction of every single man at Riley's wedding when Trinity had showed up with Thorn and Tara. That's when he'd heard she would be moving to Denver for two years to work at the hospital.

"Are you sure it's him?" Trinity asked.

"Pretty positive," he said, studying her features. She had creamy mahogany-colored skin, silky black hair that hung to her shoulders and the most gorgeous pair of light brown eyes he'd ever seen. "And it's just the way I planned it," he said.

She arched a brow. "The way you planned it?"

"Yes. After Tara called and told me about her idea, I decided to start right away. I found out from a reliable source that Belvedere frequents this place quite a bit, especially on Thursday nights."

"So that's why you suggested we have dinner here tonight?" she asked.

"Yes, that's the reason. The plan is for him to see us together, right?"

"Yes. I just wasn't prepared to run into him tonight.

Hopefully all it will take is for him to see us together and—"

"Back off? Don't bank on that. The man wants you and, for some reason, he feels he has every right to have you. Getting him to leave you alone won't be easy. I still think I should just break his damn hands and be through with it."

"No."

He shrugged. "Your call. Now we should really do something to get his attention."

"What?"

"This." Adrian leaned in and kissed her.

Trinity was certain it was supposed to be a mere brush across the lips, but like magnets their mouths locked, fusing in passion so quickly that it consumed her senses.

To Trinity's way of thinking, the kiss had a potency that had her insides begging for more. Every part of her urged her to make sure this kiss didn't end anytime soon. But the clinking of dishes and silverware made her remember where they were and what they were doing. She slowly eased her mouth away from Adrian's.

She let out a slow breath. "I have a feeling that did more than get his attention. It might have pissed him off."

Adrian smiled. "Who cares? You're with me now and he won't do anything stupid. I dare him."

He motioned for the waiter to bring their check. "I think we've done enough playacting tonight," he said smoothly. "Ready to leave?"

"Yes."

Moments after taking care of their dinner bill, Adrian took Trinity's hand in his and led her out of the restaurant.

Chapter 2

"So how did things go with Trinity last night?"

Adrian glanced up to see his cousin Dillon. The business meeting Dillon had called that morning at Blue Ridge Land Management had ended and everyone had filed out, leaving him and Dillon alone.

He'd never thought of Dillon as a business tycoon until Adrian had returned home to work for the company his family owned. That's when he got to see his Denver cousin in action, wheeling and dealing to maintain Blue Ridge's ranking as a Fortune 500 company. Adrian had always just thought of him as Dillon, the man who'd kept the family together after a horrific tragedy.

Adrian's parents, as well as his uncle and aunt, had died in a plane crash more than twenty years ago, leaving Dillon, who was the oldest cousin, and Adrian's oldest brother, Ramsey, in charge of keeping the family of fifteen Westmorelands together. It hadn't been easy, and Adrian would be the first to confess that he, Aidan, Bane and Bailey, the youngest four, had deliberately made things hard. Coming home from school one day to be told they'd lost the four people who had meant the most to them had been worse than difficult. They hadn't handled their grief well. They had rebelled in ways Adrian was now ashamed of. But Dillon, Ramsey and the other family members hadn't given up on them, even when they truly should have. For that reason and many others, Adrian deeply loved his family. Especially Dillon, who had taken on the State of Colorado when it had tried to force the youngest four into foster homes.

"Things went well, I think," Adrian said, not wondering how Dillon knew about the dinner date with Trinity even when Adrian hadn't mentioned anything about it. Dillon spoke to their Atlanta cousins on a regular basis, especially Thorn Westmoreland. Adrian figured Tara had mentioned the plan to Thorn and he had passed the information on to Dillon.

"Glad to hear it," Dillon said, gathering up his papers. "Hopefully it will work. Even so, I personally have a problem with the hospital administrator not doing anything about Dr. Belvedere. I don't give a damn how much money his family has or that they have a wing bearing their name under construction at the hospital. Sexual harassment is sexual harassment, and it's something no one should have to tolerate. What's happening to Trinity shouldn't happen to anyone."

Adrian agreed. If he had anything to do with it, Trinity wouldn't have to tolerate it. "We'll give Tara's idea a shot and if it doesn't work, then—"

"Then the Westmorelands will handle it, Adrian, the right way…with the law on our side. I don't want you doing anything that will get you in trouble. Those days are over."

Adrian didn't say anything as he remembered *those* days. "I won't do anything to get into trouble." He figured it was best not to say those days were completely over, especially after the suggestion he'd made to Trinity about breaking Belvedere's hands…something he'd been dead serious about. "Do you know anyone in the Belvedere family?" he asked Dillon.

"Dr. Belvedere's older brother Roger and I are on the boards of directors of a couple of major businesses in town, but we aren't exactly friends. He's arrogant, a little on the snobbish side. I heard it runs in the family."

"Too bad," Adrian said, rising from his chair.

"The Belvedere family made their money in the food industry, namely dairy products. I understand Roger has political aspirations and will announce his run for governor next month."

"I wish him the best. It's his brother Casey that I have a problem with," Adrian said, heading toward the door. "I'll see you later."

An hour later Adrian had finished an important report his cousin Canyon needed. Both Canyon and another cousin, Stern, were company attorneys. So far, Adrian was the only one from his parents' side of the Westmoreland tree who worked for Blue Ridge, the company founded by his and Dillon's father more than forty years ago.

At present there were fifteen Denver Westmorelands of his generation. His parents, Thomas and Susan Westmoreland, had had eight kids: five boys—Ramsey, Zane, Derringer and the twins, Adrian and Aidan—and three girls—Megan, Gemma and Bailey.

His uncle Adam and aunt Clarisse had had seven

sons: Dillon, Micah, Jason, Riley, Canyon, Stern and Bane. The family was a close-knit one and usually got together on Friday nights at Dillon's place for a chow-down, where they ate good food and caught up on family matters. Dates had kept Adrian from attending the last two, but now, since he was *supposedly* involved with Trinity, his dating days were over for a while.

He tossed an ink pen on his desk before leaning back in his chair. For the umpteenth time that day he was reminded of the kiss he'd shared with Trinity last night. A kiss he had taken before she'd been aware he was about to do so. Adrian didn't have to wonder what had driven him. He could try to convince himself he'd only done it to rile Belvedere, but Adrian knew it was about more than that.

It had all started when he had arrived at Trinity's place to pick her up. She must have been watching for him out the window of the house she was leasing because after he'd pulled into her driveway, before he could get out of his car, she had opened the door and strolled down the walk toward him.

He'd had to fight to keep his predatory smile from showing a full set of teeth. Damn, she had looked good. He could say it was the pretty, paisley print maxi dress that swirled around her ankles as she'd walked, or the blue stilettos and matching purse. He could say it was the way she'd worn her hair down to her shoulders, emphasizing gorgeous facial bones. Whatever it was, she had looked even more appealing than when he'd seen her at Riley and Alpha's wedding.

Adrian sucked in a sharp breath as more memories swept through his mind. Never had a woman's mouth tasted so delectable, so irresistibly sweet. She had been pretty quiet on the drive back to her place last night.

Just as well, since his body had been on fire for her. Big mistake. How was he supposed to stop Belvedere from getting his hands on her when all he could think about was getting his own hands on her?

He stood and stretched his tall frame. After shoving his hands into the pockets of his pants, he walked over to the window and looked out at downtown Denver. When Tara had called him with the idea of pretending to be Trinity's lover, he had shrugged, thinking no problem, no big deal. A piece of cake. What he hadn't counted on was his own attraction to Trinity. It was taking over his thoughts. And that wasn't good.

Frustrated, he rubbed his hand down his face. He had to have more control. She wasn't the first woman he'd been attracted to and she wouldn't be the last. Taking another deep breath, he glanced at his watch. He was having dinner at McKays with Bailey and figured he would surprise her this time by being on time.

He had one more file to read, which wouldn't take long. Then, before leaving for the day, he would call Trinity to see how things had gone at work. He wanted to make sure Belvedere hadn't caused her any grief about seeing them together last night at Laredo's.

"So how did things go last night with Adrian?"

Trinity plopped down on the sofa in her living room after a long day at work. She'd figured she would hear from Tara sooner or later, who would want details.

"Great! We got to know each other while eating a delicious steak dinner. And Dr. Belvedere was off today, which was a good thing, given that he saw me and Adrian together last night at dinner."

"He did?"

"Yes."

"Coincidence or planned?"

"Planned. It seemed Adrian didn't waste time. Once he had agreed with your suggestion he found out where Belvedere liked to hang out and suggested we go there. Only thing, Adrian didn't tell me about his plan beforehand and when Dr. Belvedere walked in, I was unprepared."

"I can imagine. But you do want to bring this situation to a conclusion as quickly as possible, right?"

"Yes. But…"

"But what?"

"I hadn't counted on a few things."

"A few things like what, Trinity?"

Trinity nibbled on her bottom lip, trying to decide how much information she should share with her sister. Although there was a ten-year difference in their ages, they had always been close. Even when Tara had left home for college and medical school, Trinity had known her sister would return home often. After all, Derrick Hayes—the man Tara had dated since high school and had been engaged to marry—lived there.

But then came the awful day of Tara's wedding. Her sister had looked beautiful. She'd walked down the aisle on their father's arm looking as radiant as any bride could look. Trinity had been in her early teens and seeing Tara in such a beautiful gown had made her dream of her own wedding day.

But then, before the preacher could get things started, Derrick had stopped the wedding. In front of everyone, he'd stated that he couldn't go through with the ceremony because he didn't love Tara. He loved Danielle, Tara's best friend and maid of honor.

Trinity would never forget the hurt, pain and humiliation she'd seen in her sister's eyes and the tears that had flowed down Tara's cheeks when Derrick took Danielle's hand and the two of them raced happily out of the church, leaving Tara standing behind.

That night Tara had left Bunnell, and it had been two years before she had returned. And when she had, motorcycle celebrity Thorn Westmoreland had given her a public proposal the town was still talking about ten years later. Trinity's brother-in-law had somewhat restored her faith in men. He was the best, and she knew that he loved her sister deeply.

"Trinity? A few things like what?" Tara repeated, pulling Trinity's concentration back to the present.

"Nothing, other than I wish Adrian wasn't so darn attractive. You wouldn't believe the number of women staring at him last night."

She decided not to mention the fact that he had kissed her right in front of a few of those women, although he'd done it for Dr. Belvedere's benefit. She hadn't expected the kiss and she had gone to bed last night thinking about it. Today things hadn't been much better. Burying herself in work hadn't helped her forget.

"Yes, he is definitely handsome. Most Westmoreland men are. And don't worry about other women. He's single, but now that he has agreed to pretend to be your boyfriend, he's going to give you all his attention."

Trinity sighed. In a way, that's what she was afraid of. "Adrian doesn't think Dr. Belvedere seeing us together once will do it."

"Probably not, especially if the man is obsessed with having you. From what you've told me, it sounds like he is."

Trinity didn't say anything for a minute. "Well, I hope he gets the message because Adrian is serious about making sure the plan works."

"Good. I think you're in good hands."

Trinity wasn't so sure that was a positive thing, especially when she remembered the number of times last night she had thought about Adrian's hands. He had beautiful fingers, long and lean. She had wondered more than once how those fingers would feel stroking her skin.

"Trinity?"

She blinked, realizing she had been daydreaming. "Yes?"

"You're still keeping that journal, right?"

Tara had suggested she keep a record of each and every time Casey Belvedere made unwanted advances toward her. "Yes, I'm still keeping the journal."

"Good. Don't worry about anything. I wouldn't have suggested Adrian if I didn't believe he would be the right one to help handle your business."

"I know. I know. But…"

"But what?"

Trinity breathed in deeply. "But nothing. I just hope your idea eventually works."

"Me, too. And if it doesn't we move to plan B."

Trinity lifted a brow. "What's plan B?"

"I haven't thought of it yet."

She couldn't help but laugh. She loved her big sister and appreciated Tara being there for her right now. "Hopefully, there won't have to be a plan B."

"Let's keep hoping. In the meantime, just enjoy Adrian. He's a fun guy and you haven't had any fun lately. I know how it is, going through residency. Been there. Done that. You can only take so much and do so much. We're doctors, not miracle workers, Trinity. We have lives, too, and everybody needs downtime. Stress can kill—remember that."

"I will."

A few moments later she had ended her call with Tara and was about to head for the kitchen to put together a salad for dinner when her cell phone rang again. Trinity's heartbeat quickened when she saw it was Adrian.

What was that shiver about, the one that had just passed through her whole body? She frowned, wondering what was wrong with her. Why was she reacting this way to his phone call? It wasn't as if their affair was the real thing. Why did she feel the need to remind herself that it was only a sham for Dr. Belvedere's benefit?

She clicked on her phone. "Hello?"

"Hello, this is Adrian. How did things go at work today?"

She wished he didn't sound as good as he looked. Or that when he had arrived to pick her up for dinner last night, he'd not dressed as though he'd jumped right off the page of a men's magazine.

She had been ready to walk out the moment his car had pulled into her driveway. So there had been no reason for him to get out of his car to meet her halfway down the walkway. But he had done so, showing impeccable manners by escorting her to his car and opening the door for her. However, it wasn't his manners the woman in her had appreciated the most. He was so tall she had to look up at him, into a pair of eyes and a face that had almost taken her breath away.

She sighed softly now as the memory rushed through her mind. Only then did she recall the question he had asked her.

"Today was okay, probably because Dr. Belvedere is off for the next two days so I didn't see him. I'm dreading Friday when he returns."

"Hopefully things won't be so bad. We'll keep up

our charade until he accepts the fact that you already have a man."

A pretend man but, oh, what a man, she thought to herself. "Do you think after seeing us together last night he believes we're an item?"

"Oh, I'm sure he probably believes it. But for him to accept it is a whole other story. It's my guess that he won't."

Trinity nibbled on her bottom lip. "I hope you're wrong."

"I hope I'm wrong, as well. Enjoy tomorrow and we'll see what happens on Friday. Just to be on the safe side, let's plan a date for the weekend. How about a show Saturday night?"

"A show?"

"Yes, one of those live shows at the Dunning Theater. A real casual affair."

She thought about what Tara had said, about Trinity getting out more and not working so hard. Besides, she and Adrian needed to be seen around town together as much as possible for Dr. Belvedere to get the message. "Do you think Belvedere will be attending the show, as well?"

He chuckled, and Trinity's skin reacted to the sound. Goose bumps formed on her arm. "Not sure, but it doesn't matter. The more we're seen together by others, the more believable our story will be. So are you good for Saturday night?"

"Yes. It just so happens I'm off this weekend."

"Good. I'll pick you up around seven."

Chapter 3

This is just a pretend date, so why am I getting all worked up over it? Trinity asked herself as she threw yet another outfit from her closet across her bed.

So far, just like all the other outfits she'd given the boot, it was either too dressy, not dressy enough or just plain boring. Frustrated, she ran her hands through her hair, wishing she had her sister's gift for fashion. Whenever Tara and Thorn went out on the town they were decked out to the nines and always looked good together. But even before Tara had become Mrs. Thorn Westmoreland, people had said she looked more like a model than a pediatrician.

Trinity glanced at her watch. Only an hour before Adrian arrived and she had yet to find an outfit she liked. Who was she kidding? A part of her was hoping that whatever she liked he would like, as well. She seldom dated and now, thanks to Casey Belvedere, it was being forced upon her.

Maybe she should call Adrian and cancel. Immediately she dismissed the idea from her mind. So far the week had been going smoothly. Dr. Belvedere had been off, even on Friday. It seemed everyone had breathed a lot easier, able to be attentive but relaxed. No one had had to look over their shoulders, dreading the moment when Belvedere showed his face. She wasn't the only one who thought he was a pain in the rear end.

Deciding she would take Tara's advice and have fun for a change, Trinity settled on a pair of jeans and a green pullover sweater. Giving both a nod of approval, she placed them across the chair. It was the middle of March and back home in Florida people were strutting around in tank tops and blouses. But in Denver everyone was still wearing winter clothes.

Trinity doubted she would ever get used to this weather.

"Which is why getting through your residency is a must," she mumbled to herself as she headed for the bathroom to take a shower. "Then you can leave and head back to Florida where you belong."

A short while later she had finished her shower, dressed and placed light makeup on her face. She smiled as she looked at herself in the mirror, satisfied with what she saw. No telling how many dates Adrian was giving up by pretending to be her man. The least she could do was make sure she looked worth his time and effort in helping her out.

She glanced at her watch. She had twenty minutes, and the last thing she had to do was her hair. She was about to pull the curling iron from a drawer when her cell phone rang, and she saw it was Adrian. She wondered if he was calling to say something had come up and he couldn't take her out after all.

"Hello?"

"Trinity?"

She ignored the sensations floating around her stomach and the thought of how good he sounded whenever he pronounced her name. "Yes?"

"I'm here."

She lifted a brow. "Where?"

"At your front door."

"Oh." She swallowed. "You're early."

"Is that a problem?"

She glanced at herself in the mirror. "I haven't done my hair yet."

"I have three sisters, so I understand. I can wait... inside."

Trinity swallowed again. Of course he would expect to wait inside. To have him wait outside in the car for her would be downright tacky. "Okay, I'm on my way to the door."

Glad she was at least fully dressed, she left her bedroom and moved toward the door despising the tingle that continued to sweep through her body. "Get a grip, girl. It's just Adrian. He's almost family," she told herself.

But when she opened the door the thought that quickly went through her mind was, *Scratch the thought he's almost family.*

As her gaze swept across him from top to bottom, she willed herself not to react to what she saw and failed miserably. She was mesmerized. If she thought he'd looked good in his business suit days ago, tonight his manliness was showing to the nth degree. There was just something about a tall, handsome man in a pair of jeans, white shirt and dark brown corduroy blazer. The Stetson on his head only added to the eye-candy effect.

"Now I see what you mean, so please do something with your hair."

His comment had her reaching for the thick strands that flowed past her shoulders. When she saw the teasing smile on his lips, she couldn't help but smile back as she stepped aside to let him in. "That bad?"

"No. There's nothing wrong with your hair. It looks great."

She rolled her eyes as she led him to her living room. "There're no curls in it."

He chuckled. "Curls aren't everything. Trust me, I know. Like I said, I have three sisters."

And she knew his sisters and liked them immensely. "Would you like something to drink while you wait?"

"Um, what do you have?"

"Soda, beer, wine and lemonade."

"I'll take a soda."

"One soda coming up," she said, walking off, and although she was tempted to do so, she didn't look back.

When she opened the refrigerator, the blast of cold air cooled her somewhat; she couldn't believe she'd actually gotten hot just looking at him. Closing the refrigerator, she paused. Some sort of raw, erotic power had emanated off him and she inwardly admitted that Adrian Westmoreland was an astonishing specimen of masculinity. The kind that made her want to lick him all over.

"Nice place."

She jerked around to find the object of her intense desire standing in the middle of her kitchen. For some reason he appeared taller, bigger than life and even sexier. "As you can see there's not much to it. It was either get a bigger place and share it with someone or get this one, which I can afford on my own."

He nodded. "It suits you."

She handed him the drink and their hands touched slightly. She hoped he hadn't noticed the tremble that passed through her with the exchange. "In what way?"

His gaze gave her body a timeless sweep and she felt her heartbeat quicken. His eyes returned to hers as he took his glass. "Nice. Tidy. Perfect coloring with everything blending together rather nicely."

Was she imagining things or had Adrian's eyes darkened to a deep, rich chocolate? And was his comparison of her to her home meant to be flirtatious? "Enjoy your soda while I work on my hair."

"Need help?"

She smiled as she quickly headed out of the kitchen. She didn't want to imagine how his hands would feel on her head. "No, thanks. I can manage."

Adrian took a long sip of his drink as he watched Trinity leave her kitchen. Nice-looking backside, he thought, and then wished he hadn't. Tara would skin him alive if he made a play for her sister. And if Tara told Thorn, there would be no hope for Adrian since everybody knew Thorn was a man not to toy with.

Then why did you flirt with Trinity just now? he asked himself, taking another sip. *You're only asking for trouble. Your job is to pretend the two of you are lovers and not lust after her like some horny ass. You've already crossed the line with that kiss—don't make matters worse.*

He took another sip of his soda. What could be worse than wanting a woman and not being able to have her?

A smile touched his lips, thinking that Dr. Casey Belvedere would soon find out.

"I'm ready."

He turned slightly and almost choked on the liquid he'd just sipped. She'd used one of those styling-irons to put curls in her hair at the ends. The style looked good on her. She looked good. All over. Top to bottom.

"You look nice."

"Thanks. You look nice yourself. You didn't say what show we'll be seeing."

"I didn't? Then I guess it will be a surprise. I talked to Tara earlier today and asked her about your favorite dessert. She told me about your fascination with strawberry cheesecake, so I made arrangements for us to stop for cheesecake and coffee on our way back."

"That's thoughtful of you."

"I'm a thoughtful person. You ready to go?"

"Yes."

He placed the empty glass on the counter and crossed the room to link his arm with hers. "Then let's go."

"You're driving a different car tonight," Trinity noted when they reached the sleek and sassy vehicle parked in her driveway. The night he'd taken her to dinner he'd been driving a black Lexus sedan. Tonight he was in a sporty candy-apple-red Lexus two-seater convertible.

"And I own neither. A good friend owns a Lexus dealership in town and when I returned to Denver he sold me a Lexus SUV. But he figures as much as I'm seen around town with the ladies that he might as well let me use any car off his lot whenever I go out on a date. He's convinced showcasing his cars around town is good publicity. And it has paid off. Several people have come into his dealership to buy his cars."

"And I bet most were women."

He chuckled as he opened the door for her. "Now why would you think that?"

"A hunch. Am I right?"

"Possibly."

"Go ahead and admit it. It's okay. I've heard all about your dating history," she said, buckling her seat belt.

"Have you?" he asked, leaning against the open car door.

"Yes."

"From who?"

"I'd rather not disclose my sources."

"And you think they're reliable?" he asked.

"I see no reason why they shouldn't be."

He shrugged before closing the door. She watched him sprint around the front to the driver's side to get in. He buckled his own seat belt, but before pressing the key switch he glanced over at her. "There's only one reliable source when it comes to me, Trinity."

She lifted a brow. "And who might that be?"

He pointed a finger at his chest. "Me. Feel free to ask me anything you want…within reason."

She smiled. "Then here's my first question. More women have purchased cars from your friend than men, right?"

He returned her smile as he backed out of her driveway. "I'll admit that they have."

"I'm not surprised."

"Why not?"

"Several reasons," she said, noticing the smooth sound of the car's engine as he drove down her street.

"State them."

She glanced over at him. He had brought the car to a stop at a traffic light. "I can see where some women would find you persuasive and lap up anything you say as gospel."

A smile she wouldn't categorize as *totally* conceited touched his lips. "You think so? You believe I might have that much influence?"

"Yes, but mind you, I said *some* women."

"What about you? Are you ready for a new car?"

She held his gaze. "Unless it's free, I'm not interested. A car payment is the last thing I need right now. The car I presently drive is just fine. It gets me from point A to point B and if I sing to it real nice, it might even make it to point C. I can't ask for anything more than that."

"You can but you won't."

His comment was right on the money but she wondered how he'd figured that out. "Why do you say that?"

The car was moving again and he didn't answer until they reached another traffic light a few moments later. He looked over at her. "You're not the only one with sources. I understand that beneath those curls on your head is a very independent mind."

She shrugged as she broke away from his look to glance out the window. "I can't handle my business any other way. My parents raised all of us to be independent thinkers."

"Is that why you didn't go along with Tara's plan at first?"

She looked back at him. "You'll have to admit it's a little far-fetched."

"I look at it as a means to an end."

"I just hope it works."

"It will."

She was about to ask why he felt so certain when she noticed they had pulled up for valet parking. The building was beautiful and the architecture probably dated back to the eighteen hundreds. Freestanding, it stood as an immaculate building with a backdrop of mountains. "Nice."

"Glad you like it. It was an old hotel. Now it's been renovated, turned into a theater that has live shows. Pam's group is working on a production that will be performed here."

Trinity knew Dillon's wife, Pam, used to be a movie star who now owned an acting school in town. "That's wonderful."

"I think so, too. Her group is working hard with rehearsals and all. It will be their first show."

When they reached the ticket booth the clerk greeted Adrian by name. "Good evening, Mr. Westmoreland."

"Hello, Paul. I believe you're holding reserved tickets for me."

"Yes sir," the man said, handing Adrian an envelope. Adrian checked the contents before smiling at her. "We're a little early so we might as well grab a drink. They serve refreshments while we wait."

"Okay."

When they entered the huge room, Trinity glanced around. This area of the building was nicely decorated, as well.

"What would you like?" Adrian asked her.

"What are you drinking?"

"Beer."

"Then I'll take one, as well."

Adrian grabbed the attention of one of the waiters and gave him their order. It was then that a couple passed and Adrian said, "Roger? Is that you?"

A man who looked to be in his late thirties or early forties turned and gave Adrian a curious glance. "Yes,

I'm Roger. But forgive me, I can't remember where we've met."

Adrian held out his hand. "Adrian Westmoreland. We've met through my brother Dillon," he lied, knowing the man probably wouldn't remember but would pretend that he did.

A huge smiled appeared on the man's face as he accepted Adrian's handshake. "Oh, yes, of course. I remember now. And this is my wife Kathy," he said, introducing the woman with him.

Adrian shook her hand. He then turned to Trinity and smiled. "And this is a very *special* friend," he said. "Roger and Kathy, I'd like you to meet Dr. Trinity Matthews."

Trinity couldn't help wondering what was going on in that mind of Adrian's. She soon found out when he said, "Trinity, I'd like you to meet Roger and Kathy Belvedere."

Trinity forced herself not to blink in surprise as she shook the couple's hands. "Nice to meet you."

"Likewise," Roger said, smiling. "And where do you practice, doctor? I'm familiar with a number of hospitals in the city. In fact," he said, chuckling and then bragging, "my family is building a wing at Denver Memorial."

"That's where I work. I'm in pediatrics, so I'm familiar with the wing under construction. It's much needed and will be nice when it's finished," Trinity said.

Roger's smile widened. "Thanks. If you work at Denver Memorial then you must know my brother Casey. He's a surgeon there. I'm sure you've heard of Dr. Casey Belvedere."

Trinity fought to keep a straight face. "Yes, I know Dr. Belvedere."

"Then I must mention to him that Kathy and I ran into the two of you."

"Yes, you do that," Adrian said, smiling.

After the couple walked off, the waiter approached with their beers. Trinity looked over at Adrian. "You knew he was going to be here tonight, didn't you?"

He looked at her. "Yes. And there's no doubt in my mind he'll mention seeing us to his brother."

Trinity nodded as she took a sip of her beer. Tonight was just another strategic move in Adrian's game plan. Why was she surprised...and sort of disappointed?

At that moment someone on a speaker announced that seating for the next show would start in fifteen minutes. As they finished their beers, she decided that regardless of the reason Adrian had brought her here, tonight she intended to enjoy herself.

Chapter 4

As he'd planned, after the show Adrian took Trinity to Andrew's, a place known in Denver for having the best desserts. While enjoying strawberry cheesecake topped with vanilla ice cream, Adrian decided he liked hearing the sound of Trinity's voice.

She kept the conversation interesting by telling him about her family. Her father owned a medical practice and her mother worked as his nurse. Her two older brothers were doctors, as well, living in Bunnell.

She also talked about her college days and how she'd wanted to stick close to home, which was why she'd attended the local community college in Bunnell for two years before moving to Gainesville to attend the University of Florida. Although it was a college town, the city of Gainesville provided a small-town atmosphere. She'd enjoyed living there so much that she'd remained there for medical school.

She also told him how she preferred a small town to a big one, how she found Denver much too large and how she looked forward to finishing up her residency and moving back to Bunnell.

He leaned back in his chair after cleaning his plate, admitting the cake and ice cream had been delicious. "Aw, come on," he joked to Trinity. "Why don't you just come clean and admit that the real reason you want to hightail it back is because you have a guy waiting there for you."

She made a face. The way she scrunched her nose and pouted her lips was utterly cute. "That is totally not true…especially after what Derrick did to Tara. The last thing I'd have is a boyfriend that I believed would wait for me."

He had heard all about the Tara fiasco from one of his cousins, although he couldn't remember which one. He couldn't believe any man in his right mind would run off and leave someone as gorgeous as Tara Matthews Westmoreland standing in the middle of some church. What a fool.

"What happened to Tara has made you resentful and distrustful of giving your heart to a hometown guy?"

She shrugged her shoulders and unconsciously licked whipped cream off her fork. In an instant his stomach tightened. Sexual hunger stirred to life in his groin. He picked up his glass of water and almost drained it in one gulp.

"Worse than that. It taught me not to truly give my heart to any man, hometown or otherwise."

He studied her, seeing the seriousness behind the beautiful pair of eyes staring back at him. "But things worked out fine for Tara in the end, didn't they? She met Thorn."

He saw the slow smile replace her frown. "Yes, she did, and I'm glad. He's made her happy."

Adrian nodded. "So there are happy endings sometimes."

She finished off the last of her cake before saying, "Yes, sometimes, but not often enough for me to take a chance."

"So you don't ever intend to fall in love?"

"Not if I can help it. I told you what I want."

He nodded again. "To return to Bunnell and work alongside your father and brothers in their medical business."

"Yes."

He took another sip of his water when she moistened the top of her lip with the tip of her tongue. "What about your happiness?" he asked her, shifting slightly in his chair.

She lifted a brow. "My happiness?"

"Yes. Don't you want to have someone to grow old with?"

She turned the tables when she asked, "Don't you?"

He thought about the question. "I intend to date and enjoy life for as long as I can. I'm aware at some point I'll need to settle down, marry and have children, but at the moment there're enough Westmorelands handling that without me. It seemed every time I came home for spring break, I would have a wedding to attend or a new niece, nephew or second cousin being born."

"Speaking of cousins…mainly yours," she said as if to clarify. "I've heard the story of how the Denver Westmorelands connected with the Atlanta-based Westmorelands, but what about these other cousins that might be out there?"

He knew she was referring to the ongoing investigation by Megan's husband, Rico, who was a private investigator. "It seems my great-grandfather Raphel Westmoreland was involved with four women before marrying my great-grandmother Gemma. Three of the women have now been accounted for. It seems none were his wives, although there's still one more to investigate for clarification."

He paused and then said, "Rico and Megan found out that one of the women, by the name of Clarice, had a baby by Raphel that he didn't know about. She died in a train derailment but not before she gave the child to another woman—a woman who'd lost her child and husband. A woman with the last name of Outlaw."

He could tell by the light in Trinity's eyes that she found what he'd told her fascinating. He understood. He was convinced that if there were any more Westmoreland kin out there, Rico would find them.

Adrian glanced at his watch. "It's still early yet. Is there anything else you want to do before I take you home?"

She glanced at her own watch. "Early? It's almost midnight."

He smiled. "Is it past your bedtime?"

"No."

"Then plan to enjoy the night. And I've got just the place."

"Where?"

"Come on and I'll show you."

A half hour later Trinity was convinced she needed her head examined. She looked down at herself and wondered how she had let Adrian talk her into this. Indoor mountain climbing. Seriously?

But here she was, decked out with climbing shoes, a harness, a rope and all the other things she needed to scale a man-made wall that looked too much like the real thing.

"Ready?"

She glanced over at Adrian who was standing beside her, decked out in his own climbing gear.

Ready? He has to be kidding.

She saw the excitement in his eyes and figured this was something he liked doing on a routine basis. But personally, she was not an outdoorsy kind of girl.

So why did you allow him to talk you into it?

It might have had everything to do with the way he had grabbed hold of her hand as he'd led her out of Andrew's and toward his car. The tingling sensation that erupted the moment his hand touched hers had seemed to pulverize her common sense. Or it could have been the smile that would creep onto his lips whenever he was on an adrenaline high. Darn, it was contagious.

He snapped his fingers in front of her face, making her realize she hadn't answered his question. "Hey, don't start daydreaming on me now, Trinity. You need your full concentration for this."

She looked over at the fake mountain she was supposed to climb. He claimed this particular one was for beginners, but she had serious doubts about that. She glanced up at him. "I don't know about this, Adrian."

His smile widened and she felt the immediate pull in her stomach. "You can do this. You look physically fit enough."

She rolled her eyes. "Looks are deceiving."

"Then this will definitely get you in shape. But to be honest, I don't see where there needs to be improvement."

She swallowed. Had he just flirted with her for the second time that night? "So, have you ever climbed an

outdoor mountain? The real thing?" she asked, recheck-
ing the fit of her gloves.

"Sure. Plenty of times. I love doing it and you will,
too."

She doubted it. Most people were probably in bed
and here she was at one in the morning at some all-night
indoor mountain climbing arena.

"Ready to try it?" Adrian asked, breaking into her
thoughts.

"It's now or never, I suppose."

He smiled. "You'll do fine."

She wasn't sure about that, and did he *have* to be
standing so close to her? "Okay, what do I do?"

"Just grab or step on each climbing hold located on
the wooden boards as you work your way to the top."

She glanced up to the top and had to actually tilt
her head back to see it. "This is my first time, Adrian.
There's no way I'll make it that far up."

"You never know."

She did. She knew her limits…even when it concerned him. She was well aware that she was attracted
to him just as she was well aware that it was an attraction that could get her into trouble if she didn't keep
her sense about her.

Trinity moved toward the huge structure and proceeded to lift her leg. When she felt Adrian's hands on
her backside, she jerked around and put her leg down.
"What are you doing?"

"Giving you a boost. Don't you need one?"

She figured what she needed was her head examined.
Had his intention been to give her a boost or to cop a
feel? Unfortunately her backside didn't know the difference and it was still reacting to his touch. Heat had
spiked in the area and was spreading all over.

"No, I don't need one, and watch your hands, Adrian. Keep them to yourself."

He gave her an innocent smile. "I am duly chastised. But honestly, I was only trying to help and was in no way trying to take advantage of a tempting opportunity."

"Whatever," she muttered, not believing him one bit. However, instead of belaboring the issue, she turned and started her climb, which wasn't easy.

Beginner's structure or no beginner's structure, it was meant to give a person a good workout. Why would anyone in their right mind want to do this for fun? she asked herself as she steadily and slowly moved up one climbing hold at a time. After each attempt she had to take a deep breath and silently pray for strength to continue. She had made it to the halfway point and was steadily moving higher.

"Looking good, Trinity. Real good."

It wasn't what he said but rather how he'd said it that made her turn slightly and look down at him, nearly losing her footing in the process. Climbing this structure was giving her backside a darn good workout. She could feel it in every movement, and there was no doubt in her mind that he could see it, too. While she was struggling to get to the top, he was down below ass-watching.

"That's it." Frustrated with him for looking and with herself for actually liking the thought of him checking her out, she began her descent.

"Giving up already?"

She waited until her feet were on solid ground before she stood in front of him. Regarding him critically, she answered, "What do you think?"

Dark lashes were half lowered over his eyes when he said, "I think you're temptation, Trinity."

Whatever words she'd planned to say were zapped from her mind. Why did he have to say that and why had he said it while looking at her with those sexy eyes of his? The last thing she needed was for heat surges to flash through her body the way they were doing now.

"Considering the nature of our relationship, you're out of line, Adrian."

He leaned in closer and she got a whiff of his manly scent. She watched his lips curve into a seductive smile. "Why? And before you get all mouthy on me, there's something you need to consider."

"What?" she asked, getting even more frustrated. Although she would never admit it, she thought he was temptation, as well.

"I'm *supposed* to find you desirable. If I didn't, I couldn't pull off what needs to be done to dissuade Belvedere. My acting abilities can only extend so far. I can't pretend to want a woman if I don't."

Trinity went still. Was he saying he wanted her? From the way his gaze was darkening, she had a feeling that assumption was right. "I think we need to talk about it."

"At the moment, I think not."

When she opened her mouth to protest, he leaned in closer and said in a low, sexy tone, "See that structure over there?"

Her gaze followed his and she saw what he was referring to. It was huge, twice the size of the one she'd tried to scale, designed to challenge even the best of climbers. "Yes, I see it. What about it?"

The look on his face suddenly changed from desire to bold, heated lust. "I plan to climb all over it tonight. Otherwise, I'll try my damnedest later to climb all over you."

Chapter 5

Some words once stated couldn't be taken back. You just had to deal with them and Adrian was trying like hell to deal.

He had taken his climb and had done a damn good job scaling a wall he'd had difficulty doing in the past. It was amazing what lust could drive a man to do. And he was lusting after Trinity. Admitting it to her had made her nervous, wary of him, which was why she was hugging the passenger door as if it were her new best friend. If he didn't know for certain it was locked, he would be worried she would tumble out of the car.

"I won't bite," he finally said as he exited the expressway. *But I can perform a pretty good lick job,* he thought, but now was not the time to share such information.

"Pretending to be lovers isn't working, Adrian."

"What makes you think that?" he asked, although

he was beginning to think along those same lines. "Because I admitted I want you, Trinity?"

"I would think that has a lot to do with it."

Adrian didn't say anything for a minute. Watching Trinity's backside while she'd climbed that wall had definitely done something to him; had brought out coiling arousal within his very core. And when the crotch of his jeans began pounding like hell from an erection he could barely control, he'd known he was in trouble. The only thing that had consumed his mind—although he knew better—was that he needed to have some of her.

"I thought I explained things to you, Trinity. You're a sexy woman. I'm a hot-blooded male. There're bound to be sparks."

"As long as those sparks don't cause a fire."

"They won't," he said easily. "I'll put it out before that happens. I'm no more interested in a real affair than you are. So relax. What I'm encountering is simple lust. I'll be thirty-one in a few months so I think I'm old enough to handle it." And he decided, starting now, he would handle it by taking control of himself, which is why he changed the subject.

"So what are your plans for tomorrow?" he asked.

He heard her sigh. "You mean *today,* right? Sunday. It's almost two in the morning," she said.

"I stand corrected. What are your plans for today?"

"Sleep, sleep and more sleep. I seldom get the weekends off and I can't wait to have a love affair with my bed. It will be Monday before you know it."

A love affair with her bed. Now why did she have to go there? Images of her naked under silken sheets were making his senses flare in the wrong directions.

He could imagine her scent. It would be close to what he was inhaling now but probably a little more sensual. And he could imagine how she would look naked. Lordy. His body throbbed at the vision. His fingers twitched. When he had touched her backside while giving her that boost he had actually felt the air thicken in his lungs.

"What about you? What do you have planned?"

If he was smart, he would go somewhere this weekend and get laid. Maybe that would help rid his mind of all these dangerous fantasies he was having. But he'd said on their first date that he would see her and only her until this ordeal with Belvedere was over. "Unlike you I won't be sleeping late. I promised Ramsey that I would help him put new fencing in the north range."

"I understand from Tara that you're not living on your family's land, that you lease a place in town."

"That's right. I'm not ready to build on my one hundred acres quite yet. Where I live is just what I need for now. I have someone coming in every week to keep things tidy and to prepare my meals, and that's good enough for me."

A short while later he was walking her to her door, although she'd told him doing so wasn't necessary. She had told him that the other night, as well, but he'd done so anyway.

He watched as she used her key to unlock the door. She then turned to him. "Thanks for a nice evening and for walking me to the door, Adrian."

"You're welcome. I'd like to check inside."

She rolled her eyes. "Is that really necessary?"

"I think so. After what happened with Keisha last year, I would feel a lot better if I did."

He figured she had heard how his cousin Canyon's wife, Keisha, had come home to find her house in shambles.

Trinity stepped aside. "Help yourself. I definitely want you to feel better."

Ignoring the sarcasm he heard in her voice, Adrian moved past her and checked the bedrooms, kitchen and bathrooms. He returned to the living room to find her leaning against the closed door, her arms crossed over her chest.

Her gaze clashed with his. "Satisfied?" she asked in an annoyed tone.

Suddenly a deep, fierce hunger stirred to life inside him. That same hunger he'd been hopelessly fighting all night. He told himself to walk out the door and not look back, but knew he could no more ignore the yearnings that were rushing through him than he could not breathe. She had no idea how totally sensuous she looked or the effect it was having on him.

He walked toward her in a measured pace. When she turned and reached for the door to open it for him to leave, he reached for her. The moment he touched her, fiery heat shot straight to his groin.

Before she could say anything, he pressed her back against the door and swooped his mouth down on hers with a hunger he needed to release. He couldn't recall precisely when she began kissing him back—all he knew was that she was doing so, and with a greed that equaled his.

He pressed hard into her middle, wanting her to feel just how aroused he was, as his tongue tangled with hers in a duel so sensuous he wasn't sure if the moans he heard were coming from her or from him.

No telling how long the kiss would have lasted if they hadn't needed to come up for air. He reluctantly released her mouth and stared down into the fierce darkness of her dazed eyes. She appeared stunned at the degree of passion the two of them had shared, which was even more than the last time they'd kissed.

He leaned in close to her moist lips and answered the question she'd asked him moments ago. "Yes, I'm satisfied, Trinity. I am now extremely satisfied."

He then opened the door and walked out.

Trinity stood there. Astonished.

What on earth had just happened? What was that sudden onslaught of intense need that had overtaken her, made her mold her mouth to his as though that was how it was supposed to be? And why did her mouth feel like it was where it belonged when it was connected to his?

She shook her head to jiggle out of her daze. The effects were even more profound than before. It had taken days to get her mind back on track after the last kiss; she had a feeling this one would take even longer.

Her brows pulled together in annoyance. Why had he kissed her again? Just as important, why had she let him? She hadn't been an innocent bystander by any means. She could recall every lick of his tongue just as she could remember every lick of hers.

She hadn't held back anything. She'd been just as aggressive as he had. What did that say about her? What was he assuming it said?

As she moved toward her bedroom to strip off her clothes and take a shower, she couldn't help but recall something else. Watching him climb that wall. He was in great shape and it showed. He'd looked rough and so darn manly. Every time he lifted a jeans-clad thigh as he moved upward, her gaze had followed, watching how his muscles bulged and showed the strength of his legs. The way his jeans had cupped his backside had been a work of art, worthy to be ogled. And when he removed his shirt, she had seen a perfect set of abs glistening with his sweat.

The woman in her had appreciated how he'd reached the top with an overabundance of virility. That was probably why she'd lost her head the moment he'd taken her into his arms and plowed her with a kiss that weakened her knees. But now he was gone and once she got at least eighteen hours of nonstop sleep, she would wake up in her right mind.

She certainly hoped so.

Chapter 6

With little sleep and the memory of a kiss that just wouldn't let go, Adrian, along with his brothers and cousins, helped his older brother Ramsey repair fencing on a stretch of land that extended for miles.

Ramsey had worked as CEO for a while alongside Dillon before giving it up to pursue his first love: being a sheep rancher. Adrian's brothers Zane and Derringer preferred the outdoors, too. After working in the family business for a few years, Zane, Derringer and Ramsey, as well as their cousin Jason, joined their Montana Westmoreland cousins in a horse breeding and training business.

Ramsey's wife, Chloe, had arrived with sandwiches, iced tea and homemade cookies. Everyone teased Adrian's cousin Stern about his upcoming wedding to JoJo, who Stern had been best friends with for years. The two had been engaged for more than six months and Stern was anxious for the wedding to happen, saying he was tired of waiting.

Adrian didn't say anything as he listened to the easy camaraderie between his family. Leaving home for college had been hard, but luckily he and Aidan had decided to attend the same university. As usual, they had stuck together. Their careers had eventually carried them in different directions. But Adrian knew that eventually his twin would return to Denver.

Aidan's plans were similar to Trinity's, regarding returning to her hometown to practice medicine. He could understand her wanting to do that, just as he understood Aidan. So why did the thought of her returning to Florida in about eighteen months bother him? It wasn't as if she meant anything to him. He'd already established the fact that she wasn't his type. They had nothing in common. She liked small towns and he preferred big cities. She wasn't an outdoor person and he was. So why was he allowing her to consume his thoughts the way she had been lately?

"So what's going on with you, Adrian? Or are you really Aidan?"

Adrian couldn't help but smile at his brother Zane. It seemed that while he had been daydreaming everyone had left lunch to return to work. "You know who I am and nothing's going on. I'm just trying to make it one day at a time."

"So things are working out for you at Blue Ridge?"

"Pretty much. I can see why you, Ramsey and Derringer decided the corporate life wasn't for you. You have to like it or otherwise you'd hate it."

Adrian liked his job as chief project officer. His duties included assisting Dillon when it came to any construction and engineering functions of the company, and advising him on the development of major projects and making sure all jobs were completed in a timely manner.

As they began walking to where the others were beginning work again, Zane asked, "So, how are things going being the pretend lover of Thorn's sister-in-law?"

Adrian glanced over at Zane, not surprised he knew. How many others in his family knew? Bailey hadn't mentioned anything the other night at dinner so she might be clueless. "Okay, I guess. I'm busy trying to establish this relationship with her for others to see. The first night I made sure the doctor saw us together and last night I went to a show that I knew one of his family members would be attending."

Zane nodded. "Is it working?"

"Don't know yet. The doctor's path hasn't crossed with Trinity's since we started this farce."

"Hmm, I'm curious to see how things turn out."

Adrian looked at his brother. "If he's smart, he'll leave her alone."

"Oh, I'm not talking about her and the doctor."

Adrian slowed his pace. "Then who are you talking about?"

Zane smiled. "The two of you."

Adrian stopped walking and Zane stopped, as well. "Don't know what you mean," he said.

Zane shrugged. "I saw her at Riley's wedding. She's a looker, but I expected no less with her being Tara's sister and all."

Adrian frowned. "So?"

Zane shoved his hands into the back pockets of his jeans. "So nothing. Forget I said anything. I guess we better get back to work if we want to finish up by dusk."

Adrian watched his brother walk off and decided that since he'd gotten married, Zane didn't talk much sense anymore.

"Dr. Matthews, I trust you've been doing well."

Immediately, Trinity's skin crawled at the sound of the man's voice as he approached her. She looked up from writing in a patient's chart. "Yes, Dr. Belvedere. I've been fine."

As a courtesy, she could ask him how he'd been, but she really didn't want to know. She tried ignoring him as she resumed documenting the patient's chart.

"I saw you the other night."

Her heart rate increased. He had come to stand beside her. Way too close as far as she was concerned. She didn't look up at him but continued writing. "And what night was that?"

"That night you were out on a date at Laredo's."

She glanced up briefly. "Oh. I didn't see you." That was no lie since she had intentionally not looked in his direction.

"Well, I saw you. You were with a man," he said in an accusing tone.

She hugged the chart to her chest as she looked up again. "Yes, I was. If you recall, I told you I was involved with someone."

"I didn't believe you."

"I don't know why you wouldn't."

Belvedere smiled and Trinity knew the smile wasn't genuine. "Doesn't matter. Break things off with him."

Trinity blinked. "Excuse me?"

"You heard what I said."

Something within Trinity snapped. Not caring if anyone passing by heard her, she said, "I will not break things off with him! You have no right to dictate something like that to me."

A smirk appeared on his face before he looked over his shoulder to make sure no one was privy to their conversation. "I can make or break you, Dr. Matthews. If you rub me the wrong way, all those years you spent in medical school won't mean a damn thing. Think about it."

He turned to walk off, but then, as if he'd forgotten to say something, he turned back. "And the next time you decide to report me to someone, think twice. My family practically owns this hospital. I suggest you remember that. And to make sure we fully understand each other, I've requested your presence in the next two surgeries I have scheduled, which coincidently are on your next two days off. What a pity." Chuckling to himself, he walked off.

Trinity just stared at him. She felt as if steam were coming out of her ears. He'd just admitted to sabotaging her time off. *How dare he!*

Placing the patient's chart back on the rack, she angrily headed to the office of Wendell Fowler, the chief of pediatrics. Not bothering to wait on the elevator, she took the stairs. By the time she went up three flights of stairs she was even madder.

Dr. Fowler's secretary, an older woman by the name of Marissa Adams, glanced up when she saw her. "Yes, Dr. Matthews?"

"I'd like to see Dr. Fowler. It's important."

The woman nodded. "Please have a seat and I'll see if Dr. Fowler is available."

She hadn't been seated a few minutes when the secretary called out to her. "Dr. Fowler will see you now, Dr. Matthews."

"Thanks." Trinity walked around the woman's desk and headed for Wendell Fowler's office.

Less than a half hour later Trinity left Dr. Fowler's office unsatisfied. The man hadn't been any help. He'd even accused her of dramatizing the situation. He'd then tried to convince her that working in surgery on her days off under the guidance of Dr. Belvedere would be a boost to her medical career.

Feeling a degree of fury the likes of which she'd never felt before, she walked past Ms. Adams's desk with her head held high, fighting back tears in her eyes. If Dr. Belvedere's goal was to break her resolve and force her to give in to what he wanted, then he was wasting his time. If she had to give up her days off this week, she would do it. She refused to let anyone break her down.

Chapter 7

Adrian leaned back in the chair behind his desk and stared at the phone he'd just hung up. He'd tried calling Trinity from a different number and she still wasn't taking his calls. He rubbed his hand across his jaw, feeling totally frustrated. So they had kissed. Twice. Big deal. That was no reason for her to get uptight about it and not take his calls. This was crap he didn't have time for.

It had been well over a week since that kiss. Ten days to be exact. He'd heard of women holding grudges but this was ridiculous. Over a kiss? Really? And no one could convince him she hadn't enjoyed it just as much as he had. All he had to do was close his eyes to relive the moments of all that tongue interaction. It had been everything a kiss should be and more.

The text signal on his cell phone indicated he had a message. He pulled the phone out of his desk drawer and tried to ignore the flutters that passed through his chest when he saw it was from Trinity.

Got your calls. Worked on my days off. Belvedere's orders. Spent last 10 days at hospital. Tired. Can barely
stand. Off for few days starting tomorrow a.m.

Adrian sat straighter in his chair. What the hell! Trinity had worked on her days off? And it had been Belvedere's orders? Adrian's hands trembled in anger when
he texted her back.

On my way 2 get you now!

She texted him back.

No. Don't. I'm okay. Just tired. Going home in the a.m.
Will call you then.

Adrian frowned. If Trinity thought that message satisfied him, she was wrong. Who required anyone to
work on their days off? There were labor laws against
that sort of thing. And if Belvedere had ordered her to
do so then the man had gone too damn far.

There was a knock on his office door.

"Come in."

Dillon stuck his head in. "I'm leaving early. Bailey's
watching the kids while Pam and I enjoy a date night."

His cousin must have seen the deep scowl on Adrian's face. He stepped into the office and closed the door
behind him, concern in his eyes. "What's wrong with
you, Adrian?"

Adrian stood. Agitated, he paced in front of his desk.
It was a few moments before he'd pulled himself together enough to answer Dillon's question. "I hadn't
heard from Trinity in over a week and was concerned
since I knew Belvedere had seen us together that night
at dinner. She texted me a few moments ago. The man

ordered her to work on her days off. She's worked ten days straight, Dil. Can you believe that?"

Before Dillon could answer, Adrian added, "I've got a good mind to go to that hospital and beat the hell out of him."

"I think you need to have a seat and think this through."

The hard tone of Dillon's voice had Adrian staring at him. And then, as Dillon suggested, he sat. "I'm sitting, Dillon, but I still want to go over to that hospital and beat the hell out of Belvedere."

"Sure you do. But I'm telling you now the same thing I told you the day you came home after whipping Joel Gaffney's behind. You can't settle anything with a fight."

Maybe not, Adrian thought. But if he remembered correctly, he had felt a lot better seeing that bloody nose on Gaffney. Adrian had wanted to make sure Joel thought twice before putting a snake in Bailey's locker again. "It was either me or Bane," Adrian said. "And I'm sure Gaffney preferred my whipping to Bane's. Your kid brother would not have shown any mercy."

Dillon rolled his eyes. "Again, I repeat, you can't settle anything with a fight. Belvedere will file charges and you'll end up in jail. Then where will Trinity be?"

"Better off. I might be in jail, but when I finish with Belvedere he'll never perform surgery on anyone again. I'll see to it."

Dillon stared at him for a long moment before crossing the room to drop down in the chair across from Adrian's desk. "I think we need to talk."

"Not sure it will do any good. If I find out Belvedere made Trinity work on her off days just for spite, I'm going to make him wish he hadn't done that."

"Fine, then come up with a plan that's within the law, Adrian. But first know the facts and not assumptions. It could be that she was needed at the hospital. Doctors work all kinds of crazy hours. You have two siblings who are doctors so you should know that. Emergencies come up that have to be dealt with whether you're scheduled to be off or not."

Adrian knew what Dillon was trying to do. Come up with another plausible reason why Trinity had been ordered to work on her days off. "And what if I don't like the facts after hearing them?"

"Then like I said, come up with a plan. And if it's one that makes sense, you'll get my support. I don't appreciate any man trying to take advantage of a woman any more than you do. In the meantime, you stay out of trouble."

Dillon stood and headed for the door. Before he could open it, Adrian called out, "Thanks, Dil."

Dillon turned around. "Just do as I ask and stay out of trouble. Okay?"

"I'll try."

When Dillon gave him a pointed look Adrian knew that response hadn't been good enough. "Okay. Fine. I'll stay out of trouble."

Trinity believed that if she continued forcing one foot in front of the other she would eventually make it out of the hospital to the parking lot and into her car. But then she would have to force her eyes to stay open on the drive home.

Never had she felt so tired. Her body ached all over. Not from the hours it had missed sleep but because of the other assignments given to her on top of her regular job…all deliberately and for the sole purpose of making her give in to Dr. Belvedere's advances. If she'd ever had an inkling of attraction to him, did he really think she would let him touch her after this? Did it matter to him that she was beginning to hate him? He didn't see her as a colleague; all he saw was a body he wanted. A body he would do just about anything to get. A conquest.

When she stepped off the elevator on the main level, Belvedere stood there waiting to get on. Her eyes met his and she gritted her teeth when he had the nerve to smile. "Good morning, Dr. Matthews."

"Dr. Belvedere," she acknowledged and kept walking.

"Wait up a minute, Dr. Matthews."

She had a mind to keep walking, but it would have been a show of total disrespect for a revered surgeon, so she paused and turned. "Yes, Dr. Belvedere?"

He came to a stop in front of her. "Just wanted to say that you did a great job in surgery the other night."

"Thank you," she replied stiffly. She was tempted to tell him just what he could do with that compliment.

"I think we should have dinner to discuss a few things," he added smoothly. "I'll pick you up tonight at seven."

"Sorry, she has other plans."

Trinity's breath caught at the sound of the masculine voice. She turned to see Adrian walking toward them. Why was her heart suddenly fluttering like crazy at the sight of him? And why did seeing him give her a little more strength than she had just moments ago?

Even with the smile plastered on his lips, his smile didn't quite reach his eyes. He was angry. She could feel it. But he was holding that anger back and she appreciated that. The last thing she needed was him making a scene with one of her superiors.

Because of his long strides, he reached her in no time. "Adrian, I didn't expect to see you here."

He slid his arms around her waist, placed a kiss on her lips and hugged her. "Hey, baby. I figured the least I could do after you worked ten days straight is be here to take you home."

She glanced over at Dr. Belvedere and swallowed. Unlike Adrian, Dr. Belvedere wasn't smiling. She figured he realized that, dressed in blue scrubs, he failed miserably to compare to Adrian, who was wearing a designer suit that looked tailor-made for his body.

Before she could make introductions, Adrian turned to Belvedere. "Dr. Belvedere, right?" he asked, extending his hand to the man. "I've heard a lot about you. I'm Adrian Westmoreland, Trinity's significant other."

From the look that appeared in Belvedere's eyes, Adrian knew the man hadn't liked the role he'd claimed in Trinity's life. It took every ounce of control Adrian could muster to exchange handshakes with Belvedere. He wanted to do just what he'd told Dillon and beat the hell out of him. Even so, the memory of Dillon's advice kept him in line. Though he couldn't resist the opportunity to squeeze the man's hand harder than was needed. There was no way the doctor didn't know he'd purposely done so.

Let him know what I can do to those precious fingers of his if I'm riled.

Adrian turned back to Trinity and inwardly flinched when he saw tired eyes and lines of exhaustion etched into her features. He needed to get her out of here now before he was tempted to do something he would enjoy doing but might regret later. "Ready to go, baby?"

"Yes, but my car is here," she said, and he noticed

that like him she had dismissed Dr. Belvedere's presence. Why the man was still standing there was beyond Adrian's comprehension.

"I'll come back for it later," he said, taking her hand. He didn't even bother to say anything to the doctor before walking away. He just couldn't get the words *It was nice meeting you* from his lips when they would have been a bald-faced lie.

When they exited the building Trinity paused and glanced up at him. "Thanks."

He knew what she was thanking him for. "It wasn't easy. Just knowing he had you work on your off days made me angry." He paused. "Were you needed or did he do it for spite?"

She looked away, and when she looked back at him, he saw the anger in her eyes. "He did it for spite."

If it wasn't for the talk he'd had with Dillon he would go back into the hospital and clean up the floor with Belvedere. But what Dillon had said was true. In the end, Adrian would be in jail and Belvedere would make matters worse for Trinity.

"Come on, my car is parked over there. I lucked out and got a spot close to the entrance."

"I'm glad. I don't recall the last time I was so tired. It wouldn't be so bad if I'd been able to sleep, but Belvedere made sure I stayed busy."

"The bastard," Adrian muttered under his breath.

"I heard that," she said. "And I concur. He is a bastard. What's so sad is that he actually thinks what he's doing is okay, and that in the end I'll happily fall into his arms. He's worse than a bastard, Adrian."

Adrian wasn't going to disagree with her. "We need to come up with a plan."

She chuckled softly and even then he could hear her exhaustion. "I thought we had a plan."

"Then we need a backup plan since he wants to be difficult."

"He actually told me to get rid of you, and told me he deliberately scheduled me on my days off. I went to see Dr. Fowler, who is chief of pediatrics, and he accused me of being dramatic. It's as though everyone refuses to do anything where Belvedere is concerned."

Adrian pulled her closer when they reached his car. He helped her inside and snapped her seat belt in place. "Go ahead, close your eyes and rest a bit. I'll wake you when I get you home."

Doing as Adrian suggested, Trinity closed her eyes. All she could do was visualize her bed—soft mattress, warm covers and a firm pillow. She needed to go to the grocery store to pick up a few things, but not today. Right now she preferred sleeping to eating. She would take a long, hot bath…not a shower…but a soak in her tub to ease the aches from her muscles. She planned to sleep for an entire day and put everything out of her mind.

Except.

Except the man who had showed up unexpectedly this morning to drive her home. Seeing him had caused her heart to thump hard in her chest and blood to rush crazily through her veins. She knew for certain she had never reacted to any other man that way before. That meant she was more exhausted than she had thought. And it was messing with her hormones.

Why this effect from Adrian and no one else? Why was Adrian's manly scent not only flowing through her nostrils but seeping into her pores and kicking sensations into a body that was too tired to respond?

In the deep recesses of her mind, she was trying not to remember the last time they'd been together. Namely, the kiss they'd shared. It had been the memory of that kiss that had lulled her to sleep when she'd thought she was too tired to close her eyes. The memory of that kiss was what she had thought about when she had needed to think of pleasant things to keep going.

There was no doubt in her mind that when it came to kissing, Adrian was definitely on top of his game. Even now, she remembered how his mouth had taken hers.

She had kissed him back, acquainting herself with the shape and fullness of his lips, his taste. It had been different from the first kiss. Longer. Sweeter. She had allowed herself to indulge. In doing so, it seemed her senses had gone through some sort of sensitivity training. Her head had been spinning and her tongue tingling. She'd been stunned by the force of passion that had run rampant through her.

Then there was the way he had held her in his arms. With his hands in the center of her back, he had held her with a possession that was astounding. She had felt every solid inch of him. Some parts harder than others, and it was those hard parts…one in particular…that had her fantasizing about him since.

"Wake up, Trinity. We're here."

She slowly opened her eyes. She glanced out the window at her surroundings. Slightly disoriented, she blinked and looked again before turning to Adrian. "This isn't my home."

A smile touched his lips. "No, it's mine. When I said I was taking you home, I meant to my place."

Now she was confused. She sat straighter in her seat. "Why?"

"So I can make sure you get your rest. Undisturbed. I wouldn't put it past Belvedere to find some excuse to call or show up at your place uninvited."

The thought of Dr. Belvedere doing either of those things bothered her. "Do you think he'd actually just drop by?"

"Not sure. But if he does, you won't be there. The man has issues and I wouldn't put anything past him."

Trinity hated saying it but neither would she. Still… To sleep at Adrian's place just didn't seem right. "I don't think it's a good idea for me to stay here."

"Why?"

She shrugged. "People might think things about us."

He chuckled. "People are *supposed* to think things about us, Trinity. The more they do, the better it is. Belvedere will look like a total ass trying to come on to a woman already seriously involved with another man. It will only show how pathetically demented he is."

What Adrian said made sense, but she was still wearing her scrubs and she wanted to get out of them. "I don't have any clothes."

"No problem. I'll loan you my T-shirt that will cover you past your thighs, and after you get a good day's rest, I'll take you to your place to get something else to put on. The main thing is for you to get some sleep. I'm going into the office once I get you settled in."

"I can't hide out here forever, Adrian."

"Not asking you to do that. I just think we need to continue to give the impression that we're lovers and not just two people merely seeing each other."

He paused a moment and then asked, "Why are you afraid to stay at my place?"

Good question.

"It's not that I'm afraid to stay here. It's just that I was looking forward to sleeping in my own bed."

An impish, feral smile curved his lips. "You might like mine better."

That's what I'm afraid of.

Why had his tone dropped a notch when he'd said that? His raspy words had resonated through her senses like a heated caress.

Quickly deciding all she wanted was to get some sleep, regardless of whose bed it was, she agreed. "Fine. Let's go. Your bed it is. And...Adrian?"

"Yes?"

"I sleep alone, so no funny business."

He chuckled. "I give you my word. I won't touch you unless you touch me first."

Then there shouldn't be any problems, she thought, because she wouldn't be touching him. At least she hoped not.

Chapter 8

Adrian glanced around the conference room at the four other men sitting at the table. All wore intense expressions. Since joining the company and regularly attending executive board meetings, he'd discovered that they all wore that look when confronted with major decisions involving Blue Ridge Land Management.

Today's discussion was about a property they were interested in near Miami's South Beach. He'd given his report and now it was up to the board to decide the next move. It was Dillon who spoke, addressing his question to Adrian. "And you don't think a shopping complex there is a wise investment for us?"

"No, not from an engineering standpoint. Don't get me wrong, South Beach is a nice area, but there are several red flags such as labor issues and building costs that we don't want to deal with. One particular company is monopolizing the market and deliberately jacking up prices. It's not a situation we should get into right now. Besides, whatever development we place there will only be one of the same kind of complex that's already there. Even that's spelled out in the marketing report."

He knew his report hadn't been what they'd wanted to hear. For years, Blue Ridge had tossed around the idea of building a huge shopping complex in South Beach. The timing hadn't been right then and, as he'd spelled out in his report, the timing wasn't right now.

Because he'd been taught that when he was faced with a problem he should be ready to offer a solution, he said, "There's a lucrative substitute in Florida that I'd like you to consider."

"And where might that be?" Riley asked, taking a sip of his coffee. "West Palm Beach?"

"No," Adrian replied. "Further north. It's one of the sea islands that stretches from South Carolina to Florida, right along the Florida coast. Amelia Island."

A smile touched Dillon's lips. "I went there once for a business conference. Took Pam with me and we stayed for a week. It's quaint, peaceful, totally relaxing…and—" his smile widened "—there are about six or seven beautiful golf courses."

"So I heard. And while you were enjoying your time on those golf courses, what was Pam doing?" Adrian inquired.

Dillon scrunched his forehead trying to remember. "She visited the spa a few times, otherwise she hung out by the pool reading."

"Just think of what choices she could have made if we had a complex on the island," Adrian said. "The clientele flocking to Amelia Island can afford to jet in on private planes, spend seven days golfing and dining at exclusive restaurants. They can certainly afford the type of luxury complex we want to build."

Adrian could tell he had their interest.

"What about labor issues and building costs?" Stern asked.

"Nearly nonexistent. The only problem we might run into is a few islanders not embracing change, who might want the island to remain as it is. But the person I spoke with this morning, who happens to be a college friend of mine who lives on the island, says that segment of the population is outnumbered by progressives who want the island to be a number-one vacation spot."

Providing everyone with the handouts he'd prepared, Adrian told them why placing a development on Amelia Island would work. A huge smile touched Canyon's face. "So, I suggest we see what we can do to make it happen."

An hour later, Adrian was back in his office. Since the meeting had been scheduled for ten o'clock, that had given him time to pick up Trinity from work and get her settled into his place. By the time he'd left for the office she was in his Jacuzzi tub. He expected that she was asleep now and that's what he wanted. That's what she needed.

And because his housekeeper had just been in, his place was in decent order and his refrigerator well stocked. Trinity had even complimented him on how neat and clean his place was and how spacious it was for just one person.

He had another meeting to attend today, a business dinner. But he was looking forward to returning home. Just to check on her, he told himself. Nothing more. She wasn't his first female houseguest and she wouldn't be the last. But then there was the fact that he had been thinking of her all day, when he hadn't wanted to. So what was that about?

He was pulling a folder from the In tray on his desk when his cell phone rang. He couldn't help smiling when he saw the caller was his twin.

"Yes, Dr. Westmoreland?"

The chuckle on the other end was rich. "Sounds good, doesn't it?"

"I always told you it would. How're things going?"

"Fine. When are you going to pay me a visit?"

Adrian leaned back in his chair. "I had planned to visit Charlotte this month but—"

"You're too involved with some female, right?"

Adrian chuckled. "Should I ask how you know?"

"You're letting off strong emotions."

Adrian didn't doubt it, and he blamed Belvedere for making him want to hurt somebody. "I have a lot going on here." He told his brother about the charade he and Trinity were playing.

"Trinity Matthews? I like her. I spent a lot of time talking to her at Riley's wedding."

"I noticed."

"Oops. Someone sounds jealous."

"No jealousy involved. Just saying I noticed the two of you had a lot to say to each other." He paused and added, "But I figured you were doing it to get a rise out of Jillian."

"If I was, it didn't work."

"Now what are you going to do?"

"Move on and not look back."

"Can you do that?" Adrian asked.

"I can try." Aidan paused. "Now back to you and Trinity. Has that doctor taken the bait and left her alone?"

"No, in fact he told her to break things off with me and when she refused he made her work longer hours and on her days off. And both days were assisting in surgery."

"Is the man crazy? An exhausted doctor can make costly mistakes, especially during surgery. The man isn't fit to be a doctor if getting a woman in his bed is more important than the welfare of his patients. That disgusts me."

"It disgusts me, as well," Adrian said. "That's why I refuse to let him use her that way."

"I'm feeling your emotions again. They are pretty damn strong, Adrian. Unless you plan on doing something with those feelings for Trinity then you should try keeping them in check."

"I suggest you do the same with Jillian," Adrian chided. "Just like you feel my emotions, remember I can also feel yours."

"I guess I do need to remember that."

After Adrian ended the call with his brother he couldn't help wondering if Aidan would be able to move on from his breakup with Jillian and not look back as he'd claimed. Adrian's thoughts shifted to Trinity. Was she still sleeping? The thought of her curled up in a bed in one of his guest rooms sent strong, heavy heartbeats thumping in his chest.

When he recalled how exhausted she was, barely able to stand on her feet, a muscle jumped in his jaw. No one should have to work in that state. All because Belvedere had tried breaking her down.

Anger poured through him at the thought. He was only soothed in knowing that for the time being she was safely tucked away under his roof. He rubbed the back of his neck. Aidan was right about keeping his emo-

tions in check where Trinity was concerned. Doing so
was hard, and he didn't like the implications of what
that could mean. Especially when he was in a mad rush
to leave the office and go home to see her. That wasn't
good. He needed a diversion.

Adrian knew the one woman he could always count
on. He picked up his phone and tapped in her number.
He sighed in relief when she answered.

"Bailey Westmoreland."

"Bay? How would you like to do a movie tonight?"

He smiled when she said yes. "I have a business
dinner in a few hours and will pick you up afterward.
Around seven."

Trinity shifted in bed and curled into another position beneath the covers. When had her mattress begun
to feel so soft? She slowly opened her eyes and looked
around the room. Beautiful blue curtains hung at the
window, the same shade as the bedspread covering her.
Blue? Her curtains and bedcoverings weren't blue. They
were brown. Pushing hair back from her face, she pulled
herself up in a bed that wasn't hers. She then recalled
where she was. Adrian's place.

Although she had been too exhausted to appreciate the décor when she'd first arrived, she remembered
being impressed with the spaciousness of his condo as
well as how tidy it was. He'd told her he had a housekeeper who came in twice a week, not only to keep the
place looking decent, but also to do his laundry and
prepare his meals.

That was a nice setup. Although she had a fetish for
keeping her own place neat, she couldn't help but think
about all the laundry she had yet to get to. And as far as
cooked meals, she only got those when she went home

to Bunnell. Otherwise she ate on the run, and mostly at fast-food places.

This was a nice guest room, she thought. Not too feminine and not too manly. The painting on the wall was abstract and she appreciated the splash of color that went with the drapes, the carpeting and the dark cherrywood furniture. There had been a lot of pillows on the bed, which she had tossed off before diving under the covers.

She pushed those same covers back as she eased out of bed, suddenly remembering that the only stitch of clothing she wore was the T-shirt Adrian had loaned her. It barely touched her mid-thigh. The material felt soft against her skin.

Moments later, after coming out of the connecting bathroom, she slid her shoulders into a silk bathrobe Adrian had placed across the arm of a chair. Her gaze lit on the clock on the nightstand. It was a little after seven. Had she really slept more than ten hours?

Since she felt well rested, she figured her body must have needed it. What had Belvedere been thinking to make her work such long hours, which was clearly against hospital policy? She knew very well what he'd been thinking and it only made her despise him that much more.

Her stomach growled and she left the bedroom for the kitchen. As she passed by several rooms on her way downstairs, she couldn't help but appreciate how beautiful they looked. When she got downstairs to the living room, she was surprised at the minimal furnishings. Although the place was more put-together than her own, it had the word "temporary" written all over it.

Once in the kitchen she opened the refrigerator and saw that Adrian's housekeeper had labeled the neatly arranged containers for each day of the week. Did that mean he ate in every day? What if he missed the meal for that day? Did it go to waste?

If that was true, today wouldn't be one of those days. She pulled out the container labeled for today and pulled off the top. *Mmm.* The pasta dish smelled good. Recalling that Adrian had told her to eat anything she wanted—and it seemed he definitely had more than enough to share—she spooned out a serving onto a plate to warm it in the microwave. Meals cooked and at your disposal was a working person's dream. Life couldn't get any better than this.

This kitchen was nice, with stainless steel appliances. She thought about her drab-looking kitchen and figured she could get used to living in this sort of place.

She ate her food, alone, and couldn't help but appreciate how Adrian had showed up at the hospital this morning to pick her up. He'd known her body would be racked with exhaustion and he had thought about her welfare. Dr. Belvedere, on the other hand, hadn't thought of anything but his own selfish motives.

Now that she was well rested, she recalled how Adrian had looked. Already dressed for work, he had been wearing a business suit that fitted perfectly over his broad shoulders, heavily muscled thighs and massive biceps. He had walked toward her with a swagger that had nearly taken her breath away. No man should have a right to look that good in the morning. His shirt had looked white and crisp, and the printed tie made a perfect complement. The phrase "dress to impress" had immediately come to mind, as well as *mind-blowingly sexy.*

It didn't take her long to eat the meal and tidy up the kitchen after loading the dishes in the dishwasher. The clock on the kitchen wall indicated it was almost eight. Adrian hadn't mentioned anything about working late. Now that she was rested she could go back to her place. Her only problem was that she didn't have her car.

She glanced down at herself. The bathrobe covered more than the T-shirt, but still, she didn't feel comfortable parading around any man's home not fully dressed. Going into the living room, she decided to call her sister with an update on what Belvedere had done.

"Why am I not surprised?" Tara said moments later. "He reminds me so much of that doctor in Kentucky who tried forcing me into a relationship with him. But Belvedere really did something unethical by forcing you to work. And the nerve of him telling you to end your relationship with Adrian. Just who does he think he is?"

"I don't know but his actions only make me despise him more. And he saw firsthand that I won't end things with Adrian this morning. Adrian came to the hospital to pick me up."

"Adrian picked you up from work?"

"Yes." Trinity proceeded to tell her sister how Adrian had been there to drive her and, instead of taking her home, had taken her to his place to get undisturbed sleep.

"That was nice of him."

"Yes, it was," Trinity said, glancing at the clock on the wall again. "He hasn't come home yet, so I guess he's working late." She wouldn't mention that she was slightly disappointed he hadn't called to check on her. "He'll be taking me home when he gets here."

"Well, I'm glad you got undisturbed sleep."

"I'm glad, too. I honestly needed it."

Trinity had washed the clothes she'd worn that morning and was tossing them in the dryer when she heard

Adrian's key in the door lock. Finally he was home. It was close to ten o'clock and he'd known she was stranded at his place without her car. The least he could have done was call to see how she was doing, even if he needed to work late.

But what if he hadn't been working late? What if he'd been with someone on a date or something? She frowned, wondering why her mind was going there. And why she was feeling more than a tinge of jealousy.

Why are you trippin', Trinity? It's not as if you and Adrian got the real thing going on. It's just a charade. How many times do you have to remind yourself of that? On the other hand, he had said he wouldn't see anyone else.

"If the rules changed, he should have told me," she muttered angrily, leaving the laundry room and passing through his kitchen. She'd made it to the living room by the time he walked inside.

She willed herself not to show any reaction to how good he looked with his jacket slung across his shoulder. But then she noticed other things: his tie was off and she picked up the scent of a woman's perfume.

Trinity took a calming breath, thinking a degree of civility was required here. But then she lost it, and before Adrian had a chance to see her standing there, she said in an accusing tone, "You've been with someone."

Chapter 9

The moment Adrian saw Trinity a jolt of sexual desire rocked him to the bone. She was angry, hands on hips, spine ramrod straight and wearing his bathrobe, which drooped at her shoulders and almost swallowed her whole. But damn, nothing would satisfy him more than to cross the room and kiss that angry look off her lips.

But, suddenly, it occurred to him that she had no right to be angry. She was the reason he hadn't come home when he could have. Too much temptation under his roof. Too many thoughts of her had floated through his head all day. He hadn't enjoyed the movie for thinking of her.

And what had she just accused him of? *Being with someone?* So what if he had? What he did and who he did it with was his business. Period.

Tossing his jacket onto a wing-backed chair, he

crossed his arms over his chest and rocked back on his heels a few times. "And what of it?"

He didn't need his PhD to know that was the wrong answer.

Her eyes cut into him like glass and she took a step toward him.

"Did you not bring me here, Adrian?"

He shrugged a massive shoulder. "Yes, I brought you here with the intent of you getting uninterrupted sleep. What does that have to do with how I spent my time this evening and with whom?"

He wasn't used to this form of inquisition, especially after having spent the past several years making sure no woman assumed she had the right to make any demands on his time. The last time he'd looked, his marital status was still *single*.

"The only reason I brought it up is because you agreed to the pretend affair with me. And in doing so you indicated you would forgo dating for a while," she said.

"And I have."

"Then what about tonight?" she asked brusquely.

He stared at her. "Why the questions, Trinity? Are you jealous or something?"

He could tell from her expression that his question hit a nerve…as well as exposed a revelation. She *was* jealous. He inwardly smiled at that. It looked as if he wasn't the only one plagued with emotions.

"Of course I'm not jealous," she said, dropping her hands from her waist. "I just thought we had an agreement, that's all."

"And we do. Like I said, I wanted you to get uninterrupted sleep, so after my business dinner, I called Bailey and invited her to a movie."

"Bailey?"

"Yes. My sister Bailey."

"Oh."

"That's all you have to say?" he asked, deciding not to let her off so easily.

"Yes, that's all I have to say...other than I'll be ready to go home when my clothes finish drying, which shouldn't be too long. I'll check on them now." She turned to head toward the laundry room, but he reached out and snagged her arm. He tried ignoring the spike of heat that rushed through him the moment he touched her, but it was obvious that she felt it, as well. "Hey, wait a minute. You owe me an apology."

She lifted her chin. "Do I?"

"What do you think? You all but accused me of lying to you. It was an unnecessary hit to my character and I feel wounded."

Trinity rolled her eyes. "Getting a little carried away, aren't you?"

If only she knew just how carried away he felt. Every cell in his body was sizzling, all the way to the groin. Especially the groin. Desire throbbed all through him, and an urgency he'd never felt before began overtaking his senses. Pushing him on. That had to be the reason he was still holding on to her arm. Something she noticed.

"Why are you touching me, Adrian?"

She was visibly annoyed and visibly turned on. He could see both in her eyes. There were frissons of heat in the dark depths staring back at him. He'd been involved with enough women to know when sexual hunger was coiling inside them. Some women tried ignoring it, pretending they didn't feel a thing. Calling Trinity out on it would only increase her anger.

"You had no right to question me just now," he said,

speaking firmly, not liking the way she was making him feel. Or the way he'd been feeling all day while thinking of her.

"You're right. I didn't. But that's not giving me an answer as to why you're touching me."

No, it didn't. If she wanted an answer he would give her one. "I like touching you. I also like kissing you." He saw the way heat flared even more in her gaze, and his body pounded in response.

Then, although he knew she wouldn't like it, he added, "Probably as much as you like kissing me back."

She pulled away from his hold. "Only in your dreams."

He smiled. "Trust me, baby, you don't want to go there. You couldn't handle knowing what my dreams are like."

"I don't want to know," she said, giving him a chagrined look before walking off. Adrian was right on her heels. "About that apology, Trinity."

She turned around so suddenly, she collided with his chest. His arms were on her again, this time to steady her and keep her from falling. And not one to miss any opportunity, he tightened his hold, leaned in close to her lips and whispered, "Since you won't give me an apology, I guess I'll take this instead."

Then he proceeded to ravage her mouth.

The man was a master at kissing.

The last thing Trinity wanted was for Adrian to know how much she wanted him, wanted this. But for the life of her, she couldn't stop responding to his kiss. She was engaging in the exchange in a way that probably told him everything she didn't want him to know. How was she supposed to deal with these emotions he could

arouse in her so easily? How was she supposed to deal
with him period?

He fit snugly against her. She felt the outline of his
body, every single detail. Especially an erection that
was as hard as one could get. It was huge, pressing into
her middle as if it had every right to let her know just
how much it wanted her. And this kiss…

Lordy, it should be outlawed. Arrested. Made to
serve time for indecency. Who did stuff like this with
their tongue? Evidently Adrian Westmoreland did. And
what he was doing was driving her crazy, pushing her
over the edge. Goading her into wanting things she
didn't need. Trinity followed his lead and kissed him
back with a craving she felt in places she had forgotten existed.

The kiss made her remember it had been a long time
since she'd engaged in any type of sexual activity. There
had been that one time in college—when it was over
she'd sworn it would be the last time. It had been a waste
of good bedsheets. It was obvious Ryan Morgan hadn't
known what he was doing any more than she had.

Since then, although she'd dated from time to time,
and she'd been attracted to one or two men, there hadn't
been anyone who'd impressed her enough to get her
in his bed. Plenty had tried; all had failed…especially
some of the doctors she'd worked with. She had a rule
about not connecting her personal and professional lives
since doing so would only result in unnecessary drama.
But it seemed Casey Belvedere didn't know how to
take no for an answer. He was causing drama anyway.

But then Trinity stopped thinking when Adrian intensified the kiss, sinking deeper inside her mouth like
he had every right to do so. He used his tongue to lick
her into submission. What was he doing to her? Images

flashed in her mind of scandalous things… all the other things he could do with that tongue. She began tingling all over, especially between her legs. When she felt something solid against her back she knew he'd somehow cornered her against the wall.

She heard herself moan and felt a tightening in her chest. Is this how it felt to desire a man to the point of craziness? Where she was tempted to tear off his clothes and go at it with no control? And all from a little kiss. Well, she had to admit there was nothing little about it, not when her own tongue was swelling in response, doing things it normally wouldn't do, following his lead. And talk about swelling… The erection pressing against her had thickened and poked hard against her inner thigh.

She instinctively shifted to direct his aim right for the juncture of her thighs. Ah, it felt so right. Yes, there. He evidently thought so, too, because he began moving his body, grinding against her, holding tight to her hips.

He suddenly broke off and took in a slow breath. She did the same. How long had they gone without breathing? Not long enough, she figured, when he stared hard at her without saying anything. The dampness of his lips said it all. He'd gotten a mouthful and wanted more.

"You taste good, Trinity," he said huskily, reaching up to touch her lower lip with his finger.

Why was she tempted to stick out her tongue and give that finger a slow lick? Or, even worse, suck it into her mouth.

She shook her head hoping to shake off the craziness of that thought. "We've gone too far," she said in a voice she barely recognized as her own.

A seductive smile touched his lips as he used that same finger to slowly caress the area around her mouth, causing shivers to run up her body. "And I don't think we've gone far enough."

He *would* say that, she thought. She shifted her body to move away from him, but he pulled her closer. His body seemed to have gotten harder.

She squared her shoulders, or at least she tried to do so. "Now, look, Adrian—"

"I am looking," he interrupted throatily, while staring at her mouth, "And I like what I see."

The fingers that had moved away from her lips to her chin were warm and soft, long and strong. She needed all the control she could garner. Adrian was making her feel things she'd never felt before. How? Why? She was losing it. That was the only explanation for why she had gone almost eight years without wanting a man and now passion was eating away at her.

"Trinity?"

She lifted her chin, that same chin he was caressing, and held tight to his gaze. "What?" Those long, strong fingers slowly eased to the center of her neck, touching the pulse beating there.

"I do things to you."

If he thought she would admit to that, he was wrong. "Is that what you think?"

He chuckled softly, sensuously. "That's what I know. I can tell."

She was dying to ask how he could tell, but decided to claim denial for as long as she could. "I hate to crush that overblown ego of yours, but you're wrong."

He chuckled again. "Let me prove I'm right, sweetheart."

Trinity pulled back from his touch. She'd had enough of this foolishness. "If you don't mind, I need to get my clothes out of the dryer and get dressed so you can take me to the hospital to get my car."

"Not tonight. It's late." He took a step back and dropped his hands to his sides.

She frowned. If he thought they would share space under the same roof tonight, he needed to think again. "Then I'll call a cab."

"No, you won't. You're staying put until tomorrow. I'll drop you off at the hospital for your car on my way to work in the morning."

And then he had the nerve to walk off. She couldn't believe it. Steaming, she was now the one on his heels. "I can't stay here tonight."

He turned so quickly she almost bumped into him. She caught herself and moved back. He stared at her. "Why not?"

"Because I don't want to. I want to sleep in my own bed."

He crossed his arms over his chest. "And I want you in mine."

She swallowed. "Yours?"

"Yes, you have the guest room all to yourself. And if you need another T-shirt to sleep in, I'll get you one."

Although he hadn't suggested they share the same bed, she was growing angrier by the minute. She told herself it wasn't because he hadn't invited her to be his sleeping partner. That had nothing to do with it. "What I need for you to do is to take me home."

She wished his stance wasn't causing her to check out just how good he looked. Long legs, masculine thighs, slim waist, tight abs. Why did the air in the room suddenly feel electrified? Was that a crackling sound she heard? Why did his eyes look so penetrating, so piercing? Why was she letting him get next to her again?

With a mind of its own her gaze lowered to his crotch. He still had an erection? Lordy! Could a man really get that big and make it last that long?

Her gaze slowly lifted to his eyes. The moment they made eye contact she was snatched into a web of heated desire. What in the world was wrong with her?

"We can't continue to deny we want each other, Trinity. Hell, I don't like it any more than you do," he admitted, grabbing her attention.

She swallowed and went back into denial mode. "What are you talking about?" she asked softly.

He took a step forward, coming to a stop just a few feet in front of her. "I'm talking about the way you're looking at me, the way I'm looking at you. You and I have nothing in common on the outside. But…"

She didn't want to ask but couldn't help doing so. "But what?"

He took another step closer. "But on the inside, it's a different story. Point blank, what I want more than anything is to make you come while screaming my name."

Chapter 10

Adrian believed in saying what he thought and what he felt. He had no qualms stating what he wanted. And he wanted Trinity. He had wanted her from the first time he'd laid eyes on her at Riley's wedding, and when he'd heard she was moving to Denver he'd wanted to put her on his to-do list. But her close association with Thorn had squashed that idea. Everyone knew Thorn was overprotective when it came to people he cared deeply about.

Adrian had heard stories about how Thorn had scared off guys who'd wanted to date his sister Delaney. The other brothers had been just as bad, but Thorn had been the worst. He'd had no problem backing up his threats. And Adrian didn't want to give Thorn any reason to kick his behind, family or no family.

If Adrian knew the score, then why was he willing to skate with danger? Because Trinity, standing there wearing his T-shirt and looking sexier than any woman had a right to look, made him willing to risk it all to find out what she had on beneath that cotton. He wanted her. And when a man wanted a woman, nothing else mattered.

"Scream your name? You've got to be kidding me. No man will get a scream out of me."

Her words made him study her expression. She was actually grinning as if what he'd said was amusing. "Why do you find what I said so far-fetched?"

She rolled her eyes. "I find it more than far-fetched. The notion is so ridiculous it really isn't funny. Don't you know a woman who screams while having sex is just doing it to make her partner think he's doing something when he isn't?"

He leaned back against the side of the sofa table and stared at her, his arms crossed over his chest. "You don't say?"

"Yes," she said as a smile touched her lips. "I'm disappointed. I thought you had more smarts in the bedroom."

He should have been insulted but he wasn't. Instead he was amused, especially at her naïveté. She was wrong and he would just love to prove it. But that was beside the point. He couldn't help wondering why she was convinced she was right.

"I have plenty of bedroom smarts, Trinity. But it seems you've been disappointed along the way by some man who wasn't up to snuff."

She frowned. "It's not just me. It's about women in general. We talk and at times exchange notes, and the comparison is usually the same."

"Really?"

"I wouldn't say it if it wasn't true. I'm a doctor, so I

know the workings of the human body. I know about orgasms being a natural way to release sexual buildup. I get that. That's not the problem."

"Then what's the problem?"

"Men, and some women, believing it's all that and a bag of chips when it's more like a stick of gum. When they discover it's not what they heard or what they thought, then they're too embarrassed to admit it was a disappointment. They end up faking it instead of fessing up."

"And you know women who have *faked* it."

"Yes. Can you say with certainty that you don't? Are you absolutely sure that every woman you made scream wasn't doing it to stroke that ego of yours?"

If she was trying to make him doubt his ability in the bedroom, she had a long way to go. "Yes, I can say with one-hundred-percent certainty any screams I helped to generate were the real thing."

She stared at him, probably thinking his conceit had gone to his head.

"Well, believe what you want," Trinity said, rolling her eyes.

"You don't believe me?" he asked, looking at her questioningly.

"No, and before you say it, I have no intention of letting you prove I'm wrong. I'm aware of that particular game men play and don't intend to be a participant."

He couldn't help but smile. "So it's not the orgasm you don't believe in, just the degree of pleasure a woman can feel."

She shrugged her pretty shoulders. "Yes, I guess that's right. I know two people can generate passion, and they can do it to the degree that they lose control. I get that. But what I don't buy is that they can generate passion to the point where they're screaming all over the place while sharing the big O. That's the nonsense that sells romance novels. And I'm a reality kind of girl."

Adrian slowly nodded. *A reality kind of girl.* He was going to enjoy every single minute of proving her wrong, and he would prove her wrong. It wouldn't be a game for him. It would be one of the most serious moments of his life. He would be righting a wrong done to her, whatever had made her think faking it was necessary…and, even worse, that doing so was okay.

He needed time to come up with a plan. "It's late. We can finish this conversation in the morning, *after* I've had my first cup of coffee. Towels, washcloths, extra toiletries, including an unused toothbrush are beneath the vanity in your bathroom. Good night."

Trinity tried not to stare as Adrian left the room. Sexiness oozed from him with every step he took. He had a walk that made the tips of her nipples hard. Lordy, the man had such a cute tush…. The way his pants fit his backside was a sight to behold. She could imagine her hands clenching each firm and masculine cheek. The fantasy unnerved her. Never before had she focused on any part of a man's anatomy.

Since she wasn't sleepy after having slept most of the day, she decided to stay busy. After folding the clothes she'd taken out of the dryer, she went back into the kitchen. Adrian's housekeeper was good at what she did. Trinity couldn't help looking in the cabinets, impressed at how well stocked and organized things were.

She made a cup of tea and enjoyed the beautiful view of downtown Denver out the living room window. She took a deep breath then sipped her tea, hoping it would stop her heart from pounding. Even when she'd folded clothes and messed around in his kitchen, the erratic pounding in her chest that had started when he'd walked away hadn't stopped. It was as if knowing they were under the same roof and breathing the same air was getting to her. Why?

Trying to put thoughts of him out of her mind she turned back to the view. There was a full moon tonight. Adrian lived in the thick of downtown and the surrounding buildings were massive, the skyscrapers numerous. But he still had a beautiful view of the mountains.

Her own house was on the outskirts of town in the suburbs. Adrian's condo was definitely closer to the hospital.

Adrian.

Her heart pounded even faster. The nerve of him saying bluntly that he wanted to have sex with her. Just who did he think he was? Maybe pretending to be lovers had gone to his head. Maybe it hadn't been a good idea after all. So far all she'd gotten out of it was Belvedere making her work on her days off out of spite.

That wasn't completely true. Being Adrian's pretend lover had been an eye-opener. It had made her realize how sex-deprived she was. That had to be the reason she was so attracted to him and why he was awakening passion inside of her that she didn't know she had. As she'd told him, she knew orgasms relieved sexual tension, but before meeting him sexual tension was something she hadn't worried about. Sexual urges were foreign to her. Now, with him being so sinfully attractive, her heart was overworked with all the pounding and the lower part of her body constantly throbbed.

"Trinity?"

She gasped at the sound of her name and turned from

the window. Adrian stood in his pj bottoms, which rode
low on his hips. He looked even sexier than he had earlier that night. "Yes?"

"Why aren't you in bed?"

Seeing him standing there almost took her breath
away. And if that wasn't enough, his masculine scent
reached out to her, sending her entire body into a heated
tailspin, engulfing her with crazy thoughts and ideas.
"Why aren't you?" she countered, trying to stay in control.

A slow smile touched his lips and her body tingled in
response. That erratic pounding in her chest returned.
Had it truly ever left? "I couldn't sleep," was his reply
and she watched as he rubbed a hand over his face.

"You need to go back to bed. You work tomorrow. I
don't. Besides, thanks to you, I got a lot of rest today."

"No need to thank me. I did what was needed."

He was getting next to her with little or no effort. She
glanced down at her cup and came up with the perfect
excuse to leave the living room. "Well, I've finished
my tea. I guess I'll go to bed now. Maybe more sleep
will come."

Her only regret was that she had to walk past him
to get to the kitchen. As she walked by he reached out,
took the cup from her hand and placed it on the sofa
table before wrapping a strong arm around her waist
and pulling her to him.

"What do you think you're doing?" she asked, making a feeble attempt to push him away.

"Something I should have done earlier tonight."

She saw his head lowering to hers and opened her
mouth to protest. But he seized the opportunity and
slid his tongue between her parted lips. Immediately
her traitorous tongue latched on to his and before she

could fully grasp what was happening, she was kissing him as hungrily as he was kissing her. Never had she wanted or needed a kiss as much as she wanted and needed this one.

Not understanding why, she molded her body to his as if it was the most natural thing, and instinctively wrapped her arms around his neck. She felt those strong, hard fingers on her backside, pressing her closer. She felt him, long, solid and erect against her.

Her brazen response prompted Adrian to deepen the kiss.

Desire felt like talons sinking into her skin, spreading through her body in a heated rush, making her moan deep in her throat. He was the first man to ever make her moan, but she still wasn't buying that screaming claim he'd made earlier.

Then he began grinding against her body. She nearly buckled over; the juncture of her legs felt on fire. She broke off the kiss and unwrapped her arms from his neck before taking in a deep breath. "You don't want this, Trinity. You don't need this. You've got self-control, girl. Use it," she muttered softly under her breath.

Adrian heard her. "What are you saying?" he asked, dipping his head low to hers.

Trinity stared up into penetrating dark eyes. Was he aware that his eyes were an aphrodisiac? Just staring into their dark depths caused crazy things to happen to her. She nervously licked her lips, really tempted to lick his instead.

"Trinity?"

She recalled he had asked her a question. She decided to go for honesty. "I'm trying to talk myself out of taking something that I want but don't need."

He lifted a brow. "Really?"

"Yes."

He placed his hand on her shoulder. "Keep talking. You might convince yourself to walk away, but I have a feeling you won't."

She sucked in a breath. A spark of energy passed between them from his touch, making her fully aware she was being pulled into something hot, raw and sensuous. "You don't think I have any resolve?" she asked him.

"Not saying that. But I know in most cases desire can overrule resolve, no matter what kind of pep talk you give yourself."

She didn't want to agree with him, but unfortunately she was living proof that he might be right. "Why? Why don't I have self-control around you?"

"Maybe you don't need it."

"Oh, I need it," she said. "But…"

"But what?"

"I'm beginning to think I need you more." She paused. "I don't want to make a fool of myself."

"What makes you think you will?"

"Because I'm not good at this."

"Good at what, Trinity?"

"Seduction."

His lips curved into a smile as he reached for her. Those penetrating eyes held hers again as the palm of his hand settled in the center of her back.

"Baby, give me the opportunity and I'll teach you everything you need to know and then some."

I can't mess this up.

That thought raced through Adrian's mind as he dipped his head to capture Trinity's lips. As soon as he was planted firmly inside her mouth he deepened the kiss, ravishing her mouth with a greed that had soaked into his bones. There was no stopping him now. He would sort out what the hell was going on with him later. Much later.

He had tried to come up with a plan for the best way to handle Trinity, but he'd decided a plan would appear too calculating and manipulative. So instead he'd decided to let desire take its course. And it had. He felt it in the way she was kissing him back, letting him know that she was as far gone as he was.

With a mind of their own, his hands moved, traveling from the center of her back to her shoulders before moving lower to cup her shapely backside. She felt good.

When he felt himself harden even more he knew it was time to take things to the next level. He ended the kiss, but kept his hands firmly planted on her backside, making sure their bodies remained connected.

"I want you," he whispered. "I want to take you into my bedroom and make love to you, Trinity."

He saw the indecision in her gaze and knew he had to be totally honest with her. As much as he wanted her, she needed to know where he stood. That was the only way he handled a woman. Trinity would be more than just a quick romp, but he wasn't making any promises of forever. Besides, weeks ago they had already established the fact that they wanted different things out of life.

"Before you answer yea or nay, I just need to reiterate that I'm not the marrying kind," he told her.

He saw the way her eyes widened. "Marry?" she asked in surprise. "Who said anything about marriage?"

"Just saying. Some women expect a lot after a roll beneath the sheets. Just wanted to make sure we're clear that I don't do forever."

"We're clear," she said with one of those matter-of-fact looks on her face. "I guess I should issue that same disclaimer since forever isn't in my future, either."

"Good. We're straight."

And before she could change her mind as to how the night would end for them, he swept her off her feet and into his arms. Quickly headed for the bedroom.

Chapter 11

Trinity sat cross-legged in the middle of Adrian's bed, where he'd placed her, and watched him slowly ease the pj's down his legs. He was looking at her as if she was a treat he intended to devour. And heaven help her she wanted to devour him, as well.

When he stepped out of his pajama pants, all thoughts left her mind except for one: his engorged manhood. Why did he have to be so well-endowed? No wonder he was conceited and arrogant.

She moved her gaze away from him, figuring that doing so would stop her heart from beating buck-wild in her chest. The décor of his room, like the rest of the house, was fantastic. The dominating colors of avocado and chocolate gave it a manly air. The room was a lot bigger than the guest room she'd been given. At least, it appeared that way since his furniture was positioned to give a very spacious feel.

Adrian walked toward her, completely naked, with that slow and sensual stride that he had down to a tee. Her gaze raked over him and she could imagine touching those tight abs, that muscular chest, those broad shoulders. And that flourishing manhood filled her head with all sorts of ideas.

When he reached the bed and placed a knee on it, she figured it was time to remind him of what she'd said earlier. "I'm not good at this."

"Let me be the judge of that," he said, reaching for the hem of her T-shirt.

In a blink, he had whipped it over her head, leaving her in black panties and matching bra. But from the way he looked at her one would have thought she wasn't wearing anything at all.

With a flick of his wrist, he unsnapped the front clasp of her bra. Before she could react, he had worked the garment from her shoulders and tossed it aside. Her stomach clenched when she saw his gaze focus on her breasts and the hardened tips of her nipples. His attention made them harder.

She nearly moaned out loud when he licked a swollen nipple then sucked it into his mouth. How had he known doing something like that would make her womanhood weep? She wrapped her hands around his head to hold him to her breast. Was there anything his tongue wasn't capable of doing? She doubted it. It was made to give pleasure. No wonder Adrian was so high in demand. If this was part of his seduction then he could seduce the panties off a nun.

He released one nipple and started on the other. That was when his hand moved lower, easing beneath the waistband of her panties. As if he'd given a silent order,

her legs parted to give him better access. It didn't take
long for his fingers to find what they were seeking.

She groaned deep in her throat when he slid a finger
inside her womanly core, finding her wet. She doubted
he expected she'd be otherwise. Then, with the same
circular motion his tongue was using, his finger moved
likewise inside her, massaging her clitoris. There was no
doubt in her mind he was readying for the next phase,
but she was already there.

Then he moved his mouth to her lips, swallowing her
groan and thrusting his tongue deep. He kissed her with
a hunger that he mimicked with the movement of his
finger. At some point he'd added a second finger. Together the two were stroking her into a heated frenzy.
Of their own accord, her hips began moving, gyrating
to the rhythm of his fingers. She thought she would pass
out from the sensations swamping her.

When he finally released her mouth, she gasped, and
he took the opportunity to shimmy her panties over her
hips and down her legs. Instead of tossing them aside
as he'd done with her bra, he lifted them to his nose, inhaling deeply and closing his eyes as if he was enjoying
heavenly bliss. Watching him sent sensual chills escalating through her body. She moaned again.

He opened his eyes and tossed the panties aside. He
held her gaze as he lowered himself to the juncture of
her thighs. And when he licked his lips, she felt her
inner muscles clench. It was then that he leaned up and
whispered close to her ear, "Last chance to back out."

He had to be kidding. There was no way she would
back out, although her common sense was telling her
that she should. Instead she'd decided based on feelings, and, at the moment she was dealing with some
pretty heady emotions.

"I won't back out."

"If you're certain, now is when I tell you my technique."

"Your technique?" she asked, barely able to get the words out. Surely he wasn't into anything kinky? Although right now, he could come up with just about anything and she would go along with it.

"Yes, my technique. When I make love to you, I'm going to give you all I've got."

She swallowed slowly. "All you've got?"

"Every single inch."

Trinity swallowed again as a vision flashed through her mind. Her skin burned for him and her womanly core throbbed.

"Ready for me?"

She wasn't sure. All she knew was that when he touched her she felt good. When he kissed her she felt even better. She figured making love to him would be off the charts.

"And, Trinity?"

She looked at him. "Yes?"

"I *will* make you scream and it *will* be the real thing."

Now that he'd given her fair warning, Adrian went about taking care of business. Wrapping his arms around her, he brought them chest to chest. The protruding tips of her nipples poked into him, and he liked the connection.

He eased Trinity onto her back while kissing her, doubting he would ever get tired of tasting her. He loved the way she kissed him, devouring him as much as he devoured her. How could any woman have so much passion and not know it?

He broke off the kiss. When her head touched one

pillow, he reached behind her to grab another. Lifting her hips, he placed the pillow beneath her and then used his knee to spread her legs. He licked his lips in anticipation as he gazed at her wet womanly folds.

Adrian ran a hand up and down her thigh, loving the feel of her naked flesh. She had soft skin and the scent of a woman. She was perfectly made. He'd thought so when he'd seen her in clothes and he thought so even now that he'd seen her out of them.

"Adrian?"

He met her gaze and saw impatience. He wouldn't be rushed. If she thought he was one of those be-done-with-it kind of guys, she was mistaken. When it came to sex, he was so painstakingly thorough it was almost a shame. Before the night was over, she would discover just how wrong she was about the sexual experience for a woman. No woman left Adrian Westmoreland's bed unsatisfied; he made sure of it.

And Trinity was a special case because he could tell from their conversations that she had limited experience in the bedroom. He intended to remedy that. Tonight.

He kissed her, letting his tongue mimic what his manhood intended to do once he was inside her. But first, one taste led to another. Her scent was driving him insane.

Adrian moved his hands all over her body, loving to touch her. He trailed kisses from her mouth to the center of her throat. He sucked her, intentionally branding her. He wasn't sure why, especially when he didn't believe in giving a woman any ideas regarding possession. But for Trinity, it was necessary.

Needing to touch her again, he ran a hand over her breasts and stomach before moving lower, to her thighs, brushing his fingertips over her flesh and loving the softness of her silky-smooth skin. And he loved watching her nipples harden in front of his eyes, loved seeing her light brown eyes darken and stare back at him filled with a heated lust that mirrored his own.

"I want you bad," he muttered, putting into words just how he felt. His mouth moved from her neck back up to her lips. Down below, his fingers slid back between her legs. There was something about touching her there that he found exhilarating. And he liked the way her legs spread open of their own accord. When he stroked her nub, she threw her head back and moaned. He loved the sound and wanted to hear more.

He licked her lips, wanting more of her taste. Now. He eased his body downward to lower his head between her legs. When his tongue slid between the slippery wet folds of her womanhood, she moved against his mouth.

When it came to oral sex he was a master, and he was about to show Trinity just what a pro he was. Doing so would be easy because she tasted so damn good.

He heard her release a deep groan and he smiled. She hadn't felt anything yet. He was just getting started. In a few more minutes she would be pulling his hair. With a meticulousness he had perfected over the years, Adrian devoured Trinity's sweetness, moving his tongue inside her from every angle.

Her legs began to quiver against the sides of his face. She dug into his scalp while bringing her hips off the pillow. But what he wanted to hear more than anything were her luscious whimpers that escalated into a full-blown moan.

She was trying to hold in what she was feeling. He wasn't having any of that. He knew the sound he wanted to hear and decided to use his *deep tongue* technique on her. Within seconds, her moans became screams.

He held her as she jerked, an orgasm sweeping through her. It might have started between her legs but he could tell from the intensity of her scream that she'd felt it through her entire body.

He didn't let up. Another scream arrived on the heels of the last and it was only when she finally slumped back against the pillow that he lifted his head. Leaning back on his haunches, he looked at her. Her hands were thrown over her eyes and her breathing sounded as if she'd run a marathon.

When she sensed him staring at her, she dropped her hand and stared back.

He smiled, licked his lips and asked, "Was that the real thing or were you faking it?"

Trinity wasn't sure she was capable of answering. Her throat felt raw from her screams. Never in her life had she experienced anything quite like what Adrian had just done to her. The man's mouth, his tongue, should be outlawed. She had screamed—actually screamed—and there hadn't been anything fake about.

"Still not sure? Then I better step up my game."

He had to be kidding. But when he shifted his body, she saw that he wasn't. His bigger-than-life manhood stood at full attention.

"Adrian," she whispered. He reached into the nightstand to pull out a condom packet. She swallowed, moistening her lips while watching him put it on. How could a woman get turned on by that? Easily, she thought, seeing how expertly he shielded himself. Thick, protruding veins ran along the sides of his erection and the head was engorged. An eager shiver raced through her.

He reached for her and she went to him willingly,

not caring that he could probably see the desire all over her face. "We start off doing traditional and then we get buck wild," he murmured against her lips.

He tilted her hips toward him and entered her, inch by slow inch. She closed her eyes in sexual bliss. Her body felt tight even as it adjusted to the size of him. He stretched her, lodging himself deep, to the hilt.

"You okay, baby?"

Trinity's fingernails dug into his shoulders and she inhaled a deep breath. He had gone still, but she could feel him throbbing inside her. She held tight to his gaze as a tremor ran through her. She could tell from the look in his eyes that he felt it. He got harder, bigger.

And then he began to move. If she thought his tongue needed to be outlawed, then his manhood needed to be put in jail and the key thrown away. Something inside her ignited. He thrust in and out, going deeper. She felt him, every hard inch, with each slow, purposeful stroke.

Emotions she'd never felt before raced through her. Instinctively, her hips moved, mimicking his. Sensations overwhelmed her as he continued to pump, going fast and then slow and then fast all over again.

Something started at her womb, spreading through every part of her. Her legs began to tremble; a sound erupted at the base of her throat.

He was hitting her G spot, H spot, Q spot—every spot inside her—driving her closer to the edge with every thrust. He pumped harder, longer, the intensity of his strokes triggering hot, rolling, mind-blowing feelings.

And then the world seemed to spin out of control. An orgasm tore through her. She screamed, louder than before. Waves of ecstasy nearly drowned her in pleasure. She screamed again. This time she screamed out his name. As if the sound propelled him, he thrust inside her as another climax claimed her. Then his body bucked hard and she heard her name on his lips.

Moments later, he slumped against her and then shifted their bodies so she was on top of him. He gently rubbed his hand up and down her back. "You screamed my name," he rasped huskily.

"And you screamed mine." She raised her head from his chest to point that out.

A crooked smile touched the corners of his mouth. "So I did." He didn't say anything for a long moment. "I asked you before, Trinity. Were your screams the real thing?"

She wished she could lie and say they weren't, but to do so wouldn't serve any purpose. He had proved her wrong in the most shocking yet delicious manner. It was a lesson she doubted she would ever forget.

"Yes," she whispered softly. "They were the real thing."

She placed her head back down on his chest.

She should not have been surprised about his vast knowledge of ways to pleasure a woman, but she couldn't help wondering how many women he'd been involved with to obtain that experience.

"Tired?"

She lifted her head again. "Exhausted."

In one smooth movement he shifted his body and had her on her back again so he could stare down at her. "Then I guess this time I'll do all the work."

This time? She stared at him. Surely he didn't have another round of sex on his mind. Evidently he did, she thought, watching him grab another condom from the nightstand drawer. "Time to swap out," he said, smiling at her.

He eased off the bed and trotted naked toward the bathroom. Lordy, the man had the kind of butt cheeks that made her want to rub against them all day and all night. The kind that tempted her to pinch them for pleasure.

"You can do whatever you like," he said, turning around and grinning at her.

Jeez. Did he have eyes in the back of his head? Or was he a mind reader? "I have no idea what you're talking about."

He chuckled.

"Don't let me prove you wrong again, Trinity."

Then, after winking at her, he went into the bathroom and closed the door behind him.

Chapter 12

Before daybreak Adrian had proved Trinity wrong in more ways and positions than she'd known existed. He'd made love to her through most of the night, guiding her through one mind-blowing orgasm after another.

Although she was one hell of a passionate woman, her sexual experience was limited. He had no problems teaching her a few things. He couldn't recall ever enjoying making love to any woman more. It had been an incredible night, which was why he was awake and had been since four that morning.

His heart was still pounding from when she had gone down on him. The first time she'd ever done so with any man, she had admitted. He had felt honored. He had no problem telling her what he liked and she had readily complied. Whether she knew it or not, she had a mouth that was made for more than just kissing.

He glanced over at her, naked and curled beside him

with her leg tossed over his. She was luscious temptation, even asleep. It wouldn't take much for him to shift a little and ease inside her.

Without a condom? He blinked. What the hell was he thinking? He'd never even imagined making love to a woman without wearing protection, regardless of what form of protection she was using. That wasn't Adrian Westmoreland's way. But it also wasn't his way to let a woman spend the night at his place, either. For any reason. However, she had. And why did it look as if she belonged here, naked in his bed beside him?

Not liking the direction of his thoughts, he gently detangled her leg from his before quietly easing out of the bed. While sliding into his pj bottoms he glanced over at her. Immediately, he got hard. Trinity was too damn desirable for her own good. After making love to her, she had become an itch he wanted to scratch again and again.

Closing the bedroom door behind him, he took the stairs two at a time. He needed a drink, something highly intoxicating. But because tomorrow was a workday, he would settle for a beer instead. And he needed to talk to someone. The two people he could relate to the most were Aidan, his twin, and his cousin Bane.

Aidan was probably asleep and no telling what Bane was up to. Last time they'd talked, Bane was leaving for an assignment and couldn't say where. Adrian had a feeling Bane was enjoying being a navy SEAL.

He tried Bane's number, but when he didn't get an answer, he dialed Aidan. A groggy Aidan answered on the fourth ring. "Dr. Westmoreland."

"Wake up. We need to talk."

It took a while for Aidan to respond. "Why?"

"It's Trinity."

Adrian heard a yawn, followed by yet another one-word question. "And?"

Adrian rubbed a hand down his face. "And I might have gone beyond my boundaries."

There was another pause. This one just as long as the last. "I told you I felt your emotions and they were strong. What did you expect, Adrian?"

"Damn it, Aidan. I expected to have more control, and not to forget Thorn is her brother-in-law. He thinks of her as a sister. Tonight I've been only thinking of one thing." *To get more of her.*

"Now that your common sense has returned, what do you plan to do?"

Adrian sucked in a deep breath. He wasn't at all sure his common sense had returned. What he should be doing was hiking back upstairs, waking Trinity to tell her to get dressed so he could take her to the hospital to get her car. Then, if he really had any sense, he would tell her that pretending to be lovers wasn't working and that she should come up with another plan to get Belvedere off her back. However, he could do none of those things.

"Adrian?"

"Yes?" He took a huge sip of his beer.

"So what do you plan to do?"

Adrian wiped the back of his hand across his lips. "Not what I should be doing." He placed the half-empty beer bottle on the counter. "It's late. Sorry I bothered you."

"It's early and no bother. Just don't get yourself into any trouble. I'm not there to bail you out if you do."

Adrian couldn't help but smile. "Like you ever did. If I recall correctly, most of the time whenever I got in trouble it was because of you, Bane or Bailey."

"All right, if that's what you want to believe."

"That's what I remember."

"Whatever, Adrian. Good night"

Adrian still held the phone in his hand long moments after he'd heard his twin click off the line. He knew Aidan was dealing with his own issues with Jillian, and Adrian pitied him. He wouldn't want to be in his brother's shoes when Dillon and Pam found out Aidan had been messing around with one of Pam's sisters. Everyone knew how protective Pam was of her three sisters.

Probably the same way Tara is of hers.

Adrian picked up his beer bottle and took another swig. He didn't want to think about overprotective sisters tonight. But then, what he did want to think about was liable to get him in trouble.

Going back to bed was out of the question. Since he wasn't sleepy, he went into his office to get a jump start on the day's work. In addition to the mall complex on Amelia Island, they were looking at building another hotel and mall in Dallas.

In other words, he had too many things on his plate to be standing in his kitchen at four in the morning, remembering how great it felt being between Trinity's luscious pair of legs.

Sunlight hit Trinity in the face. She snatched open her eyes. Glancing around the room she remembered in vivid detail what had happened in this bed.

She moved and immediately felt soreness in her inner muscles, reminding her of the intensity of the lovemaking she and Adrian had shared. And she had screamed. More than once. The look on his face had been irritatingly smug. Too darn arrogant and self-satisfied to suit her.

And speaking of conceited eye candy, where was he? Why was she in his bed alone? Flashes of what had gone down last night kept passing through her mind. Actually, *she* had gone down.

She vividly recalled taking the thick, throbbing length of him in her hand, marveling at its size, shape and hardness, fascinated by the thick bulging veins. She had leaned down to kiss it, but once her lips were there, she had opened her mouth wide and taken him inside. That was the first time she'd done such a thing and now the memories set every nerve ending inside her body on fire.

A sound from downstairs cut into her thoughts. Was that the shower running in one of the guest bedrooms downstairs? It was still early, not even six o'clock. Why was Adrian using the shower downstairs instead of the one he had in his master bath?

A part of her figured she should stay put and wait until he returned to the room. But another part—the bold side she'd discovered last night—wanted to see him now.

Refusing to question what was going through her mind, she eased out of bed. Looking around for her T-shirt, she found it tossed over a chair. Slipping it over her head, she opened the door and proceeded down the stairs, following the sound of the shower.

She opened the guest bedroom door. It was just as nice as the room she'd used. Nerves made her hesitate when she reached the bathroom door, but she didn't announce her presence. Instead she pushed the door open and stepped inside.

Adrian stood inside the shower stall as jets of water gushed over his naked body. She placed her hand to her throat. *Oh, my.* Water ran from his close-cropped hair to broad shoulders, a powerful chest and muscular legs. The area between her own legs throbbed just like the night before. Maybe worse.

She leaned back against the vanity, and continued to stare at him. She might as well get an eyeful since he hadn't detected her presence yet. His back was to her and those masculine wet butt cheeks were definitely worth ogling. She couldn't help but appreciate how they clenched and tightened whenever he raised his hands to wash under his arms.

For crying out loud, when did I begin drooling over any man's body?

Even as she asked herself that question, she knew she'd never drooled over anyone until Adrian.

He must have heard a sound—probably the pounding in her chest—because he turned around. The moment their gazes locked, a surge of sexual energy jolted her.

He opened the shower door. With water dripping from his body, he said, "Join me."

Need spread through her as she moved toward the shower stall, pausing briefly to whip the T-shirt over her head and toss it aside.

The moment she stepped into the shower, he joined her mouth with his, burying his long, strong fingers into her hair. Water washed over them. Closing her eyes, she sighed when the taste of his tongue met with hers. Awareness of him touched every pore of her body. Her desire for him was burning her to the core.

He let go of her hair, his hands cupping her face as he kissed her as though his very life depended on it. The kiss was everything she'd come to expect from him—dominating, powerful and methodically thorough.

He dropped his hands from her face and wrapped strong arms around her, bringing her wet body closer to his as water rained down on them. He ended the kiss then reached behind him to grab the soap and begin lathering both their bodies. He ran his hands up her arms, around her back and gave special attention to her buttocks and thighs. Her heart rate escalated with every glide of his hands.

Then he lifted her and pressed her back against the marble wall.

"Wrap your legs around me."

Automatically she obeyed, feeling his hard length against her stomach. He tilted her body, widening the opening of her legs, and in one smooth sweep, slid inside her. She felt every inch of him as he drove into her deeper.

Warm water sprayed down as he pumped hard and fast. She clung to him, digging her fingernails into his back. Her body wanted even more. Somehow Adrian knew it, and he gave it to her. His hand slid under her bottom, touching the spot he wanted, right where their bodies were joined. He stroked her there.

She couldn't take any more. She sank her teeth into his shoulder. Her action drove him on, unleashing the erotic beast in him. He released a deep, throaty groan that triggered a response inside her.

She screamed his name, then sobbed when spasms took her deeper into sexual paradise. The magnitude of the pleasure made her scream again.

And even with water pouring down on them, she felt him spill inside her. Hot, molten liquid flooded her, messing with her senses and jumbling her sanity.

She met his gaze. "More."

That single word pushed him, making him hard all over again. The feel of him stretching her even more than before had her thighs and backside trembling.

Then he moved again, going in and out of her in quick, even thrusts, a sinfully erotic hammering of his hips. He stared down at her, the intensity and desire that filled his eyes more torture than she could bear.

"Adrian."

She murmured his name in a heated rush just before a powerful force rammed through her. She felt each and every sensation, the next more powerful than the last. She bit into Adrian's shoulder to keep from screaming and arched her back to feel it all.

He tossed his head back and called out her name, exploding inside her yet again. He cupped her buttocks and kept coming, giving her the *more* she wanted, what she'd demanded.

"Satisfied?" he asked against her wet lips.

Even after all of that, desire for him was still thick in her blood.

She placed a kiss on his lips as a jolt of sexual pleasure rocked her to the bone. She couldn't help but smile, and then she whispered, "Very much so."

Chapter 13

"Didn't you get any sleep last night, Adrian?" Stern Westmoreland asked with a grin. "We expect you to start snoring at any minute."

Adrian blinked. Had he been caught dozing off during a meeting? He glanced around the room and saw the silly grins on the faces of his cousins Riley and Canyon, and a rather concerned look on Dillon's features. Adrian sat straighter in his chair. "Yes, I got plenty of sleep," he lied.

"Oh, then we must be boring you," Canyon observed, chuckling.

Dillon stood as he closed the folder in front of him. "I've caught the three of you snoozing a time or two, so leave him be."

Adrian knew Dillon's words were to be obeyed... for now. But he knew his cousins well enough to know that he hadn't gotten the last of the ribbing from them.

He stood to leave with Dillon. He wouldn't dare stay behind and tangle with the three jokesters.

Dillon glanced over at him as they headed down the corridor to their respective offices. "So, how is that situation going with Trinity?"

If only Dillon really knew, Adrian thought, the muscles of his manhood throbbing at the memory. He'd had the time of his life last night and wouldn't be surprised if he really had been dozing during the meeting. He'd gotten little sleep, but the sex had been off the charts. He would even go on record as saying it had been the best he'd ever had. And just to think, she was still practically an amateur.

But he intended to remedy that. Last night might have been their first time between the sheets, but it wouldn't be their last. He wasn't sure how Trinity felt about it, though. She hadn't had much to say this morning during the drive over to the hospital to get her car. In fact, she had taken the time to get more sleep. He'd left her alone, figuring she needed it.

Before he could ask when they could get together again, she had muttered a hasty, "See you later," and had quickly gotten out of his car and into hers. There hadn't been a goodbye kiss or anything.

"Adrian?"

The sound of Dillon's voice cut into his thoughts. "Yes?"

"I asked how that situation is going with Trinity."

"Fine." He tried to ignore the scrutinizing gaze his cousin was giving him.

"And how did things work out a few days ago when Dr. Belvedere requested that she work on her days off?"

Anger flashed in Adrian's eyes. "It was just as I suspected. According to Trinity, Belvedere came on to her again, even mentioned the night he'd seen us out together. He told her to drop me or else."

Adrian saw a mirror image of his own anger in Dillon's eyes. "Did she report it?"

"Yes, but the chief of pediatrics accused her of exaggerating, causing unnecessary drama." Adrian paused. "I met Belvedere face-to-face."

Dillon lifted a brow. "When?"

"Knowing how tired she would be I decided to pick Trinity up from work yesterday morning. And wouldn't you know it, he was there in her face, insinuating he would be picking her up for a date that night, after having made her work on her days off. It didn't occur to him that she might need to rest."

"What did you do?"

"Not what I wanted to do, Dil, trust me. You should have seen her. She was so exhausted she could barely stand. With self-control you would have been proud of, I introduced myself to Dr. Belvedere as her significant other and told him that Trinity had other plans for the evening. Then we left. I drove her to my place instead of taking her home. I figured Belvedere would be crazy enough to drop by her home, regardless of what I'd told him. Besides, I wanted to make sure she got uninterrupted sleep."

Dillon nodded. "Did she?"

"Yes. She slept all day while I was at work, and it was late when I got in last night after that dinner meeting with Kenneth Jenkins and a movie date with Bailey. But when I got home I could see that she'd gotten plenty of rest."

Dillon nodded again. "Then you took her home?" he asked, giving Adrian another scrutinizing gaze. It took everything Adrian had not to squirm beneath his cousin's intense examination.

"No. It was late, so she stayed the night."

"Oh, I see."

Adrian had a feeling Dillon was beginning to see too much and decided now was the time to make a hasty exit. "Well, I'll check with you later. I have that Potter report to finalize for Canyon."

He quickly walked off but stopped when Dillon called out to him. "Adrian?"

He turned around. "Yes?"

"Will you be available for tomorrow's chow-down?"

Adrian shrugged. "I'm free tomorrow night so there's no reason I won't be there."

Dillon smiled. "Good. It's JoJo's birthday and although she doesn't want to make it a big deal, you know Pam, she will make it a big deal anyway."

"Then I'll make it my business to be there."

"You can invite Trinity to join us if you like."

Adrian stared at his cousin. "Why would I like?"

"No special reason—just a suggestion. Besides, it might be a good idea to give the family an update. If Belvedere keeps it up, we might have to present a show of unity. The Westmorelands have just as much name recognition in this town as the Belvederes."

Adrian nodded. "Okay. I'll give it some thought."

He walked away giving it a lot of thought. Trinity was no longer a pretend lover. Last night he'd made her the real thing.

Trinity sat at her kitchen table finishing her dinner with a cup of hot tea. After Adrian had dropped her off at the hospital for her car, she had driven home, shivered and gone straight to bed. She'd appreciated her second day of nonstop sleep and inwardly admitted she'd been nearly as tired this morning as she had been the day before. Just for a different reason.

She had spent most of last night making love with Adrian. Now it was late afternoon and other than sleeping, she hadn't gotten anything done. Definitely not the laundry she'd planned to do today. Instead she had mentally berated herself for her brazen behavior last night. Who begs a man to ejaculate inside her, for Pete's sake? She cringed each and every time she remembered what she'd said and how he'd complied.

But while her mind was giving her a rough time about it, her body was trembling at the memory. All she had to do was close her eyes to remember how he'd felt inside her—stretching her, pounding into her then exploding inside her.

That's what she kept remembering more than anything. The feel of him exploding. He'd gotten harder, thicker…and then *wham!* His hot release had scorched, triggering her own orgasm.

She tightened her legs together when an ache of smoldering desire pooled right there.

What in the world is wrong with me? she asked herself. *I go without sex for years and then the first time I get a little action I go crazy.*

She took a deep breath, knowing it was more than just getting a little action. More than getting a *lot* of action. She was reacting to becoming involved with a man who knew what to do with what he had. Buffed, toned, sexy to a degree that couldn't even be defined, and on top of that, he knew how to deliver pleasure to the point that he'd made her scream. Lordy, she had screamed her lungs out like a banshee. It's a wonder none of his neighbors had called the police.

To think they had gotten careless and engaged in un-protected sex. Luckily she was on the pill and he had seemed quite relieved about that fact when she had told him later that night. He told her that making love to a woman without using a condom was unlike him. His only excuse was that he had lost control in the moment. She understood because so had she. Once it was estab-lished that they were both in good health, he hadn't used a condom for the rest of the night.

She stood now and gathered her dishes to place them in the sink. Then why, after behaving in a way so un-becoming, were her fingers itching to call his number, hear his voice, suggest that he come over?

She shook her head, inwardly chiding herself for let-ting a man get next to her to this magnitude. Besides, she had to work tomorrow and the last thing she needed was another night filled with sex.

Later she had washed the dishes, cleaned up the kitchen and tackled the laundry when there was a knock at her door. It could have been anyone but the way her body responded signaled it had to be one particular person. Adrian.

She could pretend she wasn't at home but that wouldn't stop the way her heart was beating. Only Adrian had this kind of effect on her and it annoyed her that he knew it.

She crossed the room to the door. "Who is it?" As if she didn't know.

"Adrian."

Why did he always have to sound so good?

"What do you want?"

"Do you really have to ask me that?"

Her heart skipped a beat. How on earth had she gone from a woman who didn't date to a woman who'd made a man's booty-call list? Annoyed by the very thought, she unlocked the door and snatched it open.

She also opened her mouth to give him the dressing down he deserved when suddenly that same mouth was captured by his.

This, Adrian thought as he deepened the kiss, was what he'd been thinking about all day....

She returned the kiss with the same fierce hunger he felt. It was hard to tell whose tongue was doing the most work. Did it matter when the result was so damn gratifying?

He pulled back, ending the kiss. It was either that or take her right there at her front door. A vision of doing just that immediately popped into his mind. Damn, he had it bad.

"You coming here wasn't a good idea."

"I happen to think the opposite," he said, maneuvering past her.

"Hey, wait. I didn't invite you in."

He smiled. "No, but your scent did."

She rolled her eyes as she closed the door. "My scent? What does that have to do with anything?"

He chuckled. "I'll tell you later. This is for now," he said, holding up a bag from a well-known Chinese chain. "I brought dinner."

She crossed her arms over her chest. "Thanks, but I've eaten."

"I haven't. Join me at the table. Besides, we need to talk."

Trinity stared at him and nodded. "Yes, we do need to talk."

She led him to the kitchen and he followed, appreciating the sway of her shapely hips in the cute little skirt she was wearing. He remembered how those same hips had ridden him hard last night.

And then he was drinking up her scent—a scent he remembered from last night. The scent of a woman who wanted a man—and he would admit he was just that arrogant to assume the man was him.

She took a seat at the table while he moved around her kitchen as though he'd spent time in it before. He opened cabinets and pulled out whatever he needed for his meal. From the look on her face he could tell she wasn't thrilled.

"Sure you don't want any?" he asked, emptying the contents of the carton into a bowl. When she didn't respond he glanced over his shoulder and met her gaze. He'd gained the ability to read her well and he smiled when he recalled what he had asked her. The desire in her gaze was her undoing. "I was asking if you want any of *my food,* Trinity. Not if you want any of me. Besides, I already know that you do."

"I do what?"

"Want me."

She stood and narrowed her gaze at him. "You've got a lot of nerve saying something like that."

"Then call me a liar. But be forewarned, if you do, I'll make sure before leaving here to prove I'm right."

Trinity gnawed on her bottom lip. More than anything she would like to call him a liar but knew she couldn't.

Sighing dismissively, she studied the man standing in the middle of her kitchen as if he had every right to be there. It was obvious he had dropped by his place to change clothes. Gone was the designer suit he'd worn that morning. Now he wore a pair of jeans and a V-necked sweater. Blue. Her favorite color. No matter how much she fought her drumming heart, she couldn't get a handle on it.

"Don't look at me like that, baby."

His words made her blink. It was then that she realized just how she'd been looking at him. She glanced away for a moment and then back at him. "I think last night might have given you the wrong idea."

He chuckled. "You think?" he asked, opening her refrigerator.

"I'm serious, Adrian."

"So am I," he said, turning back to her with a bottle of water in his hand. "To be honest, you didn't give me any ideas but you gave me a drowsy day. I dozed a few times in a meeting with my cousins."

Trinity could certainly understand that happening. She shrugged as she sat down. "It wasn't my fault."

"No, it wasn't your fault," he said, coming over to join her at the table with his bowl and bottle of water. "It was mine. I couldn't get enough of you."

She gave him time to sit and say grace, while her mind reeled. Did he have to say exactly whatever he thought? "Well, regardless, no matter how much you couldn't get enough, I think we need to agree here and now that what happened last night was—"

"Don't you dare say a mistake," he said, before opening the water bottle to take a sip.

"What do you want to call it?"

"A night to remember," he said huskily, taking her hand in his.

The instant he touched her, she felt it; the same sensations she'd felt last night. The same ones that had gotten her into trouble. Slowly she pulled her hand from his and looked at him pointedly. "A night we both should forget."

"Don't count on that happening." And then he changed the subject. "So how was your day?" He slid the water bottle he'd taken a drink from just moments ago over to her. "Take a sip. You look hot and it might cool you off."

Chapter 14

The next move was hers, Adrian thought, holding Trinity's gaze.

She was obviously a mass of confusion, saying one thing and meaning another. He knew the feeling. He had walked around the office all day thinking he had gotten carried away last night. Nothing could have been *that* good. But by the time he'd left the office and gone home, he'd admitted the truth to himself. Of all the lovers he'd ever had, Trinity took the cake. Last night had been simply amazing. The best he'd ever had. For a man who'd had his share of lovers since the age of fifteen, that was saying a lot.

Now, since arriving on her doorstep, she had tried to make him think she hadn't enjoyed the night as much as he had. He'd listened and now it was time for action. First, he'd help her acknowledge the truth, which meant admitting they had a thing for each other. And it wasn't going anywhere.

"I don't need a drink to cool off. I'm not hot."

So she was still in denial. "You sure?" he asked, holding her gaze intently.

"What I'm sure about, Adrian, is that our little farce has gone too far. We were supposed to only pretend something was going on between us."

"And what's wrong with making it the real thing?"

"Plenty. I don't have time to get involved in a relationship, serious or otherwise. My career is in medicine. It is my life. I told you my goal. I'm leaving here. I don't do large cities. I want to return to Bunnell and nobody is going to make me change my plans."

Adrian was thinking she had it all wrong, especially if she assumed he was looking for something permanent. He wasn't. But then, what was he looking for? A part-time bed partner? An affair that was destined to go nowhere? Both were his usual method of operation so why did those options bother him when it came to her?

"I don't want to be a booty call for any man, Adrian."

Now Adrian was confused. She didn't want an exclusive relationship nor did she want a casual one, either. "Then what do you want, Trinity? You can't have it both ways."

She lifted her chin. "Can't I be satisfied with having neither?"

The answer to that was simple. "No. Because you're a very hot-blooded woman. You have more passion in your little finger than some women have in their entire bodies. I can say that because I was fortunate enough to tap into all that fire last night. The results were overwhelming. And now that I have tapped into it, for you to go back to your docile life won't be easy. It's like a sexual being has been unleashed and once unleashed, there's no going back."

He paused, finishing the last of his meal and then pushing the bowl aside. "So what are you going to do about it, Trinity? Are you going to drive yourself crazy and try to ignore the passionate person that you are? Or will you accept who and what you are and enjoy life… no matter where it takes you? It's your life to do with it whatever you want, for as long as you want. So do it."

Adrian could see her mind dissecting what he'd said. He didn't know what her decision would be. He could see she was fighting a battle of some sort within her. For the past few years she had been so focused on her medical career that the idea of shifting her time and attention to anything or anyone else was probably mind-boggling to her. But as he'd told her, after last night there was no way she could go back.

They didn't say anything for a long moment. They merely sat staring at each other. He was certain she was feeling the sexual tension building between them. The desire in her eyes was unmistakable. It made his already hard body harder. But whatever she chose had to be her decision.

Minutes ticked by. Then, as he watched, she picked up the bottle of water and slowly licked the rim of the opening—the same place his mouth had touched earlier—before taking a sip. Then she placed the bottle down and licked her own lips as if she'd not only enjoyed the water but the taste of him left behind.

His stomach clenched. The pounding pulse in his crotch was almost unbearable. She had made her decision.

Yearning surged through his every pore and coiling arousal thickened his groin.

When the desire to have her became too strong, he pushed back in his chair and patted his lap, making his erection obvious.

"Come and sit right here."

Trinity felt the pooling of moisture between her legs. It was the way he was looking at her, was the way his huge arousal pressed against the zipper of his jeans. And he wanted her to sit on it? Seriously?

Her gaze slowly moved back to his eyes. She knew he intended for her to do more than just sit. She'd discovered last night that when it came to sex, the man came up with ideas that were so ingeniously erotic they should be patented.

He was right in saying he had tapped into something within her last night, something she hadn't known she possessed. An inner sexual being that he had definitely unleashed.

She would be the first to admit that today, upon waking from her long nap, she had felt the best she'd felt in years. Working off all that stress in the bedroom had its advantages.

So what was she waiting for? As he'd pointed out, it was her life. She could do whatever she wanted, and what she wanted at the moment was *that,* she thought, shifting her gaze back to his groin.

Pushing her chair back, she stood and while still holding his gaze released the side hook of her skirt and shimmied out of it. The look of surprise in his eyes was priceless. She fought back a smile. Did he think he was the only one who could go after what he wanted once his mind was made up?

"You look good."

A smile touched her lips. Evidently, he had no prob-

lem with her standing in her kitchen wearing only a
tank top and a thong. As if not to be outdone, he stood,
kicked aside his shoes, unbuckled his belt and relieved
himself of his jeans.

Lordy, was it possible for him to have gotten even
bigger since this morning? Her expression must have
given away her thoughts because he said, "It's just your
imagination."

She frowned, not liking that he knew what she was
thinking.

"But why take my word for it? You can always check
it out for yourself," he added.

She lifted her chin. "I intend to do just that."

Boldly, she walked over to him and cupped him. He
felt engorged, thick, hard. Deciding the outside wasn't
telling her everything, she fished her hand beneath the
waistband of his briefs.

Oh-h, this was it. She brazenly stroked him. She
needed the full length so she shoved his briefs down
past his knees and he stepped out of them.

"That's better," she said in a whisper when she had
him gripped in her hand once again.

"Is it?"

The throaty catch in his voice was followed by a deep
moan when her fingers stroked the length of him from
base to tip and back again. She met his gaze and saw
the fiery heat embedded in the depths of his eyes. The
tips of her nipples hardened in response. "Yes. And I
still think it's bigger than last night. That's amazing,"
she said.

"No, you are."

She smiled, appreciating Adrian's compliment.
"What's with all these flattering remarks?"

"I wouldn't say them if you didn't deserve them. I don't play those kinds of games."

So he said, but as far as she was concerned this was definitely game playing. There was nothing else to call it. They weren't having an affair. Not really. And she wasn't into casual sex. At least not the way most would define it. To keep things straight in her mind she *had* to think of what was between them as a game. That would keep her from getting too serious because with every game there were rules. And when it came to Adrian Westmoreland she needed plenty.

First of all, he was a man a woman could give her heart to, and that wasn't a good thing because he didn't want a woman's heart. For him, it was all about sex. He didn't have a problem with that since she was a willing partner with her own agenda. But she had to make sure she didn't slip and mistakenly think that since the sex was so good, there had to be more behind it.

She looked up at him as she continued to intimately caress him. If anyone had told her that one day she would be standing in the middle of her kitchen half naked, stroking the full length of a man's penis, she would not have believed them.

"Enjoying yourself?"

"Yes, I'm enjoying myself. Having the time of my life. How do you feel about now?"

"Horny."

She chuckled. "I have a feeling you were already in that state when you arrived on my doorstep. I'm not crazy, Adrian. You only came here tonight for one thing."

The smile that curved his lips made her fingers grip him even tighter. "Actually, two things," he said.

Before she could ask what that second thing was, in

a move so smooth she didn't see it coming, he quickly sat and pulled her onto his lap to straddle him.

He shoved aside her thong and entered her before she could utter any word other than, *"Oh."*

Then it was on. She wasn't sure who was riding whom or who was emanating the most heat. All she knew was that her hips were moving in ways they had never moved before, settling on his length and then raising up just enough to make him growl before lowering again. Over and over. Deeper and deeper. Fast and then slow.

She managed to lean in and kiss the corners of his lips, and then she used the tip of her tongue to lick around his mouth. She got the response she wanted when he grabbed her and thrust deeper.

Then it seemed the chair was lifted from the floor as he began pounding harder and harder into her. He froze, holding his position deep inside her. Her inner muscles clenched him, squeezing him tight. That's when he exploded. She felt it, she felt him and then she came, screaming out his name.

He held firm to her hips, keeping their bodies connected while they shared the moment. She dropped her head to his shoulder and inhaled his scent. She wrapped her arms around him and felt the broad expanse of his muscular back. Perfect. He was as perfect a lover as could be.

Lover...

Is that what he was to her? No longer a pretend lover but the real thing? For how long? Hadn't she told herself just a few hours ago that this wouldn't happen again? Then why had it?

Because you wanted it, an inner voice said. *You wanted it and you got it.*

She leaned back and their gazes locked. Before she could say anything, he lowered his mouth to hers. The kiss was slow, languid, penetrating and as hot as any kiss could be. His tongue wrapped around hers…or had hers wrapped around his?

Did it matter?

Not when he was using that tongue to massage every inch of her mouth from top to bottom, front to back. The juncture of her legs began to throb again as if they hadn't been satisfied just moments ago.

She broke off the kiss to look into eyes that were dark with desire once again. And she knew this was just the beginning.

Later, Adrian would question how Trinity had managed, quite nicely and relatively thoroughly, to get into his system. He would also question why, after making love to her at least two more times in the bedroom, he was still wanting her in a way he had never wanted another woman.

"Tell me your other reason," she asked, breaking into his thoughts.

She was spread on top of him. Her hair was all over her head, in her face. Her mouth looked as though it had been kissed way too many times. Her eyes were still glazed from a recent orgasm or two, possibly three. She looked simply beautiful.

"My other reason?" he asked, his brow rising.

"Yes, your other reason for dropping by here tonight. You said there were two."

So he had. "Tomorrow night. Do you have any plans?"

She seemed to think about his question for a quick second. "Granted I get to leave the hospital on time without Belvedere finding a reason to make me work late…no, I don't have any plans. Why?"

"I want to invite you to dinner. In Westmoreland Country."

She nervously licked her lips. "Dinner with your family?"

"Yes."

She didn't say anything for a minute. "They know about us?" she asked. "About this?"

He shook his head. "Depends on what part you're referring to. They know I've been your pretend lover, but as far as the transition to the real thing, no."

She pulled back slightly. "What would they think if they found out the truth?"

He chuckled. "Other than thinking Thorn is going to kick my ass, probably nothing."

"Why would Thorn do that?"

"He thinks of you as a kid sister."

She shook her head. "He used to. Now he thinks of me as an adult. I guess he's mellowed over the years."

He wondered if they were talking about the same Thorn Westmoreland. "If you say so. So what about it? Will you go with me to the chow-down tomorrow night?"

"Yes."

For some reason her answer made his night. "I'll pick you up around six, okay?"

"All right. I'll be ready."

Adrian gathered her close to him, thinking, *So will I.*

Chapter 15

As Trinity moved through the hospital corridors checking on her patients, she couldn't help but notice she felt well-rested, although for two nights straight she'd participated in a sexual marathon. That she had left Adrian in her bed after a romp of the best morning sex ever was something she tried not to think about, but when she did she couldn't help but smile.

He'd told her he'd wanted to make sure she left for work with a smile on her face and that was one mission he'd accomplished. She was in a cheerful mood this morning and was determined not to let anything or anyone ruin her day, including Dr. Belvedere.

She had seen him when she'd first arrived but he'd been rushing off to the operating room. According to one of the nurses, he was scheduled for surgery most of the day. That only added to her cheerfulness. The less she saw of the man, the better.

She pulled her phone out of her jacket when she heard a text come through. She smiled even wider after reading the message.

Think of me today.

She smiled and texted back.

Only if you think of me.

Adrian's reply was quick.

Done.

She chuckled to herself and put her phone back in her jacket.

"I see something has you in a good mood, Dr. Matthews."

Her body automatically cringed at the sound of Casey Belvedere's voice. He moved to stand in front of her, still wearing his surgical attire. Why wasn't he still in surgery? "Yes, Dr. Belvedere, I am in a good mood."

"And you look well rested," he noted.

"I am." *No thanks to you,* she thought but said, "The nurses said you had several surgeries this morning."

"I do, but the one I just completed was finished ahead of schedule so I have a little time to spare. Share a cup of coffee with me?"

"No, thank you. I need to check on my patients."

"Not if I say you shouldn't."

She lifted her chin and fought a glare. "Surely you're not asking me to put my patients' needs on hold just for me to share a cup of coffee with you, Dr. Belvedere?"

He frowned and took a step closer under the pretense of looking at the chart she was holding. "Don't ever chastise me again, Dr. Matthews. Don't forget who I am. All it would take is one word from me and I can ruin your career before it gets started. And as far as that boyfriend of yours, I meant what I said. Get rid of him. You'll be doing yourself a favor.

"I had him checked out. He's one of *those* Westmorelands. Although he and his family might have a little money, I recall that he, his siblings and his cousin were known troublemakers when they were younger. Nothing but little delinquents. My parents sent me to private schools all my life just so I wouldn't have to deal with people like them. I come from old money, his family comes from—"

"Money that's obtained from hard work and sacrifices," she said curtly, refusing to let him put down Adrian or his family.

Belvedere opened his mouth to say something just as his name blasted from the speaker requesting that he return to the surgical wing. He glared at her. "We'll finish this conversation later." Turning quickly, he was gone.

Trinity felt shaken to the core. The look on Belvedere's face had sent chills up her spine. The man definitely had a problem. If her pretend-lover plan wasn't working and if the hospital administrators and the chief of pediatrics also refused to acknowledge his continued harassment of her, then there was nothing left for her to do but to put in a request to be transferred to another hospital, one as far away from Denver as she could get. She would start the paperwork later today.

"So what do you think?"

After having read Stern's assessment report on the Texas project slated to start in the fall, Adrian smiled. "I think you outlined all the legal ramifications nicely.

We were lucky to get top bid on that property, especially since Dallas is booming."

"Yes it is," Stern agreed, dropping down into the chair in front of Adrian's desk. "So, are you joining the family tonight for the chow-down?"

"Yes, and I'm bringing Trinity with me."

Stern nodded. "How are things going with the two of you pretending to be having an affair? Has that doctor backed off yet?"

"No." Adrian spent the next ten minutes telling Stern about Belvedere's treatment of Trinity.

"I can't believe the bastard," Stern railed angrily. "Who the hell does he think he is? He better be glad he's dealing with Trinity and not JoJo. She would have kicked his ass all over the hospital by now."

Adrian fought back a smile knowing that was true. Stern's fiancée, Jovonnie Jones, was not only an ace in martial arts but she could handle a bow and arrow and firearms pretty damn nicely, as well.

"Trinity has to be careful how she handles the situation, man. The Belvedere name carries a lot of weight in this city and the administrators at the hospital refuse to do anything to stop him."

"Why wait for them? I wouldn't even be having this conversation with the old Adrian. He would have whipped somebody's behind by now. He would not allow anyone to mess with his girlfriend."

"Trinity is not my girlfriend."

"But the doctor doesn't know that and he's given you no respect. Who the hell does he think he is to hit on another man's woman? Man, you've mellowed too much over the years."

"Just trying to keep the family's name clean, Stern. You should understand that, considering my history.

Besides, Dillon gave me a warning not to take matters into my own hands."

Stern leaned closer to the desk. "As far as I'm concerned, in this case, what Dillon doesn't know won't hurt him."

"I agree," a deep voice said from across the room. "So when can we go kick the doctor's ass?"

Stern and Adrian turned. Towering in the doorway, and looking more physically fit than any man had a right to look, was Bane Westmoreland.

"And you're sure that's what you want to do, Trinity?"

Trinity could hear the concern in her sister's voice and she knew she had to assure Tara she was okay with her decision. "Of course it's not what I want to do, Tara. If I had my way I would finish up my residency in Denver but that's not possible. Putting in for a transfer is for the best."

"You and Adrian pretending to be lovers didn't help, I guess?"

"No. Belvedere expects me to break up with Adrian. He's just that conceited to think I will drop someone for him."

"There has to be another way."

"I wish there was but there's not. I could go beyond the hospital administrators to the commissioner of hospitals for the State of Colorado, but then it would be Belvedere's word against mine. The case might drag out for no telling how long. Or worse yet, he might try to turn the tables and claim I'm the one who came on to him. It will take time and money to prove my case, and I don't have either. All I want to do is complete my residency, not waste time facing Casey Belvedere in court. Besides, if I pursue this, his family might stop the funding for a children's wing that's badly needed at Denver Memorial."

When her sister didn't say anything, Trinity added, "Hey, it won't be so bad. You transferred to another hospital during your residency and did fine. In fact, by doing so you were able to connect with Thorn."

"Yes, but I left Kentucky because I wanted to leave, not because I felt I had to."

"I appreciate all you tried to do," Trinity said after a pause. "Coming up with the idea for me and Adrian to pretend to be lovers was wonderful. Any other man would have backed off. But not Belvedere. The word *entitled* is written all over him. He assumes he has the right to have me, boyfriend or no boyfriend—how crazy is that?"

She glanced at her watch. "I need to get dressed. Adrian invited me to the Westmorelands' for dinner tonight. It's their weekly Friday night chow-down."

"That was nice of him."

"Yes, it was," Trinity agreed.

"Are you going to tell Adrian about the transfer?"

"Nothing to tell yet. I just put in for it today and it will probably take a few weeks before a hospital picks me up. I'll mention it when I know where I'll be going. He's been so nice about everything." She wouldn't tell Tara how their relationship was no longer a pretense because she knew even that was short term.

"Well, the two of you won't have to pretend to be lovers anymore now."

No, they wouldn't, Trinity thought. Why did that realization bother her? Trinity pulled herself up from the sofa. "Okay, Tara, I need to get dressed."

"Tell everyone I said hello and I look forward to seeing them at Stern's wedding in June."

"I will." Trinity knew if things worked out the way she wanted with the transfer, by June she would have left Denver and would hopefully be working at some hospital on the east coast.

After clicking off the phone with Tara, Trinity headed for the bedroom. She refused to question why she was anxious to see Adrian again.

"When did you get home?"

"Does Dillon know you're here?"

"What's been going on with you?"

"We haven't heard from you in over a year."

Bane Westmoreland grinned at all the questions being thrown at him. "I came straight here from the airport and, no, Dil doesn't know I'm here. I've been busy and you haven't heard from me because of assignments I can't talk about. All I can say is it's good to be home, although I'll only be here for a few days."

Adrian studied his cousin and noted how much Bane had changed over the years. When Bane had left home to join the navy he had been angry, heartbroken and disillusioned. Personally, Adrian had given the navy less than six months before they tossed out the badass Bane. But Bane had proved Adrian wrong by hanging in and making the most of it. Now Bane stood taller, walked straighter and smiled more often. Although there was no doubt in Adrian's mind his cousin was still a badass.

"So where's Dillon? All his secretary would say is that he's away from the office," Bane said.

"He had a meeting with several potential clients and won't be back until later this evening. He's going to be surprised as hell to see you," Adrian said, grinning. He couldn't wait to see Dillon's face when Dillon saw his baby brother. Of all the younger Westmorelands that Dillon had become responsible for, Bane had been the biggest challenge. Dillon was the one who had finally talked Bane into moving away, joining the military to get his life together…and leaving Crystal Newsome alone.

Crystal Newsome…

Adrian wondered if Bane knew where Crystal was or if he even cared after all this time. All the family knew was that the two obsessed-with-each-other teens had needed to be separated. Crystal's parents had sent her to live with an aunt somewhere and Dillon had convinced Bane to go into the military.

"You returned home at the perfect time, Bane," Stern noted. "Tonight is the chow-down and we're celebrating JoJo's birthday."

Bane smiled. "That's great. How is she doing? I heard about her father's death a while back. She's still your best friend, right?"

It occurred to Adrian that because Bane had been on assignments and hadn't been home since Megan and Rico's wedding, he didn't know about any of the family's recent news—like the babies, other family weddings and the engagements.

Bane had a lot of catching up to do and Adrian couldn't wait to bring his cousin up to date.

Chapter 16

Trinity watched herself in the mirror as she slid lipstick across her lips. Why had she gone to such great pains to make sure she looked good tonight when all she was doing was joining Adrian and his family for dinner? No big deal. So why was she making it one?

One second passed and then another while she stood staring at her reflection, thinking of the possible answers for that particular question. When her heart rate picked up, she frowned at the image staring back at her.

"No, we aren't going there. I am *not* developing feelings for Adrian. I am *not!* It's all about getting the best sex I ever had. Any woman would become infatuated with a man who could give them multiple orgasms all through the night, without breaking a sweat."

And she didn't want to think about the times he had sweated. *Lordy!* Those times were too hot to think about.

She turned when she heard her cell phone ring and disappointment settled in her stomach. That special ring meant it was the hospital calling because she was needed due to an emergency. That also meant she would have to cancel her dinner date with Adrian.

She clicked on her phone. "This is Dr. Matthews."

"Dr. Matthews, this is Dr. Belvedere."

Trinity stiffened at the sound of the man's voice and tried to maintain control of her anger. Why was he calling her? Typically, whenever there was an emergency, the call would come from one of the hospital's administrative assistants, never from any of the doctors. Most were too busy taking care of patients.

"Yes, Dr. Belvedere?"

"Just wanted you to know I'll be leaving town for two weeks. They need medical volunteers to help out where that tornado touched down in Texas. They want the best so of course that includes me."

She rolled her eyes. "Is there a reason you're informing me of this?"

"Yes, because when I get back I expect things to change. I'm tired of playing these silly games with you."

Silly games with her? Her body tensed. "You're tired of playing games with me? I think you have that backward, Dr. Belvedere. I'm the one who is tired of your games. I told you I have no interest in a relationship with you. I don't understand why you can't accept that as final."

"Nothing is final until I say so. I would suggest you remember that. When I get back I want changes in your attitude or you'll be kicked out of the residency program."

She wanted to scream that he didn't have to waste his time kicking her out because she was leaving on her own, but she bit back the words. She would let him find that out on his own. Hopefully it would be after the approval for a transfer came in.

"Do whatever you think you need to do because I will never go out with you. Goodbye, Dr. Belvedere."

"We'll see about that. You've got two weeks."

Refusing to engage in conversation with him any longer, she clicked off the phone, closed her eyes and sucked in a deep breath. He had ruined what had started off as a cheerful day, and she simply refused to allow the man to ruin her evening, as well.

Adrian pulled into Trinity's driveway feeling pretty good about today. Bane's arrival had been a surprise for everyone and catching him up on family matters had been priceless. Bane was shocked as hell to find out about all the marriages that had taken place—Zane's especially. And for Bane to discover he was an uncle to Canyon's son Beau was worth leaving the office and sharing drinks to celebrate at McKays.

That was another thing that had been priceless. News that Bane had returned home for a visit traveled fast, and when he walked into McKays it was obvious some of the patrons were ready to run for cover. Bane's reputation in Denver preceded him and it hadn't been good. But some were willing to let bygones be bygones, especially those who'd heard Bane had attended the naval academy—graduating nearly top of his class—and was now a navy SEAL. They took the time to congratulate him on his accomplishments. Everyone knew it had taken hard work, dedication and discipline—things the old Bane had lacked. The badass native son had returned and everyone told him how proud they were of him.

Then there was Bane's reunion with Bailey. Canyon

had called to tell her Bane was in town and she'd met them at the restaurant. She was there waiting and one might have thought she and Bane hadn't seen each other in years. Seeing them together, hugging tight, made Adrian realize just how the four of them—him, Aidan, Bane and Bailey—had bonded during those turbulent years after losing their parents. They'd thought that getting into trouble was the only way to expel their grief.

Getting out of his car now, Adrian headed toward Trinity's front door. He couldn't wait to get her to Westmoreland Country and introduce her to Bane. His cousin had heard enough of Adrian's conversation with Stern to know what was going on with Trinity and Dr. Belvedere. Bane agreed with Stern that Adrian should work the doctor over. Specifically, break a couple of his precious fingers. Adrian was still trying to follow Dillon's advice.

Trinity opened the door within seconds of his first knock and all he could say was *wow*. Adrian wasn't sure what about her tonight made him do a double take. He figured he could blame it on her short sweater dress, leggings and boots, all of which put some mighty fine curves on display. Or it could be the way she'd styled her hair—falling loosely to her shoulders.

But really he knew that what had desire thrumming through him was nothing more than Trinity simply being Trinity.

"Aren't you going to say anything?"

He forced his attention away from her luscious mouth to gaze into a pair of adorable brown eyes. He took her hand, entered her home and closed the door behind him. "I'm known as a man of few words, but a lot of action," he said in a husky voice as a smile curved the corners of his mouth.

He tugged her closer while placing his hand at the small of her back. They were chest to chest and he noted her heartbeats were coming in just as fast and strong as his. His gaze latched on to the lips he'd been mesmerized by just moments ago. Their shape had a way of making him hard anytime he concentrated on them for too long. And tonight they were glazed with a beguiling shade of fuchsia.

He leaned in and licked the seam of her lips. Her heart rate increased with every stroke of his tongue. When her lips parted on a breathless sigh, he took the opportunity to seize, conquer and devour. He hadn't realized just how hungry he was for her taste. How could kissing any woman bring him to this? Wanting her so badly that needing to make love to her was like a tangible force.

She suddenly pulled back, breaking off the kiss. She touched her lips. "I think they're swollen."

He smiled. "Better there than there," he said, moving his gaze to an area below her waist. His eyes moved back up to her face and he saw the deep coloring in her cheeks. Honestly? She could blush after everything he'd done to her between those gorgeous legs?

"Your family is going to know."

He quirked a brow. "What? That I kissed you?"

"Yes."

She was right—his family would know. They had a tendency to notice just about everything. But Bane's surprise visit might preoccupy them. However, his family was his family and preoccupied or not, they had the propensity to pick up on stuff. So, if she thought they could keep what was really going on between them a secret, then she wasn't thinking straight. He decided to let her find that out for herself.

He took her hand. "Ready?"

"I need to repair my lipstick."

"All right."

He watched her walk off toward her bedroom and decided not to tell her that before the night was over, she would be repairing it several more times.

A few hours later Trinity was remembering just how much fun being around a family could be. The Westmorelands, she'd discovered whenever she visited Tara in Atlanta, were a fun-loving group who enjoyed spending time together. And it seemed the Denver clan was no different.

It appeared tonight was especially festive with the return of the infamous Brisbane Westmoreland, whom everyone called Bane. Although he'd mentioned he would be home for only three days before embarking on another assignment, his family already had a slew of activities for him to engage in while he was here.

Bane mentioned he would not be attending Stern's wedding in June, saying he would be out of the country for a while. Trinity figured he would be on some secret mission. He looked the part of a navy SEAL with his height and his muscular build, and he was definitely a handsome man. His eyes were a beautiful shade of hazel that blended well with his mocha complexion. As far as she'd seen, no other Westmoreland had eyes that color. When she asked Adrian about it, he'd said their great-grandmother Gemma had hazel eyes, and so far Bane was the only other Westmoreland who'd inherited that eye color.

Everyone was sitting at the table enjoying the delicious dinner the Westmoreland ladies had prepared.

It amazed her how well the women in this family got along. They acted more like sisters than sisters-in-law. Pam had told Trinity that hosting a chow-down every Friday night was a way for the family to stay connected. Earlier, they had gathered in the living room to sing happy birthday to Stern's fiancée, JoJo.

Adrian sat beside Trinity and more than once he leaned over to ask if she was enjoying herself. And she would readily assure him that she was.

"I hope you don't mind, Trinity, but Dillon mentioned the trouble you're having with some doctor at the hospital," Rico Claiborne, who was married to Adrian's sister Megan, said.

She looked down the table to where Rico sat beside Megan and across from Bane. "Yes. Adrian and I thought claiming to be in an exclusive relationship would make him back off, but it didn't. He even had the gall to tell me to end my relationship with Adrian or else." She could tell by the expressions on everyone's faces that they were shocked at Belvedere's audacity.

"Have you thought about recording any of the conversations he's having with you?" Rico asked. "Evidently the man feels he can say and do whatever suits him. There is such a thing as sexual harassment no matter how many hospital wings his family builds."

Trinity nodded. "No, I hadn't thought about it. I assumed taping someone's conversation without their knowledge was illegal."

"That's true in some states but not here in Colorado," Keisha, Canyon's wife, who was an attorney, advised. "Only thing is, if he suspects the conversation is being recorded and asks if it is, you're legally obligated to tell him yes. Otherwise it's not admissible in a court of law," she added.

"Recording his conversations might be something you want to consider, Trinity," Adrian said thoughtfully.

She nodded. It was definitely something she would consider. Although her plan now was to leave Denver and transfer to another hospital, what Rico suggested might be useful if Belvedere tried to block the transfer or give her a hard time about it. At this point she wouldn't put anything past him.

"That might be a good idea," she conceded. "At least I'll have him out of my hair for two weeks." She then told everyone about the phone call she had received earlier from Casey Belvedere and the things he had said. By the time she finished she could tell everyone seated at the table was upset about it.

"Why didn't you tell me about that call when I came to pick you up?" Adrian asked.

She could tell he could barely control his anger. "I didn't want to ruin our evening, but it looks like I did anyway. Sorry, everyone, I shouldn't be dumping my problems on you."

"No need to apologize," Dillon said, seated at the head of the long table. "The plan that Tara came up with for you and Adrian to pretend to be in an exclusive relationship didn't work, so now you should go to plan B. I agree with Rico that getting those harassing conversations recorded will help."

"I can almost guarantee they will," Rico said, leaning back in his chair. "And I've got the perfect item you can wear without anyone, including the doctor, knowing his words are being recorded. It resembles a woman's necklace and all you have to do is touch it to begin taping. Piece of cake. Let's meet right before the doctor gets back in town and set things up."

Trinity smiled. "Okay. That sounds like a great plan."

* * *

"I had such a great time tonight, Adrian. Your family is super. Thanks for inviting me."

Adrian followed her through the door, closing it behind them. He had gotten angry when Trinity had told everyone what Belvedere had said to her, and he hadn't been able to get his anger back in check since. The man had a lot of damn nerve.

"Adrian?"

Upon hearing his name he glanced across the room. Trinity had already removed her jacket, taken off her boots and was plopping down on her sofa.

"Yes?"

"I was telling you how much I enjoyed myself tonight, but you weren't listening. You okay?"

"Yes, I'm fine," he lied, moving to join her on the sofa. Truth of the matter was, he wasn't okay. A part of him was still seething. He had a mind to forget about what Dillon had said and go over to Belvedere's place and do as Bane had suggested and give him a good kick in the ass. How dare that man continue to try to make a move on his woman and...

It suddenly hit him solidly in the gut that Trinity wasn't *his* woman. However, for the past couple of nights she'd been his bed partner. He cringed at the sound of that. He'd had bed partners before, plenty of them, so why did classifying her in that category bother him?

She twisted around on the sofa to face him, tucking her legs beneath her. "No, I don't think you're fine. There's something bothering you, I can tell. You were even quiet on the drive back here, so tell me what's going on."

It was on the tip of his tongue to reassure her again

that he was okay but he knew she wouldn't believe him. He decided to be honest. "Belvedere's phone call has me angry." He shook his head. "He has a lot of damn gall. And what's so sad is that he doesn't see anything wrong with his behavior, mainly because no one has yet to call him out on it. He feels he can get away with it. You should have told me about that call earlier, Trinity."

She frowned. "Why? It would only have ruined our evening. I regret mentioning it at all. The man was behaving as his usual asinine self."

Adrian stared at her, finally realizing the full impact of the crap she'd been going through for the past six months. This hadn't been just a few words exchanged now and then, but bull she'd had to put up with constantly.

He cupped her face in his hands. "Neither you nor any woman should have to put up with that. I don't just want Belvedere gone, but I want the top administrator of the hospital gone as well. The moment you went to him and complained, something should have been done."

"I agree, but that's politics, Adrian, not just at Denver Memorial but at a number of hospitals. That's how the game is played. Some people with money assume their wealth comes with power. The Belvederes evidently fall within that category. They are big philanthropists who support great causes. Only thing is, their gift comes with a price. Maybe not to the hospital who's grateful to get that new wing, but to innocent people…in this case women who are—doctors, nurses, aides. Women they can prey on sexually. Yes, there are laws against that sort of thing, but first the law has to be enforced."

She paused and then added, "I doubt it would have made any difference to Belvedere if I was married. A husband would not stand in the way of getting whatever he wanted. And I bet I'm not an isolated case. There were probably others before me. He's trying to hold my career hostage to get his way. Some other woman might feel forced to eventually give in to him. But not me. However, I know fighting him is useless, which is why I've completed paperwork for a transfer to another hospital."

Thunderstruck, Adrian's blood pounded fast and furious at his temples. "Transfer? You've applied for a transfer?"

"Yes."

His muscles tensed. "To another hospital here in Denver?"

"No. I don't know of any hospital in this city that the Belvedere name is not associated with somehow. I'm hoping to relocate to the east coast, closer to home."

He was quiet as he absorbed what she'd said. In a way he shouldn't be surprised. She'd told him more than once that she didn't like big cities and Denver hadn't really impressed her. All she'd been doing since moving here was putting up with crap. Still…

"When were you going to tell me about the transfer?" he asked. The thought that she had put in for one and hadn't mentioned it bothered him.

"I planned to tell you once I got word it went through. There was no reason to tell you beforehand. I just put in the paperwork today."

No reason to tell him. Of course she would feel that way since all you are is a bed partner, man.

"But why today? Did something else happen that you haven't mentioned?" When she had left for work this morning she'd been in a good mood. He'd made certain of it.

She shrugged. "Nothing other than Belvedere being

his usual narcissistic self. But he did something today that really got to me."

"What?"

She hesitated, as if trying to control her emotions. "I had patients to see, yet he wanted me to forget about their needs to go somewhere and have a cup of coffee with him. How selfish can one man be? I couldn't stand him as a man but after that conversation I no longer respected him as a doctor. It was then that I decided not to put up with it any longer."

"Just like that?"

"Yes, just like that."

He could appreciate her decision since no one—man or woman—should have to put up with a hostile work environment, especially when that environment was supposed to be about the business of caring for people.

"So, if you plan on leaving the hospital anyway, why did you lead Rico to believe you want to record one of those harassing conversations with Belvedere?"

"Because I do. The paperwork for the transfer will probably take a while to get approved. Once he finds out about it he might try blocking it or give me a low approval rating where no other hospital will take me. I can't let that happen. I need leverage and I will get it."

He heard the determination in her voice. She had worked hard for her medical degree. He of all people knew how hard that was since his twin, Aidan, had gone through the process. No person should have the right to tear down what it took another person more than eight years to build.

Adrian agreed that she needed peace of mind in her work, so she didn't have to worry about some crazy jerk trying to force her into his bed. The thought of her leav-

ing Denver and moving on should have no bearing on
him or his life whatsoever, but somehow it did.

At the moment, he didn't want to try to figure it out.
All he knew was that she didn't need him anymore.

"Since you're moving to plan B, I guess that pretty
much concludes plan A," he said, standing. He had been
plan A.

She looked up at him, confused. "What do you mean?"

"You're going to expose Belvedere with that recording, so we don't have to pretend to be lovers anymore."

He watched her expression and knew the thought
hadn't crossed her mind. She stood, sliding off the sofa
in a fluid movement any man would appreciate. She
wrapped her arms around his waist. "We stopped *pretending* to be lovers that night at your house, Adrian."

He felt the way her heart was beating, fast and powerful, a mirror of his own. And he saw the look in her
eyes, glazed with desire. "Define our relationship, Trinity." He wanted her to establish her expectations.

She nervously licked her lips and his gaze followed
the movement. A spike of heat hit him in the gut, making his erection throb. He wanted her and was, as usual,
amazed at the intensity of his desire for her.

"It will be an affair with no promises or expectations, Adrian. I'm leaving Denver as soon as the transfer comes through and I won't look back. We're good
together. You make me feel things I've never felt before. I want to get it all while I can. I figure the next
few years of my life will involve working harder than
ever to rebuild the momentum I've lost here. An involvement with anyone won't happen for a long time."

A fleeting smile touched her lips. "That means I need
you to help me stock up on all the sex I can get. Think
you can handle that?"

Oh, he could handle it, but...

Why did accepting her terms feel so difficult for him? Hadn't he presented the same terms—no promises or expectations—to a number of women? He didn't like being tied down, he liked dating, and he enjoyed the freedom of having to answer to no woman. And he definitely enjoyed sex. So why did her definition of what they would be sharing bother him? He should be overjoyed that she was a woman who thought the way he did.

He looked down at her, and knew he would accept whatever way she wanted things to be. "Yes, I can handle it."

"I knew you could."

She lowered her hands from his waist and cupped him through his pants. He didn't have to ask what she was doing because he knew. She was going after what she wanted, and he had no intention of stopping her.

She undressed him, intermittently placing kisses all over his body as each piece of clothing was removed. And then he undressed her.

"Make me scream, Adrian," she whispered when she stood in front of him totally naked.

"Baby, I intend to. All over the place."

He swept her into his arms and headed toward her bedroom.

Chapter 17

"I am definitely going to miss this," Trinity said, collapsing on the broad expanse of Adrian's chest. The memory of a back-to-back orgasm was still vivid in her mind, its impact still strong on her body.

"Then don't go."

She somehow found the strength to raise her head and gaze into a pair of dark brown eyes. Although he had a serious look on his face, she knew he was joking. He had put his social life on hold while pretending to be her lover, and she knew the minute she left Denver it would be business as usual for him.

"You're just saying that because you know I intend to wear you out over the next few weeks," she said, leaning up to lick the underside of his jaw.

She watched him smile before he said, "I'd like to see you try."

Inwardly, she knew there was no way she could try

and live to boast about it. The man had more stamina than a raging bull. He definitely knew how to make her scream.

Scream...

She had done that aplenty. It was a wonder her neighbors hadn't called the police. He shifted positions to cuddle her by tightening his arms around her and throwing his leg over hers. It was such an intimate position being spooned next to him. There was nothing like having his still engorged penis pressed against her backside.

She looked over her shoulder at him. "Tell me about your childhood with your cousins. I heard that you, Aidan, Bane and Bailey were a handful." She wouldn't mention that Dr. Belvedere had referred to them as little delinquents.

Adrian didn't say anything for the longest moment, and she began to wonder if he would answer when he told her in a low tone, "You don't know how often over the past eight to ten years that the four of us have probably apologized to Dillon, Ramsey...the entire family for our behavior during the time we lost our parents. That had to be the hardest thing we had to go through. One day they were here and the next day they were gone, and knowing we wouldn't see them again was too much for us.

"But Dillon and the others were there, trying to do what they could to make the pain easier to bear, but the pain went too deep. The state tried forcing Dillon to put us in the system, but he refused, and had to actually fight them in court."

He paused again. "That's one of the main reasons I work so hard now to make them proud of me, to show the family that their investment in my future, their undying love and commitment, didn't go to waste."

She heard the deep emotion in his voice and flipped onto her back to stare up at him. "Were the four of you *that* bad?"

"Probably worse than you can even imagine. We didn't do drugs or anything like that, just did a lot of mischievous deeds that got us into trouble with the law."

"Gangs?" she asked curiously.

He chuckled. "The four of us were our own gang and would take on anyone who messed with us. I truly don't know how Dillon dealt with us. Convincing Bane to leave home for the military was the best thing he could have done. And Bailey finally got tired of getting her mouth washed out with soap because of her filthy language."

"Dillon must be proud of the men and woman the four of you have become."

Adrian smiled. "He says he is, although he considers us works-in-progress. We're older, more mature and a lot smarter than way back then. But he probably can't help but get nervous whenever the four of us get together."

"Dillon seemed relaxed tonight."

"He was to a degree, probably because Aidan was missing. I figure it will be a while before he completely lets his guard down where the four of us are concerned."

"But I'm sure that day will come," she said with certainty. "Now I want to know about your college days. Did you have a lot of girlfriends?"

He chuckled. "Of course. But they could never be certain if it was really me or Aidan they were dating. We're identical and there's only one way to tell us apart."

She lifted a brow. "And which way is that?"

He eyed her as if trying to decide if she could be trusted with such valuable information. "Our hands."

"Your hands?"

"Yes." He held up his right hand. "I have this tiny scar here," he said, indicating the small mark right beneath his thumb. "I got this when I was a kid, trying to climb a tree. Before that, no one could tell us apart. Not even Dillon and Ramsey."

"So you played a lot of tricks on people."

"You know it. Basically all the time. Even freaked out our teachers. We liked dong that. I think the only people who could tell us apart without checking our hands were Bane and Bailey."

Then they talked about her childhood. She practically had him rolling in laughter when she told him how she'd tried to get rid of one of her brother's girlfriends that she didn't like. And she told him of the one and only time she'd gotten into trouble in school.

"You were a relatively good girl," he said.

"Still am. Don't you think I'm *good*?"

He grinned. "No argument out of me."

She returned his grin. "You're a softy."

"No," he said as his gaze suddenly darkened. "I'm hard. Feel me."

She did. Now his erection was poking her in the thigh. If anyone would have told her she would find herself in this position with a man a few months ago, she would not have believed them.

"You leave for work early in the morning—are you ready to go to sleep?"

"I should be ready, shouldn't I?"

"Yes."

She had shared his bed for three days straight now

and she couldn't help wondering how things would be when she left Denver and he was no longer there to keep her warm at night. What would happen when those tingling sensations came and he wasn't there to satisfy them?

She felt his already hard penis thicken against her thigh. He'd practically answered the question for her. No, she wasn't ready to go to sleep and it seemed neither was he.

"Have I ever told you how much I love touching you?" he asked, running a hand over her breasts, caressing the tips of her nipples. The action caused a stirring in the pit of her stomach.

"I don't think that you have."

"Then I'm falling down on the job," he said, moving his hand away from her breasts to travel to the area between her thighs. She knew he would find her wet and ready.

"And speaking of *down*." He shifted his body to place his head between her thighs. After spreading her legs and lifting her hips, his tongue began making love to her in slow, deep strokes.

He held tight to her hips, refusing to let them go. She groaned and as if he'd been waiting to hear that sound, he began flicking his tongue. She grabbed hold of his head to hold him there. *Yes, right there.*

She closed her eyes, taking in the sound of him, the feel of him. This had to be one of the most erotic things a man could do to a woman. And she was convinced no one could do it better than Adrian.

Her body was poised to go off the deep end, when suddenly Adrian released her hips, flipped her around, tilted her hips and entered her in one smooth thrust.

"I like doing it this way," he whispered, taking her in long, powerful strokes as he placed butterfly kisses along the back of her neck.

She liked doing it this way, too. Trinity cried out as spasms consumed her body. He kept going and going and she was the recipient of the most stimulating strokes known to womankind.

When he let out a deep, guttural growl, she felt him, the full essence of him, shoot into her. That's when she lost it and let out a deep, soul-wrenching scream of ecstasy.

Eventually he gathered her into his arms and pulled her to him. Their breathing labored, he cuddled her close to his chest. The last thing she remembered was the deep, husky sound of his voice whispering, "Now you can go to sleep, baby."

And she did.

Several days later, Adrian scanned the room, seeing eager expressions on the faces of his family members. Rico had called this meeting to give them an update. For the past year Rico's PI firm had been investigating the connection of four women—Portia, Lila, Clarice and Isabelle—to their great-grandfather, Raphel Westmoreland.

For the longest time the family had assumed their great-grandmother Gemma was their great-grandfather's only wife. However, it had been discovered during a genealogy search that before marrying Gemma, Raphel had been connected to four other women who'd been listed as his wives.

The mystery of Portia and Lila had been solved. They hadn't been wives but women Raphel had helped out of sticky situations. It was, however, discovered that the woman named Clarice had given birth to a son that Raphel had never known about. Upon Clarice's death in a train accident, that son was adopted by a woman by the name of Jeanette Outlaw. Rico's firm was still trying to locate any living relatives of the child Jeanette had adopted. The news Rico had just delivered was about the woman named Isabelle.

"So you're saying Raphel's only connection to Isabelle was that he came across her homeless and penniless? After she had a child out of wedlock and her parents kicked her out? He gave her a place to live?" Dillon asked.

"Yes. The child was not Raphel's. He allowed her to live at his place since he was not home most of the time while riding the herds. As soon as she got on her feet, she moved out. Eventually, Isabelle met someone. An older gentleman, a widower by the name of Hogan Nelson who had three children of his own. Isabelle and Hogan eventually married. Your grandfather Raphel was introduced to your grandmother Gemma by Isabelle. Gemma was Hogan and Isabelle's babysitter."

Megan nodded. "So that's why Gemma and Isabelle were from the same town of Percy, Nevada."

"Yes," Rico said, smiling at his wife. "It seems your great-grandfather had a reputation for coming to the aid of women in distress. A regular good guy. Of the four women, the only one he was romantically involved with was Clarice."

"Have you been able to find out anything about the family of Raphel and Clarice's son, Levy Outlaw?" Pam asked.

Rico shook his head. "Not yet. That's an ongoing investigation. We traced the man and his family to Detroit but haven't been able to pick up the trail from there."

A few moments later the meeting ended. Adrian was about to leave when Dillon stopped him.

"You okay?"

He smiled at his cousin. "Yes, Dil, I'm fine."

He nodded. "I talked to Thorn last night and he told me about Trinity putting in for a transfer. How do you feel about that?"

Adrian decided to be honest about it. "Not good. I knew she would eventually leave Denver, but she is being forced to leave and I don't like it one damn bit. Denver Memorial has not treated her fairly."

Dillon nodded. "No, they haven't."

Adrian ran a frustrated hand down his face. "I can't help wondering what happens when Trinity leaves. Who will Belvedere target next? He has to be stopped."

Trinity wished the days weren't passing so quickly. Two weeks were almost up and in a few days Casey Belvedere would be returning. She had hoped her transfer would have come through by now but it hadn't.

She had met with Rico and he had given her the necklace and had showed her how it worked. He'd stressed the importance of setting it to record the minute Belvedere began talking. He also said she shouldn't deliberately lead the doctor into any particular conversation. She didn't want to make it seem as if she was deliberately trapping him. It had to be obvious that he was the one initiating the unwanted conversations.

She stopped folding laundry when she received a text on her phone. She smiled when she saw it was from Adrian.

Want to go out to dinner? Millennium Place?

She texted him back.

Dinner at MP sounds nice.

Great. Pick you up around 7.

Trinity slid her phone back into the pocket of her jeans. Adrian had taken her at her word about wanting to be with him as much as possible. Every night they either slept at her place or she spent the night at his.

The more time she spent with him the more she discovered about him and the more she liked him. He hated broccoli and loved strawberry ice cream. Brown was his favorite color. In addition to mountain climbing, he enjoyed skiing and often joined his cousin Riley on the slopes each year.

Trinity glanced at her watch. Adrian said he would pick her up at seven, which would only give her an hour to get ready. Millennium Place was one of those swanky restaurants that usually required reservations well in advance. Evidently, Adrian had a connection, which didn't surprise her.

At seven o'clock Adrian rang her doorbell and after giving her outfit and makeup one last check in the full-length mirror, she answered the door, trying to ignore the tingling sensations in her stomach.

The sight of him almost took her breath away. He looked dashing in his dark suit. He handed her a red, long-stemmed rose. "Hi, beautiful. This is for you."

She accepted the gift as he came inside. "What's this for?"

"Just because," he said, smiling. "You look gorgeous."

"Thanks and thank you for the rose. And I happen to think you look gorgeous, as well."

He chuckled. "Ready to go? Dinner is awaiting this gorgeous couple."

Smiling, she said, "Yes, I'm ready."

She bit back the temptation to say *"for you always,"* and wondered why she would even think such a thing. She knew it wasn't possible.

Chapter 18

Adrian held up his glass of champagne. "I propose a toast."

Trinity smiled and held up hers, as well. "To what?"

"Not to what but to whom. You."

She chuckled. "To me?"

"Yes, to you *and* to me. It was a month ago tonight we went out on our first date. Regardless of the reason, you must admit it ended pretty nicely. You have to admit it's been fun."

"Yes," she said. "It's been fun."

Their glasses clinked. As Adrian took a sip of the bubbly he recalled his conversation with Dillon. On the drive over to pick up Trinity he'd kept imagining how his life would be once she left town.

He placed his glass down and studied her. He'd made a slip a few days ago and asked her not to go. She hadn't thought he was serious. He had been serious. Unfortunately, he and Trinity didn't have the kind of relationship where he could ask her to stay.

Then change it.

He frowned, wondering where the heck that thought had come from. Before he could dwell on it any longer, the sound of Trinity's voice broke into his thoughts.

"This is a beautiful place, Adrian. Dinner was fabulous. Thanks for bringing me here."

He smiled at her. "Glad you approve."

"I do. And the past two weeks with you have been wonderful, as well. I needed them."

He'd needed them, as well, for several reasons. His eyes had opened to a number of things. She had become very important to him. "Want to dance?"

"I'd love to."

As he led her onto the dance floor he thought of their other nights together. Lazy. Non-rushed. Just what the two of them needed. Usually on workdays they got together during the evenings. They would order out for dinner or settle in with grilled-cheese sandwiches. Once or twice he'd brought work from the office and while she stretched out on the sofa reading some medical journal or another, he would stretch out on the floor with his laptop.

He was aware of her every movement. She felt comfortable around him and he felt comfortable around her. She had allowed him into her space and he had allowed her into his. He'd never shared this kind of closeness with any woman. Frankly, he'd figured he never could. She'd proved him wrong.

And their mornings together had been equally special. He would wake up with her naked body pressed against his after a night of nearly nonstop lovemaking. Usually he woke before she did and would wait patiently for her eyes to open. And when they did, he welcomed her to a new day with a kiss meant to curl her toes.

That kiss would lead to other things, prompting them to christen the day in a wonderful way, a way that fueled his energy for the rest of the day.

And she would soon be leaving.

"How did the meeting with your family go?"

He had mentioned Rico's investigation, and this morning before they had parted he had told her that a meeting had been called. He gazed into her beautiful features as he held her in his arms on the dance floor. He told her everything that Rico had uncovered.

"At least now you know the part all four women played in your great-grandfather's life. I guess the next step is finding those other Westmorelands, the ones from the son Raphel never knew he had. The Outlaws."

"Yes. I think Raphel would want that. My great-grandfather went out of his way to help others. He was an extraordinary man."

"So is his great-grandson Adrian. You went out of you way to help me."

"For what good it did."

"It doesn't matter. You still did it. And I will always appreciate you for trying." She placed her head on his chest and he tightened his arms around her.

Moments later, she lifted her eyes to his and the combination of her beauty, her scent and the entrancing music from a live band made the sexual awareness between them even more potent. As if on cue, they moved closer. The feel of her hands on his shoulders sent heat spiraling through him.

The tips of her breasts hardened against his chest, something not even the material of his shirt could con-

ceal. Wordlessly they danced, his gaze silently telling
her just what he wanted, what he would be getting later.

To make sure she fully understood, he moved his
fingertips down the curve of her spine. He drew slow
circles in the spot he'd discovered was one of her erog-
enous zones. Whenever he placed a kiss in the small of
her back she would come undone. Already he felt her
trembling in his arms.

He leaned down, close to her ear. "Ready to leave?"

She answered on a breathless sigh. "Yes."

He led her off the dance floor.

Trinity didn't have to wonder what was happening to
her. She was having an Adrian Westmoreland moment.
Nothing new for her. But for some reason, tonight was
more intense than ever before.

She could attribute it to a number of things. The romantic atmosphere of the restaurant, the delicious food
they'd eaten or the handsome man who was whisk-
ing through traffic to get her home. From the moment
Adrian had picked her up for dinner, he had been attentive, charming and more sexually appealing than any
man had a right to be.

All through dinner she had watched him watching
her. The buildup of sexual awareness had been slow
and deliberate. She'd discovered Westmoreland men
had a certain kind of charisma and there was nothing
any woman could do about it. Except enjoy it.

And she had. All through dinner she had known she
was the object of his fascination. He had captivated her
with an appeal that wouldn't be denied. Now, as far as
she was concerned, they couldn't get back to her place
fast enough.

It was then that she noticed they weren't returning

to her home. Otherwise, he would have gotten off the interstate exits ago. He was taking her to his place.

She glanced over at him, and as if reading her thoughts, he briefly took his gaze off the road. "I want you in *my* bed."

His words made her already hot body that much hotter. She gave him a smile. "Does it matter whose bed?"

"Tonight it does."

She was still pondering his response when he opened the door to his condo a few minutes later. Usually, whenever she visited Adrian's place, she took in the view of the majestic beauty of the surrounding mountains. But not tonight.

Tonight, her entire focus was on one man.

He closed the door behind them, locking them in. He beckoned her with his eyes, mesmerizing her. He was challenging her in a way she'd never been challenged before. And it wasn't all physical. Why was he going after the emotional, as well?

Before she could give that question any more thought, he began moving toward her in slow, deliberate steps. As she watched him, a rush of heat raced through her. The look in his eyes was intense, hypnotic, gripping.

When he stopped in front of her, undefinable feelings bombarded her. She'd never felt this way before, at least not to this degree. She reached out and pushed the jacket from his shoulders.

And then she kissed him all over his face while unbuttoning his shirt. An inner voice told her to slow down, but she couldn't. Their time together was limited. When her transfer was approved she would be leaving. Within hours, if she had her way. She'd already begun packing, telling herself the sooner Denver was behind her the better. But now she wasn't so sure. She had that one nagging doubt…only because of Adrian.

When she reached for his belt, he said, "Let me."

So she did, watching as he stripped off the rest of his clothes before he turned and stripped off hers. Then he carried her into the bedroom.

There was something about his lovemaking tonight that stirred everything inside her. His kisses were demanding, his hands strong yet gentle. His tongue licked every inch of her body, reducing her to a mass of trembling need.

When she thought she couldn't possibly endure any more of his foreplay and survive, he entered her, thrusting deeper than she thought possible. He looked down into her eyes and she felt something…she wasn't sure what. In response, she cupped his face in her hand. "Make me scream."

He did more than that. Before it was over, she'd clawed his back and left her teeth prints on his shoulder. She was totally undone. Out of control. His thrusts were powerful and her hips moved in rhythm with his strokes, in perfect sync.

Over and over he brought her to the brink of ecstasy, then he'd deliberately snatch her back. His finger inched up toward that particular area of her back and she let out a moan knowing what was about to come.

"Now!"

With his husky command, her body exploded and she ground against his manhood as she screamed his name. It seemed her scream spurred him to greater heights because his thrusts became even more forceful.

He threw his head back and his body began quivering with his own orgasm. She felt the thick richness of his release jetting through her entire body. She was suddenly stunned by the force of need that overtook her, made her come again as he once again carried her to great heights from this world and beyond.

Moments later when she slumped against him, weak as water, limp as a noodle, she knew her world would not be the same without him in it.

Chapter 19

"You're looking rather well, Dr. Matthews."

Trinity's skin crawled. She'd known when she arrived at work this morning that her and Dr. Belvedere's paths would cross. This was his first day back at the hospital since returning to the city. She just hadn't expected him to approach her so soon. It wasn't even ten o'clock. She was wearing the necklace recorder and it was set.

"Thank you, Dr. Belvedere. I take it your trip to Texas went well."

"Of course it did. But what I want to know about is this foolishness I've heard. You've put in for a transfer?"

"Yes, sir, you heard correctly. More than once over the past six months you've made unwanted advances toward me. I've told you I'm not interested, and that I'm already involved with someone. Yet you refuse to accept my words. I feel I have no choice but to work at another hospital."

A smile touched his features. "Yes, you've made it clear that you're not interested in sleeping with me, but it doesn't matter what you want, Doctor. It's all about what I want, which is to engage in a sexual relationship with you. Only then will I be satisfied enough to let you continue your work here."

Trinity wanted him to make things perfectly clear… for the record. "Are you saying you will never let me do my job here unless I sleep with you?"

"That's precisely what I'm saying, Dr. Matthews. And it won't do you any good to report me. No one will say anything to me. They need that children's wing and my family is making sure they get it. You should consider our little tryst something for the cause. You'll be doing all those sick kiddies a favor."

"I refuse to believe there is no one here at the hospital who will put you in check."

He chuckled. "Believe it. It doesn't matter who you talk to. I am a Belvedere and I do as I please. Haven't you learned that yet?"

"I refuse to be sexually harassed, which is why I put in for that transfer."

"Unfortunately you won't be getting it. I talked to Dr. Fowler this morning and he agrees with me. Your transfer will be denied."

Anger flared within Trinity. "You can't do that. I am a good doctor."

"I can and I will. And as far as being a good doctor, show up at my place tonight and prove just how *good* you are. Seven o'clock sharp and don't be late. I'll even leave the door unlocked for you. Just find your way to my bedroom and come prepared to stay all night. I've already arranged for you to have tomorrow off. You're going to need it." Then he turned and walked away with a smug look on his face.

It took Trinity a while to gather her composure. Telling one of the other doctors that she wasn't feeling well and needed to leave for the rest of the day, she caught the elevator to the parking garage. As soon as she was inside her car she called Rico. "I think I have what we need to nail Dr. Belvedere."

Trinity called Adrian and he met her at Rico's office where the three of them listened to the recording of Belvedere's conversation with her. It took all of Adrian's effort to contain his anger.

"Well, you're right. This will nail him," Rico said, fighting back his anger, as well. "He'll willingly give you that transfer to keep this recording out of anyone's hands."

"But it shouldn't be that easy for him," Adrian snapped, unable to restrain the rage he felt. "What about other women after Trinity? How long will it take before he's hitting on another woman? Forcing her to do sexual favors against her will? Do you honestly think getting his hand spanked for coming on to Trinity will make much difference?"

Rico met Adrian's gaze. "No. But unless Trinity is willing to go public by filing a sexual harassment lawsuit, there's nothing else we can do."

Adrian turned to Trinity. "Are you willing to do that?"

She shook her head. "No, Adrian. At this point all I want is my transfer. I don't have the money to go against him and I could ruin my reputation and my medical career if I were to lose the case. I don't want to even imagine the legal fees. Even with this recording, I doubt fighting it will do any good. His family has too much power."

Adrian glanced over at Rico who shrugged. "The Belvederes do have power, Adrian. And it seems they have been allowed to get away with stuff for so long, it will merely be a matter of buying off certain people. I agree with Trinity, there is a risk she might be forced to stop practicing medicine while the case is resolved, which might take some time. Unless..."

Adrian's brow lifted. "Unless what?"

"Unless we called them out in such a way where they would have no choice but to make sure Belvedere never practices medicine again."

"Strip him of his medical license?" Trinity asked.

"Yes."

She sucked in a deep breath. "It won't happen. His family won't allow it. Right or wrong, they will still back him. In the end they will get what they want."

Trinity stood. "All I want is my transfer to be approved and after listening to that tape I'm certain the hospital administrators won't allow Dr. Belvedere to block it. If they do, then I'll go public."

"I never took you for a quitter, Trinity."

She lifted her chin. She'd known the moment Adrian walked into her house that he was still upset with her. After the meeting with Rico ended, he'd barely said two words.

"You think I'm a quitter because I won't take what Dr. Belvedere did public?"

"Yes. By not doing so you're letting him get away, letting him do the same thing to other women. You have the ability to stop him now."

"That's where you're wrong, Adrian. You heard what

Rico said. Going against that family is useless. In the end—"

"You'll risk hurting your medical career. I know. I heard him. Is your career all you can think about?"

His question set a spark off within her. How dare he judge her? "No, it's not all I can think about, Adrian," she said, angry that he would think such a thing. "It's not about me but about the children."

"What children?"

"The sick kids who really need that wing the Belvederes are building. You heard what he said in that recording. If I make waves, they will withdraw their funding."

Adrian stared at her. "The way you're thinking is no better than those administrators at Denver Memorial. They are willing to turn a blind eye to what's going on to keep money rolling in."

"Yes, it's all politics, Adrian. That's the way it's played. It's not fair but—"

"It won't stop until someone takes a stand, Trinity. He was trying to force you into his bed. He expects you to show up at his place tonight. And then he has the gall to give you tomorrow off like he's doing you a damn favor. How can you let him get away with that?"

"He's not getting away with it."

"Yes, he is. All you're doing is demanding that he not block that transfer so you can haul ass from here."

Anger erupted within her. "Yes, I want to leave Denver. Why do you have a problem with that? If I make a fuss the hospital will lose a needed pediatric wing and I could have a ruined career. All you're thinking about is losing a bed partner, Adrian."

He took a step toward her. "You think that's all you are to me, Trinity? Well, you're wrong. I've fallen in love with you. I didn't realize it until I listened to that recording. As I sat there, all I could think about was that jerk disrespecting you. You are a woman whose body I've loved and cherished for the past month. But he only considers you a sex object for his own personal satisfaction."

"You've fallen in love with me?" she asked, not believing she'd heard him right.

"Yes. I hadn't planned to tell you since I know I'm not included in your dreams and goals. But even knowing that, I couldn't stop falling in love with you anyway. Imagine that." Without saying anything else he walked out the door.

Adrian was so angry he couldn't see straight. As far as he was concerned Casey Belvedere had crossed the line big time, and the idea of him getting away with it, or not getting the punishment he deserved, made even more rage flare through him

Trinity was such a dedicated doctor that her concern was for the children who needed that new wing. As far as Adrian was concerned, the Belvedere name didn't deserve to be attached to the hospital anyway. It wasn't as if they were the only people with money.

That last thought had ideas running through Adrian's head. He checked his watch. It was just a little after noon. He decided to run his idea by Dillon and hopefully things would take off from there.

"Adrian actually told you he's fallen in love with you?" Tara asked her sister. "Evidently you forgot to tell me a few things along the way. I wasn't aware things had gotten serious between the two of you."

Trinity sighed. She hadn't told her sister about becoming Adrian's real lover. "If by getting serious you mean sleeping together, then yes. That started weeks ago and we had an understanding. No promises and no expectations."

Trinity started from the beginning and told Tara everything. "So how could he fall in love with me? He knows I hate big cities. He knows I planned to leave Denver after I completed residency. He likes outdoorsy stuff and I don't. He—"

"Don't you know that opposites attract?" Tara asked her. "And when it comes to love, sometimes we fall in love with the person we least expect. Lord knows I had no intention of losing my heart to Thorn, and if you were to ask him, he probably felt the same way about me in the beginning."

Trinity couldn't imagine such a thing. First, she couldn't envision any woman not falling head-over-heels for her handsome brother-in-law. Second, Thorn adored Tara and Trinity refused to believe it hadn't always been that way.

"Well, I have no intention of falling in love with anyone and I don't want any man to fall in love with me. My career in medicine is all I want."

"I used to think that way, too, at one time, especially after that incident with Derrick," Tara said. "Having a solid career is nice, but there's nothing like sharing your life with someone you can trust, someone you know will always have your back. There's no reason you can't have both, a career and the love of a good man."

"But I don't want both."

"Who are you trying to convince, Trinity? Me or yourself?"

Trinity nervously gnawed her bottom lip. Instead of answering Tara, she said, "I need to go. Canyon's wife,

Keisha, offered to be at the meeting at the hospital in the morning and represent me. I need to call her to go over a few things."

"Okay. Take care of your business. And…Trinity?"

"Yes."

"Having a man love you has its merits. You loving him back is definitely a plus."

Adrian spent the rest of the day at the office making calls as he tried to pull his plan together. It wasn't as easy as he originally thought it would be. Most of his friends were in debt repaying student loans. That meant reaching out to family members who were known philanthropists such as Thorn, his cousin Delaney, whose husband was a sheikh, and their cousin Jared, who was a renowned divorce attorney representing a number of celebrities.

Adrian was about to get an international connection to call Delaney in the Middle East when the phone rang. "This is Adrian."

"I've got everything arranged and everyone can attend the meeting. We can meet at McKays," Dillon said.

Adrian glanced at his watch. "Can we make it at eight? I have somewhere to be at seven."

"Okay. Eight o'clock will work."

"Thanks, Dil. I appreciate it."

Adrian really meant it. Dillon had contacted the board members of the Westmoreland Foundation, a charity organization his family had established to honor the memory of his parents, aunt and uncle. Usually the foundation's main focuses were scholarships and cancer research. Dillon had arranged a meeting with everyone so Adrian could present a proposal to add a children's hospital wing to the list.

He glanced at his watch again and then stood to put on his jacket. It was a little after six. His seven o'clock meeting was one he didn't intend to miss.

At exactly seven o'clock, Adrian walked into Dr. Casey Belvedere's home. The man had left the door unlocked just as he'd told Trinity he would do. Adrian glanced around the lavishly decorated house. At any other time he would have paused to appreciate the décor, but not now and certainly not today.

"You're on time. I'm upstairs waiting," a voice called out.

Without responding, Adrian took off his jacket and neatly placed it across the arm of one of the chairs. He then took his time walking up the huge spiral staircase.

"I've been waiting on you," Belvedere said. "I'm going to give you a treat."

Adrian stepped into the bedroom and discovered Belvedere sprawled across the bed naked. The man's eyes almost popped out of his head when he saw Adrian, and he quickly jumped up and grabbed for his robe.

"What the hell are you doing here? You're trespassing. I'm calling the police."

Ignoring his threat, Adrian moved forward and said, "You disrespected *my* woman for the last time."

Before Belvedere could react, Adrian connected his fist to the man's jaw, sending the man falling backward onto the bed. Adrian then reached for Belvedere and gave him a hard jab in the stomach, followed by a brutal right hook to the side of his face. After a few more blows, he took the bottle of champagne chilling in the bucket and broke the bottle against the bedpost. He tossed the remaining liquid onto Belvedere's face to keep him from passing out.

"Go ahead and call the police—I dare you. If I have to deal with them, I'll make sure the next time I break every one of your damn fingers. Let's see how well you can perform surgery after that."

Adrian left, grabbing his jacket on the way out, and silently thanking Aidan for convincing him to take boxing classes in college.

Chapter 20

Trinity pulled herself up in bed and ran her fingers through her hair. She couldn't sleep. Her meeting with Keisha had taken its toll on her. They'd covered every legal aspect of the meeting they'd planned to spring on Dr. Belvedere and the hospital administration tomorrow. The element of surprise was on their side and Keisha intended to keep it that way.

Another reason Trinity couldn't sleep was that this was the first time in several weeks that she'd slept alone. She had gotten used to cuddling up to Adrian's warm, muscular body. He would hold her during the night while his chin rested on the crown of her head. She hadn't realized how safe and secure she'd felt while he was with her until now.

She glanced at the clock on her nightstand before easing out of bed. It was not even midnight yet. Keisha had instructed her not to go in to work tomorrow. As her attorney, Keisha would call the hospital and request an appointment with the hospital administrator, asking that the hospital attorney, Dr. Fowler, and Dr. Belvedere be present. Just from talking to Keisha, Trinity could tell the woman was a shrewd attorney. Trinity couldn't wait to see how Keisha pulled things off.

When Trinity walked into her kitchen she realized how empty the room seemed. Adrian had made his presence known in every room of her house and she was missing him like crazy.

If I'm feeling this way about him now, then how will I cope after moving miles and miles away from here?

"I'll cope," she muttered to herself as she set her coffeemaker into motion. "He's just a man."

Then a sharp pain hit her in the chest, right below her heart. He wasn't just a man. He was a man who loved her. A man who had been willing to let her go, to let her leave Denver to pursue her dreams and goals.

Sitting down at the kitchen table, she sipped her coffee, thinking of all the memories they'd made in this very room. Adrian cooking omelets in the middle of the night; them sharing a bowl of ice cream; them making love on this table, against the refrigerator, in the chair and on the counter when they should have been loading the dishwasher.

She knew all the other rooms in her house had similar memories, and those memories wouldn't end once she left Denver. They would remain with her permanently. At that moment she knew why.

She had fallen in love with him.

Trinity sighed as a single tear fell down her cheek. She tried to imagine life without Adrian and couldn't. No matter where she went or what she did, she would long for him, want to be with him, want to share her life with him. What Tara had said earlier was true. *Having a man love you has its merits, but you loving him back is definitely a plus.*

Wiping the tear from her eye, Trinity stood and headed for her bedroom. Adrian was angry with her. He thought she was a quitter. She intended to prove him wrong. This wasn't just about her. Those kids deserved better than a hospital wing from benefactors who routinely abused power.

After talking to Keisha and thinking about what Adrian had said, Trinity had changed her mind. It wasn't just about getting her transfer approved anymore. She knew that Dr. Belvedere had to go, and he could take Dr. Fowler and all those other hospital administrators who had turned a blind eye right along with him. If it meant she had to take them on, then she would do it because she knew she had Adrian backing her up. That meant everything to her.

She picked up the phone. It was late but Keisha had told her to call at any time since she would be up working on the logistics for tomorrow's meeting.

Trinity's conversation with Keisha lasted a few minutes. She quickly stripped off her nightgown, slid into a dress and was out the door.

Adrian was soaking his knuckles and thinking about Trinity. What would she say when she found out what he'd done to Belvedere tonight? As far as Adrian was concerned, the man had gotten just what he deserved. Every time Adrian remembered walking into that bedroom finding Belvedere naked and waiting for Trinity to arrive, Adrian wished he could have gotten in more punches.

He had no regrets about admitting that he loved Trinity. It had been as much a revelation to him as it was to her, but he did love her and the thought of her leaving Denver was a pain he knew he would have to bear. She didn't love him and her future plans did not include him. Now he understood how Aidan had felt when things had ended between him and Jillian. Evidently he and his twin were destined to be the recipients of broken hearts.

Aidan had called Adrian when he'd left Belvedere's place. His brother had been concerned when he felt Adrian's anger. Adrian had assured Aidan he was okay. He had handled some business he should have taken care of weeks ago.

The meeting with Dillon, his brothers and cousins had gone well and they'd unanimously agreed to shift some of the donation dollars toward the hospital if the need arose. Adrian knew from Canyon that Trinity was using Keisha as her attorney and they planned to meet with Belvedere and the hospital administrators tomorrow. Adrian would do just about anything to be a fly on the wall at that meeting to see Belvedere in the hot seat trying to explain what he'd said on that recording.

The police hadn't arrived to arrest Adrian, which meant Belvedere had taken his threat to heart. Um, then again, maybe not, Adrian thought when he heard the sound of his doorbell. It was late and he wasn't expecting anyone. If it was the police, he would deal with them. He had no regrets about what he'd done to Belvedere. At this point, he wasn't even concerned about Dillon finding out about what he'd done.

He glanced out the peephole to make sure Belvedere hadn't sent goons to work him over. His breath caught hard in his chest. It was Trinity. Had Belvedere done something crazy and sought some kind of revenge on her instead of coming after him?

He quickly opened the door. "Trinity? Are you okay?"

A nervous smile framed her lips. "That depends on you, Adrian."

Not sure what she meant by that, he moved aside. "Come on in and let's talk."

Lordy, did Adrian always have to smell so nice? Trinity could feel heat emitting from him. At least he was wearing clothes—jeans riding low on his hips. But he wasn't wearing a shirt and it didn't take much for her to recall the number of times she had licked that chest.

"Can I get you something to drink?"

She turned around and swallowed as her gaze took in all of him. She must not have been thinking with a full deck to even consider leaving him behind.

"Coffee, if you have it. I started on a cup at my place but never finished it."

"A cup of coffee coming up. I could use one myself. We can drink it in here or you can join me in the kitchen."

His kitchen held as many hot and steamy memories as her own. That might be a good place to start her groveling. "The kitchen is fine."

She followed him and, as usual, she appreciated how his backside filled out his jeans. She took a seat at the table. She knew her way around his kitchen as much as he knew his way around hers, although hers was a lot smaller.

Trinity noticed the magazine on the table, one that contained house floor plans and architectural designs. He had mentioned a couple of weeks ago that he would start building on his property in Westmoreland Country sometime next year. She picked up the magazine and browsed through it, noticing several plans he had highlighted.

He had started the coffeemaker and was leaning back against the counter staring at her. Instant attraction thickened her lungs and made it difficult to swallow. She broke eye contact with him. Moments later she looked back at him and he was still staring.

"Nice magazine," she somehow found the voice to say. "You're thinking of building your home sooner than planned?"

He shrugged massive shoulders. "After you leave I figured I needed to do something to keep myself busy for a while. I was thinking that might do it."

She didn't say anything as she looked back at one of the designs he had marked. "I see you marked a few."

"Yes. I marked a few."

When she glanced back at him he had turned to the counter to pour coffee into their cups. She let out a sigh of relief. She doubted she could handle staring into his penetrating dark gaze right now. It would be nice if he put on a shirt, but this was his house and he could do as he pleased. It wasn't his fault she had stocked up a lot of fantasies about his chest.

She turned back to the designs. All the ones he had highlighted were nice; most were double stories and huge. But then all the Westmorelands had huge homes on their properties.

"Here you go," he said, setting the cups of coffee on the table. That's when she noticed his knuckles. They were bruised.

She grabbed his arm, glancing up at him. "What happened to your hands?"

"Nothing."

She let go of his arm and he sat across from her at

the table. Her forehead crunched into a frown. How could he say that nothing had happened when she could clearly see that something had?

"What happened to your hands, Adrian?" she asked again. "Did you injure yourself?"

A slight smile touched his features. "No, I did a little boxing."

She lifted a brow. "You can box?"

He nodded as he took a sip of his coffee. "Yes. Aidan and I took it up in college. We were both on Harvard's boxing team."

"Oh." She took a sip of her own coffee. "And you boxed today without any gloves?"

"Yes. I didn't have them with me."

Before she could ask him anything else, he had a question of his own. "So what's going on with you that depends on me, Trinity?"

She placed her coffee cup down, staring into those deep, dark, penetrating eyes. She hoped what she had to say didn't come too late. "Earlier today you said you have fallen in love with me."

He nodded slowly as he continued to hold her gaze. "Yes, I said it."

"You meant it?"

His lips firmed. "I've told you before that I never say anything I don't mean. Yes, I love you. To be honest with you, I didn't see it coming. I wasn't expecting to fall in love, and only realized the extent of my feelings today."

She nodded. What he'd just said was perfect. "In that case, hopefully you won't find what I'm about to tell you odd." She covered one of his hands with hers, being careful of his bruised knuckles. "I love you, too, Adrian. And to be quite honest, I didn't see it coming,

I wasn't expecting it and only today—after you left—did I realize the full extent of my feelings."

She watched his entire body tense as he continued to stare into her eyes. Realizing he needed another affirmation, she tightened her hold on his hand and said, with all the love pouring from her heart, "I love you, Adrian Westmoreland."

She wasn't sure how he moved so quickly, but he was out of his chair and had pulled her into his lap before she could respond. Then he was kissing her as though he never intended to stop. A part of her hoped he didn't.

But eventually they had to come up for air. She cupped his face, fighting back tears. "I will remain in Denver with you. Not sure if I'll have a job after tomorrow, but I will be here with you."

"So you won't be leaving?" he asked as if he had to make sure he had heard her correctly.

Trinity smiled. "And leave my heart behind? No way." She paused. "You were right. The children at that hospital deserve a competent staff as much as they deserve a hospital wing. I've already talked to Keisha. I want more than just a guarantee that I'll get that transfer to another hospital. I want to clean house.

"So you might want to think about whether or not you want to have your name linked with mine. I plan to go public with everything Casey Belvedere has done unless he and the hospital administrators agree to leave voluntarily."

Adrian tightened his arms around her. "Don't worry about our names being linked. I am proud of your decision and support you one hundred percent. The entire Westmoreland family does." He then told her of the meeting he'd had with Dillon and his family earlier that day.

More tears came into her eyes as she realized that

even when he hadn't known she loved him, he had gone to his family to do that for her. As she'd told him a few days ago, he was an extraordinary man just as Raphel had been.

"Don't worry about how tomorrow will go down. I will be there by your side."

She leaned up and placed a kiss on his lips. "Thank you."

He held her in his arms as if he knew that's what she needed. "When did you realize that you love me?" he asked her.

She looked up at him. "Tonight. When I woke up and you weren't there. I missed you, but I knew it was more than just the physical. I missed the mental, as well. The emotional. I also realized that even if I got the transfer I couldn't endure being separated from you. I knew I wanted a future with you as much as I wanted a career in medicine and that it didn't matter where I lived as long as we were together. You, Adrian Westmoreland, are my dream."

Adrian's features filled with so much emotion that his look almost brought tears to Trinity's eyes.

He crushed her to his chest, whispering, "I love you so damn much, Trinity. It scares me."

She tightened her arms around him and said softly, "Not as much as it scares me. But we'll be fine. Together we're going to make it."

Deep in her heart she knew that they would.

Chapter 21

The next morning Trinity glanced around the hospital's huge conference room. Keisha was seated on her left, Adrian on her right. Dillon sat beside Adrian and a man Keisha had introduced as Stan Harmer, the hospital commissioner of Colorado, sat beside Keisha. Mr. Harmer was responsible for the operations of all hospitals in the state and just happened to be in Denver when Adrian had called him that morning. Things worked out in Adrian's favor because it just so happened that the man was a huge fan of Thorn's.

"You okay?" Adrian asked Trinity.

"It would have been nice to have gotten a little more sleep last night."

He chuckled. "Baby, you got just what you asked for."

She smiled. Yes, she couldn't deny that.

At that moment the conference room door opened and a stocky man, probably Anthony Oats, the hospital's attorney, walked in, followed by Dr. Fowler, who almost stumbled when he recognized Stan Harmer. Both men uttered a quick, "Good morning," before hurrying to their seats.

Trinity noticed that Wendell Fowler refused to look at her. Instead, once seated, he bowed his head and said something to Anthony Oats who chuckled loudly and then glanced her way.

"Don't worry about what's going on across the table," Keisha whispered to Trinity. "They are playing mind games while trying to figure out what we might have other than your word against theirs. They are pretty confident you don't have anything."

Trinity nodded and when she glanced up she saw the man she had met last month, Roger Belvedere, Dr. Casey Belvedere's brother, enter the room. She was surprised to see him. She could tell by the others' expressions that she wasn't the only one.

"Why is Roger Belvedere attending our meeting?" Anthony Oats asked, standing. "This is a private hospital matter."

Keisha smiled sweetly. "Not really, Mr. Oats. And since it could possibly involve the completion of the hospital wing bearing his family's name, I felt it would be nice to include him. So I called this morning and invited him. Besides, there's a chance Mr. Belvedere might be our next governor," she added for good measure, mainly to flatter the man.

Roger Belvedere beamed, and Trinity knew he didn't have a clue what the meeting would be about. He took a seat at the table and glanced around the room. "Where's my brother?" he asked the chief of pediatrics, who suddenly seemed a little nervous.

Dr. Fowler cleared his throat a few times before answering. "He wasn't aware of this meeting until this morning. He wasn't scheduled to work today."

"I wonder why," Trinity heard Adrian mutter under his breath.

"I understand he needed to stop by his physician's office. It seems he was in some sort of accident last night."

Roger raised a brow. "Really? I didn't know that. It must not have been too serious or he would have contacted the family."

At that moment, the conference room door opened and Casey Belvedere walked in at a slow pace. Trinity gasped, and she wasn't the only one. The man's face looked as though it had been hit by a truck.

Roger was out of his seat in a flash. "What the hell happened to you?" he asked his brother.

"Accident," Belvedere muttered through a swollen jaw. He then looked at everyone around the table. Trinity noticed that the moment he saw Adrian, fear leaped into his eyes.

Trinity wasn't the only one who noticed the reaction. Dillon noticed it, as well, and both his and Trinity's gazes shifted from Dr. Belvedere to Adrian, who managed to keep a straight face. Trinity suddenly knew the cause of Adrian's bruised knuckles and she had a feeling Dillon knew, as well. Adrian had gone boxing, all right, and there was no doubt in her mind with whom.

Dr. Belvedere looked over at Dr. Fowler. "What's going on here? Why was I called to this meeting on my day off? Who are all these people and what is Roger doing here?"

It was Keisha who spoke. "Please have a seat, Dr. Belvedere, so we can get started. I promise to explain everything."

He glared across the table at Keisha as he took a seat. And then the meeting began.

Casey Belvedere was furious. "Surely none of you are going to take the word of this resident over mine. It's apparent she's nothing more than an opportunist. Evidently Mr. Westmoreland doesn't have enough money for her, so she wants to go after my family's wealth."

It took every ounce of Trinity's control not to say anything while Belvedere made all sorts of derogatory comments about her character. Keisha would pat her on the thigh under the table, signaling her to keep her cool. Trinity in turn would do the same to Adrian. She swore she could hear the blood boiling inside him.

At the beginning, when Keisha had introduced everyone present, she had surprised Trinity by introducing Adrian as Trinity's fiancé and Dillon as a family friend.

"I agree with Dr. Belvedere," Anthony Oaks said, smiling. "Mr. Belvedere and his brother are stellar members of our community. It's unfortunate that Dr. Matthews has targeted their family for her little drama. Unless you have concrete proof of—"

"We do," Keisha said, smiling.

Trinity immediately saw surprise leap into both men's eyes.

"Just what kind of proof?" Roger Belvedere asked, indignation in his tone. "My family and I are proud of the family's name. As the eldest grandson of Langley and Melinda Belvedere, I don't intend for anyone to impugn our honor for financial gain."

"You tell them, Roger," Casey Belvedere said.

Keisha merely gave both men a smooth smile. "My client has kept a journal where she has recorded each and every incident…even those she reported to Dr.

Fowler where nothing was done." Keisha slid the thick binder to the center of the table.

"And we're supposed to believe whatever she wrote in that?" Mr. Oats said, laughing as if the entire thing was a joke.

Keisha's gaze suddenly became razor sharp. "No. But I'm sure you will believe this," she said, placing a mini recorder in front of her. She clicked it on and the room grew silent as everyone listened, stunned.

Although he'd heard the recording before, listening to it fired up Adrian's blood over again. This was the first time Dillon had heard it and Adrian could tell from his cousin's expression that his blood was fired up, as well.

"Turn that damn thing off!" Dr. Belvedere shouted. "That's not me, I tell you. They dubbed my voice."

Keisha smiled. "I figured you would claim that."

She then passed around the table a document on FBI letterhead. "I had your voice tested for authentication, Dr. Belvedere, and that is your voice. For the past six to eight months you have done nothing but create a hostile work environment for my client. We didn't have to request this meeting. We could have taken this recording straight to the media."

"But you didn't," Roger Belvedere said, looking at his brother in disgust. "That means you want a monetary settlement. How much? Name your price."

Adrian shook his head sadly. The Belvederes were used to buying their way out of situations. It was sickening. But they wouldn't be able to do that this time, at least not the way they expected. Keisha was good and she was going for blood.

Again Keisha smiled. "Our *price* just might surprise you."

Adrian leaned back in his chair and inwardly smiled. He reached beneath the table and gripped Trinity's hand in his, sending a silent message that things would be okay. The Belvederes would discover the hard way that this was one show they wouldn't be running.

Wordlessly, Adrian opened the door to his home and pulled Trinity into his arms. This had been a taxing day and he was glad to see it over.

Dr. Casey Belvedere would no longer be allowed to practice medicine. He was barred not only in the State of Colorado, but also in any other state, for three years. In addition, he would go through extensive therapy. The Belvedere name would be removed from the hospital wing, but their funding would remain intact.

Dr. Wendell Fowler had been relieved of his duties. In fact, Stan Harmer had pretty much fired him right there on the spot and indicated that Dr. Fowler would not be managing another medical facility in the State of Colorado. Further, sexual harassment training would be required of all hospital staff.

To top it off, a sexual harassment suit would be filed against Dr. Belvedere and the hospital. Roger Belvedere hadn't taken that well since it would be a scandal that would affect his campaign for governor. More details would be worked out.

The money Trinity would get if she settled out of court would be enough to build her own medical complex for children, right here in Denver. But first she had to get through her residency. Her transfer was approved right after the meeting by Stan Harmer, and she had her pick of any area hospital. The man had also said Colorado needed more doctors like her. Doctors with integrity who put their patients before their own selfish needs.

She'd been given a month off with pay to rest up mentally after the ordeal Dr. Belvedere had put her through. Keisha had refused to accept Roger Belvedere's suggestion that everything be handled privately and kept from the media. She had let him know that she would be calling the shots and they would be playing by her rules.

Now, Trinity gazed into Adrian's eyes and his love stirred sensations within her.

"I want you," he whispered as he proceeded to remove her clothes.

Then he removed his own clothes and carried her up the stairs to his bedroom. Standing her beside the bed, he kissed her, tenderly, thoroughly, full of the passion she had come to expect from him.

"I want to take you to your home in Florida," he told her softly, placing small kisses around her lips. "This weekend."

"Why?"

"Don't you think it's time I met your parents? Plus, I want your father to know all my intentions toward his daughter are honorable."

She tilted her head back to look up at him. "Are they?"

"Yes. I want to ask his permission to marry you."

Trinity's heart stopped beating as happiness raced through her. "You want to marry me?"

He chuckled. "Yes. I guess we'll have to get in line behind Stern and JoJo, though. But before the year ends, I want you to be Mrs. Adrian Westmoreland. No more pretenses of any kind. We're going for the real thing, making it legal."

He kissed her again. Tonight was theirs and she intended to scream it away.

Epilogue

"Stern, you may kiss your bride."

Cheers went up when Stern took JoJo in his arms. Sitting in the audience, Trinity had a hard time keeping a dry eye. JoJo looked beautiful and when she'd walked down the aisle toward Stern, Trinity could feel the love between them.

The wedding was held in the Rocky Mountains at Stern's hunting lodge. However, today, thanks to Riley's wife, Alpha, who was an event planner, the lodge had been transformed into a wedding paradise. It was totally breathtaking. Stern and JoJo had wanted an outdoor wedding and felt their favorite getaway spot was the perfect place. Trinity had to agree.

"Miss me?" a deep, male voice whispered in her ear as she stood at one of the buffet tables. Adrian and all of his Denver cousins and brothers had been groomsmen in the wedding.

Trinity turned and smiled. Then her smile was replaced with a frown. "Hey, wait a minute. You aren't Adrian."

The man quirked a brow, grinning. "You sure?"

Trinity grinned back. "Positive. So where is my husband-to-be?"

"He sent me to find you. Told me to tell you he's waiting down by the pond."

"Okay."

Trinity saw Aidan's eyes fill with emotion as he stared across the yard. She followed the direction of his gaze to where Pam and her three younger sisters stood. Trinity had met the women a few weeks ago when they'd come home to try on their bridal dresses. She thought Jillian, Nadia and Paige were beautiful, just like their older sister.

"Aidan? Is anything wrong?" Trinity asked him, concerned.

He looked back at her and gave her a small smile. "No, nothing's wrong. Excuse me for a minute." She watched as he quickly walked off.

It took Trinity longer than she expected to reach the pond. Several people had stopped to congratulate her on her engagement. Most had admired the gorgeous ring Adrian had placed on her finger a few months ago. They would be getting married in August in her hometown of Bunnell. They planned to live in Adrian's condo while their home in Westmoreland Country—Adrian's Cove—was under construction.

She found her intended, standing by the pond, waiting for her. He held open his arms and she raced to him, feeling as happy as any woman could be. He leaned down and kissed her.

"Happy?" he asked, smiling down at her.

"Very much so," she said returning his smile. And she truly meant it.

Once the details of the sexual harassment lawsuit had gone public, the Belvederes, not surprisingly, hired a high-profile attorney who tried to claim his client was innocent. That attempt fell through, however, when other women began coming forward with their own accusations of sexual harassment. So far there were a total of twelve in all. Keisha expected more.

Casey Belvedere was no longer practicing medicine, and Roger Belvedere had withdrawn his name as a gubernatorial candidate. Consumers and women's advocacy groups were boycotting all Belvedere dairy products. Needless to say, over the past few months, the family had taken a huge financial hit.

Adrian took Trinity's hand in his and they began walking around the pond. He needed a quiet moment with the woman he loved. The past three months had been hectic as hell. They had flown to Florida where he had asked Frank Matthews' permission to marry his daughter. His soon-to-be father-in-law had given it.

Now Adrian understood what Stern had been going through while waiting to marry JoJo. More than anything, Adrian couldn't wait for a minister to announce him and Trinity as husband and wife.

"Adrian?"

"Yes, sweetheart?"

"Is something going on with Aidan and one of Pam's sisters?" Trinity asked.

He gazed down at her. "What makes you think that?"

She shrugged and then told him what she'd witnessed earlier.

Adrian nodded. "Yes. He's in love with Jillian and has been for years. No one is supposed to know that he and Jillian once had a secret affair…especially not Pam and Dillon. Aidan and Jillian ended their affair last year."

Trinity stopped walking and raised a brow. "Why?"

He told her the little about the situation that he knew.

"Do you think they will work everything out and get back together?" Trinity asked softly.

"Yes," Adrian said with certainty.

Trinity glanced up at him. "How can you be so sure?"

Adrian stopped walking and wrapped his arms around Trinity. "I can feel his determination, and the only thing I've got to say is that Jillian better watch out. Aidan is coming after her and he's determined to get her back."

Not wanting to dwell on Aidan and his issues, Adrian kissed Trinity once, and planned on doing a whole lot more.

* * * * *

BACHELOR UNLEASHED

To the love of my life, Gerald Jackson, Sr.

Special thanks to Sharon Beaner,
who took the time to enlighten me about the job
of a mediator. This one is especially for you.

Give, and it will be given to you. A good measure,
pressed down, shaken together and running over,
will be poured into your lap.
—*Luke* 6:38

Prologue

There was nothing a woman was left wanting before, during and after making love with Xavier Kane. And Farrah Langley was caught now in the throes of one of those heated, satisfying moments.

She had known she was in for a sensual treat the minute she'd opened the door to him earlier. With a bottle of wine in his hand, he'd stood there looking sexier than any man had a right to look, arriving for what had become known as one of his infamous booty calls. Now with three orgasms behind her in less than an hour and her body climbing greedily toward a fourth, she reached the conclusion that Xavier Kane was a pleasure-producing maniac.

They were in the middle of her bed, on top of the covers, naked, soaked in perspiration, their limbs entwined, their bodies connected, making out like sex-deprived addicts who couldn't get enough of each other.

It was always this endless need that drove them out of control and over the edge. Something about the feel of his hot, sweaty flesh rubbing against hers as he thrust in and out of her body made her g-spot literally weep.

The room exuded the scent of raw sex, the aroma of a virile man, and she was drenched in the fragrance of a deeply satisfied woman. A woman who was his most willing partner and was doing everything to keep up with him. The man's sexual appetite was voracious, and he delivered just as much as he procured. She had no complaints, just compliments. Xavier definitely knew how to conduct business in the bedroom.

It was storming outside, and they were having their own monsoon inside. Only with him did she experience such a downpour of torrential sensations, such a deluge of emotions…some she knew were best kept under wraps. But he had a way of pulling them out of her anyway. He had the ability to make her want things she was better off not having. More than once with him she'd let her guard down, allowed her body's own greedy wants and needs to betray her, which was a transgression that could cost her.

It was nearly two years since her divorce from Dustin Holloway had become final. Dustin, her college sweetheart, a man she had vowed to always love. A man who'd vowed to love her forever as well. But four years into their marriage she'd begun noticing things. Like him wearing a scent that wasn't hers. Him moaning out a strange name during sex, and him sneaking out of bed in the wee hours of the night to make private calls on his cell phone.

She had finally confronted him, and without any remorse, he'd confessed that for the past two years he'd been living a double life. He not only had a mistress but also a child, and he wanted a divorce to marry the other woman and be a father to his daughter.

It had taken a full year for the hurt to go away, and she would admit remnants of it still lingered, making her cautious, wary and adamant even at twenty-seven years of age never to give her heart to another man again.

"Let your pleasure rip for me now, Farrah."

Xavier's deep, husky command struck a delicious chord, sent sensuous shivers up her spine, sank deep into her sensitive flesh and touched her everywhere, especially at the juncture of her thighs where their bodies were joined.

She forgot everything except how he was making her feel. Her body fragmented into a cascade of gratifying prisms that ran from the top of her head to the soles of her feet. She was flooded with more sensations than she could sink her teeth into...so she sank them into him, biting his shoulder as she found herself drowning in total and complete sensual abandonment.

It was then that he skillfully lifted her hips in order to thrust deeper into a spot he always reserved for last. Her legs tightened around his waist, and she released one hellacious scream as pleasure tore through her.

Farrah was convinced his ear drums were damage-proof, just as she figured the power and strength of his erection should be patented. While she let go and continued to take one merciless fall into ecstatic oblivion, she knew the moment the sexual tension that had been building inside him popped, and with it went his control. His body responded to hers, and following her lead, he went off the deep end. His thrusts became harder, stronger, went deeper, and his hold on her tightened as she locked him between her thighs. And then came the

Xavier Kane growl that pierced the air and only made her want him even more.

"Xavier, please. More."

And he continued to give her more, giving in to her shameless plea. Heat built as he stroked her while pushing her thighs apart with his knee to go even deeper. His thrusts were the strokes of rapture, and the skill with which he was delivering them was the pinnacle of pure sensual delight. They were what continued to spark that foolishness in her head that whispered what they were sharing was more than just great sex. It was about a man and woman so in tune to each other's wants and needs, so in harmony to each other's desires that practically anything—a touch, a lick, a breathless groan—nipped at their nerve endings and pushed them to this.

As she continued to tumble over the edge, she didn't want to be reminded that he'd become her weakness, nor that she'd made a decision as to how she would handle it. As much as she preferred not taking such drastic actions, her decision was one that couldn't be helped. Not if she wanted to retain her sanity and peace of mind. And she couldn't put it off any longer.

Tonight she would end things between them.

She pushed the thought to the back of her mind. She didn't want to dwell on all the pleasurable lovemaking hours she would be giving up. She would just have to learn to deal with it.

For now she wanted nothing more than to keep falling into the most sensuous waters a woman's body could plunge.

Xavier reluctantly eased out of Farrah's body, sighed deeply and then slid out of bed. The first thing he no-

ticed was that it was no longer storming outside. Calm
had settled over the earth.

The second thing he noticed was the absence of Farrah's even breathing, which meant even after all those
powerful orgasms she was still awake. Usually she
would have fallen into an exhausted sleep.

He glanced over his shoulder and met her hazy gaze
and thought he saw two things in the dark depths of her
eyes—regret and resolve.

"We need to talk, Xavier," she said softly.

For some reason he didn't like the sound of that.
Usually when a woman informed a man they needed
to talk right after they'd made love it meant she had a
bomb to drop. The first crazy notion that ran through
his mind was that she was going to tell him that somehow, although she was on the pill and he always wore
a condom, she'd gotten pregnant. The chances of that
happening were probably less than one percent, but it
was the one percent that had him feeling kind of nervous right now.

He studied her features and thought, as he always
had, that she was an utterly beautiful woman who wore
that "just made love to" look well. And just the thought
that he'd given her that look, dressed her in it real good,
sent primitive shivers of male pride and possessiveness
down his spine. Hell, if he was a cave man, he would
be beating on his damn chest about now.

"Let me take care of things in the bathroom first and
then I'll be right back," he said. And with every step
toward the bathroom he couldn't help wondering what
this discussion would be about.

If she was going to inform him that he was going to
be a daddy, the thought didn't send him into panic for
some reason. He was thirty-two, closer to thirty-three if

you wanted to be more specific, and he was pretty well-off, so he could handle child support payments without breaking a sweat, just as long as a woman didn't try taking him to the cleaners. He knew, after being Farrah's lover for almost a year, that she was not the greedy type.

Except for when they were in bed. Between the sheets, her sexual appetite could just about rival his. But he had no complaints. And he knew that, like him, she had this thing about commitments. They'd both gotten burned once, he with an ex-girlfriend and she an ex-husband, so a no-strings affair was all they'd ever wanted from each other.

They hadn't meant for things to last as long as they had. He'd been with her longer than any other woman... except Dionne Witherspoon. However, he refused to go there tonight. He would not think about the woman he'd fallen in love with while attending law school at Harvard. Dionne had only sought out his affections so he could provide the help she needed for her law exams. Once she aced them all, she had dropped him like a hot potato.

Xavier returned from the bathroom a short while later accepting there was a strong possibility that, regardless of whether he and Farrah wanted to play the commitment game or not, they would be forced to do so if she was pregnant. After all, he much preferred being a real father to his child rather than just a child support check. He wanted to be the type of parent to his child that his father had been to him. Benjamin Kane had been a top-notch dad. He still was.

Instead of getting back in bed, Xavier picked up his jeans and slid into them, then he eased down in the wingback chair across the room from the bed. He had followed Farrah's lead. She was no longer naked but was wearing a robe. It was short and showed a lot of thigh. He thought she had luscious thighs, the kind a man loved to hold on to and ride. Farrah Langley made any man with red hot testosterone appreciate being a man. Hell, he was getting another hard-on just looking at her.

"Tonight was it for us, Xavier."

He pulled his gaze from her thighs to her face, not sure he had heard her correctly. He stared at her for a long, silent moment, and when he saw the regret and resolve he'd caught a glimpse of earlier, he asked, "What did you say?"

She sat down on the side of her bed to face him. "I said, tonight was it."

He fought to keep back the shock from his face. "It?"

"Yes. We started this thing between us almost a year ago, longer than either of us intended. It was never meant to last more than a couple of months, if even that."

He nodded, knowing that much was true. For him the practice of self-preservation was a way of life. He abhorred emotional involvements of any kind. He and Farrah had established the boundaries up front, basically on that first night.

And he could recall that first night well…

They had met at the Racetrack Café, a popular hangout here in Charlotte. He'd been there with a close friend by the name of Donovan Steele, and Farrah had been with her best friend, Natalie Ford. Before the night was over, Donovan and Natalie had paired off and so had he and Farrah. He'd thought she was ultrabeautiful, hot. There had been something about her that had immediately made his mouth water, his tongue tingle, and he'd known from the jump that he wanted some of her.

And he had been able to tell from her body language that the feeling was mutual.

A few nights later he had shown up at her front door with a bottle of wine in his hand and a hard-on in his pants. She had opened the door and let him in, fully aware of the nature of his visit. And things had been that way between them since. No commitment, just great sex.

And now she wanted to end things.

Before he could fix his mouth to ask why, she said in a teasing voice that he really didn't find amusing, "I wouldn't want to threaten your standing as a member of that club."

He knew exactly what club she was referring to. It was one he and his five godbrothers had formed a few years ago—the Bachelors in Demand Club. They were men who enjoyed their single lives with no plans of settling down. All six of them had their own issues with commitment and were basically guarding their hearts. Now there were only five of them left, since one of his godbrothers, Uriel Lassiter, had gotten married last year.

"Donovan and Natalie's wedding reminded me of all the reasons why I don't want to be seriously involved with anyone again," she went on to add.

He drew in a deep breath. As much as he preferred things continuing between them for a little while longer, the decision to split now was hers to make, and he respected that. And then maybe she was right. Things had lasted longer than either of them had planned, and things were beginning to get too complacent between them. Hell, he could recall speeding away from Uriel's wedding reception like a mad man trying to make it to her place. And wasn't it just last weekend they had virtually burned the sheets off the bed at the Ritz-Carlton in New York after Donovan and Natalie's wedding reception?

He didn't need a rocket scientist to see that things could start getting serious between them if they weren't careful. She had the ability to unleash feelings within him he preferred staying locked away. So maybe they should make a clean break before things got messy and complicated. Those were two words he didn't like having in his vocabulary.

He eased out of the chair and stood. "Hey, no problem. It was nice while it lasted, sweetheart." He not only meant that from the bottom of his heart, but also from the head of his penis that was already swelling in protest with his words. He was definitely going to miss sharing all those bedroom hours with her.

"You do understand, right?"

"Of course I do," he said, ignoring the tightening in his chest. He slowly crossed the room and reached out and pulled her into his arms. "I will always appreciate our time together and if you ever need me for anything, you know how to reach me. Don't ever hesitate to call, all right?"

Farrah nodded. "All right. Thanks."

He cupped her chin in his hand before leaning down and capturing her mouth in a kiss that she felt all the way to her toes. She thought being a good kisser was just another quality he possessed. His tongue tangling with hers elicited all kinds of lust that began rushing through her veins in a matter of seconds. It didn't take much to get her wet again.

When he finally released her mouth to step back, she eased back down on the edge of the bed to watch him dress. He slid his jeans back down his tight, muscular thighs before grabbing his briefs to put them on. Her gaze studied his erection, the object that had given her so much pleasure over the past year. It was still hard, thick and so engorged its veins seemed ready to explode.

Desire thrummed through her, and she began remembering how his shaft felt inside of her, how good it tasted, and she quickly decided there was no use letting a good hard-on go to waste. Especially since it was one she wouldn't be seeing again. "Xavier?"

He glanced over at her as he reached for his jeans. "Yes?"

"How about one more for the road?"

A slow smiled tugged at the corners of what she thought was a pair of ultrasexy lips. She watched him slide underwear back down his legs and toss them aside before walking back over to her. He then said in a deep, husky voice, "Baby, I'll give you something better than one more for the road. Get ready because we're about to take flight. I'm about to take you on the ride of your life on the interstate."

And with that said, he tumbled her back onto the rumpled bedcovers.

Chapter 1

Six months later

"So, what are your plans for the holidays, X?"

Xavier leaned back in the leather chair and propped his legs up on his desk while glancing out the window at New York City's skyline. The Empire State Building was in his direct line of vision and looked massive against the dark blue sky overhead.

He had arrived in New York a few days ago to wrap up a business deal between the Northeast Division of Cody Enterprises and Oxley Financial Services. Cameron Cody's takeover of the investment firm was a done deal, and as the executive attorney for all Cameron's affairs, Xavier needed to be in place to make sure everything was handled as it should be. Not only was he considered Cameron's right-hand man, they were very close friends. That friendship had begun back at Harvard when the two had been struggling students, determined to become successful in life.

And now, just like then, they looked out for each other, so he wasn't surprised by Cameron's question. Cameron knew that Xavier's parents had left for their annual six-month missionary crusade—this year to Haiti—and wouldn't be returning back to the States until sometime in the spring. "I'm not sure yet, Cam. I have a number of invitations out there."

Cameron's deep chuckle sounded over the speakerphone. "Hey, don't brag about it. Not everyone is blessed to have five sets of godparents."

A frown settled on Xavier's face that was best not seen by anyone. "That could be a blessing or a curse," he said, shaking his head pensively. "Currently it might be the latter. Now that Uriel has married, some of the godparents are eyeing the remaining five of us. I'm not sure I want to be included in any of their get-togethers for the holidays. Thanksgiving was hard enough."

"I bet."

Everyone had been invited to Uriel and Ellie's place on Cavanaugh Lake. Former neighbors on the lake, the two had remodeled both their homes once married, combining them into one with an enclosed walkway. That meant plenty of space for sleepovers.

And it was nice having all six godfathers present as they retold the story of how they'd met at Morehouse and become close friends, and how on graduation day they'd promised to stay in touch by becoming godfathers to each of their children, and that the firstborn sons' names would carry the letters of the alphabet from U to Z. And that was how Uriel Lassiter, Virgil Bougard, Winston Coltrane, Xavier Kane, York Ellis and Zion Blackstone had come into existence.

"Well, you know you can add me and Vanessa to your list," Cam was saying. "You're always welcome to our place. We're doing Christmas in Jamaica this year."

Xavier couldn't help but smile. His friend sounded happy and contented. What man wouldn't be once he'd finally gotten the woman of his dreams? The former Vanessa Steele had been determined not to become involved with Cameron after his attempt to take over her family's business. Cameron, on the other hand, had been just as determined to win her over. Not surprisingly, Cam had succeeded and was a happily married man with a baby on the way.

"Thanks, Cam, but I think I'm going to use the two weeks I'll have off during the holidays to chill and relax. I'm even thinking about going someplace quiet. I might decide to visit Zion in Rome," he said.

Moments later after hanging up the phone with Cameron, Xavier stood to stretch, ignoring the pile of work sitting on his desk. Not only was he executive attorney to Cameron Cody, he also managed the legal affairs for several well-known Hollywood celebrities, which was the reason he had an office in Los Angeles as well.

Of all his clients, Cam kept him the busiest, which accounted for Xavier's additional offices in London, Jamaica and Paris. And since Cameron's newest brother-in-law, Quade Westmoreland, had a first cousin who was married to a sheikh, Cameron and Sheikh Jamal Yasir were anticipating a business venture that could now take Xavier to parts of the Middle East.

"Mr. Kane, those reports you ordered are ready."

He glanced over at the intercom on his desk before leaning over to press a button. "Thanks, Vicki. Please bring them in."

"With pleasure, sir."

Xavier shook his head. Vicki Connell, the woman who'd replaced Christine James, his New York administrative assistant, while she was out on an extended maternity leave, was determined to get inside his pants one way or the other. He knew the signs and had read those hidden seductive looks in her pretty dark eyes plenty of times whenever he came to town. All of that would be fine and dandy if he was interested, but he wasn't. And he downright hated admitting that he hadn't been gung ho about any woman getting into his pants since splitting with Farrah almost a half a year ago.

He didn't know what the hell was wrong with him since, typically, he wasn't the brooding type. He'd certainly never given a woman any lasting thoughts once things between them had ended. So why was he doing so now?

He walked over to the window and glanced out again. If the forecaster's predictions held true, a snowstorm would be hitting the city by Sunday, and Xavier wished he could return to Charlotte before that happened. He could kiss that wish goodbye since he was due to remain in New York for another week or so.

He heard the door opening behind him and then an ultra sexy feminine voice said, "Here are the reports, Mr. Kane. Will there be anything else?"

He slowly turned around at the same time Vicki was smoothing her short skirt down her thighs, at least as much of them that could be covered. He was convinced if she were to bend over he would find out what color her panties were.

He had to admit her outfit looked fine on her, but did nothing for him, other than reminding him how inappropriate it was for the workplace. But then the same thing held true for the outfit she'd worn yesterday. One

of his godbrothers, York, who lived in New York, had
dropped by the office to take him to lunch and had
mentioned a number of times during their meal how
good he thought Vicki had looked. Apparently he was
impressed with her attire.

"Yes, there will be something else," Xavier replied
to Vicki. As he spoke he watched lust flare in her eyes.

"Yes?" she asked, with anticipation flowing in her
voice.

"Please have a seat."

She lifted a brow. "A seat?"

"Yes."

"In the chair?"

He inwardly smiled. Evidently she'd been hoping
he meant spread-eagle on the desk. "Yes, Vicki, please
sit in the chair."

When she did so, the hem of her skirt barely covered
her thighs. "Yes, Mr. Kane?"

"How old are you, Vicki?"

After probably trying to figure out why he was asking, she said, "I'm twenty."

He nodded as he leaned against his desk. "And I understand you're attending classes at the university at
night and working for a temp agency part-time."

She shifted in her seat to deliberately show more of
a bare thigh. "Yes, that's right. I'm hoping to get hired
here full-time during the summer so I can qualify for
an internship next fall."

He wasn't surprised to hear that. Cody Enterprises
had several internship programs available. Going to college had been a financial hardship for Cameron, so he
was a firm believer in assisting college students whatever way he could. The internship program he had in
place was just one way of doing so.

"I see no reason why that can't happen for you, other than for one."

She looked surprised. "And what reason is that?"

"You need to improve your attire in the workplace."

She actually looked offended. "I was told there wasn't a dress code here."

"There isn't one per se. However, a person trying to move up in a company needs to care about the image she projects."

She lifted her chin. "And just what kind of image am I projecting?"

"An image of someone who enjoys getting a lot of attention. You've become a distraction. Deliberately so. Every man in this building finds some excuse to come to this floor every day and your work is suffering because you're spending more time entertaining than taking care of business matters. I've yet to get that report that was due yesterday."

"It's not my fault those guys drop by and take up my time."

Xavier's gaze roamed up and down her outfit. "Isn't it?"

He didn't say anything, wanting to give her time to consider everything he'd said. "That will be all for now, Vicki," he finally said. "I hope we don't have to discuss this issue again and I hope to have that report on my desk before I leave today."

He took his seat behind his desk and watched her quickly leave the room. Moments later, while sitting staring into space, the truth hit him right between the eyes as to why he wasn't attracted to other women. He hadn't gotten Farrah out of his system.

Considering everything they'd shared for close to a year, that was understandable. Usually his affairs with women rarely lasted a couple of months. That was when the women began to get possessive, and Xavier had no interest in being tied down to one woman.

With Farrah things had been quite different. She'd never stamped a claim to any kind of ownership on him. He'd liked that. He'd liked her. And dammit, he missed her. He still wasn't sure why she had ended things between them, but he did have a hunch.

They had started getting too comfortable with each other, had fallen into one of those relationship routines where they just couldn't get enough of each other. That sort of addiction between two people was kind of scary since there was no telling where it could lead. Straight to their hearts was out of the question since falling in love was in neither of their plans. Still, the thought of doing something as drastic as ending things between them hadn't crossed his mind.

He'd been perfectly satisfied with how things had been going. She didn't ask for anything but gave everything. Hell, no woman could compare to her in the bedroom. And she had never questioned his activities when they weren't together. But then in his mind she'd had exclusive rights as his bed partner, although he'd never given them to her verbally. It had been something understood between them. He'd known she hadn't dated anyone else during the time he'd been her lover, and neither had he.

He reached for the report Vicki had delivered to him and, after flipping through a few pages, decided his concentration level wasn't where it needed to be today. This was New York. There was no reason he couldn't get back in the groove and begin enjoying life again. He had the phone number of a few ladies living here who were laid back and easy. The latter was the key word.

He should give one a call, invite her to meet him somewhere for a drink. And then afterward, they could go to her place for a roll between the sheets. Hell, skip the drink, he would just go for the roll between the sheets. He hadn't had sex with a woman since Farrah. What was he waiting on? Christmas?

He glanced over at his calendar. And speaking of Christmas…it was only three weeks away, so if he was waiting on Christmas, he didn't have long, but he doubted his testosterone could last until then.

Xavier shrugged off the feeling that something was missing in his life. Instead, he thought about the woman he would pay a visit later tonight. Beth Logan was a flight attendant he'd met a couple of years ago and was a sure bet if she was in town. It wouldn't bother her in the least that they hadn't connected in over a year. She was known to be hot and ready whenever they got together in one of their uninhibited passionate romps.

He smiled. Yes, making a booty call tonight was definitely in order. All he needed was to stop somewhere to grab a bottle of wine, and he would be all set.

"So there you have it, Farrah," Frank McGraw said, handing the file to her. "The judge recommended the women seek mediation before officially going to court."

Farrah nodded as she scanned the file. She'd reviewed it already while on the plane from Charlotte since Frank's secretary had faxed a copy to her that morning before her flight. The case was interesting. Two best friends from high school, Kerrie Shaw and Lori Byers, had started a line of cosmetics right after college, investing equally in the start-up. Lori had eventually lost interest when she married and became a mother. Kerrie, still single, had continued to make the business prosper and, with Lori's blessings, had even moved things in another direction when she created an antiaging cream. Though Lori hadn't been actively involved in the company in over ten years, her new husband wanted Kerrie to buy out Lori's share at a percentage Kerrie felt was unreasonable, considering she was the one who'd made CL cosmetics into the mega-company it was today.

"So what do you think?" Frank broke into Farrah's concentration to ask.

She glanced up. "Like all the others, I find this case interesting."

"Well, you're the best damn mediator this firm has. I'm just glad you were able to change your schedule to accommodate us."

Farrah smiled. "What woman would turn down a chance to come to New York, especially in December? I plan to do some major holiday shopping while I'm here."

Frank chuckled. "Good luck. Forecasters predict a snowstorm by Sunday. Personally, I think it might be before then. If that happens, you won't get much shopping done."

Farrah stood, stuffing the file into her messenger case. "Hey, no problem. If that happens, then I'll stay in my hotel room with a bottle of wine and a good mystery novel and be just as happy. Then I'll fly out as planned and return next week to wrap up things when the weather is more cooperative. When I return I'll just tack on a few additional days for shopping and a Broadway show."

Frank smiled. "That sounds nice." He leaned back in his chair. The look in his eyes shifted from professional to predatory. "How about dinner tonight, Farrah?"

Farrah shook her head. She should have known the

moment she mouthed the word *bed* that Frank wouldn't waste time trying to get her into one. He'd been trying for a few years now and hadn't given up yet. The man just didn't get it, although she'd tried explaining it to him several times—and not even mincing her words while doing so. She thought her ex-husband had been scum, but Frank—who'd divorced his wife for the younger woman hired to nurse his wife after a near-fatal car accident—was no bargain either. Professionally, he was a skilled negotiator who deserved every penny of the six figures he made. As a man, he was as low on the totem pole as you could get. The only satisfaction she took was in knowing that eventually Frank's second wife had dumped him for a younger man, but not before cleaning out his bank account.

"Thanks, Frank, but I don't think so."

"Not this time?"

"Not ever."

"I won't give up."

"I wish you would," she threw over her shoulder as she moved toward the door. She was determined to prove she was just as stubborn as he was persistent.

"Will you continue to hate all men because of what your ex-husband did to you, Farrah?"

She continued walking, thinking his question didn't even deserve a response. She didn't hate all men because of Dustin. She just knew what she did or didn't want out of a relationship these days. Where she had once been the happily-ever-after kind of girl, the one who believed in white picket fences and everything that went along with it, she now knew that nothing was forever, especially a man's love. She refused to look at things through rose-colored glasses ever again.

A few moments later Farrah caught the elevator

down to the lobby and exited the Stillwell Building to step out onto the busy sidewalk. She loved New York and thought there was no place quite like it. She tilted her head back to look up at all the tall buildings. Being here was always so invigorating.

Times Square. This was the heart of Manhattan. She could pick up the scent of fresh baked breads, see all the digital billboards flashing bright lights and watch people move so fast that if you didn't keep pace they would practically knock you over. For the few times a year she had to come here on business, she not only put up with it, she loved it.

Deciding not to take a cab since she wasn't too far from the hotel, she looked forward to a brisk walk. One of her coworkers had taken her out for a prime rib lunch. It was so scrumptious she'd even loaded the baked potato with butter and sour cream. She pushed guilt aside because this was December, the one month she ate whatever she wanted. She'd jump on the weight loss train like everyone else the first of the year. This was the season to be merry, so what were some extra calories now?

She thought about the case she would be working this week. She loved her job as a mediator at Holland and Bradford and couldn't imagine doing anything else. And as long as there were disputes to be ironed out, she would always be employed.

The reason her profession would remain in demand was because mediation was definitely less expensive than litigation, and in addition to the financial advantage, there was also the time saved. You didn't have to wait on court time, the worry of witnesses disappearing on you, or people not remembering facts occurring years before. Also, the sooner you could resolve a dispute, the sooner people's lives could get back to normal.

Lives getting back to normal...

A lot could be said for that, including hers. It had been six months since she and Xavier had ended things, and she was still trying to work him out of her system. It was as if she'd become addicted to the man. No matter how many times she'd washed her sheets, she couldn't get his scent out of them. After a while, she'd stopped trying and just went to bed each night breathing him in.

But that wasn't good because his scent reminded her of what they'd done between those sheets. She often dreamed about him, and in her dreams he did every single thing to her that he'd done while they'd been together and then some. More than once she had awakened the next morning with the covers tossed haphazardly on her bed and feeling like someone had ridden her all night. But that had only made her crave the real thing even more.

Breaking things off had been the right thing to do. She had begun anticipating his visits, wondering what he was up to during those days and nights he wasn't with her, getting antsy when he didn't call or acting like a bubbly sixteen-year-old when he did. Bottom line was that she had begun getting attached, and she'd sworn after Dustin that she would never get attached to another man again.

She tightened her coat around her, glad she'd worn boots because her toes were beginning to freeze. Seeing a wine shop ahead, she decided to stop in and make a purchase. There was nothing like a glass of wine to take the chill off. Besides, if it got too cold to venture out tomorrow, she would make good on what she'd told Frank.

She'd stay in bed and enjoy the wine and the book she'd already purchased from a bookstore at the airport.

Farrah quickly opened the door to the wine shop and bumped into the person who was walking out. "Excuse me."

"No problem."

She snatched her head up. The sound of his voice and the scent of his cologne sent shock waves through her body. She gazed up into the man's dark eyes, recognizing them immediately. "Xavier!"

Chapter 2

It was quite obvious to Farrah that Xavier was as surprised to see her as she was to see him. Had it been six
months since they'd last communicated? Six months
since she'd had the best sex of her life?

She could remember, just as if it had been yesterday, the last time he had taken her—hard. And how
the mouth she was staring at now had inflamed every
single inch between her legs while she'd held on to his
wide shoulders and cried out her pleasure.

She forced that thought from her mind, not wanting to go there, although her body was defying her and
doing so anyway. As if on cue, the tips of her nipples
felt sensitive against her blouse and a telltale ache was
making itself known between her legs.

"What are you doing in New York?" she asked, and
then felt silly for doing so when she quickly recalled that
Cody Enterprises had one of their offices here. Damn,

he looked good, and seeing him again unnerved her, had her remembering just how he looked naked. He was wearing a full-length coat, but he didn't have to remove the coat for her to know the suit he wore looked as if it had been tailored just for him, and probably had been.

And there was his masculine physique—tall, well-built with a broad chest, massive shoulders and tapered thighs. Yes, she especially remembered those thighs. He worked out regularly at the gym which accounted for him being in such great shape. He was a man who took care of himself. He certainly had taken care of her.

"I'm here working. What about you?" he asked, as a smile touched his lips.

She wished he wouldn't smile. Seeing his mouth stretched wide was doing things to her. Making her remember other times he'd smiled at her and the reasons he'd done so. Like right after she'd licked him all over before taking him into her mouth.

"I'm working as a mediator for a case I've been assigned." She glanced down at the wine bottle in the bag he was carrying in his hand, and immediately knew what it meant. He was on his way to make a booty call. Whenever he'd done so with her, he'd always showed up with a bottle of wine. She remembered that oh, so well.

"How have you been?" she heard herself asking, glancing back up at him while fighting off anger at the thought he had probably reverted back to his old ways fairly easily, when she'd found it difficult to get back to hers. She hadn't slept with another man since him. The thought of doing so had turned her body off for some reason.

"I've been doing fine," he replied. "What about you?"

"Great. Just busy."

"Same here. How long will you be in New York?" he asked.

She wondered why he wanted to know. Did he not think this city was big enough for the both of them? That thought annoyed her. In fact, if she were to be honest with herself, she would admit to being annoyed with the whole split, although it had been her idea. A part of her hadn't expected him to agree to it so easily. When he'd left that night, not once had he looked back. She knew that for certain because she had watched him from her bedroom window until he'd gotten into his car and driven off.

According to her best friend, Natalie, who was married to Xavier's good friend Donovan, Xavier hadn't asked about her once. He could have, even if for no other reason than to inquire how she was doing. For all he'd known, she could have fallen off the face of the planet.

"I'm scheduled to fly out on Friday, but if the parties involved in the case don't reach a resolution by then, I'll be returning to New York sometime next week. At least I hope to return, but that will depend on the weather. A snowstorm is supposed to be headed this way on Sunday," she said.

"So I heard, but I'll be here for another week, so if it does come, I'll be here with it."

Farrah nodded. "Well, I guess I'd better let you go. I wouldn't want you late for your date."

Too late she wished she could bite off her tongue. Had she just sounded like a jealous ex? She hoped not because it shouldn't matter one way or the other if he was on his way to see another woman.

"Who said I had a date?"

He asked the question in a deep, husky voice, which stirred something within her. She found the tone just as mesmerizing as his scent, which was all male. His signature cologne certainly knew how to make a woman hot and bothered. And then there was the way he was looking at her, with those gorgeous dark eyes of his, as if he knew he was making her panties wet.

She shrugged as she glanced back down at the wine bottle in the bag he was holding. "I just assumed you had one."

"I will if you'll have dinner with me."

She lifted a brow. "Dinner?"

"Yes. There are several restaurants around here. We can get caught up. I'd like to know how you've been doing since the last time I saw you."

He really didn't want to know, Farrah thought. He didn't need to know. It was best if they didn't go there. But, heaven help her, she would like to know what he'd been doing since the last time she saw him. "You sure you want to do that?"

"Why not? I see no reason why we shouldn't. I'd like to think, although we're no longer lovers, we're still friends."

Friends? Could two people go from being lovers to friends? After all, they'd shared a bed off and on for close to a year, longer than some people remained married.

She met his gaze, and the eyes looking deep into hers were robbing her of the ability to think straight. Instead she was overcome with memories of a satisfied woman, stretched out naked on a bed. And that woman was her. At least it had been her when they'd been together.

"So, since we're here in New York together, the least we can do is share dinner," he added in that resonant voice that could make her want to toss her panties to the wind any time and any place.

But then she knew that wasn't all he could make her toss to the wind. Her ability to resist his potent male charm topped the list. He already had the wine, so all he needed was a willing woman to share his bed…or for him to share hers.

Farrah drew in a deep breath as she thought about his invitation. Didn't she turn down Frank's invitation to dinner less than an hour ago? Why shouldn't she turn down this one as well? She really should, but for some reason, she couldn't fix her mouth to do that.

Going to dinner with him wouldn't be a big deal unless she made it one. And she wouldn't. She could handle it. And there was no reason why she couldn't handle him. He was just a man who'd been a past lover. And it was only dinner, and it didn't necessarily mean she would do anything foolish like sleep with him again. No way. No how.

"I'd love to join you for dinner, Xavier, but I'd like to go back to the hotel and change first."

"All right. What's the name of your hotel? I'll swing by and pick you up later. Let's say within the hour."

"I'm staying at the Waldorf Astoria."

She tried to ignore the flutter in her stomach when he smiled and said, "It's right up the street. Why don't I walk you there now and hang in the lobby while you change."

Farrah shook her head. "I can't ask you to do that. I'm sure you—"

"I don't mind waiting. I have some work I need to look over anyway," he said, lifting up his briefcase. "That would be easier than for me to go all the way to my home on Long Island and then come back," he added.

She knew in addition to the home he owned in Charlotte, he also had residences here in New York, Los Angeles and Florida. "You sure?" she asked.

"Positive."

"Okay, then, give me a minute to buy my wine."

"Sure."

At least he hadn't said anything about her sharing his, which meant after dinner there was still that possibility he would make one of his infamous booty calls to some woman. Why did she care? And why did the thought irk her?

She figured he would wait to the side for her to make her purchase. She hadn't counted on him following her when she walked up to the counter. And when he stood directly behind her, she could actually feel heat emanating from his body to hers. She was sure she'd felt it… or was she just imagining things?

She shook off the thought. Just the very idea that she had run into him—in New York of all places—was enough to torment her in one way and make her giddy in another. It wouldn't be so bad if she hadn't thought of him often. She had missed him, and although she would never admit such a thing to him, she would and could admit it to herself.

After making her purchase, she turned around to Xavier and smiled. "Thanks for waiting."

"No problem."

As they left the wine shop to head over to her hotel, she silently kept reminding herself that her days of lusting after Xavier had ended six months ago. Still, every time she felt his gaze on her she couldn't help but wonder if accepting his invitation to dinner had been a smart move after all.

Chapter 3

"I won't be long," Farrah said, giving Xavier a smile as she stepped on the elevator.

"Take your time. I'll be waiting down here in the lobby."

The elevator door slid shut, and it was only then that Xavier allowed himself a chance to breathe deeply. What were the odds of him running into the one woman he just couldn't seem to forget? And in New York of all places. A place that held memories for them both. At least they weren't back at the same hotel they'd been in for Donovan's wedding, he thought, settling down on one of the sofas in the lobby. Had that happened, it would have been one hell of a coincidence.

Still, just the thought of her going up to her room and taking off her clothes was doing all kinds of things to his libido…as if it wasn't out of whack already. The moment she'd bumped into him at that wine store and their bodies had touched, he had felt a frisson of heat consume him that could only be ignited by one woman. He'd known before looking into her face it was Farrah.

He settled back against the cushions of the sofa and recalled the last time they'd been in New York together, the first week in June for Donovan and Natalie's wedding. After the wedding he'd been invited to join Donovan's six cousins from Phoenix, his godbrothers as well as another good friend, Bronson Scott, for a night on the town. But the only night he'd wanted was in Farrah's bed, and as soon as the wedding reception had ended, he hadn't wasted any time going to her hotel room. And then a week later she had ended things between them.

Now they were both back in New York, and he would give anything for a repeat performance of what they'd shared the last time, although he knew doing so would be asking for trouble. And speaking of trouble, he pulled the cell phone from his pocket to call Beth to cancel his late night visit. He really didn't consider his time with Beth a "date," so he really hadn't lied to Farrah when she'd asked about it. As far as his mind and body were concerned, there was only one woman who had total control of his thoughts right now.

He leaned back and glanced around. This was a nice hotel, drenched in all kinds of history and decorated to the nines in elegance. He bet a lot of romantic trysts took place within these walls. He could see himself spending the night in one of those rooms upstairs if Farrah was so inclined. They would make love all night. He would make damn sure of it.

He reached down for his briefcase, and after placing it across his lap, he opened it up and pulled out a file. He might as well try to concentrate on something other than getting into Farrah's body and then hearing her scream after pumping her into an orgasm.

Moments later, after reading over several reports, he glanced beyond the huge glass doors and saw it had gotten dark outside already. He had a private car at his disposal twenty-four hours a day, but since the restaurant was just a block away there was no reason for them not to walk.

He closed his files, deciding to think about the eleven months he and Farrah had spent together after all, since his concentration was at an all-time low. She hadn't wanted a big deal made about their affair, so they hadn't made one. Although neither had announced it or flaunted it, he had been aware that his friends and hers suspected they were involved. But not at first.

Of course her best friend, Natalie, had known, which meant Donovan hadn't been clueless. And Cameron had known he was seeing some woman on a regular basis. His friend had never inquired as to whom, and Xavier had never openly shared the information.

His godbrothers—although they'd known he was sniffing real bad behind some woman—hadn't officially met her until Donovan's wedding. After that, they'd grilled him about why he'd gone to such pains to keep her a secret. And then he'd had to quickly spread the word at the wedding among the single men that she was taken after one of Donovan's cousins from Phoenix had tried hitting on her.

What he couldn't explain to anyone, least of all to himself, was the degree of possessiveness he felt toward Farrah. He'd felt the need to keep her all to himself and not share her or her time with anyone. Whenever he'd traveled on business, he'd found himself looking forward to returning to Charlotte to spend time with her.

They had developed a routine and rarely ventured out beyond the walls of her house, preferring to remain inside—namely in the bedroom. That was the way they'd both wanted it. For some reason they'd enjoyed being detached from the outside world whenever they were together.

Showing up at her place, usually after eight at night, with his bottle of wine, had become the norm whenever he was in town, and they would often joke about it. He knew the wine was the reason she'd figured he was about to make a booty call tonight, and she had been right.

But what Farrah didn't know was that he hadn't been sexually involved with a woman since her, and Beth would have only been a substitute for the one woman he truly wanted. The woman he was sitting in the lobby waiting for at that very moment.

As if he conjured her, the elevator door opened, and Farrah stepped out. He blinked as he stared at her. She was wearing a long coat so he couldn't see her outfit, but just seeing her made his erection spring to life. He was grateful his briefcase was still placed across his lap, and he kept it strategically placed in front of him when he stood, trying to get control of his mind and body.

"You look nice, Farrah," he said, reaching for his coat on the sofa beside him.

"Thanks. If you'd like, you can leave your briefcase and wine at the front desk until we return, or I can take it back up to my room," she said sliding her hands into a pair of black leather gloves.

He preferred her taking it back up to her room so he'd have an excuse to go up there when they got back. Or he could go back up to her room with her now to leave the items. But if he were to follow her up to her hotel room, that would be asking for trouble. Seeing Farrah made him realize just how much he'd missed her. How much he still wanted her.

"I can leave them at the front desk. That's no problem," he heard himself saying, knowing that was the best option.

"You sure?"

Yes, he was sure—if she wanted to keep her clothes on for the rest of the night. "Yes, I'm sure. Ready to go?"

She nodded. "Yes."

Together they strolled over to the front desk, and he completed a claim slip for his belongings. Moments later they were walking through the hotel's glass door to exit the building. The temperature had dropped dramatically, and the cold air seemed to blast down on them the moment they stepped onto the sidewalk.

"Wow, it's freezing out here," Farrah said, tightening her leather coat around her.

Instead of responding, on instinct Xavier wrapped his arms around her waist to bring her closer to his side. The moment he touched her, a shot of something akin to hot liquid fire exploded through his veins and he nearly groaned out loud. But he kept his arms around her to share his heat, grateful for his own wool coat. However, nothing could stop his reaction to the feel of her being plastered to his body.

That made him remember how it was being skin to skin with her while they made love, sliding in and out of her body, feeling her moist heat clench him in a way that could make him moan out her name.

She didn't look over at him. Instead she stared straight ahead. He didn't have a problem with that; in fact, he much preferred it. If their gazes were to connect now, he would be tempted to take her mouth and to tongue her right in the middle of the sidewalk.

He decided talking would be much safer, so he asked, "Warmer now?"

She nodded. "Yes and thanks. We have cold weather back in Charlotte, but this seems to be a different kind of cold. I'm even wearing an extra layer of clothing."

Telling him what she had on her body wasn't helping matters, he thought, especially when he was having visions of her not wearing anything at all. He always enjoyed seeing her naked. But then her clothing was known to be sexy as well. He recalled arriving one night when she'd worked late at the office and she'd been wearing a two-piece suit. She'd looked professional as well as sensual.

Even now he couldn't help wondering what she was wearing underneath her long coat. All he could see was a nice pair of chocolate-colored suede boots.

"Is the restaurant far?" she interrupted his thoughts to ask.

He smiled, hearing the shiver in her voice. His woman was cold. He frowned. He'd never thought of any female as "his woman" before. That had definitely been a slip of the senses.

"No, in fact it's right on the corner. Otherwise, I would have called for a car. However, I did call ahead and made reservations while you were upstairs getting dressed."

"Good. I could eat a horse about now."

And he could eat her. Pushing that thought out of his mind, he tried dwelling on what she said. One of the things he'd always liked about Farrah was that she had no problems filling her plate with the takeout he'd bring with him to her place. How she managed to stay in such fantastic shape was beyond him. She had the kind of curves that would make any man take a second look and moan, then take another look and wish.

"Here we are," he said, opening the door to the Chinese restaurant. He knew how much she enjoyed Asian foods and had immediately remembered this place. He had eaten here a few months ago while in New York on business and had thought of her then. But to be honest, he'd thought of her a lot since they'd ended things between them.

"Nice place," she said, glancing around.

He followed her gaze. Like them, several couples had braved the cold temperatures to eat out this evening.

After providing the hostess their names, they followed the woman to an area in the back where a fireplace had a blaze roaring, emitting plenty of heat. He assisted Farrah in removing her coat to hang it up on a nearby rack. When he saw her outfit, his heart began pounding in his chest and his body tightened in ways only she could make it do.

She was wearing a short tan-colored wool skirt, brown tights and a multicolor V-neck cardigan sweater. The way the sweater draped over her skirt emphasized her small waist and those nice curves he'd been thinking about earlier. His gaze traveled the full length of her physique, from the curly shoulder-length hair, past a well-endowed chest, down her thighs and to shapely legs encased in a pair of knee-high boots.

While removing her gloves, she seemed not to notice the way he was staring at her. A muscle jerked in his jaw as he watched her slide into her chair. He felt sort of off balance, and he realized the depth of his desires for this particular woman was…well, getting exposed. Trying to get a grip, he moved away slightly to remove his own coat and proceeded to place it on the rack next to Farrah's before taking the chair across from her.

"How did you find out about this place?" she asked, smiling, while picking up the menu a waitress placed in front of them.

He met her gaze, and a sensual shiver ran through him. He had been attracted to her from the first time they met, and over a year later he was still very much attracted to her. "Cameron and I came here for a business meeting in September. Like you, he enjoys Chinese food, and not surprisingly, he knew about this place."

She nodded. "And how is Mr. Cody doing these days? Natalie mentioned Vanessa's pregnant and they're expecting a baby in the spring."

Since Vanessa was Donovan's cousin, Xavier was aware Farrah had met Vanessa at a bridal shower given for Natalie last spring, but Farrah hadn't met Cameron until the wedding.

"Cameron is fine, and yes, Vanessa is due in April, and they already know it's going to be a little girl. He's excited about that. I can see her wrapping her dad around her little finger."

During one of their pillow talk sessions, he'd told her a lot about Cameron, and how their friendship began back at Harvard. He'd even shared with her how determined his friend had been to win Vanessa Steele's love.

"It seems strange," Farrah said, taking a sip of her water.

He arched a brow. "What does?"

"Being here with you. This is the first time we've ever gone out on a real date."

She was right. By mutual consent, they hadn't had that kind of relationship. From the beginning, they'd only wanted one thing from each other—a good time in bed.

"First time for everything," he said, studying his own menu and dismissing her observation as nothing more than that and not a complaint.

"I know, but it just seems strange."

He decided not to tell her what really seemed strange was them *sitting* at a table, instead of him having her naked body spread across it and eager to have her for his meal, or getting ready to thrust into her. Xavier shifted in his seat at the memories of both and felt his persistent erection press hard against his zipper.

He would be the first to admit he'd considered asking her out on a number of occasions but had changed his mind. He'd known from the get-go that she had a problem with any type of serious involvement, and although she'd never really gone into details as to what her ex-husband had done that had resulted in the breakup of her marriage, he'd gotten the lowdown anyway from Donovan, who'd gotten it from Natalie. And just thinking about what the man had done to her filled him with anger. No man should hurt a woman the way her ex had hurt her, and on that same note, no woman should intentionally use a man the way Dionne had used him.

"See anything you like?"

He glanced over at her. It was on the tip of his tongue to tell her that yes, he saw what he liked and she was sitting across from him. There was so much about her he'd enjoyed during the months they'd shared a relationship. Even now he would love to go back to her place or take her to his and make love to her like he used to do, all night long.

There was something about being inside of her that would often make him pound into her almost nonstop, never to cause pain, only intense pleasure for the both of them. And during those times when she'd locked her hot lips around his shaft, gently scraping her teeth across his most sensitive flesh, his pleasure had been almost unbearable.

He picked up his cold glass of water and took a huge gulp, appreciating how good it felt flowing down his throat to cool his heated insides. But that only lasted for a little while. All it took was a glance over at her, to see the creamy brown texture of her skin, the long lashes fanning her dark brown eyes, the high cheekbones with a dimple in each and the shape of her mouth to know even after their separation, he was still very much in lust with her.

"Xavier?"

He then realized that he hadn't answered. "Yes. I think I'm going to try the pepper steak with onions and white rice. I had it the last time I was here and thought it was good." *But not as good as you,* he thought to himself. *Nothing is as good as you.*

"That sounds like a winner and I think I'll have that, too."

Moments later, after placing their order with the waitress, Farrah settled back in her chair recalling what had filled her mind when Xavier had removed his coat. His tall, muscular frame always excited her whether he was in a suit or a pair of jeans. Business or casual wear, it didn't matter. He exuded an air of total masculinity in anything he put on his body.

And then there were his facial features—definite eye candy of the sweetest kind. His strong, sensuous jaw, full lips, sculpted nose and chocolate brown eyes. And the dimple in his left cheek, she thought, added the finishing touch.

What she'd told Xavier earlier was true. Being with him, sitting across from each other in a restaurant, felt strange mainly because they'd never actually gone out on a date before. Their relationship had been defined from the beginning. She'd told him the night they'd met at the Racetrack Café that the last thing she wanted was an involvement in a serious relationship. She'd been there and done that with her marriage and had no intentions of doing so again.

She had explained, and quite specifically, that all she wanted was an occasional bed partner, a lover who wouldn't get underfoot and become possessive and be a nuisance. She wanted a man who would know and understand the only rights he was entitled to were the ones she gave him.

Xavier had agreed to her terms without batting an eye because his wants and desires from a relationship had been identical to hers. She didn't know the whole story, since it hadn't been her business to ask him. But out of curiosity she had asked Natalie, who had heard what had happened from Donovan. It seemed some chick in college, whom he'd fallen in love with, had done him in, and as a result he'd erected a stone wall around his heart. Probably similar to the stone wall she had around her own.

From the first, they'd gotten along marvelously. Since they both traveled a lot in their professions, there had been times when they hadn't seen each other for weeks. That hadn't bothered her since she appreciated her space and didn't like overcrowding of any kind. He had, however, on occasion given her a call during those times to see how she was doing. She merely took those as him being thoughtful and nothing more. She had never returned the gesture, although he had given her his business card with all his contact information.

For some reason, she'd never felt inclined to hold a conversation with him outside of their pillow talk. It was only then, while her body had been recuperating from the effects of mind-blowing orgasms, that he had shared things about himself. He'd never said a whole lot, just enough to let her know he was an okay guy who didn't have a lot of the issues that some men did. He had learned from his past mistakes the same way she had learned from hers. Emotional involvements weren't what they were cracked up to be and were best left alone.

He had told her about his five godbrothers and the story of how their fathers had made a pact upon graduating from college. She'd met them at Donovan and Natalie's wedding and thought they were really nice guys and admired their close friendship.

"So tell me about the case you're here working on, Farrah."

The sound of his sexy voice made her glance up, and immediately she wished she hadn't. Intentional or not, he had a look in his eyes that stirred desire she hadn't felt since the last time she'd seen him. The last time she'd shared a bed with a man. Just remembering made the area between her thighs ache like crazy.

She shifted in her seat before saying, "What I have are best friends from high school who started a cosmetics company together after college." She filled him in on the details of the case, then explained, "The new husband wants her to sell her share at what the other partner sees as an outlandish amount since she hadn't been involved in the day-to-day operations of the business."

Xavier nodded. "Doesn't matter. If she's still listed

as a partner, whether she contributed to the success of the company or not, she's entitled to her share, usually a fifty-fifty split, unless it can be proven that such an oral agreement was made."

Farrah couldn't stop the smile that touched her lips. "Everything you've said might be true from a legal standpoint, but I'm a mediator and not an attorney. My concern is not who is right or wrong in this case. My job is to facilitate a process of resolution, to help them work through the issue and resolve it."

"You enjoy your work?" He realized he'd never asked her that before.

"Um, I find it rewarding. The people I deal with usually can come to an amicable decision on most issues and I like helping them get there," she said.

At that moment the waitress returned with their food, which Xavier felt was timely since it gave him a chance to ponder all the things he didn't know about her, despite having been involved in an affair with her for almost a year. He'd known the basics—like what she did for a living, her marital status and that her parents were divorced and she'd been an only child. He'd also known from observation that she was an extremely neat person, which he could appreciate since he was as well.

"What about you, Xavier? Do you enjoy your work?"

He glanced over at her. Just as he'd never inquired about her work, she'd never inquired about his until now. Once in a while after making love, he would share things with her, just for conversational purposes, nothing more. "Pretty much, although some days are more hectic than others. Cam keeps me busier than any of my other clients, but he's pretty good to work for."

"I'd think being a counselor for someone who is also a close friend would be hard."

He chuckled. "It's not hard because we try and keep it real. My job is to protect his interests and he knows I have his back and will give him the best advice. It's all about trust."

They didn't say anything for a while as they ate their food, but he couldn't help wondering what she was thinking. Was she thinking that going on a date with him wasn't so bad and perhaps they should do it again? He didn't have a problem with it if she didn't.

"This is good."

He glanced over at her and saw the smile on her face. "I'm glad you think so."

Xavier resumed eating and tried to get out of his mind how good she looked. She'd always looked good before, but today she looked even better. It might just be his mind messing with him since he hadn't seen or talked to her in a while.

"So what have you been up to lately?" she asked.

He glanced up again and watched as she put food in her mouth and began chewing. Damn, she even turned him on just by chewing her food.

He dropped his gaze to his plate to gain control of his senses before lifting them again to her. "I've been doing a lot of international traveling, mostly to the Middle East."

"The Middle East?"

"Yes, a country call Mowaiti. Natalie might have mentioned that one of her cousin in-laws, Quade Westmoreland, has a cousin who is married to a sheikh."

"She did. I met Cheyenne at one of Natalie's bridal showers and got to meet Quade at the wedding. They have adorable triplets."

He smiled. "Quade introduced Cameron to Sheikh Jamal Yasir, and they're discussing a possible joint business venture in Dubai. I had to be on hand during those talks."

Farrah flashed him another smile. "Cameron is definitely a mover and a shaker, isn't he?"

"Yes, he is."

She would probably be surprised to know that Xavier thought she was a mover and a shaker as well. She had certainly moved his libido up a monumental notch since knowing her, and she was shaking his common sense right out of his head, making him think of all kinds of naughty things he'd like to do to her. He wondered what her response would be if he were to ask to share her bed tonight. For old times' sake.

He drew in a deep breath, knowing that doing something like that wasn't a good idea. Their relationship had ended months ago, the decision mutually accepted by both, and they'd moved on. Or had they? She seemed to have handled the split well, and on his good days, he thought so had he. But now he wasn't so sure.

He was definitely due for a cold shower when he got home. But as he continued to watch her eat, getting turned on every time she took a bite of her food, he knew that a cold shower wouldn't put an end to what he was feeling or the raw, primitive need growing inside of him.

And he would be the first to admit that that wasn't good.

Xavier Kane will not break down my defenses tonight!

Those words echoed in Farrah's head while she buttoned her coat after dinner. The meal had been more than delicious, and the conversation between them enjoyable. Her misgivings regarding the breaking down of her defenses could have been put to rest if sometime during the course of dinner she could have stopped remembering certain things.

Every time Xavier had picked up his wine glass to take a sip and planted his mouth on the rim of the glass, she could recall him planting his mouth on certain parts of her body just that way. Xavier had a way with his mouth that surpassed that of any man she'd ever known. And now that they were about to leave the toasty warm haven of the restaurant, she needed the strength not to succumb to those memories and give him the idea that she wanted more than the dinner they'd just shared.

"Ready?" he asked after she worked her hand into the remaining glove.

She glanced up at him and met his gaze, saw the look that flashed in the dark depths of his eyes and had to compose herself quickly. He wanted her. She had seen that look many times before, and although it had flared to life in his gaze just for an instant, it had been there. The impact of that sudden and unexpected look had her pulling in a deep breath.

She was well aware that Xavier would follow her lead. He was a man who only took what was offered. There was no doubt in her mind if she gave him even the slightest indication that she reciprocated that desire, he would pounce on it. Pounce on her. Umm, the thought of him pouncing, especially on her, wasn't a bad one.

She smiled, fighting back the urge to ask if he was interested in going back to her hotel and making love to her all night long. "Yes, I'm ready to leave, although I'm not ready for what I know is awaiting me outside that door," she finally said. "I feel a chill in my bones already, just thinking about how cold it is. And I'm sure the temperature has dropped some more since we got here."

He chuckled. "It probably has. Would it make you feel better if I promise to keep you warm?"

Depends on how you go about accomplishing it, she quickly thought. It wasn't an impossible feat where he was concerned, especially since he had the ability to set her on fire whenever and however he chose to do so. "Yes, that will certainly make me feel better," she said.

"Then I'll make you that promise," he said engulfing her gloved hand in his. The glove was no buffer from the power of his touch, and automatically, sensations began swirling around in the pit of her stomach and sliding down to the lower part of her body. They were invading her feminine core and making her crave things she was better off not having—especially from the man standing in front of her looking like he could eat her alive if given the chance.

And it was a chance she refused to give him, no matter how much she was tempted. She knew now the same thing she'd known six months ago, the same thing she'd discovered the night of Natalie and Donovan's wedding reception when he'd given her the best sex of her life. Four orgasms later—or had it been five?—she'd finally reached the conclusion that after sharing his bed for nearly a year, he was the one man who could make her think of losing her heart again. And it was a heart she'd guarded, protected and shielded since being dumped by Dustin.

She decided now not to comment on his promise. Since she'd learned from experience never to trust a promise from a man, she merely smiled as he led her out of the restaurant. The moment they exited the door, a cold blast of winter air smacked her face, and she couldn't help but grin when she saw a private car waiting at the curb.

She glanced up at Xavier. "Your car and driver, right?"

"Yes."

"But how did he know to come here?" she asked.

"I called him while you were in the ladies room. He had to come pick me up anyway, so I figured he could very well do it here. It would save us the bother of walking back to your hotel in the cold. I promised to keep you warm."

And then before she could catch her next breath, she was swept off her feet into a pair of strong arms. "Xavier! What are you doing?"

"Carrying you to the car to make sure you don't slip."

She couldn't resist burying her nose for a quick second in his chest. Her face may have touched wool material, but her nose inhaled the scent of a man. A man who used to be the best lover she'd ever had.

His driver opened the door, and Xavier deposited her on the backseat of the car with the ease of a man who knew just how to take care of a woman, and she knew that he did.

She scooted over when he slid in beside her, but not for long. The moment the driver closed the door, he pulled her against his side.

"Thanks, Xavier. You didn't have to do that," she said removing her gloves and placing them in the pocket of her coat.

"Yes, I did," he said, reaching out and letting his fingertips stroke the side of her face. "I like taking care of you, Farrah."

His words oozed liquid heat that sizzled along her nerve endings. She tilted her head to look up at him, and he stared back, watching her with an expression that turned the sizzle into a flame and sent shudders racing through her. How had he managed to do that with just a look?

She knew the answer before the question fully blossomed in her mind. It was there in the darkness of his gaze, a red-hot hunger that had the ability to strip her control, eradicate her resistance and make her crave the kind of pleasure that only Xavier Kane could deliver.

"Xavier." She heard herself moan his name, unable to hold it back any longer. And while she continued to watch him, taking in how his lashes fanned over the intensity of his dark gaze and how his lips formed a curve like they always did right before he got ready to devour her mouth, she felt a deep need spiral between her thighs.

She was tumbling into forbidden territory and couldn't stop herself. He was there, but he wouldn't lift one finger to keep her from falling. She knew that. In fact, he was poised, ready to push her over the edge if he had to. But she couldn't let that happen, not for her peace of mind and her survival.

However, what she could do and what she would allow was a way to satisfy them both for a little while. A kiss. They could even turn their kiss into a full make-out session. It would be a quick moment of satisfaction, but it would be well worth it, she told herself. No harm, right?

How could tangling her tongue with his cause any harm as long as it didn't lead to anything? She convinced herself that it wouldn't as she eased her body closer to his on the leather seat. She felt his finger move from her face to the back of her neck and begin stroking her there. Her body automatically responded to his touch.

When he lowered his head and met her lips, she heard herself groan in a way that only he could make her do. And she knew before it was over she would do more than moan.

Chapter 4

Xavier felt as if he'd come home the moment his tongue invaded Farrah's mouth. It was as if he had been away from his favorite place and was returning to a hometown welcome of the most sensuous kind.

He relished the taste of her with a primitive longing and with an urgency he couldn't deny. Not that he was thinking about denying it. He didn't intend to leave any part of her mouth untouched, untapped or unstroked. He loved her taste. He had missed it. And he was damn near starving for it.

He was kissing her with an intensity he felt in every part of his body, including the erection that nearly burst his zipper. Only Farrah had the ability to make him want to toss caution to the wind, say the hell with it and take her as he pleased. There had been so many times he had ached to take her without wearing a condom, wanting the feel of her flesh clenching him instead of the latex separating them.

And now it wouldn't take much for him to take her right here. His driver, Jules, had had the good sense to use the privacy shield and was probably driving around Manhattan at his leisure since he was certain they would have been back to Farrah's hotel by now.

The backseat of the car was dark and intimate and had the scent of pure woman. She was kissing him back with an intensity that matched his own, and the way she was sucking deep on his tongue was bringing to life every erotic bone in his body. She tasted hot, untamed, and he knew they were both on the verge of unleashing sensations they had kept bottled up for too long.

She pulled her mouth away and drew in a deep breath, evidently needing to breathe. Personally, he needed more of her taste, but would give her a moment. He watched as she glanced out of the car window. Although they could see out of it, no one could see them inside because of the window's darkened tint. "Where are we?" she asked.

Xavier smiled, refusing to remove his hand from her neck, liking the feel of the soft skin his fingertips were stroking. He curved his hand around her neck even more, making sure she didn't try easing away from him. "Driving around the city."

She glanced back at him and smiled. "On a sight-seeing tour?"

He returned her smile. "If that's what *Jules* wants to think, but I think we know better, don't we?"

"Yes."

And then he reached out and lifted her out of the seat and into his lap and captured her mouth once again.

Farrah wrapped her arms around Xavier's neck while he continued to plunder her mouth with a hunger that had her moaning again. She wasn't sure how long the ride would last, but she planned to take advantage of every tormenting and satisfying minute.

Even through his coat she could feel the hardness of his erection poking her in the backside, but she didn't mind. In fact, she relished the feel and regretted that clothing separated their bodies.

Evidently he felt the same way when he released the back of her neck, and his fingers went to the buttons of her coat while his tongue was still inside her mouth. She wanted him so bad she was almost consumed by the mere idea of being here, in the backseat of a car in his lap while he kissed her senseless. His tongue was teasing and tormenting her into sweet oblivion, and there was nothing she could do about it. There was nothing she wanted to do about it.

She felt him spread open her coat before his fingers went about tackling the buttons of her cardigan. She knew this was lust of the most potent kind, and it was probably time for her to rein him back in, but when he eased free a button and touched a spot above her bra, she could do nothing but moan.

He knew what touching her breasts did to her, and she had a feeling he was about to get downright naughty. And when he eased open the next button, she knew she was right.

She pulled her mouth away from his. "Xavier?"

"Umm?" he asked, taking the tip of his tongue and licking the area around her chin.

"What are you doing?" She knew it was a stupid question, but she asked it anyway. It was quite obvious that he was seducing her.

"Letting you know how much I've missed you."

That was definitely the wrong answer because she

knew, although she would never admit it, that she'd missed him, too.

"I think I've gotten the message," she said in a soft tone when he released yet another button.

He tilted his head and met her gaze. "Not sure you have yet and not to the degree that I want you to know," he said in a deep, husky voice. "By the time you get back to your hotel room tonight, there will be no doubt in your mind just how much I've truly missed you, Farrah."

That meant he planned to torture her some more, probably a whole lot more, before it was all over. How far would he go? How far would she let him? Those questions slipped from her mind when her cardigan opened, exposing her lace bra to his view. She knew blue was his favorite color. Had she worn a blue bra for that reason tonight? And one with a front clasp?

He released the front hook, and her body began vibrating in pleasure when he lowered his head to take a hardened nipple into his mouth. "Xavier." She whimpered his name on a breathless sigh and grabbed ahold of his head. Not to push him away but to keep his mouth right there to feast on her.

Shudders tore into her, touching every part of her body, tearing at nerve endings with every stroke of his tongue on her nipple. She tightened her legs, feeling a throb between them so deep she wanted to scream. She was on the verge of one hell of an explosion. She knew it, and from her past history, he had to know it as well.

It didn't take penetration to make her come. Xavier's mouth anywhere on her was known to do the trick. She had a feeling this would be one of those times, because tonight he was being generous *and* naughty, a combination that could cost her. At that moment, though, noth-

ing seemed more important than having him suck her
nipples like he was doing now.

Unless he decided he wanted to…

The thought of his tongue sliding between her womanly folds had her releasing a trembling breath, and
when she felt his hand work its way under her skirt to
touch a thigh, she couldn't help but groan out loud. She
needed to get laid and bad. The hot ache between her
thighs was all but demanding it, and the mouth planted
firmly on her breast seconded that motion.

"We've reached the Waldorf Astoria, Mr. Kane."

The sound of the driver's voice was a colder blast
than the one she'd felt when they'd walked out of the
restaurant. Why now, when she'd been so close to her
body fragmenting in one sensuous explosion? Talk
about lousy timing.

She looked up and met Xavier's gaze and knew he
was thinking the same thing. She also knew what else
he was thinking…

Farrah drew in a deep breath and watched as he
palmed delicately over her breasts before he began
refastening her bra. "Circle the block one more time,
Jules," he said.

"Just one block, sir?"

"Yes."

By the time the vehicle began moving again, a semblance of Farrah's common sense had returned. But the
part still lurking out there in Blissville had her worried
because she was fully aware just what an orgasm at
the hands and mouth of Xavier Kane could mean. She
would sleep well tonight and wake up tomorrow probably craving even more.

She knew she had to regain control and not succumb
to a weakness of the body nor a deep addiction for him.

When he had buttoned her sweater and pulled the lapels of her coat together, he met her gaze. And then while she was still nestled snugly in his lap, he lowered his head and kissed her again.

This kiss had all the intensity of the last, probably more so, and she could only kiss him back while shudders shook her from head to toe. When he finally released her mouth moments later, it was on the tip of that same tongue he'd just ravished to ask him up to her room for a nightcap, although they would both know the true intent of the invitation.

But a part of her kept from doing so. It was the part that couldn't forget or let go of the pain she'd felt the day Dustin had asked for a divorce to marry another woman.

"I got my bottle of wine and you have yours," Xavier said softly close to her moist lips. "How about if we…"

"Drink them separately," she finished for him.

He leaned back, lifted a brow and was probably as surprised as she that she wasn't inviting him up to her room. She would probably hate herself later, and the area between her legs would probably protest something awful, but that area of her chest where her heart was planted would eventually thank her for sparing it from further damage. It had finally gotten repaired, and she refused to let it get broken again.

"You sure you want that, Farrah?"

She decided to answer him the only way she knew how. Honestly. "No, that's not what I want, but I know that's what I need to happen, Xavier. For my sake, you're going to have to trust me on this."

He opened his mouth to say something, and then as if he thought better of it, he clamped his mouth shut. He brought her hand to his face and gently rubbed against it. "Leaving you alone tonight isn't going to be easy, Farrah," he said in a low, sexy voice.

"And having you leave me alone won't be easy, Xavier. But for my peace of mind, I don't have a choice. Please say you understand, or please try to."

He met her gaze and held it for a long moment. And then a slow smile of understanding tugged at his sensuous lips. "I'll try, but only if you agree to see me again while you're here."

"What's the point?" she couldn't help but ask.

He cupped her chin in his hand. "To prove I'm not a bad guy."

She shook her head. "I never thought you were a bad guy, Xavier. If I had thought that, you would not have shared my bed. In fact, I think you're too good to be true and that's what scares me."

"Too good to be true?"

"Yes, both physically and emotionally. I could end up getting hurt. You wouldn't hurt me intentionally, but I could get hurt just the same and I can't let that happen."

She knew she had said too much, had let her feelings become raw and exposed, but he needed to understand and accept what she was saying. He was becoming the one weakness she had to do without.

When Jules opened the car door for them, he slid out, and before her leg could touch the sidewalk, he had whisked her into his arms again. "Xavier!"

Jules raced ahead to open the glass door to the hotel, and Xavier didn't place her back on her feet until they stood in the hotel's lobby.

"I need to get my items from the front desk," he said. "But first I'll walk you to the elevator."

He tucked her hand in his and they walked toward

the elevator. "I'll call you tomorrow, Farrah. I'd like to take you to a Broadway play while you're here."

"Xavier, I—"

He placed a finger to her lips. "At least think about it. It will be just two friends going out. No big deal."

She drew in a deep breath. *No big deal? Yeah, right.* She'd assumed going to dinner with him tonight would not be a big deal either, but it turned out to be one anyway. "I'll see if I'm available."

"All right."

He leaned down and brushed a kiss across her lips when the elevator door opened. She stepped inside and glanced over her shoulder at him. "Good night, Xavier."

"Good night, Farrah."

And as the elevator carried her from the lobby up to her room, she couldn't help wondering how she was going to turn him down when he called her tomorrow.

Chapter 5

"Good morning, Mr. Kane."

"Good morning, Vicki. Hold my calls for a while. By the way, you look nice this morning."

Xavier entered his office thinking his secretary's attire, a beige pantsuit, looked more appropriate for the office than those sexy outfits she'd been wearing. He was glad she'd taken his advice.

He eased out of his jacket and then sat down in the chair behind his desk. He was ready to roll his sleeves up and get some work done. He hadn't been sure he would ever get to sleep last night, but when he had finally done so, he had basically slept like a baby. But that hadn't kept visions of a hot and ready Farrah out of his mind. At least that's how she used to be. This overly cautious Farrah would take some getting used to.

His cell phone rang and he leaned forward to pull it off his belt. "Yes?"

"When are you returning to Charlotte, X?"

He smiled at the sound of Uriel Lassiter's voice. Since he and his five godbrothers had been kids, they'd shortened each other's names to just the first letter. "Why you want to know? You miss me, U?"

"No. It's Ellie."

Xavier chuckled. "Your wife misses me?"

"No, and stop being a smart ass. Ellie's having a New Year's Eve party and wants to make sure you're coming, especially since no one knows your schedule for the holidays."

He leaned back in his chair. "I still haven't decided where I'll be for Christmas but I'm game for New Year's. And as far as when I'll be returning to Charlotte, it will depend on how soon we can close the deal here. I hope to be back in Charlotte in a week."

"And then you're taking the rest of the month off, right?"

"That's right."

"Good. Z is coming home."

Xavier sat up straight in his chair, surprised. "He is?"

"Yes. I talked to him last night." Uriel chuckled. "He couldn't tell Ellie no, so he'll be here for Christmas and New Year's."

Xavier nodded. Of his five godbrothers, Zion was the youngest, at twenty-eight, and the most well-known because of the jewelry he designed. And he was the one who at the moment was going through some major issues. Before she died four years ago, his mother had revealed to him that she wasn't sure that the man Zion thought was his father really was since she'd taken a lover during the earlier part of her marriage.

It was Zion's secret, one he'd only shared with his godbrothers. Xavier figured it would be an easy enough thing to prove or disprove, but Zion didn't want to risk his father ever finding out that the woman he'd loved so much had once been unfaithful to him. So instead of hanging around and letting something slip, Zion had escaped to Rome and built a home and an empire there. Xavier couldn't help wondering if Z had finally figured you can't run away from your problems and was now thinking about moving back to the States.

Moments later, Xavier was hanging up the phone and pulling a file off the huge stack of papers on his desk. His thoughts, however, shifted to Farrah, and he couldn't help but remember what she'd said about not wanting to get hurt again. He knew how she felt. Wasn't that the same reason he'd avoided serious involvement with women?

What he needed to do was prove they could enjoy themselves without getting all that serious. They had done so for close to a year, so there was no reason they couldn't continue. After such a long separation, he was certain if they rekindled their affair, they would be mindful of the mistakes they had begun making the last time by getting too attached.

The thought of them falling in love was scary stuff. He knew that better than anyone. But he was just as certain it wouldn't happen. There wasn't a woman alive he would give his heart to. He had no intention of getting great sex confused with any emotions of the heart. Things didn't work that way for him, and he was sure things wouldn't work that way for her either.

Her ex had damaged her emotionally on the institution of marriage, so what was the problem? Why couldn't two people who only wanted to enjoy off-the-chain sex do so without worrying about their hearts getting in the way?

It would be up to him to convince her that they could resume their no-strings-attached affair with no entanglements, and he intended to do just that.

"Mrs. Byers and Ms. Shaw, we're here to bring about an acceptable resolution to the case pending before Judge Lewis Braille. Hopefully, we'll reach an agreeable resolution so that we can avoid a costly court battle and—"

"Not unless that woman gives my wife her fair share of what is due to her."

Farrah frowned at Mr. Byers's outburst. She'd known the moment he'd walked into the room with his wife that he was bad news. For some reason, he thought he was calling the shots. He might very well do so in his marriage, but she had no intention of letting him take control of these proceedings.

"Mr. Byers, I need you to refrain from speaking out of turn. Doing so will not get us anywhere."

"Please calm down, Rudolph," Lori Byers whispered to her husband in a calm voice. "Please let Ms. Langley do her job so we won't have to go to court."

Other than a roll of her eyes, Kerrie Shaw didn't say anything, although it was evident she was angry at what Rudolph Byers had said.

When the parties had entered the room, Farrah's keen sense of observation had picked up on several points. Even with all this legal mess going on, it was plain to see that the two women had shared a very close friendship at one time, and if given the chance, without any outside interference, that friendship could be restored.

It was also quite obvious they still cared for each other. That was probably the reason Kerrie Shaw had refrained from speaking her mind a few moments ago when Mr. Byers had spoken out of line. Farrah figured she'd kept her mouth closed to spare Lori Byers's feelings. That meant during the time they'd been friends, Kerrie had had the role of protector, and Lori had been the one more vulnerable and easily swayed and misled.

Farrah glanced over at Rudolph and quickly decided that was exactly what was taking place now. Lori allowed the man she had fallen in love with to come between her and her friend. Their close relationship had started in high school and continued in college and through Lori's first marriage and birth of her two little girls. Lori had even named Kerrie as godmother for her two girls.

Both women were now thirty-four. Kerrie was engaged to be married and Lori's first husband had been killed in a car accident a few years ago. She had met Rudolph on the internet, which didn't say a whole lot to some, but definitely spoke volumes to Farrah. Not that all pickups from cyberspace were bad, but the one Farrah had landed a couple of years ago, Alvin Cornell, had made her want to toss him right back. He'd been such a jerk. She could only wonder if Alvin had an older brother by the name of Rudolph.

How two women who had been such good friends could let a man come between them was beyond Farrah. She couldn't imagine any man or woman coming in and destroying her and Natalie's friendship, which had been in existence since high school as well. After her breakup with Dustin, it had been Natalie who'd been there for her, to help her get through the worst time in her life. Natalie had known she would wallow in self-pity her first Christmas as a divorced woman and had flown into Charlotte from New Jersey to spend time with her so she wouldn't be alone, and to make her see there was life after divorce.

"Yes, let's continue," Farrah said in an authoritative voice, more so for Rudolph Byers's benefit than for the two women. "As I was saying, my goal is to resolve the complaint and conflict informally. I'm impartial. I don't know either of you, and have no ties, previous or present, to your company."

Farrah paused and then looked back and forth at the women. "My concern is not who is right. It doesn't matter to me. I'm here to work you through this, and in doing that you need to talk to me about why you think you were wronged and how we can resolve things and move forward. Are there any questions?"

"No," both women said simultaneously.

Farrah noted Rudolph had clenched down on his lips to keep from answering, but the glare he gave her let her know he wanted to say something. Probably something he had no business saying.

"I hope we can work things out," Lori said softly. "I don't want anger between me and Kerrie."

"Who cares if there's anger between the two of you?" Rudolph butted in to say, evidently not able to keep quiet any longer. "I won't let her sell that company without giving you every penny you deserve."

Farrah drew in a deep breath and shifted her gaze to Kerrie. She could tell it was taking all Kerrie's control to not lash out against Rudolph, and she knew why Kerrie was remaining silent. It was her way of protecting Lori's feelings. These two women still cared for each other, and if Rudolph dropped off the face of the earth, Farrah had a feeling there would be no need for her services here today.

But Rudolph was alive and well and sitting across

from her being a total jerk. Was greed the only factor motivating him? Farrah thought. Little did he know Farrah would be successful with this case because, whether they realized it or not, the two women's friendship had always been solid as a rock. Now it was time for Farrah to remind them of that.

"So tell me, Ms. Byers. When did your friendship with Ms. Shaw begin?" Though the woman seemed surprised, Farrah knew why she'd asked the question. She intended to make them recall why they'd become friends in the first place, in hopes they'd realize their relationship was too important to give up.

Lori glanced over at Kerrie and smiled as if remembering. "It was my first year of high school. I was thirteen and the new kid in town since my parents had moved to the city over the summer. Kerrie lived on my block and invited me to walk home with her. We became best friends immediately, and—"

"Why are we rehashing all of that stuff?" Rudolph said in a snarl. "We need to be discussing the money and—"

"Rudolph, if you're not happy with the way things are going here, you can leave!" Lori spoke up and said to her husband. It was apparent the man was surprised by his wife's sharp statement, and like a spoiled child, he pushed his chair back and stormed from the room, slamming the door behind him.

Farrah waited a beat to see if Lori would run after him. Instead, the woman seemed to remain calm, and then after a few moments she continued the story of how she and Kerrie had met.

Farrah fought to hide her smile. Now she felt they would finally get somewhere.

* * *

Xavier glanced at his watch. It was close to three in the afternoon, and he hadn't received a response yet from the text message he'd sent to Farrah earlier inviting her to a Broadway play tonight. He had decided against calling her since he hadn't known the hours she would be tied up with the case she was mediating.

When his cell phone rang, he quickly picked it up and smiled when he saw the caller was Farrah. "Yes?"

"Xavier, it's Farrah. Sorry I didn't have time to text you back earlier, but I was in mediation sessions all day."

"How did it go?"

"Rather well, actually. At least it did once the husband left. He was determined to cause problems. I spent most of the day reminding the two women why they became friends in the first place. I think another session will resolve things. That is if the wife doesn't go home and let her husband's manipulations undo all we've achieved today. He seems to have a lot of influence on her."

Xavier nodded. "Are you still at work?"

"No, I just got back to the hotel and am about to take a long, leisurely bubble bath. I'm running the water as hot as I can stand it to unfreeze my bones. It's still extremely cold outside."

Xavier paused a moment and then asked, "Have you given any thought to joining me tonight for a Broadway play? The one I thought you'd enjoy is *Hair*. And I promise to keep you warm again if you do venture out."

That's what I'm afraid of, Farrah thought, sitting on the edge of her bed. The only reason she hadn't swooned each and every time she'd thought of the kiss they'd shared in the car last night was because it had taken all of her time and energy getting Kerrie and Lori to stroll back down memory lane.

"Umm, I've always wanted to see *Hair*," she said softly.

"Here's your chance."

Yes, here was her chance. Should she take it or should she let the opportunity drift in the wind because she didn't trust herself around one particular man? Would he try kissing her again? She drew in a deep breath knowing he would and knowing she would be disappointed if he didn't.

She had gone to bed last night with that hot and sizzling kiss on her mind and too many warm, touchy-feely emotions stirring in her heart. And she knew why. During the year she and Xavier had been bed partners, he'd had a way of making her feel special and had taken whatever time was needed to bring her as much pleasure as any one woman could possibly handle. He had been more attentive to her in that one year than Dustin had been during the four years of their marriage. She had missed Xavier's attentiveness, his presence, his love-making and every single thing about him.

Now he was back, not in her life on a routine basis but just for the period of time she would be here in New York. When they returned to Charlotte, things would go back to normal, with him having his life and her having hers. Their paths would rarely cross, and on those occasions when they might run into each other, she was satisfied they'd know they could never become lovers again.

Sharing a kiss wasn't so bad, and the way he'd given attention to her breasts wasn't a sin and a shame either. But she couldn't share a bed with him. That would be her ultimate downfall. If he ever went inside her body again she would be tempted to never, ever let him out. She could possibly get hooked back on what it had taken six months to wean herself from.

Could she handle his presence, his closeness and his heat without temptation pushing her on her back with him on top of her? She nibbled on her bottom lip while thinking, yes, she would handle it, even if it almost killed her. All she would have to do was close her eyes and see Dustin's face to remember why such a thing was necessary.

"Farrah?"

She drew in a deep breath. "Yes, I'd love to go see *Hair* with you. What time does the show begin?"

"Eight. I'll be there to pick you up around seven if that's okay with you."

"That's fine. I'll be waiting for you in the lobby."

She hung up the phone knowing she needed to build up her resolve that no matter what, she would not be sharing a bed with Xavier while she was in New York.

Chapter 6

"Circle around the block a few times, Jules. I should be back out in a few minutes."

"Yes, Mr. Kane."

Xavier tightened the coat around him as he made his way toward the hotel's entrance. He was early, intentionally so, and that meant Farrah would not be in the lobby waiting on him, ready to go. He would let her know he'd arrived and ask if he could come up to her hotel room.

He was a man who usually didn't like playing games; however, under these circumstances, he wasn't averse to having a game plan. He couldn't help but smile when he thought of all the things Cameron had done to win Vanessa over. For Xavier, it wasn't that kind of party, definitely not one that serious. All he wanted was his bed partner back, not a woman to make his wife. So he wouldn't go to the extremes as Cam had done.

However, he knew the key to winning a woman over

was to discover her weakness and use it against her. He
had no problem doing that if it meant getting his libido
back on track. He needed to use the same tactic Farrah had mentioned she'd used on the two women with
whom she was holding mediation sessions. He would
force Farrah to remember what they once had and why
it was way too good to give up.

He glanced around the lobby before pulling out his
cell phone. He swiped his finger across Farrah's name
that was already programmed in his iPhone. She picked
up immediately. "Yes?"

"I arrived a little early. If you're not ready I can come
up and wait."

"No need. I'm ready."

He was surprised. "You are?"

"Yes," she said, and he could swear he heard a smile
in her voice. "For some reason I figured you might be
early."

He lifted a brow. "Did you?"

"Yes."

He didn't like the sound of that. Was she on to him
and his game plan? Hell, he hoped not. "Well, I'm here."

"And I'll be right down, Xavier."

She clicked off the phone, and Xavier was about to
return the phone to his pocket when it rang. He hoped it
was Farrah saying she'd changed her mind, and he could
come up to her room anyway. Instead, it was York.

"Yes, Y?"

"What are you doing tonight? How about coming
over for a beer and to shoot some pool?"

York, a former officer for the NYPD who now owned
his own security firm in Queens, loved to play pool and
was pretty damn good at it. There was a time he used to
participate in tournaments around the country.

"Sorry, I have a date."

He could hear York's chuckle. "Hell, you don't go out on dates, X. All you do is make booty calls. That's been your M.O. for years."

Xavier frowned. Had it? Come to think of it, yes, it had been. After Dionne, he'd made sure no other woman got close to his heart, although they'd been more than welcome to share a bed with him, preferably theirs. What he would do was select a woman, get to know her well enough to suit him and then begin showing up at her place with a bottle of wine determined to get just one thing. He'd operated that way with every woman he'd slept with.

Including Farrah.

Why did the thought of grouping Farrah with all his other bed partners leave a bad taste in his mouth? Probably for the same reason he'd stayed with her longer than the others. For him, eleven months was a long time to sleep with the same woman. Hell, normally something like that could get downright boring. But there hadn't been a damn boring thing about Farrah. She had made her bed one of the most exciting places to be. But, like the others, he'd never invited her over to his place to share his bed. Umm, he would have to remedy that one day.

"So, who is she, X?"

He couldn't very well say she wasn't someone York knew since Xavier had introduced Farrah to all five of his godbrothers at Donovan and Natalie's wedding in June. But what he could do was be evasive as hell, which wouldn't be the first time. "Why do you want to know? And aren't you supposed to be checking out Ellie's friend Darcy?"

He smiled as he could actually hear York growling

through the cell phone. "Hell, don't mess with me like that, X. The woman and I don't get along. I'm convinced she hates my guts."

Xavier laughed. Bad blood had developed between the two when, during Darcy's first week of moving to New York, she'd encountered a burglar who'd broken into her home while she slept. By the time the police had arrived, Darcy Owens had already administered her own brand of punishment to the unsuspecting criminal, who hadn't known she had a black belt in karate.

Ellie had gotten York out of bed to go across town to check on her friend. When he'd gotten there and discovered what had happened, he'd raked Darcy over the coals for placing her life in danger instead of letting the NYPD handle it. Darcy evidently hadn't appreciated York's attitude, and the two hadn't been exactly bosom buddies since. Frankly, Xavier had a feeling York liked Darcy more than he was letting on.

"You still haven't told me who's your date, X."

At that moment the bell over the elevator sounded, the door opened and Farrah waked out. Xavier smiled. *Saved by the bell.* "And I won't. Goodbye, Y."

He quickly disconnected the call and stuffed the phone in his coat pocket. His smile widened when Farrah came to a stop in front of him. She was wearing her full-length coat again, but he couldn't wait to see the outfit she had on underneath it. "Ready?"

She smiled up at him. "Yes, I'm ready."

Xavier doubted very seriously that Farrah Langley was ready for what he had in store for her tonight.

"The play was wonderful, Xavier. Thanks for taking me," Farrah said, glancing across the length of the rear car seat. She really hadn't been surprised when he'd swept her off her feet again to put her in the car at the hotel, and again when they'd arrived and left the theater. But she was surprised he had kept distance between them in the car now.

Although he'd ordered the privacy shield drawn and the lights dimmed, things were a lot different tonight than they had been last night when she'd practically sat in his lap during the car ride back to the hotel, and he'd kissed her so fervently her panties got wet.

"I thought so, too," he agreed. "And I'm glad you enjoyed it."

She glanced out the window and saw they were headed in the opposite direction from her hotel. "Where are we going?"

"I thought I'd take you for a ride across the river on a ferry boat."

"A ferry boat? In this weather?"

He chuckled. "It's a private barge and we won't have to get out of the car. I thought you'd like seeing the Statue of Liberty up close."

"You were able to arrange something like that tonight? At this hour?"

"Yes, as much as security would allow, which is understandable."

She nodded, knowing it was. She looked out the window and saw they were at the New York harbor. Several huge cruise ships were docked, and glass lanterns that were hanging from light fixtures brightened up the entire area.

"Everything is ready, Mr. Kane. Should we proceed?" the driver asked over the intercom.

"Yes, Jules, and you can darken the lights back here."

On cue, the lights in the panel of both doors went out, drenching the rear of the car in total blackness. The only illumination came from the light reflecting off the tall buildings of the Manhattan skyline.

Farrah knew the exact moment the car drove onto the huge barge, and moments later she heard the sound of the car door opening and closing. She glanced questioningly over at Xavier.

"Jules is leaving," he said. "He's joining the captain of the barge in the wheelhouse. They're old friends."

"Oh." She knew that meant that she and Xavier would be in the car alone.

Moments later she could actually feel the swish and sway of the water beneath them when the barge began moving. She had ridden a ferry once before while visiting a friend in Florida. It had been a passenger ferry, and it had been during daylight hours. However, this ferry ride provided a beautiful view of New York City at night.

She glanced over at Xavier. He was still sitting across from her and was looking at her. Although the lights reflected off his features, she couldn't see his entire face. However, knowing his eyes were on her was enough to send a luscious shiver up her spine.

Why did he have to be so mind-bogglingly handsome? Why did being here with him and sharing this space with him remind her of other times she'd shared more than space with him? She couldn't help but recall when she had shared her body, given it to him whenever and however he'd wanted it.

She decided the best thing to do was strike up a conversation to ease the heated tension flowing between them, although she doubted it would do a single thing to douse the hot-blooded desire flowing through her veins.

"We won't be running into the passenger ferry that runs twenty-four hours a day, will we?" she asked.

"No, we're taking a different route so we're safe."

She wondered just how safe she was alone with him in the darkened backseat of a car while rolling down the Hudson. There was the scent of a predatory male circulating in the air, but she was determined to stay in her corner. If anyone made the first move it would be him...although he didn't seem in a rush to do so.

Silence hovered between them for a few moments, and then he asked, "Would you like some wine, Farrah?"

She lifted a brow. "You have wine in here?"

"Yes."

He proceeded to press a button, and a compartment opened that transformed into a minibar.

"Wow, I'm impressed," she said.

He chuckled. "Are you?"

"Yes."

He uncorked the wine bottle and poured two glasses. He then leaned over and handed one to her. "Umm, you smell good," he said in a deep, throaty voice.

They were passing beneath a brightly lit building that illuminated his features. Heated lust was definitely shining in the dark depths of his eyes.

"Thanks. I think."

He smiled. "You aren't sure?"

She took a sip of her wine, liking how it tasted on her tongue. She looked at her wine in the glass and then at him. "Yes, I'm sure. I think you smell good, too. I guess our noses are in rare form tonight."

"That's not the only thing. Slide over here for a moment."

Farrah met his gaze and decided she was either a glutton for punishment or eager for pleasure. Ignoring the voice inside her head advising her to stay put, she slid over the warm leather seat toward him. What she'd told him earlier was the truth. He smelled good. Good enough to lick all over.

When she was basically plastered to his side, he stretched his arm across the back of the seat. "Now," he said when she was snuggled close to him, "this is where you belong."

"Is it?"

"Yes."

She would have thought such a statement—a bold proclamation made by him or any man about where she belonged—was out of order and deserved a blistering retort, but she didn't have time to do so when he eased the glass from her hand and placed it in the holder next to his seat.

Then he turned toward her. "You have on too many clothes," he whispered in a deep, husky voice.

"Mainly to stay warm. I get cold easily," was her response.

"I promised to keep you warm, didn't I?"

"Yes, but that was last night."

He began unbuttoning her coat. "That promise stands whenever we're together."

Farrah drew in a deep breath as she studied his face. His gaze was focused on every button he was opening as if what he was doing was a very important task. She knew she should probably tell him that when it came to promises from men, she found they didn't hold water, so he didn't have to waste his time making one that he expected her to believe. But for some reason she couldn't say it. Not when he had kept her warm last night. And not when he was taking his time now, handling her like she was a piece of fine china. He was opening each button slowly, with painstaking deliberateness, as if he was about to expose something beneath her coat other than the short blue dress she was wearing.

The dress might be short, true enough, but her black leather boots were long, stopping at her knees. Did he intend to remove them as well? Would she let him? Before she could think further on that question, he whispered, "Now scoot up a bit so I can work your arms out of the sleeves."

Like a dutiful child, she did what she was told. When she leaned forward, she placed her hand on his thigh and almost snatched it back when she felt his hard erection. Her eyes flew to his face and there was nothing apologetic about the look staring back at her. Instead it was a look that almost made her regret they were no longer bed partners.

And she didn't want to have any regrets. Although she'd found it extremely difficult to forget him and get beyond everything they'd shared, she was convinced she had done the right thing when she'd made up in her mind not to fall back in bed with him.

Fate, it seemed, was working against her now. It was as if some fragment of her brain was trying to convince her that getting back with him would be a fantasy come true and that her sex-deprived body would thank her for the chance to get laid again. But a part of her, the part that had endured pain of the worst kind at the hands of a man she'd once loved, was holding back, keeping that guardrail around her heart firmly in place. She doubted that even Xavier could knock it down.

She knew she should remove her hand from his thigh, but the feel of his erection beneath her palm was doing something to her, reminding her how it had been a vital part of her life at one time. And how it had given her so much pleasure.

She felt his erection begin to throb beneath her fingertips, a slow, steady pulsating thump that was causing her hand to tremble while causing certain parts of her body to vibrate. She was so in tune to this part of him and remembered well how once it was inside of her, it could stroke her into a frenzy of the sweetest kind. She felt the inner muscles of her feminine core clench just thinking about it.

Farrah glanced up and met his gaze when he pushed the coat off her shoulders. There was a look in his eyes that sent a delicious warmth through her body. She couldn't help wondering how she had endured a half year without this. Without him.

When her coat was off, he tossed it to the other side of the backseat and his gaze slid down the length of her outfit, which wasn't much. What little it was seemed to have his attention.

"I like blue," he said, running his fingers along the hem of her dress.

"Do you?"

"Yes. It's my favorite color. And these boots look good on you."

She smiled. "Thanks."

"So tell me," he said, easing closer to her after removing his own coat and lowering his head to whisper huskily in her ear. "What does a man like me have to do to get you out of a dress like this?"

She grinned and looked at him. "Umm, I don't know, Mr. Kane. You've always seemed to be a very innovative kind of guy. What do you have in mind?"

She couldn't help but take note that her hand was still on his thigh, still in contact with his throbbing erection. For some reason she couldn't let go just yet.

"What I have in mind is stripping you out of every

stitch of clothing you have on. Here and now. What do you think about that?"

She couldn't help but chuckle. "Umm, not sure that's a good idea."

"But you would consider it?"

She smiled upon seeing the challenging glean in his eyes. "Let's just say I don't have a problem with you trying to convince me that I should consider it."

He didn't say anything for a minute, as if giving her words some thought. "I hope you know I can be very convincing when I want to be."

"I'm very much aware of that."

She knew Xavier well enough to understand her words were like a carrot dangling in his face. A carrot he intended to devour. This was the most fun she'd had lately. The summer months had been a complete bore to her and autumn hadn't been much better. When Natalie and Donovan had returned from their honeymoon, the amorous newlyweds hadn't socialized a lot, preferring to stay inside behind closed doors, probably burning the sheets. So with no lover to sleep with, no best friend to talk to, Farrah had had a lot of free time on her hands and had wondered if she'd done the right thing in breaking things off with Xavier.

But then, all it had taken was running into Dustin, his wife and daughter at the mall one Sunday evening in mid-October to recall why it had been the only thing she could do in order to protect herself and not get hurt by any man again.

"So what do you think about the view?"

She looked past Xavier to glance out the window. It was hard to believe they were in a car, riding down the Hudson on a barge. If he had deliberately set out to impress her, he had achieved that goal. "The view is beautiful. You definitely know how to wow a girl. I'm impressed."

"Are you?"

"Yes."

"Enough to let me take this dress off you?"

She shook her head smiling. "You won't give up, will you?"

"Not until I have you naked."

There was a determination in his tone that made shivers run up and down her spine. Heat began spreading through her stomach, and she felt a tingling sensation take life between her legs. She wondered if he had any idea just what was happening to her, how much she was fighting the temptation of giving him everything he was asking for. And then some.

She looked past him out the window again. Only Xavier would go to this trouble to impress a woman. And it was working.

Farrah glanced back at him, and the look he was giving her sent a burst of desire exploding through her. She found herself leaning toward him and his masculine mouth that was so sexy it should be declared illegal.

"And once you have me naked, what's next?"

The erection beneath her hand seemed to get larger. "Then I plan to taste you all over."

With his words, blatant and hot, her thighs seem to automatically spread apart, and she couldn't help but remember how it felt to have his tongue between them, licking her with hungry strokes to sweet oblivion, fueling not one orgasm but several.

"So what do you think of that, Farrah?"

She swallowed, not wanting to think at all. Her body was pushing her to feel instead. Making her crave things she was better off not having, but making those damn hot memories invade her mind anyway. They were just too delicious to ignore.

She met his gaze, felt the heat emanating from the dark depths. And it was heat that was generating a slow yet intense sizzle within her. "Why are you doing this to me, Xavier?"

Without responding, his gaze seemed to say it all. The heat from his eyes nearly burned off her remaining clothes. Lust flowed up her spine as a fierce degree of need filled her all over. He continued to look at her, saying nothing, yet saying everything.

"I think you know the answer to that, Farrah," he finally said in a deep, throaty voice. "But in case there's a possibility that you don't, the reason is simple. I never got over you. Our split was your idea, not mine."

She lifted a brow. "But you didn't disagree."

"Because I knew it was what you wanted."

"And now?"

"And now I plan to convince you that decision was a mistake."

She saw the determination in his gaze. "What if I said you can't do that?"

A smile touched his lips. "Then I would say I intend to die trying. I want you back, Farrah."

Farrah knew he was dead serious. She forced herself to breathe in before asking, "And you think wanting me back is simple?"

A smile touched the corners of his lips. "Yes, wanting you back is simple, but *getting* you back will be the hard part." He paused and then said, "And speaking of hard…"

She held his gaze as the throb beneath her hand increased, and she could feel his erection grow and harden even more. "Yes, what about it?" she asked, not even trying to ignore the burning sensation in the pit of her stomach.

He placed his hand over hers. "For the past six months, I've been working hard, Farrah, harder than I wanted to. But I had to do it as a way to try to forget you. And I failed at doing that."

She nibbled on her bottom lip, surprised that Xavier would admit something like that. It would have been just as easy, less messy and a whole lot simpler for her to think he had moved on without any passing thoughts of her and what they'd shared. But to know he had thought of her, had worked doubly hard to forget her, yet failed, made something inside her swell to gigantic proportions, and that wasn't good.

"And can you honestly say you didn't think of me, Farrah?" he then asked.

That question was a no-brainer. Of course she had thought about him. Constantly. Every day. In the middle of the night. When she woke up in the morning. And she'd definitely thought of him during those times her body went through a physical meltdown when it needed the kind of toss between the sheets only he could give her.

She could admit such a thing now, while sitting here with him alone, in the privacy of a car where they had a spacious backseat. She had no qualms saying it because regardless of all of that, she believed she had done the right thing in ending their affair.

And she would be doing the right thing in not letting him talk her into starting things back up again between them.

"Yes, I thought about you, Xavier, but I *had* to end things between us for all the right reasons," she said quietly.

"And what are these right reasons?"

Now that would be a little harder to explain. How could she eloquently break it down so he would understand that she had to end things to keep her sanity? That with him, for the first time since breaking up with Dustin, she had begun to feel things, want things and need things that she knew could only cause her heartbreak.

How could she explain to him that every time he showed up at her place, looked at her, touched her, tasted her and made love to her until she screamed her throat raw, her heart swelled? That was the part she wouldn't try explaining since there were some things about a woman's emotions that a man didn't need to know or understand.

She had gotten a lot smarter since her Dustin days, but because of Xavier, the part of her heart that had hardened had begun to soften each time she saw him, each time he held her in his arms and kissed her with that sinful tongue of his.

"Tell me, Farrah."

Gathering her control, she removed her hand from his thigh and shifted in her seat, placing her hand into her own lap. For this she needed some semblance of detachment and distance…as much as she could get. But she was well aware that no matter how much space she put between them, she would still be able to feel his heat, the same heat that could succeed in melting the ice encasing her heart. But he needed to hear what she had to say.

"You know my history with Dustin."

He nodded. "Yes."

She drew in a deep breath. Discussing her ex-husband had never been on the agenda. But one night when

Xavier had come over she'd been caught in one of her melancholy moods. She had run into Dustin earlier that day in a department store, and he'd tried of all things to flirt with her. The bastard who'd left her for another woman had actually tried coming on to her, tried to entice her to leave the department store and have an evening of sex with him in a hotel across the street. He'd said his wife would never find out and that they would be doing it for old times' sake.

Dustin had claimed his problem with her had never been in the bedroom, but said her constant travels for her job were to blame for the loneliness that had forced him to seek out other women. He had actually tried to make her feel responsible for his adulterous behavior.

Any other woman probably would have fallen for his pitiful spiel, but she had stopped being Dustin's fool the day he'd asked her for a divorce. She doubted she would ever forgive him for the hurt and humiliation that he'd caused her.

"I don't ever want to go through anything like that again," she heard herself saying.

Xavier's mouth drew in a tight line. "I can respect that, but what does that have to do with me?"

"A good question," she murmured softly to herself. He probably didn't see the connection because, for him, there truly wasn't one. Nothing about his purpose in seeking her out then and now had changed. He was footloose and fancy-free and intended to stay that way. He shied away from serious relationships, preferring to make his booty calls whenever, wherever and to whomever he desired with no strings attached. He was a man, and he could go through that type of program without any emotional attachments. She'd tried the same but found that she just couldn't do it. Especially with Xavier.

"What it has to do with you, Xavier, is that I felt the time had come for me to take a step back from our little affair. Eleven months was way too long for me. We were getting too complacent."

She wanted to express herself in a way where she didn't come off sounding like a needy woman. God knows she didn't want that. Since her divorce she had tried not to depend on anyone—especially a man—for her happiness. But with Xavier she had found herself slipping.

When he didn't say anything, she continued. "That first night you came over we agreed to have a no-strings-attached affair, and I felt we had run our course."

He nodded. "Have there been any men since me, Farrah?"

His question surprised her. It would be so easy to say it wasn't any of his business and let him assume there had been others. After all, he'd probably slept with other women since her. Something kept the lie from forming on her lips, however. Instead she said, "No, I've been too busy." That really wasn't a total lie.

"And I haven't had another woman since you," he said in a throaty tone.

His words shocked her; in fact, they left her speechless. He hadn't had another woman since her? Xavier, the man with a sex drive that never quit? At that moment she couldn't explain the satisfied pleasure she felt blooming inside of her. Why had he denied himself?

"Seems like we have the same problem, Farrah."

She pulled herself back into the conversation, trying to tread lightly while all kinds of wicked thoughts flowed through her. "And what problem is that?"

He reached out and rubbed his thumb over her bottom lip. "We need to get unleashed. You need a man to make love to you like I need to make love to a woman. Bad. But I don't need to make love to any woman, Farrah. I need to make love to you. I so miss hearing you scream."

More sensations washed over her, wetting her panties, causing every nerve ending in her body to respond to the sensuality in his voice and the heat in his words. She had definitely missed him making her scream as well.

"So you think we need to get unleashed, huh?" she asked in a low tone, while her heartbeat throbbed in her chest.

"Yes, but due to schedule restraints, I'll just have time to prime you for now."

Oh, she knew all about his priming methods and just what setting up for that stage of seduction could do to her. They'd never made out in a car before, and just the thought of doing so was downright naughty. But she felt like being naughty tonight. She had been a good girl for a long time and felt the need to sexually unwind. But more than anything, she wanted to scream. She shuddered at the thought of all he was offering her on a sensual platter.

"So what do you think about that plan, Farrah?"

At the moment she didn't want to think. She didn't want to talk.

Instead she leaned close to him, deciding she needed to respond to him this way. She intended to start off by initiating a game they'd often played when he'd come over to her place. She leaned close and offered him the tip of her tongue. Just as expected, he swooped down quickly and all but sucked her tongue into his mouth.

She moaned deep in her throat as familiar sensations burned in her soul. The strength of the passion he was evoking within her was the same as it had been from the first. Xavier could make a woman want things she was better off not having.

As she proceeded to melt under the force of his kiss, she knew that somehow she would take whatever he was offering for now and then find the strength to walk away and not look back when their time together in New York ended.

Chapter 7

Xavier knew the moment Farrah surrendered.

He was practically on his back with her draped all over him while she took his mouth with a hunger that he was more than willing to reciprocate.

God, he wanted her with a vengeance. It wouldn't take much to zip down his pants, pull out his shaft and ease right into her. She had made it easy to do so with the way her thighs were positioned over his. He remembered—not that he could ever forget—that she preferred wearing skimpy panties, thongs or the barely-there kind. He'd bet nothing had changed in that area. Hell, he was hoping as much.

She pulled back, breaking off the kiss, and he drew in a deep breath as he gazed up into her face. She was the spitting image of a woman unleashed, a woman who knew what she wanted and planned on getting it. A woman who had gone long enough without a lover. He intended to change that. Right here. Right now.

He drew in a deep breath and swallowed hard when, not bothering to unbuckle his belt, she jerked his shirt from the waistband of his pants before proceeding to ease down his zipper. He didn't have to ask what she was about to do; he just hoped he would be able to survive the experience.

When she smiled at him while licking her lips, his heart began beating frantically in his chest. She had effectively turned the tables on him. He was supposed to be seducing her and not the other way around. What about that control he was known for? Hell, it was slipping, and there was nothing he could do about it now. At the moment he couldn't deny her anything, especially the piece of him she obviously wanted.

And when he felt her warm fingers probing inside his pants, anticipation sizzled up his spine, and it took all he could do not to moan out loud. After she pulled his erection free, he watched through lowered lashes as she studied his shaft, as if she was savoring the thought of tasting him and trying to decide the best way to go about it.

Then her fingers started moving as she began to stroke it, palmed him in her hand, pumped him with her fingers. His body shuddered, and heat surged through him, especially in his groin.

She glanced up at him and smiled as his belly clenched with the look he saw in her eyes. The fire he saw there not only sharpened his senses but had his erection expanding right in her hands.

"I'm about to show you, Xavier Kane, that you're not the only one who knows about priming. And don't you dare think about pulling my mouth away until I'm ready to let go."

She didn't give him a chance to think, let alone respond, when her mouth lowered and took him in.

"Heaven help me." He murmured the words in a heated rush of breath, closed his eyes and released a deep, guttural groan.

Her mouth seemed to expand to encompass his erection all the way from the head to the root, and when she began using her tongue in full earnest, pleasure—which he hadn't felt in six months—shot through every part of his body.

With slow thoroughness, she took her time torturing him, letting him see that she was the one in control of this, and when her mouth deliberately began exerting pressure to the head of his erection, he clenched his jaw, and his body rumbled into one hell of an explosion.

When he gripped the side of her head and tried pulling her away, she planted her teeth on him with enough pressure to remind him of her earlier order. She was in control.

When his turn came, she was going to be sorry, he thought as his jaw clenched tight and the climax shook him. He wondered if he was still breathing. Surely he had died, gotten buried and gone to heaven.

Then before he could recover from that first explosion, another one hit; this one even stronger, and he felt all kinds of sensations tear up the length of his body and back.

"Farrah!"

If he thought she was ready to let go, then evidently he was out of his mind. The latter was true anyway. He was definitely out of his mind with all the scintillating excitement thrown in the mix. And he saw that she was determined not to release him until the last shudder eased from his body.

It was then that he slowly forced open his eyes and stared at her. It took every ounce of energy he possessed to reach out his hand to caress her cheek. He wasn't sure if he was imagining things or not, but her entire face took on an ethereal beauty that was more vibrant, more soul-touchingly exquisite than ever before.

And when she tilted her lips in a smile, he dragged in a staggering breath and felt his body getting hard all over again as desire once again enflamed him, filled him to capacity. But something else happened at that moment, too. He wasn't sure just what it was, since it was something he couldn't put a name to at that moment. But he was convinced it was something he'd never felt before, and he suddenly felt totally consumed by it.

"So what do you think, Xavier?"

Instead of answering, he moved quickly, and, ignoring her shriek of surprise, he eased her back and loomed over her. He caught her chin in his hand as his mouth came down on hers, effectively absorbing whatever words she was about to say. He intended to show her just what he thought.

His kiss tried taking control of her mouth, but Farrah refused to let it. She enjoyed sharing his heat, participating in such a sensual duel as their tongues tangled. Electricity flowed through her body.

And she still wanted more.

She intended to get it, and it seemed he was just as determined to give it to her. Okay, she could handle this, she thought. Then she wasn't all that sure when she felt his hands under her dress. When he finally released her mouth, she was breathless, left in a state of pure enthrallment. Totally awestruck. Mesmerized.

"You should never have pushed me over the edge, Farrah."

She met his gaze. Had she actually done that?

"You do know what that means, don't you?"

She nodded. Yes, she knew exactly what that meant. She'd had him in her mouth, and now he intended to have her in his. He didn't waste time pushing her dress up and out of his way before pulling her barely-there panties down past her thighs.

"Xavier, don't we need to talk about this?"

"No."

And that was the last word he said before lifting her hips with his hand and lowering his head between her legs. The moment the tip of his tongue eased between her feminine folds, she cried out, closed her eyes and reached out to grab hold of his shoulders.

How had she gone without this for so long? How had she survived without the feel of his mouth on her, in her, his tongue lapping her up before delving deeper and deeper. He was feasting on her, pushing her legs apart to treat himself to more of her.

A soft moan flowed from her lips. Then another. Pleasure began rolling over her in melodious waves, pushing her over the edge while at the same time taking her under. No inner part of her was left untouched. If his tongue could reach it, it was stroked. Mercilessly so.

Farrah suddenly cried out when she couldn't take any more, and rapture struck every inch of her body. He continued to devour her, as she quivered from an orgasm that would have topped the Richter scale. When he pulled back and captured her mouth, his tongue was still hot and hungry.

And she knew he wasn't through with her yet when she heard him tear open a condom package.

Then there it was. The head of his erection probing where his mouth had been. He lifted her hips up in his hands the moment he thrust into her. The surge of pleasure that ripped through her with this coming together made her scream. That only pushed him to go deeper, made his strokes stronger.

"Xavier!"

He lifted his head to stare down at her, and the primal look in his eyes almost made her lose her breath while at the same time it triggered another explosion within her. She had wanted to be naughty, but he was making her crazy.

And then he bucked, thrust harder, went deeper and her boot-clad legs tightened around him, greedy for everything he wanted to give and ready to take it. She didn't have long to wait for his release. Hot molten liquid shot everywhere inside of her, lubricating her inner walls with the very essence of him.

"Farrah!"

He had thrown his head back and her name came out as a deep growl from his throat, and he then lowered his head to take her mouth, to feed greedily off of it, as his body continued to thrust insatiably inside of her. Harder.

She screamed again as spasms shook her. When had making love to any man been this good? And she knew at that moment it could only be this way with Xavier.

He broke off the kiss, and his forehead came to rest against hers when their bodies slowed. She breathed in a deep, trembling breath as she stared up at him.

"Satisfied?" he asked, staring down at her. His shirt was unbuttoned to his waist and he was still wearing his pants. She could just imagine how erotic things would have gotten if they'd been naked.

"Very," she said, smiling up at him and meaning

every word. He was still inside of her. Still hard. The man had more staying power than anyone she knew.

"Good." He paused a minute then asked, "So what do *you* think, Farrah?" It took her a moment to follow him. He was deliberately countering the question she'd asked him earlier.

She released a deep breath. "I can't think at the moment. Ask me again later."

He chuckled as he slowly eased out of her and proceeded to pull her panties back up and pull her dress down. He then buttoned his shirt.

"I can just imagine what your driver is probably thinking, though," she said, sitting up.

Xavier chuckled. "Jules is probably grateful he got to spend time with his old Navy buddy. He's worked for me for a while and knows—"

"How you operate?"

He glanced over at her while tucking his shirt back inside his pants. For some reason, that statement bothered him. "And how do you think I operate, Farrah?"

She leaned back against the seat of the car and closed her eyes. "Ask me later. I told you, I can't think now. I just want to savor the moment."

And he thought he wouldn't mind savoring some more of her. Not understanding why he needed to do so, what exactly was driving him, he caught her off guard when he leaned over and kissed her with the same degree of passion he'd demonstrated earlier but with far less desperation. He wanted this to be slow pleasure that was meant to be savored, relished and enjoyed. And from the unhurried and leisurely way her tongue was mating with his, he knew that it was.

When he released her mouth, her head fell back against the seat cushions, and she stared at him as if she was incapable of saying anything. He couldn't help but smile, pleased he'd kissed any words from her lips for the time being.

"What was that for?" she finally was able to ask.

"Ask me later. I can't think now," he said rezipping his pants.

She laughed and playfully punched him in the arm. "Funny. You're a regular comedian who happens to be a damn good kisser."

"Earned brownie points, did I?"

"Yes, you most certainly did. I don't know many guys like you."

"I'm glad to hear it," he said, pulling his cell phone out of the pocket of his jacket and punching a lone number. "Jules, how far are we from port?" he asked, glancing out the window while working his arms into the sleeves of his jacket. He nodded and then said, "Good."

He clicked off the phone and replaced it in his jacket and glanced over at Farrah. "When we get back to your hotel, do I get invited up for a nightcap?"

"After what we did just now do you really think you need an invitation? Better yet, do you have the energy for more?"

He couldn't help but smile at that.

She frowned at him. "Forget I asked. Silly me. How could I forget your endless amount of energy? You know, this was the first time we did it someplace other than my house," she said, reaching for her purse. He watched her pull out her makeup compact.

"First time for everything. I plan for us to start being adventurous," he said, working his tie back around his neck.

She clicked the compact closed and glanced over

at him. Surprise lit her eyes. "You do understand that nothing between us has changed."

Something fluttered in his chest. "What do you mean?" he asked.

She shrugged as if she assumed they were in one accord with what she was about to say. "Going back to our conversation earlier about restarting our affair… Spending time with you like this, here in New York, is wonderful, but when we return to Charlotte we won't be seeing each other again."

The hell we won't! He fought to keep the frown off his face while wondering just how she figured that. "I don't see why not. You've missed me. I've missed you. So there."

"Yes, which is the reason we're spending time to-gether now. A holiday fling is just what we evidently need. It's the season to be jolly, and we can even act a little loony, out of character, even behave like sex ad-dicts and all that good stuff. We're adults with needs. But when it's all said and done, eventually things have to get back to normal, and when they do, it will be life as we know it."

"And what kind of life is that?" he asked, trying to keep anger from burning the back of his throat.

"I can't speak for you, but mine will be one with no serious entanglements. I have too much baggage for any man to deal with."

Try me. He decided now was not the time to tell her that their entanglement was already as serious as it could get. He also decided not to break the news that he had all intentions of resuming what they had shared before. The only kind of life he planned on having was one with her in it.

He opened his mouth to speak but closed it when he

heard them docking back at the port. A short time later the car door opened, and he knew Jules had returned. That gave him a chance to sit and ponder why he had this burning obsession with getting back with her. And he knew the reason had nothing to do with the off-the-chain sex they'd had tonight or all those other times before. It was way too deep for him to try and dissect at this moment. Especially when she thought she'd delivered the last word.

He fully understood why she intended to keep him at arm's length again once they returned to Charlotte. She'd been burned once and didn't intend for any man to light a match to her again. Well, he had news for her. He was not going to let her lump him in with that poor excuse for a husband any longer.

"You've gotten quiet on me, Xavier."

They were back on the road again. Bright lights were everywhere as the car headed back toward her hotel. "I was just thinking."

"About what?"

"What I need to do to convince you that we need to restart our affair on a long-term basis."

She shook her head. "Don't bother. I don't do long-term."

"You did me for one month shy of a year."

"I got carried away," she said simply. "*We* got carried away. It was an abnormality for you as much as it was for me."

Yes, it had been, but he hadn't complained.

"And what about your status in the club?"

The question annoyed him. "Forget about the club."

"Why should I? And can you? You and your god-brothers are the ones who established it. What will they think?"

At the moment he didn't give a royal damn.

What had he been thinking when he'd conceived of the Bachelors in Demand Club, he wondered now. And at the time, his five godbrothers, for various reasons, had been more than happy to be a part of it.

"Xavier?"

He glanced over at her. "I'm still thinking."

She smiled. "Yes, you do that and pretty soon you'll see I'm right. What you're asking for is not what you really want. You just got caught up in the moment. You even admitted yourself that because of work you hadn't slept with another woman since me. The way I see it, you've been suffering from a bad case of horniness. Don't get your heads mixed up, Xavier. You used to be pretty good knowing one from the other."

He looked away out the window. She sounded like she assumed she had all the answers. Well, he had news for her. If she thought—

"And I think considering everything, we should forget about that nightcap."

At her interruption, he looked at her. "Are you saying you don't want me to spend the night with you?"

"I don't recall issuing you an invitation."

He frowned. "Are we into playing games now, Farrah?"

"No." She didn't say anything for a moment and then, "Look, Xavier, I'll spend every moment that I can with you while we're here in New York. I really want that. There's nothing wrong with enjoying the fun while it lasts."

There was a momentary pause, and then he asked, "But when we return to Charlotte, I can't call you or drop by like before?"

"I prefer that you didn't."

Did she really mean that? he asked himself. She was returning his stare with a straight face, and her tone of voice sounded serious enough. But still...

She was the same woman who'd come apart in his arms moments ago. The same woman who'd admitted to missing him, to trying to forget him these past six months.

He studied her features and saw the determined look in her eyes. However, he took a minute to look beyond that, and he could swear he saw something else. Was she really that scared to admit that possibly those eleven months they'd been together had meant more than just sex?

His eyebrows knit in a tight frown. This was getting pretty damn confusing. He should be in agreement with how she was thinking. She definitely expected him to be, but he just wasn't feeling it, and he needed a reality check to figure out why.

"Let's do dinner tomorrow night," he heard himself suggesting.

"That's fine, if I'm in town."

He lifted a brow. "Where will you be if not here?"

"Heading back to Charlotte if I wrap things up with my clients tomorrow. Either way I hope to be leaving by Friday."

A sense of dread felt like a sword twisting in his chest. Friday was two days away. "I want to spend time with you again before you leave, Farrah, and I agree tonight might not be a good time."

"I'll call you tomorrow, Xavier. That's the best I can do."

She was deliberately giving him little to work with, but she didn't know that Xavier worked best under pressure. He would take tonight to go home and regroup, plan a new strategy and decide just what he intended to do about Farrah Langley.

One thing was for certain. He had no intentions of letting her go. If she thought things were over between them, then she definitely had another thought coming.

Chapter 8

Farrah wrapped the huge towel around her as she stepped out of the shower. From where she stood in the bathroom she could see her bed, and if anyone would have told her she would be sleeping in it alone tonight, without Xavier, she would not have believed them.

There was no reason for him not to have spent the night…at least there hadn't been a reason until he began spouting all that nonsense about them continuing their affair once they returned to Charlotte. What could he have been thinking to even suggest such a thing?

As she slipped into her nightgown, she shook her head, totally confused. Tonight had been an adventure, definitely something new and different. She smiled, thinking she liked the idea of being naughty. She liked the idea of a holiday affair, too.

A casual relationship was all she was interested in. With Xavier, however, what had started out as a strictly no-strings affair had slipped into a hot and heavy routine, a full-blown sexual habit they couldn't kick. Not that they'd tried. The more he'd shown up on her doorstep, the more she'd wanted him to keep coming.

And that wasn't good.

He could argue with her on that point all day long, and she would not change her mind and relent. As far as she was concerned, they either agreed to indulge in a New York affair or nothing.

Then why, she thought a short while later when she slipped between the sheets of her lonely bed, was she thinking of him and all they'd done that night? What they'd shared for eleven months, and more importantly, what she'd gone without the past six months and what she would continue to go without?

If tonight had been a calculated move on his part to stir up memories, then she would be the first to say he'd succeeded. As she lay staring up at the ceiling, she couldn't get out of her mind just how he'd felt inside of her, killing her softly with every sensual stroke.

So many memories began swirling around in her head, making sleep impossible. At least for now. Instead, she couldn't help but recall the first time he'd shown up on her doorstep and how quickly and easily she'd tumbled with him into her bed. She'd opened the door, and he'd stood there, wearing a pair of jeans and a white shirt and looking as sexy as any man had a right to look. There had been something about him that had wowed her from the first time she'd seen him that night at the Racetrack Café. She'd heard about him and the bachelor club he was affiliated with, but until she'd seen him for herself, she hadn't known how any man could have that effect on a woman.

She'd known she had wanted him from the start,

passionately so, and hadn't intended to let something like protocol stand in her way. She'd seen him as a way to have fun and forget about all the hurt Dustin had caused her. She'd wanted to know how it felt to have a no-strings-attached affair and not care one iota if she saw the man again. She'd wanted an affair that was as casual as it could get.

And that's what she'd gotten in the beginning. But then she'd noticed things beginning to change, even if he hadn't. Probably because those changes had been one-sided. There was no reason to assume that he'd begun thinking about her in the wee hours of the night and anticipating the next time they would hook up. Or find himself smiling in the middle of the day after thinking of something that happened between them the night before. And she was pretty confident that when she did open the door for him, he didn't feel that funny feeling in the pit of his stomach.

Those had been the warning signs, and she'd had no reason not to heed them and put in place any and every preventive measure that she could. Nothing seemed to work. The situation seemed to get worse. And she'd known the best thing to do was to break things off with him completely.

And now he wanted to jump-start things again and had done a pretty good job giving her a reason to do so. But she couldn't. Bottom line was that she was dealing with something he couldn't understand. It was only about sex for him, but for her she was taking every memory as seriously as it could get.

She moved to another position, not that she thought that would help. It would be a sleepless night. Even after the workout Xavier had given her tonight, her feminine core was achy, in need of some intimate attention, Xavier Kane style.

Give in to him, a voice inside her head whispered. *You're a big girl. You can handle another affair with Xavier. It would be up to you to make sure it's an affair that leads nowhere. And if it did, what's another little broken heart? What's the big deal?*

The big deal was there in his eyes each and every time he looked at her. It was there on his tongue every time he kissed her. It was embedded in the fingers that touched her.

After a few tosses and turns, she discovered she still couldn't get to sleep and decided she needed to talk to someone, and there was no other person she could share her woes with than her best friend.

She glanced over at the clock and cringed when she saw it was almost one o'clock. She didn't know what kind of hours Natalie was keeping now, but before she was married, Dr. Natalie Ford Steele, esteemed chemistry professor at Princeton University, used to be up at all hours of the night.

She grabbed her cell phone off the nightstand and punched in one number that automatically connected to Natalie. The phone was picked up on the first ring. "Hey, Farrah, what's going on?"

Farrah smiled, grateful to hear her friend's bubbly voice at a minute before one in the morning. "Evidently, you are. I take it you aren't sleep."

"Heavens, no. I just finished another chapter of this book I'm working on and was sitting here cuddled on the sofa enjoying a cup of hot chocolate."

She then remembered that Natalie was working on what would probably be another *New York Times* bestseller on global warming. "Where's Donovan?"

"Oh, he went to bed hours ago. I think the triplets wore him out. We kept them earlier while Cheyenne and Quade went shopping to play Santa. They are definitely three busy beavers. Donovan and I could barely keep up with them."

Farrah chuckled. "Are you two having second thoughts about having kids of your own now?"

"Never! I want Donovan's baby so bad."

Natalie's words made something twist in her heart when she remembered how she had wanted Dustin's baby, too. Instead of giving a child to her, he'd given one to someone else. That pain reminded her why she could never give her heart to another man.

"So what's up, Farrah?"

She swallowed. There was no reason to talk anything over with Natalie now. Not with the reminder she'd just gotten. The pain was still stabbing her chest. "Nothing."

"Um, I know you, girl. You would not have called me at one in the morning for nothing. Go on. Let it out. What's bothering you?"

Farrah nibbled on her bottom lip a minute before saying, "I ran into Xavier yesterday."

There was a pause on the other end, which Farrah understood. Natalie knew why she had broken things off with Xavier. "In that case, I'm sure cold New York is probably pretty hot by now."

Farrah threw her head back and laughed, especially when she remembered how hot things had gotten while riding across the Hudson in Xavier's private car. She then cleared her throat. "Hey, what can I say?"

"You can say the two of you have decided to get back together."

The smile on Farrah's face immediately became a frown. She'd known that Natalie liked Xavier. What was there not to like? Besides being good-looking as sin, he was also a downright nice person. She would attest to that. And of course he was one of Donovan's closest friends. But all of that had nothing to do with her heart.

"No, we're not getting back together, although he suggested such a thing. I told him I'd indulge in a holiday fling while we're here in New York. That was the best I could do."

Understandably there was another pause, which was followed by a feminine snort. "I wish you would rethink that proposal, Farrah. Not all men are like Dustin."

Farrah changed positions in bed while she rolled her eyes. How many times had she heard that very thing— not only from Natalie, but from several others? "I don't want to try and weed the good from the bad. Casual affairs suit me just fine, but the one with Xavier was beginning to get too hot, heavy and addictive."

"That's not bad with the right guy, Farrah. Hey, let's run down a few things."

"A few things like what?"

"Why Xavier might be a keeper."

There was no doubt in Farrah's mind that he was a keeper. All she had to do was concentrate on the tingling between her legs to know just how much of a keeper he was. But he would be a keeper for some other woman, definitely not her. She frowned, wondering why the thought of that suddenly annoyed her.

Natalie began her checklist. "I don't have to ask if he's good in bed."

She couldn't help but laugh again. "No, please, don't bother."

"Okay, then. Is he someone you would want as a friend?"

A friend? Yes, she could see him being her friend

once they put the bedroom behind them. But when she saw him, she didn't think of friendship, just sexual satisfaction. "Yes, he's someone I'd want as a friend."

"Okay, then. Do you consider yourself happy when you're with him?"

That was a no-brainer. Of course she was happy whenever she was with him. He could do things with his mouth, tongue and erection that could keep any woman delirious. "Definitely," she heard herself saying.

"Get your mind out of the bedroom, Langley, and provide responses on a purely plausible basis."

"Not sure I can do that with Xavier. Our relationship was one that started in the bedroom."

"That's not true. If anyone's relationship started in the bedroom, it was mine and Donovan's. Your relationship with Xavier started at Racetrack Café, Farrah. You were the one who was quick to carry it into the bedroom."

Farrah thought about Natalie's accusation and had to agree that she had been the one who'd instituted a sex-only relationship with Xavier from the first. Of course he had gone along with it. What man wouldn't have? She had known the moment she'd lit her gaze upon him that night that she'd wanted him.

"Sorry, but I've conditioned myself to only think one way when it comes to men. And please, please don't tell me again that all men aren't the same."

"Maybe if I keep saying it, one day you'll believe me."

"I believe that now, Nat, but like I said, I don't have the time to find out who's naughty and who's nice. I can't risk taking a chance and being wrong."

"I think deep down you want a man who's both naughty and nice and you have both with Xavier."

Farrah released a deep sigh. "What is this? Slap-some-sense-into-my-best-friend-where-Xavier-Kane-is-concerned Day?"

"I won't even try doing that. You'll have to see for yourself what a great guy he is."

"I hate to burst that romantic bubble floating around your heart, but all Xavier wants from me is sex, too. It's not that serious. Only problem with that is that I could fall in love with him, Nat, if I'm not careful and I can't let that happen. Thanks for listening." Not waiting for Natalie to reply, she quickly ended the call. "Love you. Bye."

Finding a more comfortable position in bed, she stared up at the ceiling again as she drew in a ragged breath. Sleep continued to elude her as one thought replayed in her head. A woman was entitled to make at least one mistake in her lifetime, but a smart woman wouldn't be a fool and make two.

Xavier slipped into his robe as he eased out of bed, unable to sleep. At this very moment he should have been in Farrah's bed making love to her again. When she'd ridden the elevator up to her room, he should have been on that elevator with her, kissing her every second of the ride.

Okay, so her refusal to jump-start their affair again had thrown him for a loop. He'd figured after tonight she would have seen the merit in them hooking back up. Evidently they weren't on the same page. Not even close.

Moving through the hallway, he walked down the stairs to the kitchen. He had purchased this house on Long Island as investment property a few years ago and hadn't regretted doing so. He liked New York and whenever he came to town he much preferred staying here than in a hotel.

Grabbing a beer from the refrigerator, he slid onto a bar stool. The night was quiet, understandably so. Most sane people were in bed getting a good night's sleep. But not him. He was letting a woman tie him in knots.

He was in a bad way. Pretty messed up. Royally.

He took a huge gulp of his beer, acknowledging that he'd been delivered a setback. It wasn't the first time with a woman, but he'd never been this interested in one before. And to think that all she wanted was a holiday fling.

He took another swig of his beer while memories of their night together came tearing into him, and he couldn't help but recall when she'd gone down on him. And then later when his body had slid into hers, he'd felt as if he was someplace he could stay forever. Even stretched out as best she could on the car's backseat, she had used their limited space effectively and met him stroke for stroke. And as much as he wanted to chalk her up as a lost cause and move on with his life, he knew that he couldn't.

He knew it wasn't just about sex with Farrah, although that part of their relationship was always off the chart. But now when he took the time to think about it, it had always been more than just two bodies mating, at least in his book. She had a way of touching him everywhere and not just below the belt. From the first, he'd always felt in sync with her. Whenever she would smile, something inside of him would light up. And then there were those feelings of loneliness whenever he wasn't with her. For the past six months it had felt as if something was missing from his life. She was the only woman since Dionne who could fill him with emotions. Emotions he thought had died a hard death a long time ago.

He held his beer bottle to his lips, ready to take another healthy sip, when he was hit with a realization that had his heart pounding, his pulse racing and his esophagus tightening. This couldn't be happening to him. No way. But as he stared into space for a few seconds, he knew that it had already happened. He had fallen for Farrah, and hard.

Damn.

What had happened to that strong resolve to guard his heart? What had happened to all those instilled and painful memories of what Dionne had done to him? He wasn't sure what had happened, but he knew, just as surely as he knew Diana Ross was once a Supreme, that he was in love with Farrah Langley.

He set his beer bottle down, thinking that definitely put a whole new spin on things. It hadn't been his intent to fall in love, but it had happened and now he planned to do something about it, which didn't include running in the other direction. No, he'd confront the opposition head on. This was his heart they were talking about.

He knew without being told that if she got wind of his feelings, she would make things even more difficult. But he had news for her. Not only was he going to have his fling with her in the Big Apple, but it would continue right to Charlotte and eventually lead into marriage.

Marriage?

Yeah, marriage.

He smiled, thinking he liked the sound of that. He knew the hell she would probably give him, but he was up for the battle. All was fair in love and war, and he would do whatever it took to win her over and make her realize that regardless of what had happened in her past, he was the man for her.

It was a good thing Farrah wasn't there to see the sly smile that had formed around his lips. She wouldn't know what hit her until it was too late for her to do a damn thing about it.

Chapter 9

Farrah wasn't so sure how today's session with Kerrie Shaw and Lori Byers would pan out when Rudolph Byers strolled in by his wife's side with a smirk on his face, as if he knew something they all didn't. She couldn't help wondering if all the progress she'd made with the two women would get flushed down the toilet by the man who was determined to keep a wedge between the friends.

"Good morning, everyone, and welcome back," she said when they were all seated at the conference table. "I think we made really good progress yesterday and would like to pick up where we left off if everyone is in agreement." She held her breath, almost certain that Rudolph Byers would step in and oppose. When he did not and sat there beside his wife with that silly smirk still on his face, she continued.

"Okay, then, yesterday we ended with you, Kerrie, telling us about the early years when you and Lori worked together. Kerrie, I believe you were sharing with me how things were that first year when the two of you finished college."

Kerrie nodded, glanced over at Lori and smiled. Lori smiled back, which in Farrah's book was still a good sign. "Lori came up with this idea of how we could raise money for our first batch of makeup by getting a group of friends of ours in a band to agree to do a concert…"

Farrah leaned back in her seat listening to what Kerrie was saying, while at the same time noticing there seemed to be a bit of tension between Lori and Rudolph. Being rude, he was doing annoying things to get his wife's attention as if to remind her that he was there. At first he'd been rubbing his finger up and down the sleeve of her blouse, and now he was entwining his fingers on the table with hers. It probably would have come off as a romantic gesture if he wasn't making it so obvious, so deliberate.

Moments later when Kerrie finished talking, Lori jumped in and said, "We used to have so much fun, although we operated in the red most of the time. I can recall when we finally were able to get out of Kerrie's parents' basement and into our own store in Queens."

"That was the store given to the two of you as a gift from your parents, right?"

"Yes, I guess they figured that was the least they could do after we bummed off the Shaws for almost two years," Lori said laughing.

Kerrie joined in the laughter, and she saw Rudolph Byers flinch as if the sound of the two women sharing memories of happier times bothered him. A half hour later Farrah called for a break and wasn't surprised when he pulled Lori off to the side. It wasn't hard to tell that whatever he was saying to her wasn't nice.

Moments later Lori frowned deeply before pulling away from him, and Farrah was grateful when the man stormed out of the conference room, slamming the door behind him.

Kerrie was on the other side of the room with her back to everyone while she talked on the phone, and the loud sound made her swirl around. An apologetic look appeared on Lori's face and she hunched her shoulders in disgust when she said, "Rudolph has an errand he needs to take care of and will be back after lunch."

The expression on Kerrie's face all but clearly said *good riddance.* Farrah refrained from saying anything, but she definitely agreed with Kerrie. She had the same opinion that she had yesterday. The man was bad news and a born manipulator.

Farrah glanced at her watch; it was still early. They had an hour and a half to go before they stopped for lunch. She couldn't help wondering what Xavier was doing. She had promised to call and let him know if she was free for dinner, and she would do so. She felt she needed to see him again since she knew their days together were numbered. She had thought about it, and to avoid being alone during the holidays, if he wanted to extend things until then, she would even consider that.

She began nibbling on her bottom lip wondering why she was doing this to herself. Why not make a clean break after she left here as she'd planned, instead of looking for any excuse to spend more time with him? Maybe one of the reasons was that she could remember the last holidays so well, and he had been a part of them.

It had been the best Christmas she had had in a long time, even better than the times when she'd been married to Dustin. But especially better than the year before when she'd been prepared to spend her holidays alone until Natalie had decided to come home.

The Steeles were a large family, and from talking to Natalie, she knew that this Christmas Donovan's parents, who traveled a lot since retiring, would be returning home for a huge family get-together. That meant, Farrah thought, that more than likely she would be spending the holidays alone.

If she were to suggest to Xavier that they continue their affair at least through the holidays, would he figure out why and grant her that request, or would he decide he didn't want to be used and tell her just where she could go? Besides, chances were he'd already made plans for the holidays.

She glanced across the room and noticed Kerrie had ended her phone call and was standing at the window looking out. Lori, standing on the other side of the room, appeared lost, and from her body language and expression, it was obvious she wanted to approach Kerrie but didn't know how to do so.

Farrah shook her head. Her heart truly went out to both women. Their relationship was badly in need of repair, and neither knew the best way of going about making it happen. "Ladies, I'm ready to resume things."

When both women sat down, she thought for a minute and then said, "You know I have a best friend, who, like the two of you, has been there for me since our high school years. There's nothing I wouldn't do for Natalie and there's nothing Natalie wouldn't do for me."

A smile touched the corners of Farrah's lips. "I know her secrets and she knows mine. She knows my weaknesses and my strengths and vice versa. We understand each other, which is why we've been friends for so long.

We might not agree on everything, and I'm sure there have been times when she would have knocked my head off if she could have, but in the end, no matter what, I know our friendship is one that defies the test of time."

"I thought ours would, too," Lori said softly, looking at her when Farrah knew she wanted to glance over at Kerrie.

"I'm not going to ask what happened," Farrah said. "I just ask that no matter what, you remember what you had, what you still have and what will always be there no matter what."

At that moment, Lori did glance over at Kerrie. "You think I'm only doing this because of Rudolph, don't you?"

Kerrie met her gaze and asked, "Why wouldn't I think it, Lori? Leaving the company in my hands was your idea. Saying that you would only want half up to the day you left was also yours. You also said that we keep things as they were to avoid any messy legal entanglements. It would be unnecessary, you said, since we fully trusted each other."

Kerrie shook her head and said softly, "The sad thing is that I believed you. Stupid me."

The room got quiet and Farrah spoke up. "Is this the first time your friendship has been tested?"

Both women glanced over at her with a bemused look on their faces, so much so that she couldn't help but smile. "You both know that's what this is, don't you?"

Neither woman made a comment, and Farrah figured she had given them something to think about. She glanced at her watch. "You know, I think now is a good time to break for lunch. It's a little early but I think we deserve it today."

Instead of responding, both women nodded as they

stood. Kerrie was pulling out her cell phone while heading for the door. Lori watched her leave before turning to Farrah. She could see the tears in the woman's eyes.

"I didn't mean to hurt her," she said in a broken tone.

Farrah stood as she gathered her folders together. The last thing Lori needed was to be sent on a guilt trip, but in this case one was probably warranted. "Well, I hate to tell you this, Lori, but I think you did."

Xavier read the report spread across his desk and tried not to glance up at the clock on the wall. How many times had he done it already? He had to believe that eventually Farrah would call him. She'd said she would, hadn't she?

He threw the pencil he held in his hand down on his desk and leaned back in his chair as he squinted his eyes in thought, trying to recall exactly what she had said. *I'll call you tomorrow, Xavier. That's the best I can do.* Those had been her exact words. He recalled them clearly.

He was about to get up and pour another cup of coffee when his cell phone rang. If it was York, he was going to kill him. He'd called twice already. It seemed that York needed a life more than he did.

Xavier reached for the phone and exhaled a sigh of relief when he saw the caller was Farrah. He glanced at the clock. It was almost four. What had taken her so long? Of course he wouldn't ask her that. In fact, he intended to sound cool, calm and collected. "Hello."

"Xavier. Hi."

"And how are you, Farrah?"

"Fine. Sorry it took me so long to call but it turned out to be a long session today."

He nodded as he leaned back in his chair. "Did the women reach a resolution?"

"I wish."

"I take it that they didn't."

"You've got that right. But I can say I feel we're close. Hopefully tomorrow."

Not if it means you'll be catching the first plane out of here, he thought to himself.

"Anyway, I just wanted to let you know I'd love to have dinner with you."

He couldn't help the smile that touched his lips from corner to corner. "Good. Where are you now? Back at the hotel or still at work?"

"Still at work. I need to complete a few reports and then I'll head back to the hotel."

He glanced at the clock again. "Umm, how about around seven?"

"That's good."

"I'll send a car for you."

"A car?"

"Yes. I'm treating you to dinner at my place."

"In Long Island?"

"Yes."

There was a pause, and he waited, knowing she was rummaging through that gorgeous brain of hers for an excuse not to come. On cue she said, "You don't have to do that. I really don't want to put you through any trouble, Xavier. For me to come all the way to your place really isn't necessary."

Yes, it is, sweetheart. She had no idea just how necessary it truly was. "No trouble. Jules will be there to pick you up exactly at seven. I hope you're hungry."

She didn't say anything for a minute and then, "Yes, I'm hungry. I had a light lunch. But—"

"Good. I'll have something I know you'll like when you get here."

Another pause...and then, "Okay. Thanks."

"Don't mention it. I'll see you when you get here."

He closed his cell phone and placed it back on the desk where it had been since early morning, awaiting her call. Then he stood. It was time for him to go home and prepare dinner for the most lovable yet detached woman he knew. He planned to make things right for her or die trying.

He was well aware of why she assumed she didn't want another man in her life. His mission, which he fully intended to accept, was to convince her that she was worthy of everything life had to offer.

Especially his love.

Chapter 10

"Here we are, Ms. Langley."

"Thanks."

Jules offered Farrah his hand as she eased out of the car and glanced around. The huge triple-story house sat on what appeared to be a private lane, surrounded by a number of huge overhanging trees that formed a canopy over the impressive residence. If privacy was something Xavier was shooting for, then he had succeeded.

Pulling her coat tightly around her, she moved quickly toward the front door. She liked the sound of her booted heels as they clicked loudly against the stone pavers. She had lifted her hand to knock when the door opened.

Xavier was there, and she took a good look at him. He was eye candy of the most delicious kind. And dressed in a pullover sweater and low-riding jeans, he was the epitome of sexy. He moved out of her way as he invited her in. "Come on, I have a blaze roaring in the fireplace. I still intend to keep my promise to make sure you stay warm."

"I appreciate that."

As she followed him through his house, she noticed two things—the aroma of food cooking that made her mouth water, and the fact that he had a beautiful home. She knew this place was just one of many of his show-places. He also had homes in Los Angeles, Miami and in the Palisades section of Charlotte, where houses went for millions. At least those were the ones he'd mentioned. There was no telling how many others he might own.

They passed a spiral staircase, and she couldn't help but glance up wondering if that was where his bed-room was and if she would find out for certain later. She shook her head. She needed to get her mind off sex, but that was definitely hard when, following him, she got an eyeful of the sexiest backside any man could possibly have.

By the time she'd reined in her wandering thoughts, she only caught his last word: *weather*.

"Excuse me, Xavier, what were you saying?"

He glanced over his shoulder, stopped walking and smiled. "I said it doesn't appear the weather is getting any better," he said, reaching for her hands. He removed her gloves and took her hands in his. As if he'd known they would be cold and stiff, he began massaging them.

Immediately, she felt heated sensations run through the tendons in her palms. The feelings were so strong she clenched her legs together when she felt an unexpected throbbing there.

No, the weather was not getting any better, which was quite obvious. The temperature had dropped, and depending on which news reports you were listening to, a snowstorm the likes of which New York hadn't seen in a long time was headed this way by Sunday. But Farrah knew that regardless of how cold it was outside, she would feel hot in here even if Xavier didn't have a fire roaring in the fireplace. Together, they could generate that kind of heat.

"Make yourself at home."

She broke eye contact with him and glanced around. They were in a room that he probably used as a den. It looked rustic with dark oak plank walls, the kind you'd find in a mountain cabin, and the fireplace was encased in whitewashed stone. The furniture looked sturdy and masculine, including the gigantic pool table in the middle of the room. He had mentioned that he enjoyed playing a game of pool every once in a while.

She glanced around the room again as she removed her coat, and as if he knew what she was thinking, he said, "No, I didn't decorate the place. It was bought as is. I figured the last owner wanted the feel of the Smoky Mountains in here, which is something I didn't have a problem with. In fact I think that's what enticed me to buy it."

She nodded as he came over and took the coat out of her hands. She automatically eased down on the sofa, a little surprised she was still wearing clothes. She had really expected him to strip her naked the moment she had stepped over the threshold. It seemed he was going to take things slow. Slow was good. But if he started showing signs of wasting too much time, she knew how to take things into her own hands, literally. She inwardly smiled, thinking how she'd done that several times before.

"Here, you probably could use this to get your blood warm."

He handed her a glass filled with wine. When had he poured it? She took a sip, liking the sparkling taste, but then she'd always enjoyed his wine selections. She licked her lips and glanced across the room knowing he was watching her. That was good. Let him look. It would make things easier later when she threw her new idea out to him.

She cleared her throat. "Whatever you're cooking smells good, Xavier."

He chuckled. "Thanks, but I didn't cook it. Ms. Blackburn did it all."

She lifted a brow. "Ms. Blackburn?"

"Yes. My housekeeper, cook, gardener. You name it, she does it."

She lifted a brow again. "Umm, does she now?"

He laughed. "Except for that. For crying out loud, Farrah, she's old enough to be my mother. But I would admit to coming close to asking her to marry me one day after eating a slice of her apple pie."

"It was that delicious?"

"Honey, delicious doesn't come close."

She swallowed. No one could say the word delicious quite the way he could, and no one could do things deliciously quite like him. She'd bet no one could even come close.

"So, will you be meeting with those women again tomorrow since no closure came about today?"

She glanced over at him. He had moved to sit on a bar stool. His taut thighs strained tightly against the denim of his jeans, and his abs were outlined in his form-fitting sweater. Not an inch of flab anywhere. She knew in reality he much preferred beer to wine, but unlike some men, he didn't have a belly to show it.

And speaking of his belly…she thought he had a nice looking one, especially when it wasn't covered with clothes. She remembered quite well how a sprinkling of dark hair adorned it. And then there was that trail of hair that tapered off to his groin area. She felt her mouth watering again, and it wasn't for anything his housekeeper had left cooking on the stove.

She took a sip of her wine before saying, "Yes, I'll be meeting with them, but if everything continues in the same way as today, I'm hoping we'll wrap up by tomorrow. But that depends on—"

"One of the women's husband's involvement," he finished for her.

She nodded and smiled. "You remembered."

"Yes."

"And here I thought you were listening just to humor me and weren't really paying attention."

He met her gaze and held it. "I'm sure since we've met that you've made a number of assumptions about me that aren't true, Farrah."

She blinked, surprised he would say that. "Like what?"

"You'll find out soon enough."

She wondered what he meant by that. But then she would admit that maybe she had made a few assumptions. Being here in his home challenged one of them. She had always assumed his home, his domain, was off-limits to any woman. He'd never said that, but given the way he'd meticulously made his booty calls, she'd certainly thought so.

Xavier stood and placed his wine glass on the counter. She couldn't help the way her gaze followed his movement, especially the muscles in his thighs when they stretched. He was definitely a man who could wear a pair of jeans. But then he looked damn good in a business suit as well. And Lordy, she didn't want to think about how good he looked naked.

She blinked again, noticing his lips move. He was saying something. "Excuse me?"

He smiled, and she felt a tingle that seemed to take life in her stomach. Why did he have to have such a luscious mouth? And why did she have to remember all the things that mouth could do?

"I asked if you were ready for dinner."

She was ready for whatever he had in mind. Holding back that thought, she cleared her throat and said instead, "Yes, just lead the way."

She followed him, appreciating another chance to check out his broad shoulders and the best backside a man could possess.

Xavier glanced across the table at Farrah and decided he was going to enjoy every single plan he put into action to win her over. They were almost finished with dinner, and just in case she planned to leave any time soon, he would suggest that she stick around to help with kitchen cleanup. He glanced back down at his plate thinking she didn't have to know Ms. Blackburn had instructed him to leave everything for her to take care of in the morning.

"You should have warned me, Xavier."

He glanced back up and met her gaze. The eyes staring back at him were a serious brown. He wondered if she'd figured out his action plan for tonight. "Warned you about what?"

"That I would be so full after this meal that you'd probably have to roll me out the door."

A relieved smile touched his lips. "I did warn you. I told you how I felt after eating her apple pie."

"I thought you were exaggerating. Now I see that you weren't. I've never eaten pork chops that all but melt in your mouth. They are so tender."

He had to agree, Ms. Blackburn had done a great job with dinner. And Farrah, he thought, had done a great job with dressing. She looked good tonight. When she'd taken off her coat, his tongue had almost wrapped around his head. That was one sexy purple dress she was wearing. It was short, which showed off her legs that were encased in tights and another pair of black leather knee-high boots. He had invited her over for dinner, not to give him heart failure.

"You look nice tonight, by the way."

She smiled at his compliment. "Thanks. You look good yourself."

He pushed his empty plate aside to lean back in his chair. "Glad you think so."

"I do. Always."

She was flirting with him, and as a man, he could only appreciate it. "Would you like some dessert now?" He watched her lick her lips, and he couldn't help but shift in the chair to ease the pressure behind his zipper.

"Sounds tempting but I'll wait for a while. I'd like to talk to you about something."

He wondered what she wanted to talk about. "Sure. Let's go in the family room and sit in front of the fireplace."

"But what about the dinner dishes?"

He smiled. "We can leave them for now and you can help me clean up the kitchen later."

"All right. That's the least I can do after such a wonderful meal."

No, that wasn't the least she could do, but he would keep that little tidbit to himself.

He rounded the table to pull the chair back for her. One thing he'd liked about Farrah from the first was that she never got offended when he did gentlemanly things for her. No matter how raw and raunchy they got in the bedroom, he totally enjoyed treating her like the lady he knew she was.

And she was a downright sexy lady at that, he thought as his gaze swept over her, up and down her body. Just looking at her almost derailed any thoughts about what was the best way to handle her. He wanted to get out of her the one thing he deemed most important. For her to return his love.

He knew that was a tall order, one that would take measured, strategic planning. His goal was to convince her that he was a viable candidate for her affections, and that he was more husband material than her ex ever was.

When she walked off swaying her hips, it took all of his control not to reach out and pull her into his arms and begin removing every stitch of clothing she had on her body before tearing off his. Then it would be on, all over the place. His erection throbbed just thinking about it.

He momentarily closed his eyes while telling himself to hold tight and keep a handle on his control. It would all be worth it in the end, even though not making love to her tonight was going to drive him insane, especially when she was intentionally trying to bait him.

Xavier reopened his eyes the moment she glanced over her shoulder at him with a teasing smile on her face. "Are you coming, Xavier?"

He gave her a warning frown. He would definitely be coming if she kept it up, but he intended to resist her temptation, even if it killed him. And he had a feeling that if it did kill him, he would die an excruciating, slow death. "I'm right behind you."

And he was. As she led the way back to his family room, he was what he considered a safe distance behind her, which had its advantages if you were into ass-watching. He was, especially when that part of the anatomy was hers.

She slid down on his sofa in a movement so fluid, so damn enticing, he didn't even blink as he watched her. He waited until she was settled in her seat before crossing the room and taking the recliner across from her. He'd known resisting her wouldn't be easy, but he hadn't counted on it being such torture. The woman was almost too hot for his own good.

He cleared his throat. "So, what do you want to talk about?"

"Us."

Us? She'd never referred to them as an *us,* so in a way things sounded pretty good already. "I'm listening."

She began nibbling on her lower lips. He knew that sign. Whatever topic she wanted to broach wasn't easy for her. "I, um, I was thinking about what you said last night."

He'd said a lot of things. He'd done a lot of things, too. "And?"

"And you wanted us to continue the affair past New York."

Had she come around without much prodding from him? "Yes, I recall having said that."

She began nibbling on her lips again, and then she said, "I'd like to offer a proposal to you."

He lifted a brow. "A proposal?"

"Yes."

He leaned back in the chair as he rubbed his jaw. This had better be good, he thought. It'd better be what he wanted. "I'm listening."

"I don't have any plans for the holidays and I thought…"

She paused, but he was determined that she finish what she was saying. "You thought what, Farrah?"

She met his gaze while nibbling those luscious lips again. "That since you wanted to continue things between us for a while, that we could extend our affair at least through New Year's."

He didn't say anything. He had to make sure he fully understood what she was offering. "Are you saying that once you leave here it's okay for us to hook up in Charlotte again, with things being like they used to be with us?"

She nodded. "Yes, but only through the holidays."

He ignored the ache in his body that tried convincing him that something was better than nothing, and that he should take her up on her offer. But he wasn't in the market for just being involved in a holiday affair. He wanted the whole shebang. That meant he had no intention of letting her place limitations on their relationship.

"So, what do you think?"

He shrugged his shoulders and wondered if she was prepared for what he was about to say. "I think I'll pass."

Voices in his head were calling him all kinds of fool for not accepting her offer. One voice in particular was all but giving his brain a hard kick, screaming that if he thought he could convince her to consider a real relationship with him, he was crazy and wasting his time.

Her ex had done too much of a number on her for that to happen. How many times had she told him that she would never, ever, become involved in a serious relationship again? How many times had she reiterated that fact for his benefit?

"You'll pass?" she asked, with a mixture of shock and confusion outlining what he thought were gorgeous features. "But why?"

He held her gaze. "Because I told you what I wanted."

"For us to pick up where we left off?"

"Yes, and continue from there without any limitations, Farrah."

She shook her head. "That's not going to work, Xavier. That's why I thought it was best if we ended things six months ago."

"Whatever hang-ups there were, Farrah, were yours, not mine. The only reason I gave in to it at the time was because I convinced myself that perhaps you were right. After last night I decided you're dead wrong."

The flaring of fire in her eyes let him know she hadn't appreciated what he'd just said. It didn't take a rocket scientist to know he'd pushed the wrong button, but at the moment he really didn't give a damn. It was time they had it out. He refused to go through another long spell without her.

She leaned forward in her seat. "This new attitude of yours is all because of last night? One good blow job got you all up in arms? Got you refusing a holiday fling with me because you want more than that?"

He slid out of the chair to stand on his feet. "It's more than that, Farrah, and you know it. It's about the chemistry we stir whenever we're together. I see nothing wrong with wanting more. But after almost a year, you decided we should end things. Why? Because you had begun feeling something a lot deeper and more solid than mere orgasms."

"That's not true!" she said adamantly.

"Isn't it?"

"It was just sex, Xavier. You could have gotten the same from any woman."

"Hardly, which is why I haven't slept with another woman since you. And probably why you haven't, by your admission, been intimate with anyone since me."

He thought he'd hit a nerve, and she proved him right when she began pacing angrily. He decided to sit back in the chair and let her blow off steam, come to terms with being called out. Except he was getting more turned on by the second watching her, seeing how the hair was flying around her face with every livid step she took in boots that were definitely made for more than walking.

Her hips were not just swaying now, they were being brandished about under the sting of rejection. Something she evidently didn't care much for. Not for the first time, he noticed just how small her waist was, and how her hips flared out in an almost perfect womanly shape. And her breasts—heaven help him, they were the most luscious pair on any woman—were straining against the bodice of her dress.

While his gaze roamed all over her, she finally came to a stop mere inches from where he sat. She placed her hands on her hips. "So, what exactly is it that you want?"

He smiled and leaned forward in his chair and met her gaze without wavering. He fought the urge to tell her that what he wanted was marriage, until death do them part. Considering everything, he figured now was not a good time to share that with her.

"What I want is for us to resume our affair without

limitations. That means we go for as long as we're mutually satisfied."

She rolled her eyes. "People only do long-term affairs when they want to get serious eventually. People who want more out of a relationship. People who might even contemplate marriage."

"Not necessarily. I think we know each other's position on marriage, so we don't have to worry about us wanting anything *that* serious. However, I'm at a point in my life where I prefer long-term exclusiveness. Not only do I want a satisfying bed partner, I also want to be with someone I can take out to dinner on occasion, to a movie, to those business functions that I'm oftentimes invited to attend. I don't like women coming on to me anymore. I want to emit an air that I'm taken... even if I'm truly not."

He paused, wanting her to digest what he'd just said. Then he continued. "You enjoy my company and I enjoy yours. I see no reason why we can't continue what we had unless..."

She tilted her head and looked at him, lifting a brow. "Unless what?"

"Unless you're afraid of falling in love with me."

He eased up from his seat, ignoring the burst of longing and love he felt for the woman standing in front of him. The woman he was determined to make fall in love with him to the same degree that he was with her.

He knew now that she wasn't as opposed to restarting their affair as she put on. But she was scared of letting her heart get broken again. So he knew he had to tread lightly but at the same time push harder...if that made sense.

"Are you afraid, Farrah? If you are, then I understand

and totally agree that we should not pick up where we left off."

He immediately saw the effect his words had on her. After her jaw dropped to the floor, she went still. He was convinced she was barely breathing. And her gaze intensified, focused on him. Her eyes zeroed in on him like he was the only thing in their laser beam's target. From the distance separating them, he felt her anger, but he also felt her fear. He actually saw it in her eyes, and he knew at that moment what he'd assumed was right. She was falling in love with him, but was fighting it tooth and nail. She would never, ever admit such a thing.

So he stood there watching her, waiting to see how she planned on getting out of the neat little box he'd just placed her in.

Chapter 11

Think, Farrah!

She nibbled on her bottom lip as she tried unscrambling her brain, refusing to admit Xavier had hit a nerve, which automatically put her on the defensive. "Me? Not being able to control my emotions and fall in love? Please. That is the last thing you, or any man, have to worry about, trust me."

He shrugged. "If you say so."

She didn't like the sound of that. Did he honestly think she'd fall in love with him? Okay, she would admit—although never to him—that she had ended things between them because she'd had feelings for him and had been uncomfortable with those newfound emotions. But she would never let any man suspect she was afraid of losing her heart.

She threw her head back, sending her hair flying over her shoulders. "I'm going to only say this once and I hope you're listening, Xavier. The last thing you have to worry about, and the one thing I am *not* afraid of, is falling in love with you or any man. I've been there, done that and you can believe I'll never go that way again."

"In that case, I see no reason for us not to continue our affair beyond the holidays. In other words, there is no reason not to go back to things being the way they were. And in addition, I see no reason why we can't bring our affair out of the bedroom and start going out more…unless there's a reason you prefer not being seen with me."

Farrah's head was spinning dizzily with everything Xavier was saying. But she was coherent enough to latch on to his last statement. "For what reason would I not want to be seen with you?"

"That you're still pining away for your ex-husband and you don't want him to know you're in a relationship with someone."

If Farrah hadn't been programmed to act in a dignified manner, especially when discussing such an important topic, she would have fallen to the floor and rolled over a few times in laughter. Anyone who knew her and Dustin's history knew there was no way that she was pining for her ex. In fact, whenever she saw him, she wondered why she'd fallen in love with him in the first place. It's not that he'd ever had anything going for him that was so spectacular. But while they'd been in college, he had convinced her he was the best thing since sliced bread and that he would be going places.

She had believed he loved her, wanted to spend the rest of his life with her and they would stay together forever. She didn't even mind during their first year when he couldn't get a job and she had supported the both of them, or the times she'd put up with his dead-beat parents whose way of life was calling for loans and not paying them back.

"So, did I hit it out of the ballpark, Farrah?"

She could only assume he figured that because she hadn't yet responded to his statement. "You didn't come close, Xavier. In fact, you struck out so bad they are replacing you in the game entirely. There is no way I'd ever get back with Dustin, nor do I want to."

She didn't like the look she saw in his eyes. Although he heard what she said, she couldn't tell if he believed her.

"*If* what you say is true, then there is no reason why we can't continue what we once had without limitations, right?"

Farrah's pulse began beating wildly, anxiously, and that cloak of protectiveness she used as a shield immediately went into place. There were lots of reasons why they couldn't continue what they once had. And not imposing limitations was simply out of the question.

Although she would never admit she had developed a weakness for him, the truth of the matter was that on more than one occasion she had lost control and lowered her guard, which was totally unacceptable behavior. When she was with Xavier she had a tendency to let loose, getting buck wild and crazy. Not just in the bedroom—that she could handle. But with her heart. Only with him did she care about the here and now and not worry about the outcome.

She lifted her chin. "There *is* a reason," she said, knowing what she was about to say was an absolute lie. "Have you ever considered that the only reason I don't want to take up where we left off in an affair, Xavier, is because I just don't want to be romantically involved with you any longer?"

Darn. Instead of frowning, he was smiling, which meant he hadn't believed a word she'd just said. Hadn't taken her seriously. She watched as he crossed his arms over his chest and braced his legs apart in a ready-for-combat stance. She hated thinking it, but his standing that way and looking at her with that "I know better" smirk on his face sent a rush of adrenaline up her spine.

"You expect me to believe that, Farrah? The same woman whom I took on the backseat of a private car last night while cruising on a barge on an icy cold night down the Hudson."

She narrowed her eyes at him. "Why can't I convince you it was nothing but sex?"

He shrugged his shoulders. "I don't know, but here's your chance. Convince me. Prove you're not afraid of letting your emotions get in the way of an affair with me, and that your mind is not getting confused with the L-word. Prove to me, Farrah, that for us it's only about sex, which is the only thing we want anyway, and that we don't have to worry about anything else to the point that we establish limitations."

Her mind was spinning in confusion, and she wondered if he'd caused that to happen deliberately. All she knew at that moment was that she had a point to prove to him, several in fact. First, she was capable of keeping her emotions under wraps. Second, she was not still carrying a torch for Dustin. And last but not least, she was not afraid of falling in love with Xavier.

"Fine," she threw out heatedly. "You think you've got everything figured out, but I'm going to prove you wrong, Xavier. I'm going to give you your affair without limitations and then you're going to see just how wrong you are about everything."

Xavier couldn't ignore the burst of happiness that tore through him at that moment, and he had to fight hard to keep a smile off his lips. With some outright manipulation, which he wasn't all that thrilled about, he had moved Farrah into the spot where he wanted her for now.

She had agreed to an affair without limitations, and he doubted that she fully understood exactly what that meant, but she would find out soon enough. Although they would continue to make love just as before, they would not be spending one hundred percent of the time between the sheets. He would take her out on dates, to parties—there were always a number of them to attend this time of year—and she would get to spend time with him around people who meant a lot to him. They were family and friends who would come to love her as much as he did.

"Good, we're on the same page now," he heard himself saying as he crossed the room to her, needing to feel her in his arms, although he could tell she was still somewhat tiffed with him.

"Fine," she said, when he slid his arm around her waist and brought her body closer to his. She might not be happy with him now, but the moment he pulled her into his arms, she came willingly. And when he lowered his head to capture her mouth, there was not a single ounce of resistance in her body.

She leaned in, and he felt her warmth deep, all the way to the pit of his stomach. He wasn't surprised when he felt the shiver ease up his spine and his erection get harder. Desire sizzled through him, and he fought to push it back. This woman could set his body on fire, and at any other time he would take advantage of it. But not this time. He had his game plan tonight and didn't want to ruin it.

But there was no reason he couldn't make love to her mouth if not her body, was there? After all, when it came to kissing, they always indulged in the ultimate enjoyment. Then he remembered. The fact that he had managed to breathe six months without tasting her was a miracle, and he didn't intend to suffer through that agony again.

He finally pulled his mouth away, but their greedy tongues were still intent on doing a tangling dance, if not inside their mouths then out. They always enjoyed this type of play where they took licking and sucking to a whole new level.

And then his tongue was back inside her mouth again, and his arms tightened around her. It wouldn't take much to ease her down on the sofa, push her dress up, pull down those leggings and bury his head between her legs and do a lot of tongue play there. It wouldn't take much enticement for him to kiss every inch of her body. Unfortunately, he would save that specific activity for another day. Unknown her to, this kind of kissing was all they would be doing tonight.

Ah hell, he thought, when he felt her hands wiggle between them and her fingers tug on his zipper. He needed to stop her before she went down on him. There was no way he could resist that. With all the strength he could gather, all the control he could muster, he reached down and took hold of her hand to stop her from going further.

She pulled her mouth from his and looked up at him

with a questioning gaze. "Why are you holding my hands, Xavier?"

Before answering her question, he leaned down and took another lick around her mouth. Hell, she tasted as good as she looked. "I want to give you time to be absolutely sure I'm what you want, Farrah."

He had worded the statement carefully. Instead of saying he wanted her to be sure that the *affair* was what she wanted, he had said he wanted her to be sure that *he* was what she wanted. There was a difference, and over the next few weeks he would show her what that difference was.

"But I already know you're what I want, Xavier."

Yes, she would want him sexually, that was a given. But he wanted her to want him in a way she'd never wanted another man, a way that went deeper than mere sex. He wanted to conquer her heart. For a man who just last week had thought he didn't need the love of a woman, in the last forty-eight hours he had been proven wrong.

"Yes, but I want you to be certain because now that you've agreed to an unlimited affair with me, Farrah, there's no turning back."

She lifted her brow, as if his comment gave her pause. "No turning back" sounded kind of final in his book, so he knew it sounded likewise in hers, but now he was talking for keeps.

She didn't say anything for a long moment and then, "Why are you trying to make things so complicated, Xavier?"

"Sorry if you think I'm doing that, sweetheart, but I just want to make sure a few weeks from now you don't try kicking me out of your life again. I have to know that we want the same thing out of this relationship."

He was trying to defuse any suspicions she had that things with him weren't on the up-and-up. He only hoped when she discovered they weren't she would be too far gone to care.

She nodded slowly. "Okay, I guess that makes sense."

"It does. Besides, another reason I need to make it an early night is because Cameron is flying in tomorrow and I need to have some papers ready for him to sign when he does."

He was deliberately giving her the impression that he was putting work before her. Although she didn't say anything, he could tell she was both surprised and disappointed.

"Oh, well, then I guess I need to go."

"Not before we share dessert and not before you help me with kitchen clean up."

She smiled. "All right."

He wanted to kiss her again, and he figured before she left to return to the hotel that he would, several times. But at least she would be leaving with the knowledge that for the first time, though they'd had the convenience and the privacy to make love, they hadn't.

"Is the car warm enough for you, Ms. Langley?"

Farrah glanced over the seat in front of her at Jules. Xavier had given the driver strict instructions to see to her every comfort, and to especially make sure she was kept warm.

"Yes, thank you for asking."

She settled back against the plush leather seat, determined to replay in her mind all that had transpired tonight and to make sure she hadn't imagined anything.

She'd gone to his house fully intending to convince

him to extend their affair through the holidays, after which, they would go their separate ways again.

For reasons she was still trying to figure out, he hadn't wanted any part of that suggestion. Instead, he wanted to resume the affair with no limitations. He'd even gone so far as to suggest her reluctance to do so was because she was afraid of falling in love with him and because she still harbored feelings for Dustin.

Okay, secretly she would agree the former did have some merit, but the latter did not. To prove him wrong on both counts, she had no choice but to agree to his terms. So technically, they were now involved in a long-term, no-strings relationship.

Even more confusing to her was how, once she'd agreed, their relationship had taken a definite turn. But to where she hadn't a clue. First, it had been the way he'd kissed her. It was greedy and hungry as usual, but it seemed like he was holding back, which didn't make sense. After all, she had agreed to what he'd wanted. And no matter what she'd done, she hadn't changed his mind about sleeping with her, although she knew without a doubt that he'd wanted her.

Men!

Now here she was, riding in the car alone as she returned to her hotel. Truly, what sense did that make? He could have easily asked that she stay the night and she would have. But he hadn't. He'd even suggested she take time to think her decision through. Now, drawing in a deep breath, she decided to do just what he'd suggested.

As the car sped along the Long Island Expressway, she closed her eyes. An unlimited affair with him meant essentially no more booty calls. At least they wouldn't be termed that anymore. She had agreed that she and Xavier would start doing things outside the bedroom.

More than likely they would go out to dinner on occasion, to a movie, to business functions.

She felt a knot forming in the pit of her stomach at the thought of doing those things with him and knew the reason why. She might just begin to enjoy it too much. Her challenge was going to be keeping things in perspective. Though neither of them wanted to take things any further than they had previously, Xavier was now ready for more exclusiveness. At least she could rest assured he still wasn't the marrying kind. Good, she thought, because neither was she.

She opened her eyes and glanced down at her watch. It wasn't even midnight. Depending on how things turned out between Kerrie Shaw and Lori Byers, she could very well be back in Charlotte around this time tomorrow. Doing so would have her out of New York before the snowstorm hit on Sunday. Xavier had even offered to take her to the airport tomorrow. Getting back home might be a good thing. It would put distance between them for at least a week and would give her time to clear her head and decide on the best way to handle him.

Over ice cream and apple pie, Xavier had told her about his trip after the holidays to Los Angeles where he would be for a few days in January. Usually, she wouldn't know about his trips until he was packed and ready to go because that was the type of relationship they'd had. For him to keep her abreast of his plans was going to take some getting used to.

But for now she wanted just to concentrate on what had or hadn't happened tonight. Sex was one of the things that hadn't happened, and for a reason she didn't quite understand. A part of her believed it was intentional on Xavier's part.

She had come here fully expecting dinner followed by hot, mind-blowing sex. That was the only kind she'd ever shared with Xavier, and tonight she had been willing, but for some reason, he had held back.

After dessert he had kissed her a few times, and although she would admit the kisses had been long, drugging and delicious enough to tingle her toes and wet her panties, she had still felt him holding back on her. It was as if he was keeping himself in check, fearful of just what too many slow, deep kisses could do to them.

And then, after they'd cleaned up the kitchen together, he had helped her back into her coat and gloves, had picked her up in his arms and, instead of carrying her upstairs to a bedroom, he had carried her outside and placed her on the backseat of the private car.

He had told her that regardless of whether she stayed in New York over the weekend, he would be seeing her tomorrow and to expect his call. Why was she thinking already that, in addition to the feel of him easing back off sex, she was also losing control of the relationship? Now it seemed as if he had taken the lead role in managing just how things went between them. And she wasn't sure if she particularly liked giving any man that much control over her.

"We'll be at your hotel in less than five minutes, Ms. Langley," the driver interrupted her thoughts to inform her.

"Thanks, Jules."

As they drove into the city, she wondered what would be the best way to take back that control she had somehow lost tonight. She didn't like any man calling the shots and had dispensed with that nonsense at the moment the ink had dried on her divorce papers from Dustin.

After the divorce she had been furious, even resentful, and at one point out for blood. In a fit of spite, she'd thought about suing the other woman. North Carolina was one of a few states that still enforced a century-old case law that said a wife could sue her husband's mistress for breaking up a marriage. Her attorney had been more than happy to do it, and Dustin's attorney had scared her ex-husband shitless by informing him of a recent suit in which the duped ex-wife had gotten nine million dollars richer. Natalie had talked her out of it, but still she'd felt good knowing she had made Dustin sweat for a while.

When the driver brought the car to a stop in front of her hotel, she gathered up her things. She had been so certain about tonight that she'd put her toothbrush in her purse. In a way, she was somewhat disappointed. But then she would be the first to admit engaging in the unknown was kind of exciting. She couldn't help wondering what Xavier had planned for tomorrow. Surely he wasn't going to push for another wasted night. If he did try going that route, she would have to do something about it.

Chapter 12

"Hey, man, you okay?"

Xavier glanced across the desk at Cameron thinking that if he looked like a man who'd had a sleepless night then that was definitely right on the money. After he'd put Farrah inside the car and sent her home, he had walked around his house with a hard-on that wouldn't go down. He'd called himself all kinds of fool. Although he'd known that in the long run he had done the right thing for them, he'd gone to bed with regrets of not having made love to her.

"No, not really," he said, deciding to be honest.

The necessary documents had been signed, and now Cameron Cody owned yet another company. The negotiations had gone well, better than expected. Sleep-deprived or not, when it came to business, Xavier knew he was on top of his game. But now that he and Cameron were alone, that adrenaline high from earlier was fizzling fast.

"What's your problem, Xavier?"

He couldn't help but smile at Cameron's question. For the first time since Dionne, he was actually having a problem with a woman. Before, he'd never considered a female significant enough to cause a problem in his life, but with Farrah things were different.

"I have a lot of decisions to make and I want to be absolutely sure I'm making the right ones."

Cameron leaned back in his seat and chuckled. "I assume these decisions are about Farrah Langley."

Xavier raised a brow. He'd never discussed Farrah with anyone, although he was certain after Donovan's wedding a number of his friends—his godbrothers in particular—had figured he and Farrah were involved in a hot and heavy affair. "How did you know?"

Cameron chuckled. "Because I know you. You started paying late-night visits to the same woman on a rather frequent basis. And since you never discussed these visits or the woman with me or anyone, that was the first sign."

"Sign?"

"Yes, a sign that this particular woman meant something to you and that you thought she was different from all the others."

Xavier nodded slowly. Yes, Farrah was different from the others. At first he'd just enjoyed being in her bed, but then something had begun happening to him, although at first he hadn't known exactly what. It had taken half a year of not being with her to make him realize Farrah was more than a woman he just wanted in his bed. Once he'd seen her again, spent time with her, he'd known she was the only woman he wanted in his life for always. "I'm crazy about her, Cam," he admitted.

"Does she know how you feel?"

Xavier shook his head. "Hell, I just figured it out myself a few days ago. We broke up a week after Donovan's wedding—her idea, not particularly mine. She thought our short-term affair had gone on longer than intended and it was time to move on. I didn't argue and will admit at the time I thought maybe she was right. And then a couple of days ago we ran into each other here in New York. She's in town on business like I am. We went out to dinner that first night and a Broadway play the next. I enjoyed her company and realized just how much I had missed her. Then I knew exactly what had been truly missing from my life for the past six months."

Cameron smiled. "Now you can understand why I wouldn't let up in my pursuit of Vanessa, although it didn't take me as long as it took you to figure out I was in love, and that Vanessa was the woman I wanted in my life."

"Um, that might be true, but I have a feeling I'm going to work just as hard to win her over," Xavier said. He paused, thinking of all the things Cameron had done during his pursuit of Vanessa, and then shook his head and laughed. "Hell, I hope not."

Cameron couldn't help laughing as well. "But in the end it was all worth it."

All Xavier had to do was to see them together to know what Cameron said was true. "I'm definitely in love with Farrah, Cam." Xavier wasn't surprised how easily the words flowed from his lips.

"Good. I like her, so what's the problem?" Cameron asked.

Xavier sighed deeply. After all Cameron had gone through for Vanessa, if anyone understood his plight, it would be him. "She can't seem to get over a bad marriage. Her husband cheated on her and ended up marrying the other woman. He even went so far as to have a child with her while married to Farrah."

Cameron shook his head sadly. "Some bastards really make it hard for the rest of us, don't they?"

Xavier nodded in agreement. Farrah's ex was making it nearly impossible for him. "Yes, it's going to be difficult for her to trust another man."

"Be patient. Some scars are harder to heal than others."

Xavier understood that. It had taken him years to get over the damage Dionne had done to him. But he truly believed in his heart that Farrah and Dionne were nothing alike, and now he had to prove that fact to Farrah.

"I'm sure you have a plan, Xavier."

Xavier chuckled. Cameron knew him well enough to know just how he operated. "Yes. Last night I got her to agree to resume our affair with no limitations. That in itself wasn't an easy task, so I feel good about it. The next thing I intend to do is prove to her that there's more between us than just great sex."

Farrah had expected to get carted off to his bed last night. He could tell. A part of him believed she was somewhat confused as to why he hadn't slept with her. She had tried more than once to tempt him, and he'd known exactly what she was doing. A few times his traitorous body had almost given in, but luckily his ironclad control had ruled.

"Thanks for listening to my woes, Cam."

"Hey, no problem. That's what friends are for. Now, I'm out of here. That snow storm they had predicted for Sunday is blowing in early, and I intend to be gone before then."

Xavier glanced out the window, noticing for the first

time the weather had changed. The sky was white and heavy, the wind blustery. He needed to call Farrah to see if she planned to leave for Charlotte today. A smile touched his lips. Although he knew it would be a bad idea with all the temptation she would present, he kind of liked the idea of her getting snowed in, in the city. Of course he would invite her to move in with him until the worst of the storm passed. He could imagine how it would be if that were to happen.

"What are you smiling about, Xavier?"

He glanced up at Cameron. "Trust me, you don't want to know."

"I've made a decision about things, Ms. Langley."

Farrah glanced over at Lori. Her husband hadn't come with her today, and as far as Farrah was concerned, that was a good sign. She wondered if today would entail another long, drawn out session. They had covered a lot of ground yesterday, revisited a lot of memories, and Farrah hoped doing so had worked.

"And what decision is that, Lori?"

"That I'm fine with a seventy-thirty split. Kerrie's right in thinking that I don't deserve fifty-fifty. Besides, I admit to telling her that years ago, and I won't go back on my word now. Our friendship means more to me than that."

Kerrie glanced over at Lori. "I think you deserve more than seventy-thirty Lori. I'm willing to go back to the original contract between us and honor that."

Lori shook her head. "I won't let you do that. I walked away from the business. You're the one who made it into what it is today, and I won't be greedy about it."

Kerrie then asked, "What about Rudolph? How will he feel about it?"

Lori shrugged. "I told him my decision this morning. He's not happy about it, but it was my decision to make. He'll just have to get over it since this doesn't really concern him. These past few days have made me realize that the business was based on our friendship, our trust and love for each other. I can't let anyone destroy those things."

Farrah couldn't help but admire Lori for the decision she'd made and for standing up to her husband. She wondered if it was the first time Lori had defied him. "Well, I'm glad we've resolved the matter, and I'll get the papers ready to be signed so we can all leave before the weather worsens. It looks like it's about to start snowing any minute."

"It does," Lori said in agreement. "And I want to thank you for reminding me that true friendship will outlast anything, and that's what Kerrie and I have always had."

Kerrie nodded in agreement before reaching across the table and taking Lori's hand in hers.

Farrah drew in a deep breath, feeling good about the resolution and happy about how things had worked out in the end. She glanced at her watch, wondering if she would be able to get a flight out today before the storm hit.

An hour or so later she checked her phone and saw she'd received a text message from Xavier. All it said was—Cold outside. Car will pick you up.

Moments later when she exited the building, she saw his private car parked at the curb waiting for her. Jules smiled when he saw her and quickly opened the car door. "Mr. Kane sent me with instructions to take you wherever you want to go, Ms. Langley."

Farrah smiled as she slid onto the backseat. It was cold, and she couldn't help but appreciate the vehicle's warmth. "Please take me to my hotel. I want to get a flight out before the storm arrives."

At that minute her phone rang. She smiled when she saw it was Xavier and immediately clicked on the call. "Xavier, thanks for sending the car."

"I promised to keep you warm, didn't I?"

Her smile widened. "Yes."

"So did things get resolved today?"

"Yes," she said excitedly. "I feel good in not only resolving another case, but with this particular one, renewing a friendship. Now I'm headed back to the hotel to pack. The storm's coming and I'm afraid if I don't get a flight out today, I might get stranded here."

"I hate to tell you this but you might already be stranded. I heard on the news that they've already started canceling flights headed to New York, which means that flights leaving the city are being impacted."

Farrah frowned, disappointed. "The last thing I want is to get stranded here."

"In that case you might be in luck. Cameron is here and will be flying out in his private plane in a few hours. If you're ready to leave, then you can fly back to Charlotte with him."

Farrah blinked. "I can't impose on Mr. Cody like that, Xavier. He doesn't know me that well."

Xavier laughed. "Cam knows you're a close friend of mine. I'll make the necessary arrangements with him. You just get packed. I'll touch base with you in an hour."

Farrah clicked off the phone, thinking just how appreciative she would be if Xavier could arrange for her to leave New York before the storm hit. But to accompany Cameron Cody in his private plane, she thought, was asking too much. Although he and his wife were Natalie's cousins-in-law, as she'd told Xavier, she didn't want to impose on the man.

She shook her head, somewhat disappointed. If she left the hotel and went straight to the airport, that would mean she wouldn't see Xavier before leaving. Nor had he said anything about wanting to see her again before she left.

"We're here, Ms. Langley."

Farrah pushed her disappointment aside. This had turned out to be a happy day, and she refused to let thoughts of Xavier put a damper on it.

Xavier couldn't ignore the shiver of pleasure that ran down his spine when Jules pulled the car up in front of Farrah's hotel. And then moments later he watched the woman he loved come through the revolving glass doors pulling luggage behind her.

She looked all bundled up in her leather coat, gloves, boots and a furry-looking hat that covered her head. It was cold outside, and according to the weather reports, it was the coldest it had been in New York all year. If the forecasters were right, the following days would get even more frigid with record-breaking temperatures. Combine that with snow and it was a recipe for disaster.

Jules opened the car door for her, and the wide-eyed look of surprise and the warm smile that lit her face caused a sensual jolt to his midsection. "Xavier! I didn't think I'd see you before I—"

He didn't give her a chance to finish what she was saying. In fact he barely gave her time to get settled in the backseat before he leaned over and captured her mouth with his. Damn, he needed her taste. He needed her. And at that moment there was no doubt in his mind that he loved her.

Their mouths mated hungrily and fused passionately as their tongues tangled in a wild and frenzied exchange that had him groaning. Thankfully, Jules drew the privacy shield closed without being told, and Xavier proceeded to pull Farrah into his lap. At that moment he couldn't fight the rush of desire that suddenly consumed him, making him hot, almost causing him to overload. She was returning his kiss measure for measure while sensation after glorious earth-shattering sensation tore into him.

They finally ended the kiss, but he kept his mouth close to hers, a breath away from her moist lips. The look in her eyes almost sent him over the edge. If he were to spread her out on the seat, strip her naked and take her, she wouldn't resist. There was no doubt in his mind that she wanted him as much as he wanted her.

But he wanted her to do more than just need him. He wanted her to love him as much as he loved her. To reach that goal he had to prove to her there was more between them than just the physical. That didn't mean he would stop making love to her. He just needed to find a balance between the physical and the emotional so that she would see she was not only desired but also loved.

"Now what were you about to say?" he asked, pulling her close to him while wrapping his arms around the back of the seat.

His gaze went immediately to her lips when they began moving again. He liked kissing them, nibbling on them, licking them and doing all kinds of naughty things to them.

"I said I didn't think I would see you before I left," Farrah said.

Unable to resist any longer, Xavier leaned down and swiped a slow lick off her lips. "Did you honestly think I would let you leave without seeing you again and saying goodbye?"

"After last night I wasn't so sure."

Xavier pulled her closer to him. "Well, I am here, and in fact I intend to go back to Charlotte with you and Cam."

She blinked as if she wasn't certain she'd heard him correctly. "You're going back to Charlotte?"

"Yes, there's no reason for me to get stranded here, too. Besides, if the storm is as bad as the forecasters predict, the office will be closed anyway. I can fly back sometime next week to finalize things."

"Oh."

"I've got a favor to ask of you," he said, pulling off her gloves, needing to feel his skin enmeshed with hers.

"What?"

He entwined their fingers and felt the warmth of her flesh. He looked down at their joined hands in her lap. "I've been invited to several holiday parties and I want you to go as my date."

He felt her flinch but chose to ignore her reaction. "I had originally planned not to accept the invitations, but since we've decided to remove the limitations on our affair, I think it would be nice for us to share the holiday spirit, don't you?" Xavier figured those parties would be perfect for him and Farrah to be officially seen out together as a couple.

Farrah wasn't sure if what he was proposing would be nice or not. She certainly hadn't expected him to ask her out on a date so soon. And from what he'd said, it sounded as if it would be several dates. She knew it might sound pretty sleazy to some, but she much preferred sharing her time with him in the bedroom in a strictly physical and nonemotional affair. However, it had nothing to do with the reasons he had accused her of last night. To get him to believe that would be close to impossible.

Instead of answering his question, she posed one of her own. "How many parties are we talking about, Xavier?"

He leaned over and began nibbling on her neck, ears and the corners of her mouth. "Um, I think we're talking about three or four. And then there's the New Year's Eve party that Uriel and his wife, Ellie, are hosting at the lake."

She gazed up at him. "And you want me to attend all those parties with you?"

"Yes. Is there a reason why you can't? Have you made other plans for the holidays?"

Farrah inwardly sighed. Unfortunately, she hadn't made other plans. She figured on it being a low-key time for her. Her company was closed for ten days, and she had planned to buy a number of books and to stay in, relax and have a read-a-thon.

"Farrah?"

Why did he have to say her name in such a way that waylaid her senses and sent a ripple of desire through her? "Yes?"

"Have you made plans for the holidays already?"

"No, but—but—"

He lifted his head and stared down at her. "But what?"

How could she tell him that she wasn't comfortable dating the way normal couples did? How could she explain that she equated dating with establishing the foundation for something more serious, and she didn't do serious?

Instead of wasting her time explaining anything, she said, "Nothing. Going to all those events will be fine. Just let me know when and where and I'll meet you there."

Xavier threw his head back and laughed. "Sorry, sweetheart, but it doesn't quite work that way. I'll let you know when and where, but I'll pick you up. We won't show up in separate cars."

She nibbled on her bottom lip wondering why it mattered if they both ended up at the same place. But she didn't want to argue with him about it. She glanced out the window and noticed they had passed the exit for the airport. "Where are we going?"

"Back to my place to get luggage. When I talked to you earlier I was at the office finishing up a few things."

She nodded. "And where's Mr. Cody?"

"Cameron has his own private car and will join us at the airport at the designated time."

"Okay."

She settled back against his chest, and when he shifted positions, she could feel his hard erection pressing against her backside. What she felt was a sure sign that he wanted her, so why wasn't he taking her?

As the car sped toward Long Island, she sat cuddled in Xavier's lap, thinking and wondering just what was going on in that mind of his.

Chapter 13

A few hours later Farrah entered her home, and Xavier walked in behind her. He thought the flight from New York had gone well, with Cam and Farrah chatting amiably during most of the trip. More than once Cam had shot him a look that had clearly asked, *Why have you kept her hidden?*

He closed the door, leaned against it and watched as she moved across the room and switched on a lamp. Although it was late afternoon, it had already been dark when the plane had landed. Two private cars had sat waiting on the airstrip. One had whisked Cameron home, and Xavier had placed Farrah and her luggage with him in the other.

Swallowing thickly, he recalled how tempted he had been to take her directly to his place instead of bringing her here. In the end, his common sense had won out. He had to be patient in his handling of her.

When she moved to turn on another lamp he glanced around thinking how he had missed coming here.

"Thanks for everything, Xavier, especially for making the arrangements to get me back home."

His gaze returned to her. "You're welcome."

Xavier straightened from leaning against the door, and his stomach clenched when she walked slowly toward him. He wasn't sure what she planned to do, but from the look in her eyes, he had a feeling he was in trouble.

When she reached him, she wrapped her arms around his neck. And when she tilted her face up to him, he lowered his head to give her what she wanted. What he wanted. The moment their lips connected, he slid his tongue in her mouth and began mating hungrily with hers. She melted into him, and he deepened the kiss by widening his mouth over hers.

He needed this contact as much as he needed to breathe. And she clung to him as if she felt the same way. For him, that was a good sign, one he intended to cultivate any way that he could. He reluctantly broke the kiss and whispered against her moist lips, "Come home with me tonight."

He saw the indecisiveness in her arched brow and knew why. One of their unspoken agreements had been he would visit her here. She'd preferred things that way because it had given her a semblance of control. What she didn't know, and what she would eventually discover, was that no matter how many roadblocks she erected, he intended to rush right through each and every one of them.

When she didn't say anything, he leaned down to place kisses around her mouth. "I figure we could grab something to eat at the Racetrack Café and go to my place to watch a movie and then go to sleep."

"Sleep?" she asked in a deep, raspy tone.

"Yes, if that's what you want to do," he said in a husky voice. "But would you really want to?"

Farrah threw her head back and groaned deep in her throat when the tip of Xavier's tongue became naughty and began licking all around her mouth. The man was torturing her something awful. She tried pushing the thoughts from her mind that he was asking her to relinquish control by doing something atypical in their relationship.

However, she *had* agreed to an unlimited affair with him, hadn't she? And she did want to make love to him again, didn't she? Should it matter if it was his bed or hers? His home or hers?

"Farrah?"

She met his gaze. The look she saw in his eyes was enough to make her panties wet. "No, I don't want to sleep," she heard herself saying. "And yes, I want to spend the night at your place."

Farrah moved around her bedroom unpacking her things, while at the same time tossing a few items into an overnight bag. The private car had taken Xavier home where he would get his car and come back for her in an hour.

Snapping her overnight bag shut, she moved from her bedroom toward the living room, intent on making sure she was ready when he returned. Tremors of anticipation were racing through her at the thought that he would be taking her back to the place where they had met. A place where a number of his friends, as well as hers, hung out.

She nearly jumped when the doorbell sounded, and moved toward the door. She looked through the peephole, and sensations flooded her insides. It was Xavier, and as she had done, he had taken time to change clothes. Opening the door, she saw he was no longer wearing a suit but had changed into a pair of jeans and a shirt. And this was the first time he had appeared on her doorstep without his signature bottle of wine.

She felt his gaze roam over her, and when he smiled, she couldn't help but smile, too. "Ready?" he asked, taking her overnight bag from her hand.

"Yes."

He stepped back, and after she locked the door behind her, he took her hand and escorted her to his two-seater sports car.

"Did you enjoy your meal?" Xavier asked Farrah a short while later at the Racetrack Café.

The popular bar and grill in town was jointly owned by several drivers on the NASCAR circuit. Over the years it had become one of his favorite places to eat and to hang out, especially on the weekends.

Tonight the place was crowded, understandably so since there was a live band every Friday night. Couples were on the dance floor, and he couldn't wait to get out there himself. The need to hold Farrah in his arms was hitting him hard.

"Yes, everything was wonderful."

"Do you remember that we met here?" He wondered if she remembered that night like he did.

She smiled. "Yes, I know. It was girls night out for me and Natalie. She had her eyes on Donovan and my eyes were on you. I thought you were hot."

Xavier chuckled. One of the things he liked about

Farrah was her honesty. She was up front with her responses. "You thought so?"

"Yes, I still do," she said softly at the same time one of her bare feet intentionally rubbed against his pants leg.

He held her gaze, fully aware of what she was trying to do. It wouldn't take much to push him over the edge. She was ready for them to leave and go to his place to be alone.

"Hey, you two, when did you get back?"

He glanced up to find Donovan Steele and his wife, Natalie, standing at their table. Immediately Farrah was out of her seat to give her best friend a hug, while likewise, he stood to shake Donovan's hand and invite him and Natalie to join them.

"We decided to head back before the snowstorm hit," he said, smiling over at Donovan. "Cameron made that possible since he was anxious to return to Charlotte anyway. We caught a ride back on his private plane."

Donovan chuckled. "I can just imagine Cam wanting to get back. Now that Vanessa is pregnant, he doesn't like being away from her for too long."

"So you didn't get any shopping in?" Natalie asked Farrah, grinning.

"Are you kidding?" Farrah laughed. "You know I don't do cold weather well. I was ready to come home the minute the temperature dropped below twenty."

Xavier leaned back in his chair and noticed Farrah seemed comfortable with them being seen together as a couple tonight. During the course of their meal, several people they knew had stopped by their table to say hello.

"Since the two of you have finished eating, will you be leaving here soon?" Donovan asked.

Xavier glanced over at Farrah and saw the hopeful

look in her eyes but chose to ignore it. "Not until we get a few dances in, starting now, so please excuse us," he said, standing up and extending his hand out to Farrah when he heard the band play a slow number. She took it and stood.

He was grateful she wasn't upset that he was stalling about leaving. But he wanted her to enjoy doing things with him other than making love. He pulled her into his arms the moment their feet touched the dance floor. Wrapping his arms around her waist, he drank in her luscious fragrance. "Do you remember the first time we danced here together?" he asked, angling his head and leaning his mouth close to her ear.

She nodded, tilting her head back to look up at him. "Yes, it was right after we spent an hour or so in the game room. You beat me at everything that night. Pool. Darts. Pinball."

He chuckled. "Yes, but you weren't so bad. In fact I thought you were pretty good."

She seemed pleased with his compliment. "Really?"

"Yes, really. I think we need to play a few of those games again sometime."

She studied his gaze. "But not tonight."

He chuckled. "No, definitely not tonight."

He pulled her tighter in his arms, and she rested her head against his chest. He felt his desire for her growing and his love right along with it. He tightened his arm around her even more, and glancing over at their table, he saw Donovan and Natalie watching them with curious eyes. But he didn't care. The only thing he cared about was the feel of her in his arms. The woman whose head was pressed against his heart. A heart that belonged to her whether she knew it or not.

They moved to the slow music, and luckily for him,

when the song ended, another slow one began. And just like before, he held her close. At one point he rested his lips close to her ear and sang parts of the song to her. In between the lyrics, he whispered just what he wanted to do to her later. And he was as detailed and explicit as he could be.

When the song came to an end, before they parted, Farrah leaned closed to him and whispered, "Don't be all talk. Do it."

Xavier decided to accept her challenge. He took her hand in his and led her back over to their table. After quickly gathering their coats and her purse, they bid good-night to their friends and left.

They didn't share much conversation in the car. Instead, Farrah stared out the window at the moonless sky, although there were a number of bright stars overhead.

She figured there was nothing left to be said between them since they both knew what they wanted. But that didn't keep her from anticipating what was in store. She didn't have any regrets about them being together and couldn't help thinking how easy it had been to be out with him tonight. She had enjoyed herself before dinner, during dinner and after dinner.

They had discussed a number of topics, and when people who knew them had approached their table, it hadn't bothered her when she could tell they assumed she and Xavier were an item. Even when Donovan and Natalie had shown up and joined them, she hadn't been bothered by the knowing looks Natalie had given her.

Farrah's attention was pulled back to the present when they came to the entrance of Xavier's subdivision, and he pulled up to the security gate. Moments later he drove through. Most of the homes they passed were adorned with holiday decorations. It then dawned on her that she hadn't bothered putting up a tree since her divorce from Dustin. At one time she used to fully embrace the merriment of the season and would look forward to all the holiday festivities.

When Xavier's car pulled into the driveway to his home and the garage door went up, she felt an anxiousness in the pit of her stomach. She was here at the place he considered his primary home. After the garage door closed behind him and he'd brought the car to a stop, he killed the engine before glancing over at her and smiling. "Welcome to my home, Farrah."

There was something about what he said that sent a warm feeling through her. "Thanks for bringing me here."

And she truly meant it. There *was* something about being here, being a part of Xavier's element and sharing his personal space that had her feeling emotions she had never felt before.

He opened the car door and she watched as he moved around the front of the vehicle to open the door for her. He extended his hand to her, and she took it, and then, surprising her, he whisked her off her feet and into his arms.

"Xavier!"

He lowered his head and captured the squeal from her lips, effectively silencing her while mating his mouth hungrily and greedily with hers. His tongue was devouring her, escalating her desire and longing for him as he took her mouth with a mastery that made her groan.

Moments later he released her mouth and began walking with her toward his back door. Desire began spiraling through her when he opened the door. She didn't say a word. She just stared up at him while he continued to hold her in his arms.

He pushed the door open and carried her over the threshold. She could barely see her surroundings as he swiftly moved through his kitchen, dining room and living room and then carried her up the stairs.

Xavier walked down a hall before finally entering a dark bedroom. He placed her in the middle of the bed before turning on a lamp to bring light into the room. It was then that she looked at him and saw the heat within his gaze. Her eyes roamed all over every square inch of his muscular body after he removed his coat and tossed it aside. The muscles bulging beneath his shirt made her appreciate the fact he was a man with the ability to make her mind incapable of thought. With Xavier all she could do was feel.

He unbuttoned his shirt, then removed it to reveal one incredibly hot-looking chest dusted with hair she wouldn't mind running her fingers through or burying her nose in, while inhaling his masculine scent.

When her gaze moved from his chest to meet his eyes, he said, "In case you're wondering what I'm doing, I'm about to prove to you, Farrah Langley, that I am not all talk."

Chapter 14

No, he wasn't all talk, Farrah thought a short while later as his engorged erection pushed through her womanly folds to join their bodies as one.

Already she had climaxed from his mouth twice, and every single inch of her was still humming for more. How was he able to do that? He used his mouth in ways that should be outlawed.

Once he had stripped every stitch of clothing from her body and encased his huge erection into a condom, he had joined her in bed. A slow, sensual smile had touched his lips when he pulled her into his arms, and anticipation had rammed through her, making her want him that much more.

"At last," she whispered when she felt the strength of him continue to push through her. He lifted her hips in his big hands, holding her steady while he pushed inside of her to the hilt. And then he threw his head back and growled satisfaction. He began moving inside of her, sending sensations from where their bodies were joined to every part of her body, touching every single nerve ending and making breath whoosh from her lungs.

Each stroke, each tantalizing thrust, made her moan his name over and over. He lowered his head to her breasts and captured a nipple between his lips and began sucking on it like it was the best thing he'd ever tasted. She felt on the verge of total sensuous madness and ultimate fulfillment.

"Farrah!"

She knew the moment his body exploded, and she tightened her legs around his waist when she felt him driven to yet another orgasm. She screamed his name when she felt herself losing control, digging her fingers deep in his shoulders while doing so. He continued to thrust into her, over and over again.

It was only then he slumped off her, still keeping her in his arms and their bodies connected. Even now it seemed he wasn't ready to let her go. And for the moment, as he held her in his arms, there was no other place she'd rather be.

The sound of cabinet doors opening and closing downstairs made Xavier open his eyes to squint against the sunlight coming in through his window. He smiled, realizing he was in his bedroom. His bed. And he had made love to Farrah in it last night. To him that was a major accomplishment.

He gazed up at the ceiling remembering last night. Oh, what a night. After removing his own clothes he had proceeded to remove hers before tasting every single inch of her body. Her full sweet breasts had been heavenly, the dark nipples meant for sucking and licking.

The sounds she'd made when his mouth touched her body only made him want to do even more things to her. And they were things that had made his erection swell even more.

By the time he had eased between her legs, while she had clutched his shoulders tight and wrapped her long legs around his waist, he'd known they would be having orgasms all over the place. They had. The mere memory had his erection throbbing. He wanted her again, and he wanted her now.

Easing out of bed, he slipped into the jeans he had discarded last night. He went into the bathroom to quickly wash his face and brush his teeth and couldn't help but smile when he saw her toothbrush already in the holder beside his.

He moved slowly down the stairs, and when his nose picked up the aroma of coffee, he increased his pace. He rounded the corner to the kitchen and stopped dead in his tracks. Farrah was standing at the refrigerator, leaning over to look inside and wearing the shirt he'd worn last night. It barely covered her rear end and he could clearly see the luscious swell of her butt cheeks, which meant she wasn't wearing any panties.

It could have been his groan that made her aware he was behind her. She turned, and they stared at each other, not saying anything. It was as if time stood still.

He finally moved, crossed the room to her and, without saying a word, he lifted her into his arms, carried her over to the table and sat down in the chair with her straddling his lap. He wanted her. Now.

He took her mouth, mated with it voraciously while she took matters into her own hands by lowering his zipper to release his erection from bondage. Once free, his erection swelled in anticipation, and when he released her mouth, he whispered against her moist lips, "I want to come inside of you."

He knew just what he was saying, exactly what he was asking. They both were fully aware that since the night they'd met neither had indulged in sex with anyone else. And as far as he was concerned, they wouldn't be making love with anyone but each other from now on. They both had good health records, so as far as he was concerned, there was no reason they couldn't be skin-to-skin, flesh-to-flesh and make love with the purpose of giving each other the most primitive pleasure possible. He'd never released his semen inside a woman before but wanted to do so with her. He just hoped and prayed that she went along with it.

He watched her nervously nibble on her bottom lip, which meant she was considering his request. "Why?" she asked.

"Because every time I sank my body into yours," he whispered, "I wanted to know what it's like to feel you without any barriers and to know when I come I will fill you with the very essence of me. Not for the purpose of making a baby, but for the purpose of knowing how it feels to mingle my semen with your juices when we share pleasure."

His pulse throbbed painfully in his throat as he waited for her to make the next move. Her grip on his erection tightened, and she lifted her body off his lap so he could slide inside of her. As he began pushing forward, she groaned while her muscles clenched him all the way. And when he met her gaze he saw a mirror of desire so heated it almost took his breath away.

He pushed farther inside of her and knew the exact moment the physical and the emotional became one, merging in a way that robbed him of any coherent thought other than to be with her like this. And when he began moving, he felt her heated flesh consume him with every thrust. Unable to retain hold of his sanity, he leaned over and devoured her mouth as he gave her body and the chair one hell of a workout.

And then it happened. An explosion that nearly knocked the chair from under them. In a mad rush his semen filled her, triggering her climax. She screamed his name, and he gritted his teeth as he continued to pump into her. Hard. Fast. He was giving her all he had with no holding back. This was the way it was supposed to be, he thought. This was the way he wanted it. And from her deep, guttural scream this was the way she wanted it as well.

Little did she know that for them this was only the beginning.

Farrah sat at Xavier's kitchen table and glanced out the window that faced the majestic Palisades Golf Course. Already golfers were moving about. Luckily the curtains had been drawn when they'd made out in the very chair she was sitting in a short while ago. Xavier had assured her that even if the curtain had been open it would have been highly unlikely that anyone would have seen what they'd done in his kitchen. Still, the thought couldn't help but make her blush.

She took another sip of her coffee as she moved her gaze from the window to the man standing at the stove preparing pancakes. He hadn't bothered to snap up his jeans that hung low on lean hips, and they looked so darn good on his hard masculine thighs and fine-as-a-dime backside. Her gaze traveled upward and did a wide sweep of his hairy chest, tight abs, well-defined arm muscles and wide shoulders.

She moved her gaze upward, past his broad shoulders to his face. He had long lashes, the kind most women would kill for. And the shadow darkening his jaw indicated he hadn't bothered to shave. Then there were his lips, full and inviting. She felt heat flood her stomach when she remembered all the things those lips and his mouth had done to her.

She released a deep breath, suddenly feeling the effect of the caffeine. The effect of Xavier Kane. The man had a gorgeous body, and he most certainly knew how to use it.

"You like what you see, Farrah?"

She blinked, wondering how he'd known she was staring at him when he was supposed to be concentrating on fixing breakfast. He looked up and smiled before turning around to face her while leaning his hip against the kitchen counter.

"How could I not like what I see? You're a straight guy, pretty well-off and you look pretty darn good in a pair of jeans. And you can make me purr in the bedroom. According to some women, a man with those qualities is a rarity these days."

He lifted a brow. "Some women?"

"Yes, those looking for a mate."

"Oh, I see." He didn't say anything for a minute and then asked, "What are you doing next Saturday night?"

She blinked. His question had caught her off guard. She hesitated for a second and then said, "I don't recall having any plans. Why?"

"I'd like you to go to a party with me."

She placed her coffee cup down, feeling anxiety set in. "A party?"

"Yes."

Her anxiety increased. Although he had mentioned

attending parties with him, she wasn't prepared to do so this soon.

"It's being given by Donovan's brother Morgan and his wife, Lena. A holiday fundraiser to benefit underprivileged kids."

Instead of saying anything, Farrah picked up her cup to take a sip of her coffee. She needed to think about that. She didn't know Morgan Steele that well, but she had known Lena for years. As a real estate agent, Lena had been the one to sell her and Dustin their first home, and four years later she had sought out Lena's services to find her another place after their divorce.

"Farrah?"

She glanced up and met Xavier's gaze. His expression didn't give anything away, but she had a feeling he fully expected her to turn him down, although she *had* agreed to the affair without limitations. In a way, she felt foolish for letting past pain dictate how she lived her life.

She forced her eyes away from his to glance out the window, knowing she couldn't hide behind her pain forever. Maybe it was time to take a stand and finally move on. Something she hadn't done and something it seemed Xavier was hell-bent on forcing her to do.

She glanced back at him and swallowed deeply before saying, "Yes. I'll go to the party with you."

Chapter 15

Farrah stared at herself in the full-length mirror. When was the last time she had dressed to please a man? And as much as she'd tried convincing herself she'd purchased this dress because she'd liked it, deep down she'd bought it because she figured Xavier would like it. It was blue, his favorite color, and the style of the dress showed off her figure. Even Natalie had said so when the two had gone shopping.

At least there would be people at the party she would know besides the host and hostess. Donovan and Natalie would be there, as well as other members of the Steele family. And Xavier had mentioned a couple of his god-brothers would be in attendance as well.

Last weekend, she had ended up spending the entire time at Xavier's home. On Saturday night he had brought her back home to get more clothes and to dress for a movie.

She laughed softly to herself when she thought how Xavier had threatened never to take her to a movie again if she had to cry through the entire feature. She hadn't been able to help it, convinced during most of the film the hero was going to lose his life and never return to the heroine.

When she heard the doorbell sound, she slowly inhaled a breath of air and gave herself time to release it. Xavier had returned to New York on Tuesday to finalize a few things and had called every night to see how she was doing. He'd returned to Charlotte late last night and had called her this morning to invite her to his place for breakfast. Unfortunately, she had been on her way out the door for her hair and nail appointment.

As she headed for the door, a part of her wondered what on earth she was doing by letting another man get under her skin. But in reality, he'd done more than get under her skin. He had licked every part of it at one time or another. She would be the first to admit that although she was still trying with all her might to keep her guard in place, the time she was beginning to spend with him outside of the bedroom was awakening something within her that she thought had long ago died a brutal death. She could actually say she enjoyed spending time with a man in something other than a sexual affair.

She stopped walking and squeezed her eyes shut for a second, remembering why she had broken things off between them six months ago. Why wasn't the thought of becoming too close not scaring her out of her wits now?

A shiver ran down her spine as she opened her eyes and resumed walking. It was hard to describe what she was feeling these days. It was as if each and every time Xavier touched her he was branding her for life. She knew the idea of such a thing sounded absolutely crazy and probably was, but she couldn't let go of the question running through her head. Why was she comfortable with how things were between them now?

She opened the door, and he stood there, leaning in her doorway, and as usual, looking as sexy as ever. For some reason, he seemed even more so today, dressed in a pair of jeans, a white shirt and a chocolate brown suede jacket. He smiled at her in a way that deepened the lines around his lips and brought out a dimple she rarely saw. And then she saw something flame to life in his gaze, and her heart began pounding in her chest. She felt sensual stirrings in the pit of her stomach.

"Xavier," she said in a raspy voice that she couldn't hide. "Welcome back to Charlotte." She took a step back to let him inside.

"It's good to be back. I missed you." And then he reached out for her, pulled her into his arms and captured her mouth in his. A part of her understood his craving since it mirrored her own hunger. He said he'd missed her. She honestly didn't know what to make of that. They had been together nearly a year before and had gone weeks without seeing each other, and not once had he ever admitted to missing her.

But tonight he had.

He finally pulled his mouth away but rested his forehead against hers, drawing in a deep breath while she did likewise. He then whispered against her moist lips, "It wouldn't take much to strip you naked right now."

"What's stopping you?" she murmured, taking a quick lick of his lips and causing his erection to jump. She felt it and couldn't help but smile at his body's response to her words.

His gaze roamed over her before returning to her

eyes. "It's tempting, sweetheart, but we have a party to attend."

She leaned forward and wrapped her arms around his neck. "You mean you'd rather go to a party tonight than stay here and spend some productive time with me?"

A smile spread across his lips. "No, but I plan for us to go to that damn party and when it's over I'll bring you back here and get a lot of productive time in."

"You might be too tired."

He threw his head back and laughed. "Not on your life, sweetheart, so come on and let's go. The sooner we can make an appearance at the party, the sooner we can get back here and get naughty."

She couldn't help but smile. "I'm holding you to that, Xavier Kane."

"Will you be withdrawing your membership from the club, X?"

Xavier glanced up at one of his godbrothers, Virgil Bougard. "What gives you that idea, V?" he asked, taking a sip of his wine.

"The way you're acting with Farrah Langley. Tonight's the first time I've seen you out with a woman in a long time and unless I'm seeing wrong, you're quite taken with her."

Xavier smiled. No, Virgil wasn't seeing wrong. But then, even if he were to explain how things were, Virgil wouldn't understand.

"And what do you think you see, V?" he couldn't help but ask. He could tell Virgil was getting annoyed with his evasiveness.

Virgil frowned. "I see you acting almost as bad as Uriel. At least he's married. Just look at you now. You're talking to me but not once have you taken your eyes off Farrah."

Xavier knew that much was true. He had pretty much hung by Farrah's side most of the evening. Only when Natalie and Vanessa had come and grabbed her had he sought out Virgil's company for a while.

"Xavier?"

He glanced back to Virgil. "Yes?"

"I said that—"

"Mind if I join you guys?"

He glanced over at the woman who walked up. Marti Goshay. They'd been involved in a sex-only affair a few years ago that hadn't even lasted a month. That was all of her he could take, especially when she'd begun hinting at a serious affair that she'd wanted to end in marriage.

"Would it matter if we said that we did mind?" Virgil asked the woman.

Xavier had to keep from smiling. He'd forgotten there was bad blood between Virgil and Marti. Some claimed she was the reason her sister had dumped Virgil a few years ago over some lie Marti had told.

Ignoring Virgil, Marti turned her attention to Xavier. "I thought I'd give you my business card. I hadn't heard from you in a while and figured you probably didn't know my phone number had changed."

He nodded as he accepted the card she handed him. Not that he would use it. He intended to toss it in the trash at the next opportunity. Of course, Marti would think the only reason he hadn't contacted her in almost two years was because he didn't have her new phone number. The woman really thought a lot of herself. She was attractive, true enough, but her beauty was only on the outside. Farrah's beauty, he thought, was both inside and out.

"How would you like to attend the Tina Turner concert with me next weekend, Xavier?" she asked him.

"I'll be busy next weekend."

Virgil decided not to be so subtle. "He's involved with someone, Marti. Move on."

The woman seemed amused by that bit of news. "Who? Definitely not the woman you brought here tonight," she said smiling. "Everybody knows Farrah Langley couldn't hold on to her husband. He was involved in an affair, so what does that tell you?"

Xavier turned his dark, laser sharp eyes on Marti and said, "It tells me the man was a damn fool." He walked off, leaving Virgil to deal with her, knowing without a doubt that his godbrother could.

"I thought the party was nice, Xavier. Thanks for bringing me."

He glanced over at Farrah as they pulled out of Morgan's driveway. "Thank you for coming."

Farrah leaned back against the headrest and closed her eyes. The party had been nice, and she hadn't once felt awkward being seen out with him. In fact, she'd read a lot of envy in the gazes of a number of women. What she'd told Xavier earlier tonight was true. He would be a great catch for any woman.

Even her.

She snapped her eyes back open and glanced over at him. His full attention seemed to be on driving, but her full attention was on him. What made her put herself in the group with all those other women when she wasn't interested in a serious relationship? She didn't think of Xavier in terms of a good catch, but rather a perfect lover. What if she began seeing him in a whole new light?

She shook her head and then turned her attention to the objects outside the car window, refusing to go there. The only reason she was thinking such things was because of how good she felt. She had enjoyed a good party and now she was looking forward to an even better night. That had to be it. It couldn't be any other reason.

"What are you doing next weekend, Farrah?"

She glanced back over at Xavier. "Why do you want to know?"

"I have tickets to the *Nutcracker* and was wondering if you'd go with me?"

She drew in a deep breath. Now was the time to tell him that although she had enjoyed herself with him tonight, they shouldn't overdo it. But for some reason, she couldn't fix her mouth to say that. Especially when she enjoyed the *Nutcracker.*

"Yes, I'd love to go with you," she heard herself saying.

He smiled. "Good."

Farrah looked back out of the car's window, not sure if it was good or not.

Chapter 16

Farrah tried shifting to another position and discovered she couldn't, due to the masculine body still connected to hers. Ever since Xavier had stopped using a condom, he liked drifting off to sleep with his manhood still inside of her and one of his legs thrown over hers. More than once over the past few weeks, she had awakened from the feel of his erection stretching her inner muscles as it enlarged inside of her.

It was hard to believe that next week would be Christmas, and so far she had been Xavier's date to four parties and to the *Nutcracker*. Since they ran into most of the same people at all the events, she knew everyone thought they were having a hot and heavy love affair…and she would have to agree with them.

That thought no longer bothered her, and each and every day she was beginning to feel more and more comfortable with him and how their relationship was going. Just last week he'd flown her to New York to spend a few days with him while he'd wrapped up business there. She had stayed with him at his home, spending her days shopping and her nights in his bed.

Needing to go to the bathroom, she tapped him on the shoulder and his sleep-laden sexy eyes stared into hers. "I have to go to the bathroom," she whispered.

He lifted his leg off hers and disconnected their bodies before flipping on his stomach. From the sound of his even breathing, he had gone back to sleep within seconds. She smiled as she eased out of the bed. Poor baby, she thought. Evidently she had worn him out.

The light shining from the bathroom showed their clothes were scattered all over the floor. They had begun stripping the moment they had entered her bedroom. How they'd made it up the stairs with their clothes on was beyond her.

After using the bathroom, she was returning to the bed and decided to gather up the scattered clothing along the way and toss them on a chair. She picked a business card off the floor that evidently had fallen out of Xavier's jacket. She was about to put it back inside the pocket when she read the words someone had scrawled on the back.

Call me. You won't regret it.

She frowned when she flipped the card over. Marti Goshay, Attorney-at-Law.

Her frown deepened. Although she didn't know Marti Goshay personally, she knew of her. And she'd known from that night at the party that Morgan and Lena had guessed the woman had the hots for Xavier. Farrah had heard from Natalie that Xavier and Marti had dated a while back, and from the looks Marti had

had in her eyes whenever she'd glanced at Xavier, the woman wanted him back.

Farrah had been talking to Natalie and Vanessa that particular night and had seen Marti hand Xavier her business card. He had taken it, and at the time Farrah had wondered why. Now she wanted to know why he'd kept it. That had been almost two weeks ago. Hadn't he claimed he wanted a long-term affair with her because he was tired of women coming on to him? So why hadn't he let Marti Goshay know he was already involved?

Not even bothering to fight back the anger and jealousy she suddenly felt, she quickly moved to the bed to tap Xavier on the shoulder. "Wake up, Xavier. You need to leave. Now."

She had to tap him a couple more times before he finally awoke. "Xavier, you need to leave."

He lifted his head and flipped on his back to stare up at her with sleep-filled eyes. "What's wrong?"

"Nothing other than this," she said, dropping the business card onto his naked chest.

He rubbed a hand down his face before picking up the card. He considered it for a moment and then tossed it on her nightstand. "Come back to bed, Farrah."

His command angered her even more. "I won't, and I want you out of my bed. Now," she said, looming over him, in his face.

Instead of moving, he stretched out, placed his hands behind his head and stared up at her. "Why?"

She rolled angry eyes. "I just told you why."

"No, you didn't."

And before she could blink, he had reached out and grabbed her hands and tumbled her down in the bed with him. He shifted his position, and now she was the one on her back with him looming over her. "Now tell me why you're upset, Farrah."

"That business card fell out of your jacket."

He shrugged. "And?"

That one word seemed to make her angrier. "And that was enough."

He chuckled. "I care to differ. Marti Goshay gave me that business card at Morgan and Lena's party."

"But you kept it."

"Only because I'd forgotten about it. I had intended to throw it away." Now it was his eyes that darkened with anger. "And just what are you accusing me of?"

"What do you think?"

For a few seconds Xavier just stared down at her, and then a smile replaced his anger. "You're jealous."

That observation really riled her. "I am *not* jealous. I detest men who can't be trusted. Now get off of me."

Xavier released her and eased off the bed. He moved across the room and slumped down in the chair. "So you're saying I can't be trusted because you found a business card in my jacket?"

She sat up in bed. "A business card from an old girlfriend who said to call her."

"And you figured I would?"

"You kept the card, Xavier."

She fought back the tears. She wouldn't tell him that was the first sign she'd gotten that Dustin was cheating. It was the first one she'd gotten and the main one she'd overlooked, thinking there was nothing to it. She had been a fool not to catch the early warning signs. She wouldn't be a fool ever again.

"Does your mistrust of me have anything to do with that ass you were married to?"

"And if it does?"

He held her gaze. "Then I want you to stop."

"Stop?"

"Yes. Stop comparing me to him, Farrah." He slowly shook his head. "You still don't get it, do you?"

She crossed her arms over her chest. "And just what am I supposed to be getting?"

"The fact that no other woman interests me because I love you."

Her mouth dropped open. "Love me? That's crazy."

He eased to his feet. "Maybe. And what's even crazier is that I believe you love me back. You're just afraid to admit it. However, your overblown jealousy just proved I'm right."

She glared over at him. "You're not right. I don't love you."

He smiled. "Yes, you do, and please don't say what we've been sharing was nothing but sex. Sex between us is good—hell, it's unbelievable, Farrah. But nothing can be that good unless there's some heavy-duty love thrown into the mix. For the past three weeks I've deliberately and painstakingly tried proving to you that we're good together, in or out of bed. Think about it." He then moved to walk away.

She floundered for a response and then asked, "And just where do you think you're going?"

"To take a shower," he called over his shoulder as he kept walking. He went into the bathroom and closed the door behind him.

A frustrated Farrah reclined on her back and stared up at the ceiling when she heard the shower going. How dare he insinuate that she loved him just because she'd gotten tiffed over finding that business card. Any woman would be upset. Wouldn't she?

She turned her head toward his pillow and breathed

in deeply to inhale the scent he'd left behind. And then she closed her eyes, and memories began flooding her brain. The magic of everything she and Xavier had shared touched her deeply. Did he really mean it when he said that he loved her?

She considered the possibility for a second and knew it was true. What other man would have taken the time to deliberately take their affair out of the bedroom? And each and every time she'd gone out on a date with him, she had enjoyed it immensely. He'd been adept at balancing the physical part of their relationship with the emotional.

And she knew, believed in her heart, that he was nothing like Dustin. Xavier could be trusted. He would never deliberately hurt her, use her or abuse what they had together. He would only love her.

Tears sprang into her eyes, and she wiped them away as she eased off the bed and headed toward the bathroom. He was so right. He wasn't Dustin, and her ex couldn't compare to Xavier in any way.

He was right about something else, too. She did love him, and it was about time she showed him how much.

A spray of water poured over Xavier's body as he stood underneath the showerhead. A part of him always regretted washing away Farrah's scent; he much preferred to wear it all day.

He hoped he'd given her something to think about, although that was not how he'd wanted to blurt out that he loved her. He'd pretty much envisioned a romantic candlelit dinner on Christmas night where he would pour his heart and soul out to her before asking her to marry him. But at least now she knew how he felt, and the way she'd gotten in a tiff about Marti's business card had sent hopeful chills up his spine.

If she thought for one minute he was going to let her end things between them again, she had another thought coming. He was in for the long haul, and the sooner she admitted to herself that she loved him, the better it would be for the both of them. Then they could get on with their lives. Together.

He reached up to turn off the water when the shower door opened and she stood there. Naked. Beautiful. He leaned against the tile wall. His heart began doing jumping jacks in his chest when she stepped into the shower stall with him. "I didn't know you planned to take a shower with me," he said throatily, feeling every word torn deep in his lungs.

Instead of saying anything, she grabbed the soap and lathered her hands and then reached for his chest. He grabbed her hands to stop her. Whenever they showered together, she always lathered him all over. She was acting as if nothing had changed between them. But things had, and it was time for her to acknowledge that fact.

He held her hands tightly in his and met her gaze. "Tell me, Farrah. Don't show me anymore. Whether you wanted to or not, you've been showing me each and every time we made love. Now I want you to tell me."

She shook her head. "I can't."

He rubbed a finger gently across her cheek. "Yes, you can, baby. You're not the only one who's ever been hurt by love."

Her mouth pressed into a thin line, and for a minute he thought that maybe he had pushed her too far, had asked too much of her. But then she took a step toward him and reached up to wrap her arms around his neck while water sprayed down on them both. He reached behind him and turned off the water and turned back to her. "Tell me."

She inhaled deeply and met his gaze. "I love you, Xavier," she then said softly. "I've loved you for a long time. I've been too scared to admit it to myself. I tried denying it by sending you away. And then when I ran into you in New York, I convinced myself that a holiday fling was all I wanted. But I know now that would not have been the case. I will always love you and I want you."

He lowered his mouth to hers at the same time his hands spread across her backside to bring her closer to him. He fully understood what she'd been going through. It had taken him a while to recover from Dionne, so he knew why she'd been hesitant to give her love freely again. But each and every day he would show her, tell her, prove to her just how much she was loved, wanted and cherished.

He continued to take her mouth in agonizing pleasure, tasting her as their tongues tangled, mated in a dance of possession and non-restraint. He wasn't the only one coming unleashed. She was deliberately tempting him by rubbing her body against his, cradling his manhood between her open thighs. She moaned into his mouth, and the sound sent sensuous shivers all the way up his spine.

Xavier broke off the kiss and drew in a deep breath. He studied the face staring up at him, and it was all he could do to maintain his control and not sweep her into his arms and take her back to bed.

"I was determined to prove to you it wasn't just about sex with us, Farrah," he said, reaching out to brush back wet hair from her face.

"And you did." A smile touched her lips. "But the sex was still good."

He chuckled. "It will always be good between us. I love you."

"And I love you, too."

Xavier lowered his head, capturing her mouth again. He knew at that moment that their life together was just beginning.

Epilogue

Six months later

"I now pronounce you man and wife. You may kiss your bride, Xavier."

Xavier pulled Farrah into his arms and kissed her deeply. Moments later when he felt one of his godbrothers poke him in the side, he winced before releasing her mouth. He'd gotten carried away, but that was okay. It was his wedding day, and he intended to let everyone know just what a happy man he was.

A short while later at the wedding reception, he stood on the sidelines watching Farrah toss her bouquet to all the single ladies when one of the men standing by his side said, "You're officially out of the club now, X."

He glanced over to his godbrothers, the ones who were still bachelors in demand—Virgil, Winston, York and Zion. "I know, but I have no regrets."

He glanced back to Farrah. In her wedding gown, she looked simply beautiful. She met his gaze and smiled. He hoped one day each of his godbrothers would have a reason to lose membership in the club as well. He was convinced that nothing could replace a good woman in a man's life. Nothing.

"It's time for our dance," Farrah said, walking straight into his outstretched arms.

Her small hands felt secure in his as he led her to the dance floor. He couldn't wait until later tonight when he had her alone. In the morning, they would leave for a two-week honeymoon in Hawaii.

Xavier caught the eye of his friend Galen Steele, who was also one of Donovan's cousins from Phoenix. Galen, who'd been a devout bachelor, had gotten married himself a few months ago. From the smile he still wore on his face, Galen, like Xavier, had no regrets about moving from being a single man to a truly happily married one.

Farrah smiled up at him when they reached the dance floor. "Are you happy, sweetheart?" he asked her.

"Yes, I am truly happy. What about you?"

Instead of answering he leaned down and kissed her. After hearing a number of catcalls and whistles he figured he would let her mouth go.

"Did that answer your question?" he asked, whispering against her moist lips.

She laughed softly as she looked up at him. "Oh, yes, that pretty much summed it up."

Xavier pulled her tighter into his arms, feeling all of the love in his heart. He would have to agree. That pretty much summed it up.

* * * * *

YOU HAVE JUST READ A

HARLEQUIN®

Desire

BOOK

If you were taken by the strong,
powerful hero and are looking for the
ultimate destination for **provocative
and passionate romance,** be sure
to look for all six Harlequin® Desire
books every month.

HHARLEQUIN®

Desire

Powerful heroes…scandalous secrets…burning desires.

Use this coupon to save

$1.00

on the purchase of any Harlequin Desire® book.

Available March 2014 wherever books are sold,
including most bookstores, supermarkets,
drugstores and discount stores.

Save $1.00

on the purchase of any Harlequin Desire® book.

Coupon expires December 31, 2014. Redeemable at participating retail outlets
in the U.S. and Canada only. Limit one coupon per customer.

52611399

5 65373 00076 2   (8100)0 11910

BJINC0314COUP

REQUEST YOUR FREE BOOKS!

2 FREE NOVELS
FROM THE ROMANCE COLLECTION
PLUS 2 FREE GIFTS!

YES! Please send me 2 FREE novels from the Romance Collection and my 2 FREE gifts (gifts are worth about $10). After receiving them, if I don't wish to receive any more books, I can return the shipping statement marked "cancel." If I don't cancel, I will receive 4 brand-new novels every month and be billed just $6.24 per book in the U.S. or $6.74 per book in Canada. That's a savings of at least 22% off the cover price. It's quite a bargain! Shipping and handling is just 50¢ per book in the U.S. and 75¢ per book in Canada.* I understand that accepting the 2 free books and gifts places me under no obligation to buy anything. I can always return a shipment and cancel at any time. Even if I never buy another book, the two free books and gifts are mine to keep forever.

194/394 MDN F4XY

Name	(PLEASE PRINT)	
Address		Apt. #
City	State/Prov.	Zip/Postal Code

Signature (if under 18, a parent or guardian must sign)

Mail to the **Harlequin®** Reader Service:
IN U.S.A.: P.O. Box 1867, Buffalo, NY 14240-1867
IN CANADA: P.O. Box 609, Fort Erie, Ontario L2A 5X3

Want to try two free books from another line?
Call 1-800-873-8635 or visit www.ReaderService.com.

* Terms and prices subject to change without notice. Prices do not include applicable taxes. Sales tax applicable in N.Y. Canadian residents will be charged applicable taxes. Offer not valid in Quebec. This offer is limited to one order per household. Not valid for current subscribers to the Romance Collection or the Romance/Suspense Collection. All orders subject to credit approval. Credit or debit balances in a customer's account(s) may be offset by any other outstanding balance owed by or to the customer. Please allow 4 to 6 weeks for delivery. Offer available while quantities last.

Your Privacy—The Harlequin® Reader Service is committed to protecting your privacy. Our Privacy Policy is available online at www.ReaderService.com or upon request from the Harlequin Reader Service.

We make a portion of our mailing list available to reputable third parties that offer products we believe may interest you. If you prefer that we not exchange your name with third parties, or if you wish to clarify or modify your communication preferences, please visit us at www.ReaderService.com/consumerschoice or write to us at Harlequin Reader Service Preference Service, P.O. Box 9062, Buffalo, NY 14269. Include your complete name and address.

ROM13R

Kick back and relax with a

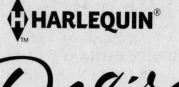

book

Passion, wealth and drama make these books a must-have for those so-so days. The perfect combination when paired with a comfy chair and your favorite drink or on the subway with your morning coffee. Plunge into a world of **hot cowboys, sexy alpha-heroes,** secret pregnancies, family sagas and **passionate love stories.** Each book is sure to fulfill your fantasies and leave you wanting more.